Rhys Alun Wilcox was born in Luton on Decimalisation Day. He does not think that missing out on shillings by a few hours has affected his life in any way.

He started writing some time between his first and second birthdays and has never looked back. Literature took a more serious turn at Portsmouth University whilst reading Media & Design. There, he found he had a lot of spare time on his hands so wrote some plays for the drama society, started his first proper novel and tried his hand at stand-up comedy.

He thinks he's funny and has only had his secondary school maths teacher tell him otherwise.

He currently exists in West Sussex with his wife and two children where he attempts to complete, at least, another dozen novels in between parenting, procrastinating and dying.

He spends the majority of his time not updating his website *www.thebloodlust.co.uk*.

Also by Rhys A Wilcox
Blood Lust
Blood Lust 2: The Carrion
Blood Lust 3: Revelations

Due to be by Rhys A Wilcox
Blood Lust 1.5: L'Hunch Est Dos
Like Father?

Rhys A. Wilcox

Aftermath

RAW!

© Copyright 2008
Rhys Alun Wilcox

The right of Rhys A. Wilcox to be identified as the author of this work has been asserted by him in accordance with the Copyright, Designs and Patents Act 1988

All Rights Reserved

No reproduction, copy or transmission of this publication may be made without written permission. No paragraph of this publication may be reproduced, copied or transmitted save with the written permission or in accordance with the provisions of the Copyright Act 1956 (as ammended).

Any person who does any unauthorised act in relation to this publication may be liable to criminal prosecution and civil claims for damage.

So there!

ISBN: 978-0-9561559-0-0

Apologies:
To those nations I may affront with my apathetic attempts at translations. It is more for effect than bilinguistic versatility – of which, I have none.

For Melanie
Without whom
I would have nothing

Epilogue: February 17th. 11:27 pm (all times local GMT)

It was a cloudless Monday night. The sky was so clear that all the stars shone with a brilliant radiance. But unlike their usual innocent twinkle they seemed to be glaring threateningly.

The stars were shining brighter because of a lack of peripheral interference. There were no man-made illuminations that would normally block out the subtle wonder of nature in favour of garish over-statements. Like streetlights that stay on during the day.

No one was looking up to admire or notice the heavens because, down on the ground, all attention was focussed on an unimposing, eight-storey office block. The building was situated on an industrial estate and was surrounded by similar non-threatening constructions. This one had an expansive forecourt that would allow for potentially sixty considerately parked cars. At this moment there were approximately thirty vehicles squeezed into the area. All were facing the building at varying angles. All had their headlights on full-beam and, those that were equipped with them, had their roof-top flashing lights flashing in the manner they were so appropriately designed for.

Over twenty police cars, half a dozen police vans and two black, window tinted, limousines were aimed at the office block starting about twenty feet away from the front doors. With each car came four pistol and shotgun armed police officers. They stood behind the relative safety of their vehicles' open doors, boot or bonnet with their weapons trained at the windows of the building. The vans carried ten special officers armed with automatic rifles and wearing body armour. They stood in orderly queues at either end of the forecourt awaiting the command to rush the premises. Other special officers had taken up positions on the rooftops of some of the surrounding buildings and aimed rifles with laser sightings. The small red dots of their attention could be seen dancing across the face of the building trying to seek out a suitable target to lock on to.

Standing outside of the limousines were eight men dressed in dark, expensive suits covered by long raincoats whose tails caught any breeze that passed their way.

Six pairs of floodlights had been erected at the back of the forecourt and lit the parts of the building the headlights could not reach.

No one looked up at the night sky because most people there thought it was still daytime. They had been watching the building for many hours but very little had been happening.

A scruffy suited man left his position from the front line and wove his way back to the limousines. He looked as if he was in his mid-fifties. He was overweight and just under six-foot. A skinny black moustache gave definition to his mouth where the lack of a top lip did not. His black hair was thinning but swept backwards in no attempt to cover up the receding hairline. His black, puffy eyes indicated he had been without quality sleep for some time.

"This is madness," he announced as he approached the group of expensive suits. He closed in on one of the men who was at least a decade older than him. He was frail looking with thick white hair and an immaculate quiff that seemed hard-set on his head.

"Inspector Roberts," the old smart suit said, "I reiterate that we need to show restraint. We need to be patient. We have to wait."

Roberts shook his head and placed his hands on his hips. "We don't even know if they're still alive."

"Oh, they're definitely alive," another suit chipped. He was a foot taller than both men and had an almost identical hairstyle to his senior colleague but in pumpkin orange. In fact, all of the suits around him had that same plaster-cast hair-do.

"How the hell can you know that, Poindexter?" Roberts demanded.

"My name is Cummings, Inspector Roberts, as well you know," the man corrected. "Agent Cummings."

"I couldn't use you as a cleaning agent," Roberts spat.

"We know that they are still alive," Cummings continued, "because we are still alive."

This stopped Roberts in his protesting tracks.

"Fair enough," he grumbled. "Can't argue with that. But how do we know that they're still in there?"

"We have the building surrounded," the old suit pointed out. "No one has come or left in the eight hours that we've been here."

Roberts wanted to say, "Nothing's fucking happened in the eight fucking hours that we've fucking been here," but unfortunately the sound of the first syllable got sucked from the back of his throat before it had the chance to pass his tonsils.

To say the building exploded would not be an understatement, per se, but more of a misinterpretation of a sequence of extreme kinetic and phonetic events.

Roberts had his back to the building so was unaware of the first event. Those officers who survived, and were still able to offer a cohesive account, stated that the walls bowed inwards. All four walls and the roof were drawn in without so much as a stress-related squeak emanating from the buckling building.

Next, all the windows gave in simultaneously but again, without a sound. Each pane of glass shattered and was sucked into its respective room. That was when Roberts lost his voice or, perhaps, when it was mugged from him. The atmospheric noise around the building stopped: the officers' breathing, the subliminal hiss of their radios and even the sound of swallowing. The sudden, absolute silence sent a couple of officers into an instant state of catatonic shock - we are always surrounded by sound, from inside and out – where their brains could not cope with the total sensory shut down.

Maybe more would have suffered similarly if the equalisation of pressure had not followed immediately after. The building's walls sprang back into shape and the air was vacuumed in like a hurricane. Masonry fired out in all directions like brick arrows from a granite bow while debris was sucked in. The officers were caught in the crossfire, cars were pummelled to scrap, bodies were shredded as if caught in a propeller and the floodlights shattered to plunge the scene into darkness.

Then the building exploded. The blast started on the ground floor and flames squirted through every orifice with a radius of thirty feet. Cars and bodies were indiscriminately set alight and hurled to the back of the queue. The second floor erupted but the reach of the flames was slightly shorter. Then each proceeding storey ignited consecutively with shorter bursts until the roof geysered with the final needle of energy trying to ignite the sky.

For the fraction of the second that each floor was alight to its maximum the building took on the appearance of a monstrous, hell spawned Christmas tree. Then the building collapsed in on itself.

As the fires subsided, molten rock rained down upon the law enforcing audience adding further injury and, in some cases, that metaphorical final nail.

When the onslaught seemed to be over, bodies began to emerge from whatever shelter they had managed to find or from whatever shelter had managed to find them. Roberts pulled himself from under the smouldering arch of two fused cars and tentatively threw aside an arm that was clinging to his shoulder. He looked around him and caught site of Cummings staggering towards him cradling an obviously broken forearm.

"Does that mean they're dead now?" Roberts asked rhetorically.

Cummings shook his head and shouted, "I can't hear you." As he got closer Roberts noticed a steady flow of blood dribbling from each of Cummings' ears. Cummings stopped walking, wobbled on his feet then fell to the floor. Roberts could not tell if he was dead or unconscious and, to be perfectly honest, at that moment, he did not care. He was alive and that was the main thing.

A couple of other suits emerged from the darkness and a few officers hobbled and crawled to this point of focus. Each person had no words. This had been an episode beyond comprehension. Those who had survived were probably going to be mentally or physically crippled for life. Maybe both. Those who died had been colleagues, compatriots and friends of the survivors. Not one person there had *ever* experienced so much personal devastation and so to even think of asking, 'Are you okay?' was beyond farcical. It would have been sadistic.

From the flaming rubble came a movement. Bricks shifted and started a cascade towards the forecourt. A couple of alert officers moved to get their guns but realised they had lost them during the blitz.

The bricks continued to pour from the centre of the wreckage where something large had survived the very heart of the attack and still had the ability to shirk off several tonnes of searing stone as if wading through a paddling pool. The officers' Walther PPK pistols probably would not have had much stopping power if they did still have access to them.

The closer wreckage parted and a black ball the size of an adult rolled out onto the charred forecourt, knocked a couple of overturned cars out of its way and made a path to the collection of survivors.

When the sphere stopped directly in front of them, it caused them to flinch more than had it tried to roll straight over them. The ball had been scorched black and now it was so close they could make out cracks spreading across the surface. Chunks of crust dropped to the floor to reveal a bright, pristine chrome surface underneath. When the sphere was completely clear it shimmered and converted to the consistency of liquid which then poured to the floor. Two figures collapsed into the puddle of silver: a male and female. Both were wearing torn, dirty and bloodied clothes. Both were torn, dirty, bloodied and bruised.

The man lifted his pain-wracked face to Roberts.

"You?" Roberts gasped and the man just concentrated on breathing.

"What happened to Evershine?" Roberts demanded.

"Dead," was all the man could manage.

"How do you know for sure?"

"Here," the man said and proffered Roberts a hand.

Roberts presumed the man needed help getting to his feet so he took the hand and braced himself to take his weight but stumbled backwards as the hand came away in his grasp.

"You check for a fucking pulse," the man growled.

Roberts looked at the hand; it had been cleanly sliced just the other side of the wrist. His eyes fell on an ornate signet ring on the middle finger; a blood-red gemstone set in the centre of a silver omega symbol.

"What the -?" Roberts muttered in awe then looked back to the man but he had passed out on the floor alongside the female. He had her enveloped in a protective embrace.

ACT 1: What It Was And What Could Be
One week earlier: Monday 10th - Saturday 15th

The most bizarre thing was, everyone knew.
    Everyone.
    It was not as if a secret Government research facility set up somewhere in New Mexico had picked up a random signal and, by an equally haphazard series of occurrences, the signal had been cracked and blah blah blah.
    Nor was it that a group of rambunctious kids had accidentally had their hobby-craft telescope pointed in *just* the right place, at *exactly* the right time, to see *exactly* what they were not supposed to see and then had to try to convince the rest of the world that blah blah blah.
    No. Strangely enough the only reason why everyone knew was because it became a conversation piece across the globe.
    The first official report came from a British regional newspaper on a Monday morning.

> Phone Home
> A constabulary in Pembroke Dock has received a record number of complaints from local residents this weekend. An astonishing 685 unrelated complaints to the police station stated they had been the victim of a female prank telephone caller. The woman claimed that aliens from another planet were coming and warned them that all life on Earth will be wiped out and then the planet destroyed within eight days. A police spokesman told us they are treating the calls as a telemarketing company going too far.

This came to the attention of one of the national tabloids who then reprinted the report in the 'aren't people stupid' section for their Tuesday edition. Had they made a couple of phone calls before going to print, they might have come across a second piece printed in a local paper from the opposite side of the country. Had they done that simple piece of research then they could have claimed to have uncovered the hottest news story during the history of humanity since, 'Man Walks on Water.'

> Mystery Fore Site
> A local information website, www.gravesend_rocks.co.uk, has had a mysterious visitor. This caller has managed to hack into the site's server and uploaded a new home page. Where any visitor to the site would normally be welcomed with a picture of St Mary's Church and a friendly paragraph summarising the pages within the site, anyone logging on now will find the rather antisocial proclamation that the end of the world is, as they say, nigh. The strangest part of this 'break in' is that the site owners cannot remove the message because they cannot find the illegal files on their server to remove them. They are requesting that people access the normal site using www.gravesend_rocks.co.uk/index2.htm.

The new 'Welcome to Gravesend' page read like this:
YOU *ARE* GOING TO DIE!
IN SEVEN DAYS!
Unless you do something very soon, a committee commissioned group will be coming to eliminate all life forms and then destroy your planet.
Do yourselves a favour and change quickly.
YOU HAVE BEEN WARNED!

As soon as the paper was circulated then the www.gravesend_rocks.co.uk hit rate increased by two thousand per cent. Its average hit count had been half a person a day (and that rate was only achieved by cheating when the authors logged on occasionally) but that upped to one thousand. Of course no one visited their index2 page. But then why would they?

Then the emails started to circulate and within two hours a further fifty thousand people from all around the globe had been informed of their imminent end. Then the emails came back, directing their friends to similar sites.

From Italy (www.desenzano_rocce.it)
LEI VANNO MORIRE!
IN SETTE GIORNI!
A meno che lei fa qualcosa molto presto un comitato ha incaricato
il gruppo verrà eliminare tutte le forme di vita e distrugge
poi il suo planet. Voi farstessi il favore ed un cambiamento velocemente.
LEI È STATO AVVERTITO!

To China (www.shenyang_yan.ch)
你將要死亡！
在七日！
除非你很很快做事委員會
受委托的團体將來到消除
所有生活形成然后摧毀你的行星。
迅速地給你們自己一贊同和變化。你被警告了！

To Mexico (www.ajo_piedras.cc)
¡USTED MORIRA!
¡EN SIETE DIAS!
A menos que usted haga algo muy pronto un comité comisionar
el grupo estará viniendo a eliminar todas formas de la vida y entonces
destruir su planeta. Háganse un favor y el cambio rápidamente.
¡USTED HA SIDO ADVERTIDO!

And America (www.pittsburgh_rocks.com)
YO *ARE* GOING TO DIE!
IN SEVEN DAYS!
Nless yo do something very soon a committee
commissioned grop will be coming to eliminate
all life forms and then destroy yor planet.
Do yorselves a favor and change quickly.
YO HAVE BEEN WARNED!

Then it came to the attention of the international press on the Wednesday and the same phone call was reported as having been received in millions of homes around the world, translated into their native language. It was just a recorded message and even though many police forces were able to monitor some of the calls they were unable to trace them.

Of course, the press still managed to tell the story from completely the wrong angle. They focussed mainly on the power of communication and how the new 'word of mouth' had become more powerful than the reach of the mass media. Some hypothesised as to the security breaches of the internet and telephone systems; how can we feel safe in our beds when it is so easy for someone to tap into the most securely encrypted satellite and computer systems in the World? Some focussed on the fan networks that were building up around the mysterious multi-lingual woman and whether *she* was actually an alien, how large her alien breasts might be and whether she had only two of them? Some papers reported stories of men having been abducted by her and her having her wicked, alien way with them. None of them seemed to believe in the concept that maybe, just maybe, someone was coming to destroy all life on the planet as we knew it. And all life as we did not know it. All life.

It was that Wednesday when the daytime sky was pocked by thousands of shadowy smudges from horizon to horizon. It was announced then that the planet Earth had been surrounded by extraterrestrial 'caretakers' and it was their responsibility to 'take care' of the Earth. They had one small matter to deal with and then all would die. They expected to start within the next couple of days and the 'caring' would be over before the following Monday.

Still nobody really got it. The human race seems to have this extraordinary ability to deny the very obvious threats to their own mortality. Everyone dies but humans still manage to wander around, day after day, trying to find more interesting ways to quicken that demise.

The top phrase is pollution. Everything about humanity is creating another method of pollution without actually calling it that. Smoking kills and yet people still smoke. Cars kill and yet people still drive too fast. Cancer kills and yet people still lie in the sun too long. A polluted atmosphere kills everything and yet people still run factories that produce products that are not needed. People use detergents with no thought of the consequences to their water supplies, people dispose of packaging without consideration for either how it was produced or where it goes from there. Everyone knows that the continued degradation of the Earth's atmosphere will ultimately lead to the demise of all life on it. But everyone still pollutes because human ethos states that 'it' always happens to someone else.

And so it was on Wednesday that life continued as per usual. Commuters went to work, parents did their weekly shopping and politicians convinced the populace that everything was going to be okay.

On Thursday a major city in every country around the World died. It happened pretty much overnight. On Wednesday evening the planet said goodnight to places like Gravesend, Pittsburgh, Ajo and Shenyang and on Thursday morning the rest of Earth knocked on their bedroom door to find out if they were going to get up at any time today and no one answered. Everyone and everything had died.

It was then that our television channels were possessed by a mid-twenties looking female. She had short, spiky blonde hair and totally non-outstanding features. She looked like the sort of person if built by someone generalising the human form: Two eyes? Check. Colour? Blue. Nose? Check. Two nostrils? Check. And so on.

She appeared on every television and her voice appeared on every radio station and cut into every telephone conversation around the world.

"People of Earth. The destruction of your planet has been delayed. The deaths of your countries' towns and cities was meant to be the start of your end but the caretakers are missing a vital part of the viral code they are using to cleanse your habitat. It is still not too late to drastically alter your lifestyle and redeem yourselves."

The transmission was cut off and replaced by a very serious man aged somewhere in his forties. He had black hair cut in a geometrically perfect bowl that tilted from the top of his eyebrows, over the tips of his ears and down to the nape of his neck. Every time he moved, his hair wafted like a grass skirt.

He was wearing a black coat buttoned to his neck. The cuffs and neckline were bordered with an inch of thick, black fur. On the index finger of his right hand was an elaborate signet ring; a silver omega symbol inset with a large red jewel.

His face emerged from his hair like the bow of a ship, his nose was the defining point and his mouth looked like it was permanently down-turned.

He very rarely blinked. Or maybe he never needed to since he peered through a needle thin gap between his eyelids. It was impossible to see what colour his eyes were or if, in fact, there were any at all.

"People of Earth," he announced. His voice was soft and wispy but not quiet. It was as if the words were being formed through a steam outlet. However, no matter how bizarre his appearance, or how freaky his voice, anyone could tell the man was just plain bored. "I apologise for the setback in our plans. It *is* just a setback and we will resume all services as promised as soon as the individual responsible has been tracked down and eviscerated. In the meantime, I advise you to make whatever peace you may feel necessary as, I assure you, no change - no matter how drastic - in your lifestyle will prevent the maintenance on your planet being carried out."

The message flickered and all machines returned to their normal activity. This time, however, the people of Earth did not. The message had finally sunk in.

Phone networks immediately jammed, roads quickly became gridlocked, riots and looting broke out all across the planet as people realised these were the last moments to do what it was they always wanted to do or try to make some meaning of it all. Those people stuck in cars were still in denial and thought that there was still somewhere to escape to.

By Friday afternoon things had slightly calmed down and humanity had the 'pleasure' of receiving the following message from the caretaker's spokesman again.

His eyes were slightly wider this time, which seemed to indicate that he was taking this broadcast a bit more serious than his previous. Unfortunately, this wider-eyed announcement meant everyone could see his sockets were obsidian black.

"Let me make this clear, you *are* going to die and your planet *is* going to be removed. At this stage you have a choice as to how these inevitables are going to happen: slowly and painfully or quick and painless. We have the girl and we know she has passed the code on and whoever has it is advised to give it back immediately or your people will die in the most horrible, *horrible*, ways imaginable. And a few you could not imagine. You have six hours."

This generated mixed emotions amongst the damned. Some saw it as a good thing, that there was someone out there doing something to try to save them all. Others saw it as things going from bad to worse, they had prepared themselves for straightforward death but now they had the idea of suffering to contend with.

There were those who took this opportunity to try to aid in the prevention of extinction by working out what this 'code' was and whom might be carrying it. This discussion found its way on to news and chat shows around the globe with each country laying claim that it was one of their 'special agents' who was responsible for keeping the aliens at bay. Many civilians took it upon themselves to hunt down the carrier in the hope of being able to trade this person for their own lives.

Six hours later and 'black eyes' was back on the air.

"Right. I'm going to make it simple. This is who we are looking for," a photo of a young man appeared on the screen. He was white, had chocolate brown hair and eyes. Again, he was a fairly non-descript person. Not an eye-catcher from either end of the spectrum.

"His name is Luke Robinson. He is 28 years old. He lives in Camden, London, Britain. He has the code. Whoever delivers him to me may live. Pick up a phone, dial 5971* and ask for me, Evershine. Six hours and then the pain starts."

The picture returned to the 'man' who called himself 'Evershine' and he slumped back in his seat. "Fucking species," he exclaimed to someone offscreen and the transmission ended.

Luke's picture and name was, of course then posted over everything: television, radio, internet, newspapers, calling cards in telephone boxes. His friends and family were badgered, beleaguered and beaten for information as to his current whereabouts. Most of his friends and family argued that if they knew that then they would not standing there talking to these people but would instead be sitting in the front row seats watching the end of the World.

Television producers needed something to fill their airtime so they started researching Luke's life and in no time at all, the World knew everything about him: date and place of birth, parentage, lineage, schooling, employment history, hobbies, skills, sexual orientation, girlfriend history and favourite position. Within three hours it was possible to have a virtual tour on the internet around Luke's flat and dress a virtual doll in his actual wardrobe.

But Luke was nowhere to be found. He had been at work the day before and had not been seen again thereafter.

Everyone said he was a quiet man, unassuming, kept himself to himself, would socialise with the lads but never be rowdy or rambunctious. He was strictly monogamous to his fiancée, Carolyn Soper. They had been seeing each other for five years, living together for three, engaged for one and were now dealing with the logistics of getting married. She said he was a very caring man, calm, non-violent and non-provocative person. To go off with a strange, female and then try to save the planet single handedly did not sound at all like the Luke she knew. She was sure there was some kind of mistake.

Six hours passed since the previous transmission and, as promised, the pain started early Saturday morning. To be fair to the caretakers, it seemed to be completely indiscriminate. The citizens of a totally random selection of towns and cities around the world were struck down by a sudden illness. Every possible illness symptom was suffered by someone in the affected areas: fevers, chills, headaches, joint and muscle aches, sore throats, muscle fatigue, diarrhoea, vomiting, stomach pains, rashes, red eyes and even chronic hiccups. Eventually this led to internal and external bleeding. People began to, literally, explode and die. Gutters ran with a viscose black liquid and corpses lined the streets. The air of these places stank like slaughterhouses. Armies and special pathogen departments were called in to try to cure or, at least, contain the contaminates.

It was later diagnosed that these places had been exposed to mutated strains of Ebola and Marburg. The usual gestation period for these is two days at their quickest so the caretakers' version must have either been introduced up to two weeks earlier or took two minutes. From the spread across the populace the incubation period must have been a maximum of two hours.

In their natural form these are evil viruses called hemorrhagic fevers because they melt the victims from the inside out and are easily communicable. However, the CDC claimed that there was no conceivable way that even these genetically adjusted variants would have the capability to wipe out all human life on the planet. The virus killed itself off too quickly.

Eventually those in control were just required to clean up the mess. The air of these places had smelled like slaughterhouses, now they smelled like barbecue.

But then that was the last they heard from the caretakers until the news broke early Tuesday morning that Evershine had been killed, the caretakers had been turned away and Luke Robinson had saved the World and every life thereon.

The skies were no longer dotted with the silhouettes of impending doom and life returned to normal for those who had survived.

ACT 2: Who He Was, Who He Became And Who He Might Be
One month later: Monday 24th

It was early morning and the sun had not yet made much of an impression on the day.

It half-heartedly sent a smatter of illumination through the north and south facing windows of a particular room. It was a really big room, so what light was filtering through did not have much chance to dent the shadows in the deepest recesses. It could have been an auditorium or maybe a theatre if there had been an obvious stage, but really it was just a big room. A really big room.

At the eastern end of the room was a huge set of oak panelled double-doors. They were at least nine foot square and ornately arched. They served absolutely no practical purpose being that big. No one in the history of humanity has ever been that big and needed that much space to get through. The really stupid thing was that the doors you had to get through to get to this door were all 'normal' seven by three so the giant who did need these ones could never have got to them anyway. Maybe the builders had run out of bricks but had these huge bits of oak left.

Once you had managed to get the doors open and entered the room you were faced with a two person wide aisle that separated two blocks of seating. The seats were of that hard, blue plastic variety. The type that stacked neatly on top of each other for efficient storage. The type that, if you stacked them more than six high, they made the stack fall over. The type that had special designed metal interlocking links at either side. The type of interlocking link that was surreptitious enough so as not to make the chair ugly but manage to stick out enough to gouge a nasty cut halfway up your shin. The type of chair that had a hole in the base of the upright, just at bum level. For some reason.

There were thousands of these chairs, twenty-five deep on both sides and one hundred rows thereof.

The ceiling was as far away so as to make its very existence negligible.

After the front row of seats was a makeshift barrier designed from solid brass plinths with a loose red cord between them. In front of this were two plain tables with three leather office chairs behind each one. On each of the tables were two jugs of water, three glasses and two microphones.

In front of that, directly opposite the aisle, was another table with seats at each end and three along the front side facing the opposing direction to everything else thus far.

Behind these chairs was a raised platform that stretched from one side of the room to the other. Centred on that was a wide podium with chairs to seat five people and a microphone for each. To the right was a pulpit with a chair inside and another microphone. To the right of the pulpit was a final chair.

In each corner of the room was a normal sized door. The west wall was covered by a square, glass panel, fifty feet as high as wide. And in the four corners of the roped off section were television cameras.

At seven o'clock in the morning, the oak doors were opened gently and a waifish female entered dressed in a black skirt, jacket and cravat, a white blouse with a gold name badge. She was immediately followed by a middle-aged couple dressed in their Sunday best. The female inspected a slip of paper in her hand as she led the couple half way down the aisle. She stopped and pointed to the seats at the far end of the row. She then gave the couple the slip of paper and walked back to the doors. The couple edged their way to the designated seats and sat. They each ripped open a small plastic bag they had carried in and removed an earpiece and a piece of paper. They both studied the paper - which must have had directions for use on - and experimented with the earpiece for comfort. Eventually they just stared towards the front of the room and, every now and then, one would lean over and whisper something to the other.

As the hours passed, the frequency of people entering the room increased. The two smaller adjacent doors were also employed and each individual who entered the room was directed to a specific seat by a similarly uniformed male or female whereupon they opened their little plastic bag, read the instructions on the paper and played with the earpiece. The people consisted of multiple races, a broad spectrum of ages and social standing. That many people in one place at that one time *must* have contained a representative from all walks of life. From the clothes that were worn, it could be seen that there seemed to be at least one representative from all the most obvious religious and cultural sects.

Despite the number of politically, sexually and religiously opposing groups, everyone took their seats with quiet dignity and respect for those around them. Unlike the usual scenes of agitated temperament that tend to accompany large groups of people and the inconvenience of having to wait, there were no raised voices, no huffing and puffing, no tutting and no rolling eyes. Eventually the seats were filled and although there was no audible talking there was a cacophony of shuffling, whispering and occasional bodily eruptions. It was a noisy silence that only a room of nearly five thousand people trying to be quiet could make.

All the doors were closed and the general attention of the audience was directed to the television cameras becoming operational. They were being controlled remotely from wherever the production booth was. The glass panel on the front wall flickered with static and then produced a giant image of the podium. There was a buzz of anticipation through the crowd and heads bobbed from side to side trying to see around corners. Of course, when someone behind the person trying to see something that is not there sees this happening they immediately presume they are missing out on something and so try to see the thing that is not being seen and then this behaviour spreads exponentially through to the very back row.

The front doors opened and three armed police officers entered the room. One stood at each door and the third made his way to the centre of the rope barrier.

The large oak doors swung open and roughly five thousand heads turned. This created quite a breeze that actually managed to ruffle the raincoat of the man who hurried in to the room. People stood, camera bulbs flashed from all around, he stopped in his tracks as he noticed all eyes were upon him. Then the waifish usher stepped in behind, placed a gentle hand on his shoulder and whispered in his ear. He held up his slip of paper and she pointed to an area in the left-hand block of seats. The four thousand, nine hundred and ninety-nine members of the audience did various tuts and groans of disappointment as the man got to his row and edged his way to the final empty seat. He apologised as he passed each person and they had to adjust themselves to let him get past.

The crowd settled down again and returned their attention to the big screen at the west of the room. They watched as the image scanned the crowd and no one felt obliged to wave, smile or mouth something to their mum at the camera as it passed them. The image settled on the doors as, once again, they were pushed open. Four men and a woman, all carrying briefcases, entered the room. They stood motionless as the cameras flashed again, then made their way down the aisle with cameras relentlessly strobing their every movement. As they approached the red cordon the officer unclipped one end of the rope and allowed them through. The three men who took the seats at the left table were clones of each other. Their suits were worn as a uniform to show they were together. They were all aged somewhere in their forties and wore suits that would show that they 'worked out regularly' - bench press statistics were probably a foremost topic of discussion. One of the men was black, the second was East Asian and the third was Asian.

The woman and last man took position at the right table. She was a slim Hispanic; her hair fell to half way down her back and was tied in a neat ponytail. She wore a delicate pair of black oval glasses of which she tended to peer over the top of more often than look through. Her associate was a skinny Caucasian. His lack of body weight seemed more to do with ill health rather than fitness. His eyes had dark rings around them and his skin was pale. They looked younger than their counterparts; late twenties? Possibly mid-thirties.

The officer replaced the rope and, again, the atmosphere calmed.

The five newcomers removed bundles of papers from their cases and arranged them on their respective tables in a manner that seemed well rehearsed. You could not help think that all of them were chosen specifically for their physical appearances: their pleasing aestheticness, their athleticism, their cross section of ethnicity. It was as if they had been plucked from a prime-time soap opera.

One camera quickly spun to focus on the doors again, the crowd got to their feet as one and then the doors swung open as if blasted by a hurricane. At that moment, the sun found a break through whatever cloud cover had been impeding it. It blasted its brilliance through the doors blinding the audience and casting the figure in the entrance in total silhouette.

The figure stepped forward into the room and looked around at the crowd. It was Luke Robinson and he was in handcuffs. He had a look of grim determination on his face as he tried to catch eye contact with every man and woman in that room. Behind him were two armed police officers, one of who gave him a nudge to continue his long walk to the tables.

Photographers cursed themselves for being awe-struck like rank amateurs and missing out on such an iconic moment. Their cameras began to flash in earnest trying to catch every nuance of this man. His hair style, the shape of his eyebrows, his fingernails, the dirt behind his ear; anything that might mean they had the photograph that would ensure Joe Public bought their paper before any of the others and, of course, ensure a fat paycheque as a result.

As they progressed along the paparazzi gauntlet, the two officers had to shield their eyes from the glare but Luke did not even blink. His pupils had tightened to a pinprick. After all, this was not the harshest light he had ever had to suffer.

He was back 'there.' He was naked and bleeding. His eyelids had been carefully, delicately and painfully stitched back to stay open and his optic muscles had been injected with a paralysing agent so he could only stare directly ahead. They had placed tiny filaments that glowed white hot an inch from each eye. Not only did the searing brightness scorch at his retinas, he could feel the tears that streamed from their ducts evaporate instantly. He had never, in his life, ever considered that you could feel such an intense pain that you could pinpoint its exact location. Usually you hurt 'in your back' or 'in your stomach' or suchlike. Both of which are pretty broad regions when considering that he could state, in absolute honesty, that he was currently 'hurting' in two half-inch circles at the back of each eyeball *and had been for almost five hours.*

Luke had been led to his seat between the man and woman and was assisted into it. Then the handcuffs were removed and he lowered his head and closed his eyes. He rubbed at his wrists and the reporters presumed he was inspecting them for injury when really he was fighting back two tears that threatened to escape in empathy of his flashback. His two escorts left via the side door.

"How are you feeling?" the female enquired.

"Tired," he muttered. "Can't sleep at the moment and I want all this to be over with."

"It should be by the end of the day," the man responded. "Just stay calm throughout and we should have a chance."

Luke gave him a disappointed look. "Aren't you the fucking optimist?"

"You know what I mean," the man explained. "They are going to cajole and goad you in an attempt to get you to ..." he trailed off.

"React," the woman added.

"'React,' right," he concurred.

"I can take whatever they throw at me," Luke told them.

All he could remember was that there was so much noise and it was coming from everywhere. He was sitting in a chair in complete darkness so he could put his hands over his ears to try to block the noise out. It was then that he found out that the noise was actually coming from the inside of his head. It was like the noise a bottle of cola makes when first opened; a high pitched release of pressure combined with an intense bubbling. It was constant, irritating and starting to hurt. The headache started just behind his ears and spread up to his temples. His eyes began to water as it slowly heightened to a migraine and flowed across his forehead and to the back of his skull. He tried to tell them *but they just would not listen.*

"Luke!" the man snapped. "Are you listening? It's not just you. What about when they do it to your family and friends? Will you be able to handle seeing your mum up there crying? What about Carolyn? Are you going to be able to stay calm as they question her about her fidelity and whether she thinks you're a psychopath or not? Are you going to be able to handle what she tells them? Luke!"

He blinked, swallowed and turned to the man. "You don't get it, do you? After all this time, you still don't get it. They're all dead. You all are."

"My final piece of advice to you?" the man whispered. "Don't say that up on the stand." He stood and picked up his briefcase. "Sorry Kat," he said to the woman, "I can't stomach to be around him any more."

"John," she exclaimed, "they'll disbar you for this."

"After all this, I need to find a new direction in my life anyway."

He turned and walked out. The flash of cameras and the snowballing mumbles of contention followed him out.

"Oh shit," Kat mumbled.

"Don't sweat it," Luke consoled, "it won't matter."

"You don't understand," she whispered and peered at the spectators from over the rim of her glasses, "I can't do this on my own."

Luke stared into her eyes. Eventually they stopped dancing around the crowd like five-year-olds on a sugar rush and settled to stare back. Her eyes were big, brown and filled with -

fear. His back was aching and his head was still ringing from the impact but for that split second that he looked into her eyes he was lost. Everything around him melted away and there was just them. Then something made him choke and *she was up and running again.*

"We'll be okay," Luke reassured. "No matter what happens. We'll get through this." He turned his attention back to staring at the podium in front of him. She was still staring at him, now at his left ear. In her bewilderment she noticed that his earlobe was missing and she remembered an interview she had seen on a daytime television show.

Luke had been sitting on a sofa next to ... damn it, she still could not remember his name. He had been famous for something and then slipped into obscurity so ended up hosting this air-filler. Luke was going through the motions of answering the same old questions and then the host noticed the difference in his ears.

"I thought your head was lopsided for a minute then," he joked.

Luke self-consciously rubbed the underside of the damaged organ and smiled sheepishly.

"It, er, fell off," Luke said.

"How on earth does an earlobe just 'fall off'?" the host laughed.

Kat had noticed that none of the studio audience had laughed with him. They were smart enough to remember the rumours that had circulated as to some of the things he had gone through in those eked forty-eight hours. And everyone remembered the photos of him from that Monday night.

Everyone apart from the host.

Luke's lips were still smiling but his eyes were not. He glared unblinkingly as he said, "They tried to dip my head in liquid nitrogen and when they pulled me away my ear had frozen. They thought it would be really funny to flick it to see if it made a ringing noise but instead the lobe 'just fell off.'"

The programme ended there and on the next day's show the host had been replaced by that woman... ah, you would know her if you saw her.

Kat shook all this from her mind but realised the distraction had managed to calm her quite considerably. She must remember that when things got a little bit tough then she would have to try to remember the names of those semi-celebrities. Either that or look at his dodgy ear. Whatever worked the best.

The two side doors opened and she heard the rising noise of craning necks trying to get a look at who was coming on next. The image on the big screen split and focussed on the five women and the man who entered the room. The women were dressed in black gowns, two of them carried chunky cases and the other three carried a pile of books each. They took the seats at the table in front of the podium. The two with the cases sat at either end and removed transcribers from the boxes and the other three took their places and spread the books out evenly in front of them.

The man was dressed in a smart black suit and sat next to the pulpit.

Kat looked at her wristwatch.

"I think this is the first time in my experience that a case is going to start right on time," she said to herself.

"Good," Luke mumbled, "because I hate waiting."

He had been sitting there for what seemed like hours.

"Fucking hate waiting."

"You might want to watch the language too," Kat warned. "Here we go."

The side doors opened again, the pulpit man stood up, the females at the front table stood, then the lawyers and the rising wave tsunamied through the crowd.

Two people entered from the left and three from the right. They took their places at the five chairs behind the podium.

The first judge was a dark-skinned female. She was in her fifties, had red-tinted, brown hair and wore a pair of bifocal glasses. She looked as if she had a tick as her head constantly bobbed up and down in little steps but really she was inspecting the audience and had to keep adjusting her view to focus.

The second judge was male and at least ninety years old. He was white and about five feet tall. He wore a white judicial wig that fell over his shoulders and made him look like a bloodhound. His gown was edged with a red fur.

The middle judge was female, black and looked the youngest of the group. She was wiry and had a very smooth, tight haircut. She wore a large, black-rimmed pair of glasses with convex lenses that sucked the sides of her head in.

The fourth judge was a stout, East Asian man. He was in his fifties and had white flecks of hair running backwards from each temple and white patches dotted around a neat beard.

The last judge was female, white and in her late fifties. Her hair was pure white and she carried a pair of red glasses on a chain around her neck. She was over six-feet tall and towered over her colleagues.

They sat down and the rest of the hall followed. The middle female judge placed her hand over her microphone and turned to her left. She said something and the East Asian and tall judge nodded. She did the same to the judges on her right and they assented. She took her hand away from the microphone and leaned slightly forward.

On the big screen behind her the camera zoomed in and the sides of her head sucked in further.

"Ladies and gentlemen," she was American, "before we commence with the days proceedings I would like to explain the details of this special hearing. This is probably more for our benefit," she indicated her colleagues, "than yours."

The two women that sat at opposite ends of the table in front of them started tapping at the keys on their transcribers.

There was a small smattering of laughter through the audience.

"Firstly I shall introduce us. My name is Judge Henley and I am from the State Supreme Court in Washington DC, USA. I have served thirty years at the bar and, in that time, have dealt with cases ranging from twenty dollar parking fines to serial killings.

"On my left is Judge Miakoto from Japan. He has been a High Court judiciary for Tokyo for twenty-five years and oversaw the controversial Nagatomi war crimes case two years ago.

"To my far left is Judge Jameson from Australia. She has been sitting on the Melbourne High Court for twenty-three years and has had significant experience with trials and hearings involving high level politicians.

"Next to me on my right is Lord Farthing from the United Kingdom. He has been an active of the British Crown Court for over fifty years and had been specially appointed barrister for the Royal Family for ten of those. He has announced that this shall be his last case.

"To his right is Judge Etienne from France. She has been serving for twenty years on the Paris High Court and has extensive experience in cases involving foreign high dignitaries.

"We have been commissioned by the United Nations to sit over this very special hearing. At no other time in the history of humanity has one case required the judicial intervention of five nations nor affected the World on a whole.

"At no time has any individual ever been in a position to receive such treatment but then this man is not just any individual. He is globally recognised as the saviour of the human race.

"The focus of this hearing is to ultimately decide whether the defendant is in a position to be judged for the crime that has been charged against him. Perhaps it is also to decide whether there are any people on this planet willing or able, to be called his peers and place a verdict and, perhaps, a punishment upon him should a guilty verdict ensue. This is a case that could be settled in one of many ways. The extremes being that he be judged singularly as any other citizen of this planet would be or he be allowed not to be judged at all and held in a position above and beyond the reach of society. But as I said, a charge has been brought against this man in one country but the result of that charge affects and involves the interest of the entire planet. Hence a carefully selected range of judiciaries from around the World are to sit.

"I cannot speak for my colleagues on this point but, personally, I am not happy about being here. This is the one case of my career that I would prefer to be a part of from the spectators' gallery rather than interact directly."

The judges on either side of her nodded solemnly.

"The People versus Luke Robinson is now in session. We will commence the proceedings with the opening statements. Messrs Umri, Singleton and Tailor for the prosecution: Ms Sabella and -"

"Ah crap," Kat whispered. "Now it starts."

"Ms Sabella?" Henley called. "You seem to be short of a partner."

Kat stood and Luke noticed her hands, although pressed as bridges on the table, were trembling.

"Yes, your honour. He had a change of heart and has left the courtroom."

Henley sat back and shook her head. "This is not a good start, Ms Sabella."

"No, your honour."

Luke raised his hand.

"Mr Robinson? You have something to say?"

Luke leaned forward to his microphone. "Yes, your honour, we're cool to carry on."

Henley's eyes looked at Kat and displayed distinct doubt. She arched an eyebrow as if to say, 'Well?'

Kat shrugged nervously and nodded.

"Very well," Henley sighed. "Let's continue. Opening statements please, gentlemen."

Kat sat down quickly.

"Relax," Luke whispered. "Don't anticipate the horror, act on the moment."

"What 'horror'?" Kat replied with sheer terror.

The girl was staring deep into his eyes and he was lost again. Despite the fact he had just been trembling so hard he had just thrown up, she was only a couple of inches from his face and looking so sincere that it switched him off. In his memory of their first 'meeting' he thought her eyes had been dark brown but now he could see they were actually red, like rust.

"Ready?" she asked.

He just nodded and took a deep breath. *They stood and ran into the room.*

The black man from the prosecution table rose to his feet.

"Your honours," he bowed his head to them then swung his right arm out over the audience, "people of the world." He was African.

"Young man," the bloodhound called Farthing interrupted. "Could you please introduce yourself to the Court?"

"My sincerest apologies," the man bowed his head again. "I am Jason Umri and my partners are Rana Singleton," he indicated the Asian man, "and Henry Tailor," to the East Asian.

"Thank you," Farthing said. "You may continue."

"Thank you, your honour."

"What a creep," Kat muttered.

"This case is not as complicated as it first appears. Although the position in our society that Mr Robinson has attained and the circumstances that pushed him to that position cannot simply be ignored. A crime *has* been committed. A law broken. An international law that God himself set in stone. Mr Robinson was directly and deliberately responsible for the death of another human being.

"His defence are going to bring forward witnesses who will vouch for his character without question and state that this is not the sort of behaviour that would normally befit him. And we will believe them. But Mr Robinson is no longer normal and we aim to reflect upon those events that took place between Wednesday the twelfth and Monday the seventeenth to show that the man they knew is no longer the man he is. We will show that he is capable, able, willing to and, did indeed, take another human's life."

Umri sat down.

"Wow, he's good," Luke said.

"Shit," Kat hissed and scrabbled for a piece of paper that might defy the laws of relativity and give her at least another six years before it was her turn to speak.

"Ms Sabella?" Henley called.

Kat turned to Luke. "I'm so sorry," she blurted and got to her feet.

"Your honours. The World." *What?* she thought. *This was all John's. He had all this in his head.*

She looked back down at her defendant and his imperfect ear and with that the imaginings of what happened to him to ensure that she was standing there, breathing, alive.

"What we aim to show today is that the prosecution's evidence is purely circumstantial. The events that transpired across *that* week may have changed Luke Robinson beyond the boundaries of how his friends, colleagues and relations may have known him. The incident that has brought him here today may be an echo of those ordeals but ... We will prove that Luke Robinson is the victim here. The resultant death from the events that took place last month on the evening of Friday the twenty-eighth was the fault of no one in particular. Just an unfortunate accident. Thank you."

She sat down and breathed for the first time since she started her speech.

"Thank you, Ms Sabella," Henley said. "Succinct and not patronising."

Umri shot the judge a hurt look.

"This is a very special case," Henley continued, "and for that reason the usual rules for witness testimonies have been changed. We have got a list of all the witnesses due to be called and the testimony you are hoping to get. We are going to call the witness, ask questions and then you will get the chance to examine and cross.

"First up? Christine Robinson, please."

The guard by the right-hand door opened it and called for Christine Robinson. After a moment, a middle-aged woman came to the door and the guard escorted her to the pulpit. She had dark brown, curly hair that wriggled to the base of her neck. She wore a plain blue jacket-and-skirt suit with a green blouse.

The man at the pulpit passed a small black book to her.

"Do you swear on the ruling deity of your life to tell the truth, whole truth and nothing but the truth?"

"I do," she said.

"Please be seated."

She sat down and looked across the room at Luke. She gave him an encouraging smile but he did not react.

"For the record, could you give your name to the court and your relationship to the defendant?" Henley requested.

She self-consciously leant forward to the microphone.

"MY NAME," she boomed and jumped back with shock. She cleared her throat.

"You can just talk as normal," the Australian judge, Jameson, told her.

"Sorry," the woman said. "My name is Christine Robinson and I am the mother of the defendant, Luke Robinson."

"Thank you, Mrs Robinson," Henley said. "Now, we are just going to ask you a few questions to try to get a better idea of who Luke Robinson is."

"Okay," Christine agreed.

"Now, Mrs Robinson, is Luke your only child?" Henley enquired.

"That's correct."

"And was there a reason for having only one child?" Henley continued.

"There were complications at the time of his birth and I was unable to have any more."

"I'm sorry to hear that," Jameson added.

"Not at all," Christine said with a cheery smile. "Luke was an accident anyway."

"Mum!"

"We hadn't actually planned to have any children at all."

"Jesus!"

"Ms Sabella," Henley called, "will you tell your client to refrain from any further outbursts."

"Were you married at the time?" Farthing enquired.

"Certainly," Christine replied offended.

"And were you happy to have a baby?" Jameson asked.

"Oh yes," Christine replied and turned her attention to Luke again. He had his face buried in his hands. "It was the most wonderful thing that could have happened to us."

Her baby boy was lying in his cot and she was just watching him. She had so much to be getting on with: there was some housework, some 'thank you' letters to write and maybe get some dinner ready but she could not drag herself away from her baby boy. He was a few months old and could not do much but wriggle and kick wherever he was put. He had stopped moving now and she noticed he was just staring at her. Their eyes locked and he gave her a smile so big that she felt her *heart burst with so much love.*

Her baby boy looked up at her from the table and their eyes locked. He was being convicted for murder and there was nothing she could do to save him. She could feel her heart breaking that something like this should be happening to him.

"Mrs Robinson?" Jameson prompted. "Would you like a moment?"

Christine realised that she was crying and became embarrassed. She rummaged in her pockets, pulled out a tissue then dried her eyes.

"I am so sorry, I was just -"

"It's okay," Jameson soothed. "When you are ready?"

"I'm fine," Christine sniffed.

"Was your son a happy boy?" Miakoto demanded.

"Very much so," Christine nodded.

"And he had many friends?" he continued.

"There were friends," Christine remembered. "Not what I would call a lot but those he did have were very good friends and are still today. He was very content to play by himself a lot."

"And he was good at school?" Farthing enquired.

"Yes. He didn't get into any great trouble. He passed all his exams, went on to university – which he seemed to enjoy – and got his degree."

The judicial bench went quiet as they all made notes on pads in front of them. Henley looked around at her colleagues. "Anything further?" They shook their heads. "Over to you Ms Sabella."

Kat stood up.

"Mrs Robinson, did you ever get Luke signed up to any youth clubs when he was a boy?"

"He tried his hand at piano for a couple of years but never really took to it. Apart from that, no."

"Was he interested in sports at all?"

"He'd play football with his friends and there was his p.e. classes at school."

"'P.E.'? Miakoto asked.

"Physical Education," Christine told him.

"So, no contact sports?" Kat asked.

"No," Christine said.

"Did he ever get in any fights at school?"

"Not that I was made aware of," Christine said. "He never came home in any bruises or scrapes."

"Thank you Mrs Robinson," Kat said then turned to the judges. "No further questions at this time." She sat down and sighed.

"Mr Umri?" Henley prompted and the three prosecutors stopped talking amongst themselves. The East Asian lawyer, Tailor, stood up.

"Mrs Robinson," he was English, "I only have a couple of questions for you. When your son was younger did he enjoy watching films?"

"Yes."

"Action films?"

"I suppose, yes."

"Cowboy films."

"Yes."

"He played 'cowboys' with his other friends."

"Yes."

"He liked to watch war films?"

"Yes."

"He played 'war'?"

"Yes, but -"

"Thank you, Mrs Robinson," Tailor said.

"- all boys -"

"Thank you," Tailor reiterated.

"Have you had much contact with your son since the events of last month?"

"Not as much as I would have liked," she told him.

"Could you elaborate?"

"He was in hospital, he was with the police, he did television interviews and then he was arrested."

"Did you notice any change in your son's demeanour?"

"His what?"

"His mannerisms. His conduct. Did you notice any change in his character?"

"Hmm, let me think," Christine mocked. "Luke had just been involved in an alien attempt to destroy the world and was then thrown into international celebrity limelight but was there a change in his character?"

"Just answer the question, please," Tailor urged.

"Yes, there was a change in his character."

"Anything that you can define for us?"

Christine's belligerence faded. "He wasn't as happy as he used to be."

"Thank you Mrs Robinson," Tailor said and sat down.

The judges stopped writing again and Henley turned to Kat. "Ms Sabella? Would you like to re-examine?"

Kat stood up.

"Mrs Robinson, when you were a girl did you use to play with dolls?"

Christine looked slightly bemused. "I did."

"And yet you *didn't* want to have children?" Kat asked incredulously.

"Objection, your honour," Umri stood and declared. "Relevance."

"What is your point, Ms Sabella?" Henley asked.

"Boys who play war do not necessarily grow up wanting to be warriors, just as girls who play with dolls do not necessarily grow up wanting to be mothers."

The judges conferred.

"We'll allow it," Henley informed the court and Umri sat down.

"One last thing Mrs Robinson, would you say that your demeanour has changed at all after the events of last month?"

"I suppose."

"Are you as happy as you were before knowing that there is other life out there and they want us all dead?"

"Not really, no."

"I have no further questions," Kat said and sat.

"Nice one," Luke commended.

"Thank you, Mrs Robinson, you may step down," Henley told Christine.

She gave her son a last encouraging smile and left the room the same way she had come in.

After another quick debate, Henley turned to Kat again. "Do you think it is necessary to call Mr Robinson as well?"

Kat was about to reply when Tailor stood.

"If it pleases your honours, we would still like him to testify."

Henley raised her hands in acceptance. "Very well, call Mr Robin Robinson."

He entered wearing a black jacket, black roll-neck jumper and charcoal grey trousers. He looked like Luke but with more wrinkles around his face and a solid moustache.

He was sworn in at the pulpit and he sat down.

"For the record, please state your name and relationship to the defendant," Henley instructed.

"My name is Robin Robinson," he declared and turned to the judges. "My parents thought they were being funny when they did that. They knew full well that it would dog me throughout my childhood and then in later life if I was ever to have any male children. Him," he indicated at Luke, "being Robin's son. Robinson. See? I am his father."

"Mr Robinson," the French judge, Etienne, welcomed. "Would you say you were the main source of discipline in your son's upbringing?"

Robin shook his head. "I think we shared the responsibility between us. If anything, I probably let him get away with more than Christine did."

"Your wife told us that you were not planning a family. Were you happy about the arrival of your son?" Henley asked.

Robin was slightly taken aback. "She said that, did she? Well, she was speaking for herself, I can assure you. I wanted children and was very pleased when Luke came along."

"You had quite a close relationship with your son, did you?" Jameson asked.

"Luke was a bit of a loner. He was always quite happy to do his own thing but never afraid to ask for help if he was having problems. I suppose we were close, we could talk easily and still can." He corrected himself, "Could."

"You cannot talk now?" Miakoto enquired.

"He doesn't talk about those few days. He won't talk to anyone."

The judges made their notes and handed Robin over to Kat. She stood.

"Mr Robinson, do you think there was anything peculiar about Luke as he was growing? Any odd behavioural traits?"

"I couldn't really comment, I'm afraid," Robin confessed. "I didn't know many children so everything he did was pretty odd."

"Well, for instance, the prosecution has tried to establish a propensity for violence by identifying Luke's interest in playing war games. Did you notice a violent streak in him?"

"Not at all, if anything that was the oddest thing about him. He wouldn't harm a fly. And I mean that literally."

He was in his bedroom finishing off some paperwork when he heard Christine scream from downstairs. He dropped everything and went running down to the living room calling, "What's wrong? What's happened?" all the way. His heart was pounding at the thought that she had been hurt or that something had happened to Luke. When he burst into the living room he saw her dancing on the sofa, bouncing from one cushion to the next in frightened little girly steps. She had her hands clasped to her chest and was staring at the floor. At first he could not see what she was focussing on and then there was a slight movement. A spider.

"For Christ's sake, Chrissy, I nearly had a heart attack," he cursed and marched forward.

"Dad, wait," Luke called from the kitchen and came running out with an empty pint glass and a postcard. He crept up on the spider and plonked the upturned glass over it. The vibration panicked the creature to run but it just bounced around in its glass prison. Its sudden movement elicited another squeal from Christine.

Luke carefully slid the postcard under the glass and edged it towards the spider, ensuring that its legs did not get trapped on the underside. When the card was fully covering the hole he flipped the whole snare over so the spider dropped to the bottom and tried running up the frictionless walls.

"You want to take a closer look, mum?" he teased and proffered the glass to her. She screamed again and told him to get rid of it. As he passed his father he wafted the glass at his face and he backed away. Luke laughed at his father's mock bravado and threw the *spider out of an open window.*

"Me?" Robin continued. "I'd stamp on the blighter and scoop it up. Him? Fetch a glass, piece of paper, chase it around the room, catch it and let it out."

"Thank you, Mr Robinson." Kat sat down and Tailor stood.

"So you think he was overly concerned for lower life forms?" Tailor asked.

"It did seem to be a bit over the top to me, yes," Robin admitted.

"And since being a boy he has taken the responsibility of rescuing these lower life forms from being killed?"

"I'm not sure I'd call it a 'responsibility' but that's what he does."

"So it wasn't totally against his character to be found saving all of humanity?"

"When you put it that way, no, I suppose not."

"Thank you, Mr Robinson." Tailor took his seat again.

"What was that about?" Luke whispered.

"They've already devalued our later testimonies trying to say it was against your character to get into a fray," Kat explained.

"A what?"

"A 'fray'. A -"

"Ms Sabella?" Henley called and Kat jumped to her feet.

Did you beat Luke? Did you sexually abuse Luke? Did you ever murder anyone? She thought about asking. The violence inherited in the system, it was called, but it had not been brought up by the prosecution because they knew Luke had come from a 'normal' family upbringing. They did not want to be seen as 'the bad guys' any more than they were already and unnecessary badgering would put them on everyone's blacklist. She certainly did not want to be on there either.

"No more questions," she said.

"Thank you, Mr Robinson," Henley said.

"Good luck, Luke," he called and gave his son a 'thumbs up' salute. Luke responded with a brave smile and a nod of his head.

When the door had closed behind Robin, Henley looked up from her paper.

"Call Gary Shepherd," Henley ordered.

A blond man of Luke's age entered. He was dressed in a white shirt, a garish *Homer Simpson* tie, denim jeans and white trainers. He skipped up to the pulpit and was sworn in. He did not stop smiling.

"For the record, please state your name and relationship to the defendant," Henley instructed.

"My name is Gary Shepherd and I am Luke's best mate," the man said.

"Pardon me," Etienne said, "You are his 'mate'?"

"What?" Gary looked blank for a second then it sunk in. "Christ no, love. Not like that. I don't know about him but not me. Nah, I'm his best friend."

"Mr Shepherd," Henley scorned, "please remember that you are in a court of law and you will act with a degree of decorum, respect and seriousness."

"Can I tell you something?" Gary responded, still smiling. "We nearly died. All of us. We were this close," he pinched his thumb and index finger together, "to being wiped out. None of this bullshit matters any more. This stuff isn't important. It's all self-satisfying wank. You've all had a major upset to your little bubbles of existence, science is flummoxed and religions have crumbled. You need to restore some balance and normalcy so you have to take control and attack the only thing that is left to upset your status quo. Your wasting your lives sitting here thinking you're doing something important and right, when these tossers could be back tomorrow to complete the job."

Throughout the spectators, hundreds of hands were pressed against their little earpieces and eyes were scrunched in concentration to keep up with the respective translators who were trying to make sense of Gary's vernacular.

Henley was leaning over to Farthing who was whispering in her ear.

"- and 'tosser' means roughly the same," Farthing finished.

"So why are you here, Mr Shepherd?" Jameson asked.

"Because I am doing what's right by trying to stop you idiots destroying one of the only people who have ever done something totally unselfish for this planet," he replied.

"How long have you been friends with the defendant?" Miakoto asked.

"I've known Luke for as long as I can remember," Gary said. "I used to beat him up in little school. Then we became friends when we moved up to middle school. I got duffed up by a bigger lad and he helped me get it together."

"Did he never try to hit back at you?" Henley asked.

"We were five years old," Gary scoffed. "I was hardly kickboxing the little snotter."

There were confused faces in the audience again.

"You have been in constant contact with the defendant since then?" Miakoto asked.

"Yep. All our schooling, then we did the same uni' and moved up to London together after graduating."

The Judges were quiet as they made their notes.

"Ms Sabella?" Henley called.

"Gary, we've had testimonies from Luke's parents stating that he was not a violent boy. You said that you were at university together?"

"I did," Gary confirmed.

"And you socialised together, did you?"

"Yes indeed."

"Did the pair of you ever experience any first-hand trouble from other people?"

"Rephrase the question, Ms Sabella," Miakoto requested.

"She wants to know if the boys ever got into any fights," Farthing explained.

"Thank you and I apologise. Yes, Gary, throughout your time together were there any instances when you were aggressively confronted by other parties?"

"Where we grew up, it happened all the time," Gary exclaimed. "Groups of lads staggering around town after closing time with time on their hands, booze in their bloodstreams and aggro on their minds."

"And did you get into any fights?"

"I'd have a go if I was in the right company and Luke was NOT the right company."

"He wouldn't fight?"

"Not at all. But it wasn't like he'd do a runner and leave you standing on your own, he would either avoid the trouble or try to quell it if it did kick off."

"How is it possible to avoid the trouble when these 'lads' are so desperately looking for it?"

"You learn to pick up on the danger signals and how not to react to provoke them. For starters, it's gone closing time and people are either moving on to a club or going home. You learn which pub routes to avoid and you behave appropriately if you do come up against rowdy lads."

"What's that behaviour? Turn around, cross the street?"

"No, no, no. That sort of thing is incitement. You keep walking, you keep talking, you keep your head up and keep looking straight in front. No eye contact. If they mouth off then you ignore it and keep walking."

"And this kept you out of trouble?"

"For most of the time, yes. But there were times when you couldn't avoid it. Some lad might walk over and ask for a light. If he hasn't got a cigarette in his hand, he's going to lamp you so you bop him right on the bridge of the nose then a knee in the nads and keep walking."

There were confused faces in the audience again.

"What if just wanted a light for a cigarette?"

"He should have known better than to approach a bunch of boys out on the street after closing time."

"And Luke always tried to avoid conflict?"

"Yeah, if we did get slapped around a bit then he'd roll himself up and they'd soon get bored."

"As far as you're aware, Luke never struck out."

"That's right."

"Thank you," Kat took her seat and Tailor stood up.

"Mr Shepherd,"

"Hallo, yes."

"When was the last time you spoke to the defendant prior to the events of the twelfth to the seventeenth?"

"I saw him that Wednesday morning before setting off to work."

"And after?"

"I got to see on his second day back. When he was in hospital."

"Wednesday the nineteenth."

"I'll take your word for it."

"How did he seem to you on that day?"
"Unconscious."
"When was the first time you had the chance to speak to him?"
"When he got home on that Saturday."
"The twenty-second."
"Whatever."
"And how did he seem?"
"Knackered."
There was confusion amongst the crowd.
"And you went out socialising again with the defendant?"
"Too right, mate. He was desperate for a drink so we went out that evening."
"Did you go anywhere special?"
"Nah. Just down to the local pub."
"And there were other drinkers there?"
"Yeah. A reasonable crowd."
"And what was their reaction to the defendant's presence?"
"We got in there and no one really paid us any attention. Then as the evening continued we noticed a few people kept staring at us and whispering amongst themselves. Then this bloke strolled up."

The pub was dingy. That was the way most of the locals preferred it. If the lights were down low enough then it meant they could not see their drunken misery reflected back at them in the faces of their drinking partners. That was why Gary chose this place; it was quiet and everyone tended to mind their own business. The landlord liked the lights to be dimmed because it saved electricity and meant you could not tell how dirty the carpet and glasses were.

They had gone in and a couple of the more sober patrons looked up but Luke had kept his head down and that was not unusual for people entering that place. Luke sat at a small table in one of the darker corners as Gary got the drinks in and took them back to the table.

"How are you doing mate?" Gary asked.

"I don't know where I am anymore," Luke replied.

"What's that mean?"

"I look at everything in a different light now," Luke told him. "We were all so close to being killed it's unreal."

"You and the girl? What was her name?"

"Tasya," Luke said. "No, I mean everyone. You, these guys, everyone."

"Well? You did good, young man, didn't you?"

"Nothing's going to be the same now," Luke muttered.

"Shut up and drink," Gary ordered and they did. Gary didn't ask any more questions about what had happened and Luke did not offer any information. They did talk about the television and radio interviews he had given over the past few days and bitched about some of the celebrities he had rubbed shoulders with. They reminisced on the old times and proposed their plans for the future.

Gary had been keeping a surreptitious eye on the other drinkers and, as the pints went by, more heads kept turning towards their direction. Eventually, the landlord had had a word with a bloke at the end of the bar who then lifted himself off his stool and lumbered over to their table.

The man was six-foot-six in height, width and breadth. He was wearing a Manchester United football top with the sleeves ripped off, a pair of khaki combat trousers with the bottoms rolled up to display the full shiny length of his seventeen hole Dr Marten Union Jack boots. His bare arms were a mass of scribbles and patterns like someone had tried to draw something really clever with an Etch-a-sketch, fouled it up and scribbled over it in frustration.

"You're 'im aren't you?" the bruiser demanded.

"I'm always me, pal," Gary replied with a cheeky grin.

"Not you," Bruiser said but did not take his eyes off Luke. "'Im."

"No," Gary said. "He's not me. You've got the wrong man."

Bruiser turned all six hundred and sixty-six pounds of attention to Gary. "You fink you're funny, gobshite?"

"I make me laugh," Gary told him.

"I can help you wiv that," Bruiser said and leaned over the table towards Gary.

"What do you want?" Luke asked but still kept his head down. Bruiser stood upright again.

"You're 'im, right? The 'ero?"

"I'm no hero."

"You saved the World. We all saw it."

"What do you want?" Luke repeated.

"Wanna buy you a drink."

"You don't owe me anything," Luke told him.

"You saved my life," Bruiser said. "And I am 'indebted'." The word came out as if he had heard it somewhere before and was trying it out for the first time. "I don't like to owe nobody nuffink."

"So you feel like you owe me," Luke surmised.

"S'right."

"Does that mean I owe those thousands of people who didn't get saved?"

Bruiser leaned forward again and put his mouth right next to Luke's ear.

"I am going to buy you a fucking drink for saving my life you snotty little fucker and that's that."

Luke turned his head and their noses nearly touched.

"You buy that drink," Luke said and Bruisers eyes relaxed slightly. "You drink it," Luke ordered, "and you fucking choke on it."

Bruiser stood up.

"I don't want anything from you, thank you," Luke said and turned back to the table.

Bruiser stood at Luke's back for a ponderous moment.

"I'll have a packet of peanuts if you're offering?" Gary said but Bruiser just turned and went back to his seat.

They were not disturbed again.

"The guy was actually pissed at Luke for being alive," Gary said.

Tailor smiled self satisfyingly and Kat noticed.

"He's got something," she muttered.

"Did the defendant's behaviour strike you as odd at all?" Tailor asked innocently.

Gary thought back and shook his head. "No."

Tailor looked down at his notebook.

"One of your rules for avoiding trouble, that you said the defendant was so adamant about doing, was no eye contact. Isn't that correct?"

"Yeah. And?"

"You just told the court that the defendant deliberately turned his head to stare directly at a man twice his size and who was acting in a threatening manner."

"Yeah?"

"That doesn't sound like a man trying to avoid or quell a potential conflict. That sounds like the sort of thing you might do to start a fight."

Kat leapt to her feet. "Objection."

"I'll rephrase, your honour," Tailor told the court. "Was that reaction consistent to the defendant's usual behaviour prior to the events of the twelfth to seventeenth? Yes or no?"

Gary gave Luke a quick glance of uncertainty. "No," he said.

Tailor sat down. "Thank you, Mr Shepherd."

"I can get us out of this," Kat whispered and got to her feet before Henley had the chance to invite her.

"Gary? Did the bruiser hit you or Luke?" she asked.

"No."

"Did he come back later and threaten you some more?"

"No."

"Were there any repercussions at all as a result of Luke's reaction?"

"No."

"So perhaps you would say that Luke had managed to quell the potential threat of violence?"

"I suppose," Gary said unsure of what was happening, then it sunk in. "Yes. Definitely. Yes."

"Thank you," Kat said and sat. Gary was excused and he left the room. The judges scribbled on their notepads then Henley consulted secretly with her associates the turned to her microphone.

"We will take a sixty minute recess," she announced.

The judges stood and started to leave. The wave of respectful compliance washed across the room. When the judges had left the east doors opened and the audience began to filter out making stretching noises and popping joints. It took so long for the room to clear that before the last people could get out, the first were coming back in again.

"I am really getting into this," Kat whispered to Luke and reached for her glass of water. Her hand trembled as she brought it to her mouth. "I'm going to make it okay."

Luke smiled at her. "I thought that too," he said.

"You think we're doing okay?"

"No, not the case," he corrected, "everything else."

"You 'thought that'?" she asked concerned. "You don't think that anymore?"

"No, I know now that we're not going to make it."

"The case?" she asked hopefully.

"No," Luke replied and it sent a chill down Kat's spine.

She waited for what she thought was a moment shy of an awkward silence.

"Luke?"

He looked up at her.

"Are we all going to die?"

"Everyone dies," he replied, "but no one believes it."

"I mean, are we going to get wiped out as a race?"

"We're doing that to ourselves already."

Kat was getting annoyed.

"Are aliens from a technologically advanced society going to return to annihilate all life on this planet?"

Luke waited for what he thought was a moment longer than an awkward silence.

"Yes."

"Why did I ask?" she said to herself.

"Especially when you already knew the answer," Luke said.

"Will you be able to save us again?" she wondered.

"Not if I'm serving a life sentence at her Majesty's displeasure."

She started rummaging around in her piles of paper. She started stacking witness profiles on top of each other as she listed. "On our side we've got Carolyn,"

Luke 'harrumphed' in disagreement.

Kat continued unperturbed, "Gordon and Sanjeet from your work. The policeman Roberts seemed very positive towards you. Bambury, the arresting officer, Mary Hopkins and the eyewitness, Malcolm Ingrams, have nothing but details of what happened and I am confident that the three boys testimonies will impeach each other. The psychiatrist, doctor and that agent Cummings are the random factors. And that's it. I'm feeling really positive about this."

"You forgot about me," Luke said and passed her a blank piece of paper.

"I'm not going to call you," Kat told him.

"But they probably will," Luke said. "Everyone wants to know exactly what happened to me in those five-and-a-half days. That's why this is so important and that's why they will definitely call me to testify. They all want to be assured that this is all over."

She could not help herself. "What did happen?"

"Things happened that no one should ever have to go through," he replied, lost in the mists of time.

There was a pain inside his body. An agonising, cramping sensation from his spine to his naval. He looked down to his stomach and discovered that the *pain was actually outside of his body.*

Luke swallowed back at something that threatened to rise up his throat. He grabbed his glass of water and knocked it back.

Kat's eyes were wide. Whatever emotion it was that she could infer from his reaction was more than any words he could have used.

"I'm so sorry," she said.

"What for?"

"Everything," she said in total sincerity. "For asking, for what happened, for all of this. I am sorry."

"You don't have to be, Kat. Really. We've all been sucked into this whirlwind of happenstance and we've all got to just go with the flow until it blows itself out."

"You make it sound like there's nothing we can do to control the outcome," Kat said.

"In the grand scheme of things? There isn't. We're on a train ride and we can do things on the train, we can do things to the train, we can pull the emergency cord to stop the train but ultimately? The train *is* going to reach its intended destination."

"You are so depressing," Kat told him.

"It amazes me that I tell people the truth and think they might turn around and start making the most of things. You know? Really start to enjoy their time with the people around them? But they don't. All they say is, 'Oh well, what's the point.' I've been given the chance to highlight to everyone that they have a choice – and it's actually the same choice we've always had – you can die happy or you can die miserable but you *are* going to die."

"Merry Christmas to you too," she replied which made Luke laugh.

"That's the first time I've ever heard you laugh," she commented. "It seems to me that you know your rules but you don't know how to abide by them yourself."

"How do you mean?" he demanded.

"You don't seem to be making the most of your last days on the planet."

"I said, 'You have the choice,' not, 'We'," he corrected her. "I didn't say anything about me dying."

Kat decided to leave the conversation alone at that point and concentrate on remembering and planning what line of questioning to use for each witness instead of ad-libbing as she had been doing so far.

She looked over at her rivals and noticed with much disdain that they were not doing much but sitting back in their seats, sipping water and idly chatting between them. Tailor looked over to their table, gave a smile to Kat and bobbed his head. Kat forced a smile in return and tried to work out why it was she felt so much animosity for those three men who were just doing their jobs. She had never felt like that in any of her previous cases. Oh sure, she might get a pang of jealousy which was easily twisted into anger when her opposition got in a clever question that turned the tide of the case. Afterwards, win or lose, she was able to have a drink and a chat with whoever it had been opposing her. For some reason she really hated those guys even though she thought she had come out tops so far. She was winning, she was right, she was the best, so really she should not even waste any emotion on the prosecution. But there they were: chatting away, minding their own business, doing what they thought was right in their own self-satisfied, selfish, arrogant, unjustifiable way.

Was it because she was the hero and they were mindless servants of an evil social order? She truly believed that Luke *was* innocent of the charges but even if he was not, after everything that he had done, should he not be allowed to 'get away with murder' in both of the saying's literal and figurative contexts?

How could anyone sleep at night knowing they were consciously battling against the World's ultimate good guy?

That was why she hated them. Regardless of whom they might be, regardless of how much money they might give to charity, regardless of anything, they had decided to fight *the* good guys. *That* made them the bad guys and you were supposed to hate the bad guys.

She changed her forced grin to a snarl and flicked her middle finger at him. He looked genuinely upset and turned to pass the news to his compatriots who then, in turn, looked at her. She held the pose so they could all get the message first hand.

"That's the definition of true evil," Luke said to her, "people doing bad things in the name of good."

"Were the caretakers evil?" she asked.

"No, not really," Luke replied.

"Just misguided? Being led by an evil leader?"

"No," Luke said. "You don't really want to know," he added. "Or rather, you don't want to realise that you already know the answer."

"I am not talking to you about this anymore," she spat. "Stop talking to me about it."

"Denial," Luke tutted. "That's the first sign."

"I'm not listening," she sang and Luke laughed again.

When *was* the last time he had laughed? He had been having so many flashbacks to those few days and every one had been an image of pain, suffering or torment. There must have been a moment of happiness. He would settle for a memory of contentment, even relief, but none would surface. Everything that had happened just brought on another life-threatening situation to escape from or another damning fact about life to accept.

He was laughing so hard that there were tears forming in the corners of his eyes. He did not know if he had ever laughed as loud or as long as that before. He managed to control himself and looked into the eyes of the man who stood before him. Those cold, black eyes.

As soon as Luke had started laughing, the man's attitude had changed completely. He had been so smug thinking he knew everything and then it became apparent, and then Luke had started laughing, and then the man had become so angry.

Luke was laughing even harder now and the tears could not be held back. They started to trickle down his cheeks and that made him laugh even more. He could feel them swelling on his lower eyelid. They filled until the meniscus finally gave way and started a trail winding their way down his blood caked face. The salt stung as the rivulets flowed through the cuts and grazes and incorporated the blood and muck it swept against. They wound their way down to his mouth and, as he licked his parched lips, he could taste the bitter mix of salt, iron and dirt.

It was all so fucking stupid. So ridiculously, hilariously, fucking stupid. He told them so many, many times that he had no idea what they were talking about and eventually they believed him. So they decided to tell him what they thought he should have known, and they told him everything, they told him what it was *all* about. That was when the laughter kicked in and the black-eyed man became irate. Oh, god, Luke was finding it so hard to breathe because he was laughing so hard.

No, hang on, he was not laughing *anymore. He was crying.*

Luke did not think that moment counted as the last memory he had about laughing because it was not a 'good' laugh. He could remember bringing a lot of enjoyment to a lot of other people who had come in contact with him. Even after they had rolled out of the office block and he knew that it was, at least for now, all over he could still not allow himself a sense of relief.

There were images constantly flashing in front of his eyes. It was dark most of the time - dark, peaceful and relaxing - but at that moment of rest another horror would show itself and send his heart racing again. Nothing happened when it did show. In fact it was such a fleeting glimpse, he was never really sure that there had been anything at all. There was a sensation that there had been something. The horror, whatever it was, seemed content just to leap out of the darkness without so much of a 'boo' and it seemed to have been going on for ages.

It was happening for so long and doing so little that eventually Luke just became plain bored with the whole situation he forced himself to wake up and open his eyes. He slammed them shut again as searing white light flooded in from everywhere. He heard himself groan from the discomfort and that irritated the back of his throat.

As consciousness filtered back, all the memories came with it. It took so much willpower to stop himself from crying because of the overwhelming deluge of misery. What trouble was he in now? Was this the time he was going to die?

"Luke?" a female called. He recognised the voice but could not place it. It could be another trick, everything had been a trick. He decided to play dead until he could assess his predicament better.

"I'm sure he just moved," the voice said again.

"Hmm," a male voice responded. "His EKG and heart rate have stabilised."

Damn their machines! He might still be able to bluff his way through this. The voice was not Evershine's which meant the man might be new and not aware of how tricky Luke could be.

He remembered giving Evershine's hand to the policeman.

Evershine was dead.

He was back on Earth.

It was over and he now recognised who the female voice belonged to.

"Mum?" he croaked dubiously.

"Luke," she called again and he felt her arms grab him around his head.

Again, he had to fight back an urge although this time it was denying an instinct to free himself from the headlock by any means possible.

He allowed the light to filter between his eyelids and, slowly, he became aware that he was in some sort of hospital room. Sensors had been attached to his temples, another had been placed over his left index finger and, from his forearm, a tube slithered its way up to a drip. Another tube emerged from under his covers and disappeared below his bed but he did not want to give that pipe too much consideration.

"How long have I been asleep for?" he mumbled through Christine's shoulder.

"Three days," she sobbed.

"How's Tasya?" he asked.

"Who?"

"The girl who was with me," he informed her.

"There wasn't anyone with you," she said and Luke's heart rate increased.

"Mum, she was there. She got out with me. If she died, tell me and I'll be upset but don't say she wasn't even there."

Christine pulled back and looked at her son with absolute sincerity.

"'There' where?" she asked. "Dad and I were here before your ambulance arrived and I am telling you that you travelled alone."

Luke's jaw tightened and his teeth ground together. It was not over, it never would be, *it had just changed direction.*

Luke blinked to reacquaint himself to his surroundings. He looked over his shoulder and was surprised to see that the room had filled again and only a few stragglers were left hurrying to their seats.

"I should've gone for a pee," Kat muttered to herself.

"Have you never heard of 'inner dialogue'?" Luke enquired and made Kat jump.

"Jesus," she spat. "I thought you were still asleep."

"I was asleep?"

"Well, your eyes were open but you were definitely snoring," she told him.

"For how long?"

"Just long enough," she said, "we're about to get started again."

The guards got to their feet, the door opened and the judges filed through to take their positions at the podium.

Before the wave of standing could hit the back row the judges had already taken their seats and the trough commenced its path.

Each judge adjusted his and her notebook and then Henley addressed her microphone. "If everyone is set to commence, we'll call the next witness."

All lawyers nodded their assent so Henley checked her papers again. "I see we have three more character witnesses to call, two of whom are from the defendant's place of employment. Is that absolutely necessary Ms Sabella?"

Kat stood up. "I believe that each witness should provide a different angle relative to their position within the company and their relationship to my client."

"One is a colleague," Henley read.

"And the other is their direct manager, your honour," Kat continued. "One's testimony from the perspective of authority will give a different slant to that from the view of a fellow employee."

Henley sighed. "As long as this is all okay with the prosecution then we shall continue." She turned her attention to the three men at which Tailor got to his feet and said, "No problem here, your honour." Then he sat down again.

"Very well," Henley shrugged, "call Gordon Baley."

A few seconds later and a skinny man dressed in a navy-blue suit two sizes too big for him walked up to the pulpit. His brown hair had been scribbled on to his head and he wore a five o'clock shadow more awkwardly than a middle-aged woman taking HRT. He was sworn in.

"Please give your name and relationship to the defendant," Henley requested.

"My name," he paused as if about to reveal a major twist in the story line, "is Gordon Baley and I work with Luke Robinson."

Luke pulled a writing pad toward him and scribbled a note. He passed it to Kat. He had written *The man is a tit.*

He seemed keen enough to help Kat scrawled back.

"How well do you know the defendant?" Jameson asked Gordon.

"We've worked together for over three years," Gordon replied.

"But how well, would you say that you know him?" Jameson reiterated.

Gordon shrugged. "We're in close proximity to each other from nine a.m. until six p.m. Monday to Friday. Regardless of however you interact on a day to day basis you are going to know one another to a fairly high degree."

What the hell is he doing? Kat wrote.

He's being Gordon, Luke replied. *The office tit.*

"Mr Baley," Henley said, "could you please try to answer the question as directly as possible."

"So would you know if a colleague was acting out of character?" Jameson continued.

"Yes, I suppose," Gordon replied. "In an office like ours -" he continued.

No! Kat scribbled desperately. *Stop talking!*

"- you tend to get sucked into a cycle of repetition. Each day is the same as the last. Your day is determined by the mode of transport by which you commute, then your transfer, then you get to your work place and you get on with your work."

What the hell is he talking about? Kat wrote and Luke started his response.

"On top of that you have to interact with your fellow employees; your daily journey passes you by the same people every day and each person in the company is either proactive or reactive."

He's written a thesis called, 'Office Politics and the Zoology of the Corporate Zoo.'

Gordon waited.

"Mr Baley," Henley started.

"Some people initiate 'good morning' whereas others will only offer 'good morning' when it is first given."

Oh Christ! What have I done? Kat scribbled.

"If there is ever a change in someone's 'good morning' it is a signal of a change in that person's out of office stimuli and can be instantly detected by those employees that person usually interacts with."

Who could possibly give a flying fuck? Kat wrote, almost by free association.

"What you're saying," Farthing interjected, "is that you don't need to know someone intimately to know when there is a change in that person as long as you have studied their long-term, daily routines."

Kat was wordless.

"That's right," Gordon affirmed.

"Mr Baley," Henley interrupted, "I am going to request that you please answer the questions as succinctly as possible."

"I am, your honour," Gordon replied in almost a whine.

"Mr Baley, if you cannot tell, you are receiving a warning from me and so answering back serves you no good."

"What sort of a person was the defendant?" Jameson asked.

"He would say, 'Good morning,' but he was picky as to who he would say it to," Gordon said.

"Was he at all temperamental?" Henley asked.

"Not really," Gordon replied. "He would come in, get on with his work and then go home at the end of the day. If something had annoyed him on the way into work then he would complain about it for a while but it wouldn't really affect his work or the way he reacted with the rest of us." Gordon gave Henley a sideways glance to see if that answer was over the top but all the judges were making their notes. They pondered then silently agreed that they had finished their questions.

"Ms Sabella?" Henley invited.

"Thank you. Hello again ti-" she stopped herself and looked down at her table to try to compose herself. "Gordon," she managed.

"Hello," he responded slightly bemused.

"Would you consider yourself to be a friend of Luke's or just a work colleague?"

"I suppose we are friends," he replied.

"Did you socialise together much?"

"We lunched together on occasion and had drinks after work but we never went out in the evenings or weekends."

"How did he feel about the management in the company?"

"We have a rather bizarre corporate hierarchy in which each department is tribalised into micro-factions. Each faction -"

Kat tried to warn him with over obvious eye contact but he was lost in his soapbox. Henley slammed her pen on the podium which made Gordon shut up instantly.

"Mr Baley!" Henley snapped. "This is your last warning. If I have to tell you again then you will be held in contempt. Just answer the question."

"Sorry," Gordon whimpered.

"Would you like me to repeat the question, Gordon?" Kat asked from behind the hand that was hiding the smirk on her lips.

"No, thank you," Gordon replied. "He didn't seem to have any real problem with any of the management. Like I said -" He stopped.

"Go on," Kat urged.

"He got on with his job," Gordon said curtly.

Kat could not help her self. "So no office subversive tendencies at all?"

Gordon went wide-eyed as he desperately wanted to go off on one again. "No," he choked.

"Thank you Gordon," Kat said and sat. She looked down at the notebook that Luke pushed towards her.

Nice try.

Tailor stood up. "Mr Baley, you mentioned earlier that the defendant was picky as to who he would say good morning to," he reminded.

"That's right," Gordon affirmed.

"Anyone in particular?" Tailor asked.

"Mainly the females of the office," Gordon replied.

"Thank you," Tailor said and sat down again.

Everyone seemed quite shocked that Tailor's had been such a quick deposition and Kat was on her feet before she really knew why. She searched her papers for inspiration and saw Luke's note book. Under *Nice try* he had added *I dare you.*

She smiled and her eyes sparkled.

"Why do you think that was?" she asked.

Henley gave her a stare that would have shot her across the room if it had anything to do with ballistics.

"Well, gender grouping within the office is an entirely different matter. The sub-classes within each department is a study on its own but a generalisation would have the males as natural combatants within the corporate gladiatorial arena. The men would fight over everything that could elevate their testosterone rating within their tribe and, as an aggregate, to compare with rival tribes. Such things as sales figures, budget margins, alcohol consumption, sexual proclivity, football statistics and so on. But as these men try to outdo each other there are some males who would travel amongst these tribes not as a contender but as an unobtrusive observer. He is able to-"

"Mr Baley," Henley interrupted calmly, "I am holding you in contempt of court. Guards please remove him from the courtroom."

"What?"

The guards stepped up to the pulpit and pulled Gordon down and away through the right hand door.

"That, Ms Sabella," Henley said, "was very cruel and most unusual."

Kat stared blankly at the judge and sat down. *Should I feel a bit guilty?* She wrote to Luke and he scribbled a reply.

This'll give him something to talk about in the office on Monday. His testosterone rating will go through the roof. And besides, he's a tit.

When the guards had returned to their positions, Henley announced, "Call Sanjeet Raj." She did not stop eyeing Kat with disdain until a thirty-year-old Asian man had taken the stand and was sworn in. Kat made sure she did not give the judge eye contact or any hint of a smile.

Sanjeet was wearing a tan suit, lime green shirt and black tie. He had a neat black beard and such white teeth that shone like a beacon each time he smiled.

"Please tell us your name and relationship to the defendant," Henley requested.

"My name is Sanjeet Raj and I am Luke Robinson's manager at Garrick Communications," he told the court.

"How long has the defendant been working for you?" Miakoto demanded.

"Two years as manager and two as team supervisor," Sanjeet replied.

"You know him well," Miakoto concluded.

"Reasonably."

"Do you know him purely from the office or on a personal level as well?" Jameson asked.

"I divine details of my staff's background from collated information over time," Sanjeet told her. "I listen and I remember. Luke is not one to offer personal details without being asked directly and I do not pry into the affairs of others without reason."

"What sort of reason would make you ask about an employee's life outside the office?" Henley asked.

"If there was a downgrade in their work. If something was interfering with the office."

"Did you ever have to that sort of a talk with the defendant?" Henley continued.

"Never," Sanjeet said. "Luke was a consistent worker and a credit to the department."

The judges went silent and passed the questioning over to Kat.

"Sanjeet, would you say that Luke was a conscientious worker?" Kat asked.

"Yes, indeed."

"He performed all his tasks in a professional manner?"

"Without question."

"Was he at all subversive?"

"In what context?" Sanjeet asked.

"Well, did he go telling tales on his co-workers? Did he complain to your manager about issues he could have dealt with you? Did he ever try to rock the boat and cause trouble?"

"Never. In the four years I worked with him there was never the need to hand out a disciplinary action, on or off the record, verbal or written."

"Thank you," Kat said and sat.

Tailor stood and read from his notes.

"You 'never' had to have a talk with him about his personal life interfering with his professional?" Tailor asked.

"That's correct," Sanjeet replied.

"Your office diary says that you had an impromptu meeting with the defendant at nine-thirty on the morning of the twelfth. Is this correct?"

"Ah, well you see, what that was -"

"Yes or no, Mr Raj," Tailor demanded.

Sanjeet's eyes thinned.

"I had a meeting with Luke that morning," he said.

"And did you discuss any element of his private life?"

"We did."

"But you 'never' had to have a talk with about his private life interfering with his professional?"

"Correct," Sanjeet said.

"Mr Raj," Henley chipped in, "I must remind you that you are under oath and it seems that your testimony is contradicting itself."

"Your honour, if the 'oh so clever' lawyer would have given me the chance to explain, I would have told him that I didn't call Luke in for a chat. He came to me."

Tailor did not look perturbed.

"And what was it that you discussed?" Tailor asked.

"A few people had not turned up to the office because of the caretakers' announcement. Luke stumbled in just before nine-thirty - an hour later than he usually would. He looked flustered. He saw me and asked if he could have a word. I said yes and he told me what had happened to him."

Luke had been one of those people who did not believe that the caretakers were going to change the world. Heck, if a change in Government did not do anything then what would a bunch of intergalactic tourists be able to do? So Luke went to work as per normal.

It was a frosty morning; the kind he liked. A deep breath of coldness invigorated his body and fuelled him with energy. He decided not to take the Underground because everyone would be on it and with the time it would take waiting, cramming his self on the sardine express, stopping between stations, blah, blah, it would not take much longer to walk and he certainly would not be in as foul a mood when he got to the office.

There were a few other pedestrians on their way to wherever they needed to get to and the traffic was thickening to the point of imminent gridlock. Luke maintained a brisk pace and wove deftly around slow movers and path obstructions.

He slipped up a side street that connected this main road with a parallel road that, in turn, fed onto a pedestrian walkway. He was passing a set of fire doors when they flew open and struck him squarely in the chest. The impact was enough to launch him off his feet and send him to the floor. The wind had been forced from his lungs and he struggled to catch his breath and fight off a rising shock. He was not hurt but could not believe what had happened.

He sucked in a lungful of air and hoisted himself back onto his wobbly legs. It was then that a noise from the other side of the doors filtered through his confused senses. There was a commotion coming from inside the building. There was a loud crack that made him flinch and then a person came running from behind the doors and he found himself on the floor again with the person on top of him. He focussed his eyes and saw the person was a woman about his age. She looked into his eyes and he saw fear.

His back was aching and his head was still ringing from the impact but, for that split second while he looked into her eyes, he was lost. Everything around him melted away and there was just them.

In retrospect he considered that there was not anything in particular that was striking about the woman but she was the first person he had ever seen in his life whose features just fit perfectly. Everyone has at least one facial flaw: their nose is too big, one eye is slightly squint, eyebrows join at the brow, but everything about her face was fine.

She looked hesitant and panicky. Then she overcame some internal struggle and spat into Luke's open mouth. She jumped to her feet and took off running again just as a couple of bloody men thundered through the fire doors. They all left Luke writhing on the floor choking in disgust and trying not to drown on someone else's saliva.

And then he was alone, lying in the road as if nothing had happened apart from the pain in his back and head, the foreign taste in his mouth and associated nausea, and the memory of those eyes and features.

He tried to get to his feet but his legs were not strong enough yet so he sat on the curb for a few minutes until a sense of composure had returned. Then he continued on his way to his work place.

It was not until he had entered the building that he discovered he was almost an hour later than he should have been, that his recovery time must have been longer than the few minutes he thought it was.

It was all too weird: the accident, the meeting, the reaction, the gobbing, and the leaving. What the hell had just happened? He felt the need to talk to someone, not for advice but just so he could hear his voice say it all so he knew it really happened.

As he breezed into his office he could see that there was less activity than a usual morning. He dumped his stuff at his desk and he looked around. There was Gordon at the opposite desk and his gums were flapping away ten-to-the-dozen about nothing in particular to no one at all. Then there was Sanjeet coming out of his side office. He listens, he would do.

Luke made a beeline for him and Sanjeet looked almost scared for a second because of this dedicated motivation.

"Can I have a word, Sanj?" Luke asked as he strolled past.

"Erm, of course," Sanjeet stuttered. "Go into my office."

Luke let himself in and took the seat in front of Sanjeet's desk. Sanjeet followed him in, closed the door behind him and took his seat across the opposite side.

They two men just stared at each other for a moment.

"You seem troubled," Sanjeet commented.

"Something odd," Luke muttered. "Something so very odd has just happened to me."

"Are you all right?" Sanjeet asked.

"I don't know," he replied. "There was a girl with -" He tried to find the right words but could not. "Eyes. She knocked me down."

"You were mugged by a woman?" Sanjeet asked in alarm.

"No, she just knocked me down then got up and ran off," Luke explained. "She was being chased by someone but there was a look in her eye that totally threw me."

"What?"

"Such passion and kindness," Luke sighed. At last he had worked out what it was he had seen behind the fear and it relaxed him so much. His eyes wandered around the room as pieces slowly fitted together.

"Luke?" Sanjeet prompted.

"Carolyn," he said, stood and walked to the office door. "Thanks, Sanj," he said and made his way back to his desk.

"You're very welcome," Sanjeet replied, totally unsure of what it was he had been thanked for.

"Are you okay, Luke?" Gordon enquired as he approached.

"Yeah," Luke replied.

"Had a word with Sanjeet did you?"

"Yeah."

"About anything in particular?"

"Nope," Luke replied and gathered his things together.

"Did you talk about me?" Gordon demanded.

Luke just stood there and stared at Gordon for a second.

"Yeah," he said and walked out of the *office and out of the building.*

"Why do you think he said his fiancée's name?" Tailor asked.

"Objection, your honour," Kat called. "Mr Raj is not in a position of expertise to determine the defendant's reasoning behind saying, er, what he said."

"Not very eloquent, Ms Sabella," Henley chided, "but point well made. Sustained."

"Was that the last time you saw the defendant?" Tailor asked.

"It was," Sanjeet answered.

"One more thing, Mr Raj. The defendant's mode of work; you said he was very conscientious?"

"That is correct."

"He did all his work according to office policy?"

"Yes. I checked his files - when it was apparent that he was not returning - and I found he had kept records of every email he had sent and received, and notes relating to conversations he had had for individual jobs. They were all cross referenced and easy to follow."

"In your experience as an office worker, would you say it was purely worker conscientiousness to go to that detail?"

"I am not sure. I have never seen any one go to that extreme."

"Let me ask this, then. Why would you keep a copy of an email sent to you?"

"In case I needed to refer back to it, I suppose," Sanjeet said.

"Under what circumstances would that happen?"

"If the person who sent it was to contradict the details of that email at a later date."

"So, you would keep copies to protect yourself?"

"Yes, you could put it that way."

"So would you say that the defendant was protecting himself from every possible angle? That this 'extreme' was almost verging on acute paranoia that someone was out to get him?"

"Objection," Kat yelled.

"Sustained," Henley responded. "Mr Tailor, the witness is not a psychiatrist."

"No further questions, your honour," Tailor said and sat. "Thank you, Mr Raj."

Kat remained standing.

"Mr Raj, would you say that the 'extreme' nature of Luke's filing allowed you to trace his work and methodology a lot easy than if he just had a few invoices lying around?"

"Absolutely."

"Thank you. No further questions." She sat down.

"Just Carolyn left, then," Luke commented.
"Is she still on your side?" Kat asked.
"I doubt it," he replied.
"When were you supposed to get married?"
"This summer."
"Wow, you must have really messed up to change her mind," Kat suggested.
"Who said *she* changed?" Luke asked.

"Call Carolyn Soper," Henley announced and the side door opened. Carolyn was possibly a few years younger than Luke was. She had an unblemished, fresh faced appearance that promoted a youthful appearance. She wore very little make-up; just a sprinkle of foundation, blush and a light red lipstick. She was wearing a cream dress suit and white blouse. She had straight blonde hair cut to a bob with an upturned 'v' flick in her fringe over her left eyebrow. She marched to the pulpit and was sworn in.

"Please tell us your name and your relationship to the defendant," Henley requested.

"My name is Carolyn Soper and I was the defendant's fiancée," she said.
"How long have you known the defendant for?" Jameson asked.
"Six years," she replied.
The judges waited for elucidation but it did not follow.
"Where did you meet?" Jameson pried.
"At university," she replied.

In retrospect, you would have to say that the students' union bar was a grotty hole. When you work and have a regular income and are able to go to restaurants and tasteful wine bars, you can look back at the regular drinking places of old and shudder at the thought of the strangely-brown, sticky carpet, the seats with frayed upholstery, missing cushions and 'substance' between the gaps. At the time though, most of the patrons were living in similarly styled residences so this place represented a hole-away-from-hole that sold cheap beer.

It was Carolyn's second week of her first year and only her third trip to the union. It had all been a bit scary mixed with a bit exciting having to be this independent. Being able to do exactly what she wanted with only herself to blame for any consequences.

She had teamed up with three other girls who lived in her halls and they shuffled their way around the room like wary sheep. If one stopped to inspect something and the others moved on, she would quickly seek the safety of the herd again. They stood out as easy game to the older boys of the union; timid fawns trying their luck at the drought season watering hole. They may have had the appearance of fawns but they had the rapid response defensive capabilities of a US battleship. As a boy would advance from one side, the girls would wheel around to support the female being attacked. The lad would limp away with nothing more to report home other than being suckered into buying four rum-and-cokes rather than just the one.

This was pretty much the course of action for their evening and, to be honest, the girls were really enjoying all the attention, the free drinks and the new knowledge of how to control these poor mindless beasts called 'men'. But then she had seen Luke across the other side of the room, having a laugh with Gary

Shepherd (although she did not know their names then) and a couple of girls. As the night went on she satisfied herself - although she was not sure why - that he was not 'with' either of the girls and nor was he 'with' Gary.

She became more interested in Luke the more she noticed that he was not interested in anyone else in the bar apart from the people he was with. Whereas practically every bloke and every girl - including her - were, at some point, scoping the rest of the students present, there might as well have been no one else in the room as far as those four people were concerned and Luke was holding court.

Then the two girls were chatting to themselves, Gary had wandered off somewhere and Luke was staring back at her. She felt her face heat up dramatically and quickly turned her back on him. She could feel his eyes burning into the back of her skull. She could feel his inspection travel down her spine all the way to her feet and then back up to settle on her bum. She screwed her courage to the sticking point and turned to face him but he was talking to the girls again. Had he looked at her? Had he even given her a second look or a cursory inspection? She was almost insulted that he had not ogled her, that he had not undressed her with his eyes, that he had not-

She had to stop herself because she suddenly realised that he had not done all the things that she hated men doing to her. It had been such an expected attitude to face in the dating arena that it had become ingrained that it was the normal behaviour. But this man did not do it. He did not display the usual chauvinistic attitude towards her and that made him different, that made him special, that made her want to be one of those girls who he was devoting his utmost attention to.

Maybe he just did not fancy her.

She nearly laughed out loud at such a foolish notion and one of her friends asked what she was laughing at and she realised that she really had laughed out loud and that she was really drunk and needed to go home right now if her legs would work.

Luke and his friends had left and she wobbled precariously on the edge of insobriety and unconsciousness.

She had almost forgotten about Luke - presuming that he had been a twisted memory of that evening and 'An Officer and a Gentleman' - until another trip to the union bar and he came and stood right next to her and said her name.

"It is Carolyn, isn't it?" he asked again.

"Why?" she asked and wanted to slap herself across the face but presumed this would make her look even more foolish than asking, 'Why?' to a perfectly innocent question.

"Sorry," Luke stuttered, "I think someone has just played a trick on me." He turned red and was turning away from her.

Was that it? Was that going to be her, 'One that got away'? Based on what? Her, 'Why?' and someone pulling his leg about something.

"Yes it is," she blurted.

"Thought so," he muttered and stomped away.

"I mean, my name," she called after him. "It is Carolyn."

He stopped and turned to her then turned back to look at a couple of guys standing by the pool tables who were eagerly watching the events unfold.

"That doesn't change anything," he said and walked back to her. "Do you know those two?"

"One of them went out with a friend of mine for a while," she replied.

Luke toyed around with a couple of phrases and associated scenarios in his head for a minute.

"They said," he paused, "that you 'might need' some help getting home." He phrased the sentence so very carefully that she was sure there was a connotation in there somewhere but she could not pick it out.

"And you thought?" she asked.

"I'd help you home," he said, slightly shocked that there might be anything else.

"Fucking wankers," she spat.

"What is it?" Luke asked and then thought that maybe he should not have and that this was something he should have just walked red-faced away from.

"It's nothing," she said. "Or rather, I don't really know what 'it' is but they've both tried it on before and were both turned down."

"Oh."

She almost blushed at her thought processes.

"Do you want to do me a favour?" she asked.

"If I can," Luke said.

She could feel her heart begin to beat that little bit faster and was not sure she was going to be able to force the next few words out. She swallowed back the rising butterflies.

"Give me a kiss then leave with me."

Luke did not blink.

"Okay," he managed.

She had to confess that it was not the best kiss she had ever had but it was by no means the worst. She presumed that it was because it was not a 'real' kiss, it was pretend, because the one he gave her a bit later *was sooooo much better.*

"You lived together?" Etienne continued.

"Not at university but when we moved to London after graduating," she told them.

"So you were also living with," Jameson rifled at her notes, "Gary Shepherd?"

"That's right."

"How long were you engaged for?" Etienne asked.

"Nearly two years."

"And you were to be married?" Etienne asked.

"Yes," Carolyn replied and bowed her head slightly. "In three months."

"You have separated now?" Etienne continued.

"Yes," Carolyn said and had composed herself so returned her head to its resolute position.

"Why?"

"Differences," she said.

"You argued?"

"Not really. There was something different about him."

The judges left it there, realising that, perhaps at last, here was a witness with some meat to her testimony.

Kat stood up.

"Carolyn, do you remember what it was that attracted you to Luke when you were together?"

Carolyn burst out laughing and covered her mouth quickly. "Sorry," she said. "I'm not sure I can what it was specifically, he was just different than other men."

She would always look at Gary first or think about what he might do. Gary was your atypical lager drinking, bird shagging, footie-watching lad. He did not seem to have any redeeming characteristics when you really got to know him apart from he would do anything for his mates. Considering that usually meant trying to start a fight, she was not sure that was redeeming in itself but maybe relatively redeeming.

After she had considered Gary, she would then have a better idea of what Luke's reaction might be because, for some reason, despite the years they had been together she still had problems trying to predict him. He just would not conform to what her idea of what a man should be and that was not a bad thing in any way shape or form.

He would go shopping with her, he would watch chick-flicks with her, he would remember, discuss and anticipate her periods and there were many other things that were the exact opposite of what her friends would complain about their men. But at some unconscious level there was something creepy about it. So when he did go out by himself and drink himself to a state of extreme nausea she actually sighed with relief that there was some 'normality' in there somewhere. She would still bitch at him in the morning about it, though.

He was not a sports spectator, he was not aggressive, he was always a considerate and passionate lover, he enjoyed cuddles after sex and he made them dinner in the evenings.

He could always surprise her and do things that would catch her emotions totally off guard. On the night he proposed to her, he was acting so odd that she thought he was about to finish it so she bawled her heart out with relief as much as happiness that they were taking the next step.

And then the wedding plans. It was not that he was unhelpful because he *did* want to be involved and was constantly asking about updates, offering advice and making necessary arrangements, but he left the entire decision making up to her saying, "What ever you want to do is fine with me." He had said that all he wanted was the result of them being together forever. The pomp, circumstance and party afterward would be a small price to pay to ensure her happiness.

She had bawled then too.

"Were you physically attracted to him?" Kat asked.

"It wasn't the first thing that I noticed but I certainly didn't think he was ugly or anything."

"Did you ever know Luke to have gotten himself in any trouble?"

"No."

"Never? Physical? Financial? Emotional? Family? Nothing like that?"

"No. He never got himself into any kind of trouble."

"What about last month with the invasion?"

"He didn't get himself into that," she endorsed, "he was dragged into it."

"What did you think when you first heard the caretakers were looking for him?"

"I thought it was a horrid joke that Gary was playing. Then later I thought it had to be a mistake."

"And later still?" Kat urged.

Carolyn closed her eyes and bit into her bottom lip. "When I got home on the Wednesday the place was a mess: broken furniture, holes in the walls, bizarre equipment and two dead bodies. We alerted the police and when Luke didn't come home they went out looking for him. When Thursday came and went and we didn't hear anything from Luke, the police or the caretakers again I thought he had to be dead. I thought we all were going to be."

"When was it that you found out that Luke wasn't dead?"

"Gary woke me up early Tuesday morning to tell me. Then there was a phone call from Christine, Luke's mum."

"And how did that make you feel?"

"I don't know," Carolyn confessed. "I was confused. Gary was jumping around the house, Christine was crying and the television just had images of so many bodies and so much smoke."

"So you weren't happy?" Kat asked surprised.

"I told you, I don't know what I was. I must have been in shock."

Kat turned to the judges. "Your honour, can we have that last comment stricken from the record on the grounds that Ms Soper is not in an experienced position to be able to diagnose what is or isn't a state of shock?"

The judges and Carolyn looked very surprised at Kat.

"Under the circumstances, yes," Henley agreed, "but I am surprised you are treating one of your witnesses with such curtness. Your reasoning is your own but I advise you to turn it down a bit."

"I am sure I do not know what you mean, your honour," Kat responded. "I simply want Ms Soper's testimony to be free of any confusion."

"You don't think it would be totally unreasonable for the defendant's intended wife to suffer shock after hearing he's not dead but had saved the entire planet from total annihilation?" Henley asked.

"Objection, your honour," Singleton shouted with an American accent and jumped to his feet.

"I beg your pardon?" Henley demanded.

"I, er, object to your statement, your honour," Singleton explained.

"On what grounds?"

"Speculation."

"That Luke Robinson saved the world?"

"That he saved the world from total annihilation, your honour."

"Sit. Down, Mr Singleton," Henley recommended then turned her steely gaze back to Kat. "Well?"

"Not at all unreasonable to suppose it could happen, your honour, but it would just be a supposition and not, as Ms Soper stated it, a fact unless it had been medically diagnosed. Your honour."

"So maybe you should just ask your witness to reword her answer rather than have it stricken from the record," Henley suggested.

Kat let her eyes wander around in their sockets for a reasonable response.

"I could," she said.

Henley shook her head in dismay. "Denied, the comments will remain in the witness's testimony. Please continue, Ms Sabella."

Kat rifled her papers to remind her where she had got up to.

"When was the first time you got to see Luke after the seventeenth?"

"I went to the hospital a few times but he was still unconscious."

"I have the visitor list from Luke's ward and it states here that his mother never left the building and yet you only went to visit a few times? Why was that?"

"It hurt me too much to see him like that."

"Were you there when he awoke?"

"No, but Christine called me shortly after so I dropped everything and went straight there."

"At that stage, did you notice any of these differences?"

"He was very distant towards me and reluctant to give me eye contact."

"And after his release, he went back to your residence?"

"Yes."

"And did your living arrangements continue as normal?"

"At first. Then after a few days we broke off the engagement and I moved out."

"Are you able to tell us the point at which you knew that your relationship was beyond saving?"

"There was a build up. He was having nightmares and would keep calling her name out."

"Whose name?"

"Hers. The woman from the messages," Carolyn spat.

"The woman called Tasya?"

Carolyn shuddered at the sound of the name. "Yes. He kept calling her name in his sleep."

"Do you know why?"

"He said it was because she had been there throughout every horrendous thing that had happened so it was logical that she would be in his nightmares as well."

"But you didn't believe him."

"I did at first but then he called me by her name."

"When?"

"I was stepping out into the road and hadn't seen a bike coming. He called her name and pulled me back."

"He saved you from a perilous situation?"

"Yes."

"And then you broke up with him?"

"He had changed," Carolyn snarled through clenched teeth. "Everyone saw it."

"Had he become violent towards you?"

"No," she said defiantly.

"Did he threaten you at all?"

"No."

"Was it him who called off the wedding?"

"No, but -"

"Did he say he still loved you?"

"N-" she started automatically. "Yes. Yes, he said he loved me. But he never said it with the same look in his eyes when he said it before he met her."

"Do you believe Luke had an intimate relationship with Tasya?"

"Yes I do."

"Did you ask him?"

"Yes, but he said he hadn't."

"But you didn't believe him and still don't. Under the circumstances that he was facing the probability of painful death and very real possibility of never seeing any of his loved ones again; do you think it would have been totally unreasonable for him to seek comfort from the only friendly face present?"

Carolyn did not even wait to think about it. "Yes," she said.

"No more questions," Kat said and sat down.

Tailor stood up.

"Did the defendant ever give you reason to believe he had been unfaithful in the past?" he asked.

"Not really," Carolyn confessed.

"A colleague of his testified earlier that he was particularly friendly to the female staff of his employment. Were you aware of this?"

"He did talk more about the women in his office than any men," she said. "I just presumed that there were more women there."

"Back to his change in personality," Tailor digressed. "Can you elaborate on any other changes other than the nightmares and name calling?"

"Whereas before, it used to be me who made all the decisions. Now he started to tell me what he was going to do. We used to do everything together but then he was going off by himself."

"Going where?" Tailor asked.

"The television interviews and things like that. He specifically told me that he didn't want me to go."

"Did he give you a reason?"

"He said he didn't want me to get mixed up in that part of his life."

"How did that make you feel?"

"Alienated. Everyone else in the world was allowed access to that part but me. It felt like he was keeping secrets."

"We heard earlier that he had become more confrontational," Tailor told her. "Were you ever a witness to this new trait?"

"Yes."

"Please go on," Tailor prompted.

"Well, like I said, he always left the decisions to me and that included things like complaining, making organisational phone calls and that sort of thing. After the seventeenth he became more assertive, he'd be more willing to voice his opinion. He'd tell people when he was dissatisfied with their service, if people were rude in the streets."

They were on their way to the jewellers to try on his wedding ring again. This was the third time they had to go back because they had got the size wrong.

"If they haven't got it right this time we should just cancel it and go somewhere else," Luke said as they got in the car.

"If you think so," Carolyn replied. "That's exactly what I said after the first time," she reminded him, "but you said to leave it."

Luke climbed into the driver's seat.

"Yeah well, that was then," he said, strapped in his seat belt and turned the ignition.

Carolyn climbed in next to him and Luke started to drive into town.

"I've been thinking," she started. "Are you sure you're absolutely okay to go ahead with the wedding? You don't want to postpone it for a while until you're totally settled?"

"Sweet-heart, I am as settled as I'll ever be," he said and indicated to turn right at a roundabout. "Besides, we've paid all the deposits that we'll not get back." He checked his rear-view mirror and pulled into the next lane.

"Under the circumstances, I am sure they would all appreciate our predicament and allow us to delay the event."

"What predicament?" he asked and pulled off the roundabout.

She turned her attention out of her side window. "Don't be facetious, Luke, please."

A set of traffic lights ahead were showing him a red so he started slowing down. The traffic was pouring from a side road and either cutting across his lane or joining it.

"There's nothing wrong with me, Carolyn," he urged. "But if you're having doubts."

The lights changed to amber before he had stopped so he took his foot off the break and applied acceleration.

Carolyn spun her head to him in anger. "Don't turn this round on me."

His car passed the lights just as the signal changed to green.

"Why's it got to be about me?" he demanded. "JESUS FUCK!" he yelled and stamped on the breaks.

A black Porsche shot across the junction in front of him. Luke rammed his fist on the horn and the driver slapped his index finger on his window at him.

"Are you okay?" Luke asked Carolyn.

She was panting heavily. "The belt winded me," she explained. "What happened?"

"That fucking idiot just jumped his red," Luke said. "Had I been a second quicker," he pondered then took a long look at how his fiancée might have been had the Porsche rammed into her door.

"Fucking idiot," he shouted and turned the car to follow in pursuit.

"Luke? What are you doing?" Carolyn gasped.

"You could've been killed," he told her.

"I'm okay. Let's just go to the shops."

"No," he told her flatly. "I need to speak to that arse."

It did not take long for Luke to catch up with the Porsche and he started flashing the driver with his lights. All this did was receive another index finger aimed at him and the driver accelerated away.

"Luke, please," Carolyn begged.

"No, things *have* to change around here," he said. "Otherwise, what was the point?"

He caught up with the Porsche again and started flashing. The driver slammed on his breaks to try to get Luke to rear-end him but he had had the good sense to stay far enough away to have plenty of time to avoid the collision. At that point, instead of breaking, Luke accelerated along side the Porsche and stopped in front of it. The Porsche slowed to a stop and both drivers stepped out of their cars.

The Porsche driver was in his early forties. He was wearing jeans, white tee-shirt and a baseball cap.

"What the fuck is your problem?" he yelled.

"You could've killed us back there," Luke told him.

"Oh, fuck off," he screamed and went to get back into his car.

"Don't walk away from this," Luke ordered and took a step forward. "We will resolve this."

The man stood up again. "Are you threatening me?"

"No," Luke stated. "I just want to know why you think the laws of the road don't apply to you?"

"Fuck. Off." The man instructed.

"Is it just because you've got an expensive, fast car," Luke pondered, "or is there something about you that makes you better than the rest of us?"

"You're pissing me off, pal," the man said and leaned inside his car to pull the boot release.

Luke felt his jaw tighten and his teeth grind together.

"Do you not even care that you might've killed yourself?" he asked.

The man opened his boot fully and rummaged inside. He stood up again brandishing the lever of a car jack. By this time a few pedestrians had stopped to watch what was going on.

"You don't want to do that," Luke advised.

"If the last week has shown me anything," the man said as he advanced, "is that life is too short to waste on pansy-arsed mother fuckers like you. So, fuck off or I might have to do some damage to you, your car and even maybe your girlfriend."

This caused a buzz of communication amongst the growing audience.

Luke sidled opposite the man's path so he stood between him and the Porsche. He stood still, opened his eyes wide and smiled.

"Come on then," he said calmly. "*If* you think you're hard enough?"

The man was slightly surprised that this conflict had turned so peaceful. It incited him even more and he swung the jack handle at Luke's shoulder but Luke was not standing there any more and the handle struck the Porsche's wheel arch.

The man was catatonic for a second as he stared at the self-inflicted dent. A couple of spectators laughed.

"You did that on fucking purpose," the man said.

"And what?" Luke demanded. "You were going to hit me by accident?"

The man swung out again but Luke stepped back and gave his arm an extra shove. His momentum sent him spinning and the handle whacked against the Porsche's windscreen that sent a crack winding along its length. That produced an, 'Oooh,' of mixed awe and sympathy from the crowd.

"Noooo!" the man screamed.

"Learn to drive considerately," Luke recommended. "Learn to live considerately. Maybe then, we've all got a chance."

The man lashed out and the end of the jack handle caught against Luke's cheek.

"That's all I needed," Luke told him and grabbed the man's hand at the handle. He pushed at his arms and the handle thumped the man on the forehead; his eyes crossed and his legs wobbled. He tried to release his grip of the weapon but Luke wrapped his hands tighter around it.

He pulled at the handle and the man automatically pulled back, Luke feigned a lurch forward and the handle smashed through the Porsche's side window. Again the man tried to drop the bar but Luke would not let him.

The witnesses told the police, when they turned up, that the men jerked backwards and forwards, each of them apparently trying to gain control of the metal bar. It hit the man twice across the temple and caused a gash to open but he still would not let go. The car's headlights were smashed, the roof dented and scratched and the front bumper got kicked off. In the final movement Luke was thrown to the floor, the man fell backwards onto the bonnet of his car and the handle flew up in the air and came down to stab into the man's thigh. He screamed and slid to the floor clutching the bleeding limb. Luke sat up holding a bloody gash on his face.

Neither the man nor police pressed charges against Luke and, after he had been discharged from the hospital with butterfly stitches to his cheek, he got into the passenger seat of their car. Carolyn was in the drivers' seat but she made no intention of setting off. This was the first time she had him to herself and she needed to get some things straight.

"Why did you do it?" she asked.

"He could've killed us," he reminded her.

"But he didn't," she pointed out. "He could've killed us when you stopped him."

"But I didn't," he replied. "What's your point?"

"You," she exclaimed. "What has happened to you?"

"I don't understand," he said but turned his head away from her.

"You always used to let stuff like that pass you by, but now you won't let anything go. Everything has to be an issue now. You are so intense."

He turned back and his eyes were waterlogged and angry. "Everything *is* a fucking issue now," he snarled, "but none *of you have a fucking clue."*

"That seems quite an extreme reaction from anyone," Tailor commented.

"That was the last straw," Carolyn said. "I dropped him off at the house and went back to my mum's."

"Did you feel threatened?" Tailor asked.

"I was petrified from the moment he chased after the Porsche," she admitted. "I was scared I was going to get hurt."

"As a result of your fiancé's actions?"

"Yes."

"No further questions, your honour." Tailor took his seat again. Kat stood up.

"Is it true that you were having doubts about your relationship before the events of the twelfth?" Kat asked.

"No," Carolyn replied defensively.

"But you were obviously not content with the relationship as it stood," Kat suggested.

"I loved Luke and I intended to marry him," Carolyn stated.

"But you said that there was something 'not right' about his unmanliness, as you described it, and that you had doubts as to his faithfulness even though he gave you no reason to think so."

"No."

"Your honour, can you remind the witness that she is under oath," Kat requested.

"I would, but you just did it," Henley said.

"You're twisting my words," Carolyn said.

Kat sighed.

"You were right to call off the wedding," she said. "Luke came back a different person who was not right for you. That is not in question here. No one would think badly of you for making that decision but you said that the machismo differences between Luke and your friends' boyfriends 'was something creepy.'

"This doesn't seem like a solid basis for a long-term, stable relationship."

Carolyn bowed her head and started to sob. "I don't understand what happened. When he was there I wanted him to be more of a man and then when I thought he was dead I mourned so hard. When he came back I felt robbed of purging those emotions. Then I found out who he had become and I knew my Luke was dead and I wished this one had never come back."

Carolyn raised her head, her tears were flowing unashamedly down her cheeks. She raised a hand out to Luke. "I'm so sorry, baby," she cried. "I wanted *you* back. Was that so wrong?"

Luke shook his head and mouthed, *I love you*.

"No further questions. Thank you, Carolyn," Kat said and sat. She pulled out a tissue and dabbed at the corner of her eye.

Carolyn was excused and the judges finished writing their notes. Jameson looked at her wrist watch then had a quick chat with her colleagues.

"We're going to recess for lunch," Henley announced. "We will recommence in two hours."

They stood, the rest of the room stood, and they left. Everyone sat.

"What's that all about?" Luke demanded. "They just had a break."

"They're getting old," Kat told him. "When they got to go they got to go, you know?"

"Not really," Luke replied. "What's the matter with your eyes?" he asked. "Are you crying?"

"I felt sorry for Carolyn," she confessed. "She loved you, you know."

"Bollocks," Luke suggested. "She possessed me and that's want she wanted; someone to own. Now, she wants to have loved me because she realises what she had lost."

"What was that, exactly?" Kat asked derisively.

"A genuinely nice guy," he told her.

Luke's two personal guards emerged from their side door and advanced on him. His jaw tightened and his teeth ground together. Kat noticed his severe reaction and placed her hand on his arm. She expected him to be so engrossed in his steely glare that he would either flinch at her touch or shirk it off in a sudden movement. He did not react at all, he did not stop staring and he did not stop grinding his teeth.

"I'm okay," he said. "I can't help myself any more."

The guards got to his table, made him stand and turn his back to them with his hands behind so he was facing Kat.

"My body seems to automatically prime itself for fight or flight," he explained to Kat. As the handcuffs snapped shut, Luke's preparatory stance washed out of him and his body relaxed.

"I'll be down in a couple of minutes," Kat said. "Can I bring you a sandwich or something?"

"Yes please," he replied and was escorted back through the side door.

She watched as the door closed behind him then began organising her papers for the next session.

As she became more engrossed in her filing, her brain filtered out the commotion of the spectators leaving the room. Then the guard's voice behind her made her jump in fear.

"Sorry, sir," the guard warned, "no unauthorised personnel are allowed past the ropes."

"I would like to speak to Katalina Sabella, please," a male voice told the guard and Kat span on her heels. She was not sure where or why this sudden burst of panic had come from but her heart was racing as she turned to face her enquirer and all she could notice were his eyes.

It had been a long couple of days for both of them. Kat and John had managed to steal about three hours sleep each out of the last forty-eight. It had been Friday evening when John wandered into the office as if he had been in a near death experience: he was pale, starey-eyed and shaky. Kat was getting ready to go home when he walked in, past her and dropped himself into his seat.

Kat waited a couple of minutes to see if he was actually going to say something or whether he wanted the dramatics to go on a bit longer. His eyes flicked over to her to see if she was paying him any attention and she rolled her eyes to the ceiling in search of divine assistance.

"It's been given to us," he announced cryptically.

"What? Hepatitus B?" she asked.

"His defence," he said.

"Whose?" she asked, becoming more wary.

"*His*," John hissed and Kat's legs started to give way so her hands searched for her seat behind her but did not stop staring in horror at her partner.

She swallowed hard.

"The Robinson hearing?" she asked and he just nodded. "But how?" she demanded. "Surely he's got enough money to go to some big U.S. partnership?"

"Apparently he's got nothing," John told her. "He's skint. You don't get paid for saving the World."

"He must be able to raise some funds. I'd send him a few pounds for saving my life."

"He doesn't want anything. He didn't even want any representation but the court appointed us and that's that."

"I …" Kat wanted to say something, anything, but words totally failed to be generated in her addled brain at that moment.

"That's exactly what I said," John told her. He was perking up now; obviously passing the panic along alleviated the bearer of some. A misery shared *is* a misery halved but it is still two people miserable rather than just the one.

"When do we start?" she managed.

"He's coming in tomorrow morning."

Her right leg started to jiggle under her desk. "It's too soon. We need time to prepare. I need to get a haircut," she rambled.

"Kat, there is nothing we can do to prepare for this," John tried to console. "We're about to be representing the saviour of human race. This man is an international hero. There has never been something like this before."

"What about Jesus and Pontius Pilate?" Kat wondered.

"The whole world only watched that in retrospect," John said. "If you happen to believe that it's a true story. And anyway, the existence of aliens has thrown an entire bundle of disrepute to a whole bunch of religions."

The fax machine started ringing and caused them to nearly fall out of their seats. John got up and walked to the machine. He held the corner of the paper as it fed through. Kat hated it when he did that. It was if he thought it was going to feed through quicker or he was going to be privy to the information a microsecond earlier. What really wound her up was when he -

"To Henwick and Sabella," he read and waited for the next line to roll through.

"Con," he deciphered before its completion. "Gratulations."

"That didn't take long," Kat commented. "Who would know already?"

"You are taking on a case that will," John continued and waited.

"The court would not have released it yet," Kat mused. "Did you tell anyone?"

"No," John replied then turned back to the fax. "Jesus," he exclaimed. "It's a death threat."

Kat jumped up. "What?"

"Congratulations. You are taking on a case that will ultimately end in your demise," he read. "You are consorting with the devil himself and many have taken a charge from God to rid the world of Satan in all his incarnations, his followers and sympathisers."

Kat thought about the words for a second as John ripped the paper from the machine.

"I'm calling the police," he stated.

"It's not actually a threat, though, is it?" she said.

"Don't do your lawyer shit with me now," John argued and dialled on his phone.

"The author of that doesn't threaten us, he's just warning us."

"I realise that, Kat," John said. "But do realise that it is probably true. Even though Luke Robinson has saved the World and all life on it, there are going to be a shit-load of fucked-off religious zealots who have lost their sole source of income to an advertising sales assistant from Camden."

"You really think we might be in danger?" she asked.

"I'd guarantee it," John said and turned his attention to his phone as he got connected.

Kat could not hear his conversation as she slipped into a trance. How can so much happen in such a short amount of time? They had been given the responsibility for the civil rights protection of the most important human being since, if you believed it, Jesus, and now someone wanted to kill them for it.

The stories that had circulated since Luke's safe return had it that he nearly died on numerous occasions for the sake of his planet and the people thereon. Did she have that same sense of morality to be able to do the same for that man? To put her life on the line for the sake of the planet's protector? Could she be so passionate about a cause, or case, that her personal safety was not an issue to her? Had there ever been a cause as big as this for her to be that passionate about?

No. She could actually answer that one. She had never been presented with a client who was so righteous that she felt she owed them her very life.

She jumped when John slammed the phone down.

"We're getting twenty-four hour, police protection," he told her.

"Just like that?"

"I told them what happened and why and they said they would sort it straight away. We've to wait until our escorts get here."

From that point on, Kat never travelled without at least two armed police offers until the moment she walked into the courtroom. The security had been so tight on that place that she felt absolutely at ease *until that man said her name.*

ACT 3: What Could Be And Who He Became

Luke's cell was not entirely uncomfortable. In fact, it looked like the proprietors had made the room up especially for Luke's temporary residence. They had even installed cable to the television and plumbed in a toilet with a cubicle around it.

Luke sat on the bed and did not turn on the television. He pondered the rest of the trial and what he was going to get out of it. The only thing that would have been on any channel would have been images of the empty courtroom, commentators giving their thoughts of how it was going so far, or vox pops from members of the audience. God knows he did not need to hear what other people thought of it so far. Nor did he care whether they thought he was guilty or not, or whether he should be put through the humiliation of a trial after what he had, supposedly, been through, or whether he was actually mentally fit to sit trial. He did not need anyone to tell him what he already knew.

It was so easy to slip into manic depression during these quiet moments of introspection because it was the self-exploration that tended to uncover what was wrong with everything else. The questions he would ask about himself could not be answered honestly without taking into consideration the rest of the World. He would never have been in this position if it had not been for 'the rest of the World.'

It was all so obvious to him and yet no one else seemed to get it. Any of it. What had happened and why it had happened. But he had been like that once, before being shown 'the light'. He remembered how little thought he had given the black spots in the sky as he walked to work that morning; how he was thinking of having to phone the coach company to make sure they had a thirty-seater available for the wedding day. It took so much to show him the truth, that he could not believe that it really needed to be that severe to get everybody else to see it his way. He thought that he had suffered for the sins of his people - although he made no pretences to think he was likeable to a deity of any kind - and all they did was take his phone number and say they would, 'give him a call some time'. That next time, probably, when the shit was slapping against the fans of impending extinction.

Of course, the worst thing for them was trying to put him in relation to their normal lives. How was he to fit in? How could any one have a normal conversation with a super hero? It was one thing to get a bit giddy and star struck in front of a Hollywood icon because that is easy to rate. The Hollywood actor is seen in the media, on the silver screen and on the television. Here is an unreachable being whom millions adore but there is the tiniest of finite chances that you *could* bump into them down at your local supermarket, in your world. Now, mankind's champion? In less than two weeks you are told you are going to die and people around you *do* die so you know it is going to happen. Then it does not happen and because you are alive you think that maybe it never really was going to happen. But you are constantly reminded that this one person who you have never met, never heard of and who had no previous experience is personally responsible for your continued existence.

HOW DO YOU DEAL WITH THAT? Especially if you then bump into him at your local supermarket and he is wearing a tatty jogging suit and buying haemorrhoid ointment.

Luke gently laid himself down on the bed and rubbed at his eyes.

What do you say to a person who you know saved your life but you are not really convinced you were ever going to die? *'You should really go see the doctor about that'*?

Luke did not want them to say anything. He had said on the television a thousand times, "You owe me nothing. I just did what I had to do." That was the only reason he agreed to do the interviews; to try to reach as many people in as quick a time possible to explain that everyone needed to change their lifestyles and that he was not anyone special and did not want special treatment.

He really *was* no one special. He really had no previous experience. He really did not have haemorrhoids, that was just an example he liked to use which, in actual fact, was always taken out of context.

How could it be so dark and *bright at the same time?*

He so wanted to open his mouth and scream so loudly that it might distract him from the agony in his eyeballs but they had clamped his mouth shout and all he could do was growl through his grinding teeth. His arms and legs were shaking violently in their restraints; the steel cuffs had made deep lacerations in his wrists and shins and blood was dripping gently on to the floor.

The light was extinguished and his growl turned into a pitiful sob. His tears started to pour forth again and a steady flow of saliva dribbled from his trembling mouth. His eyes started to accustom to the relative gloom and he could soon recognise the forms of his two captives.

They had told him straight away that they were a part of the alien invasion - that they were caretakers - but he assumed someone was taking the piss. Then they started hitting him and, eventually, he had passed out. When he awoke he found himself in this position albeit without the stitches in his eyelids and the burning at the back of his retinas.

They were a classic partnership in that they were total opposites. There was probably a back story of how they were mistakenly teamed together and they hated each other because of their differences but in the end it was those differences that brought them closer together.

Luke's sobbing had turned into manic laughter.

One was at least seven-foot tall and four wide but strangely it had not been him who was the instigator of the physical violence. No, he had been the seamstress. Luke had had to stare at his ogre sized face as his disproportionately huge fingers did such a neat, delicate job.

Luke could count the number of pock marks across the man's craggy cheek bones, he could smell the soft scent of orange on his breath and he quickly recognised the man's involuntary three blinks he made before sliding the needle through his skin again. Worst of all was Luke could see the reflection of his own eye, and the work being done on it, in the black iris of the giant. He was a perfectionist too; he took his time to make sure his work was infallible.

The other man was small and wiry and kept himself propped up on a slender, silver tipped, black cane. He had been the violent one. He had been the one to waste no time by punching Luke right on the bridge of his nose which blinded him and sent a shooting pain through to the back of his skull. After that the blows came from all around: stomach, ribs, kidneys and limb joints.

He had sat back and watched his big partner do his thing. Every now and then he might tut, or tap his fingers impatiently on the handle of his cane but he probably knew better than to actually say anything.

The strangest thing had been during the set up of their equipment.

"How's Macy?" Wiry asked.

"Yeah, she's not bad," Needlepoint replied. "She's a bit annoyed about all this but I have to keep explaining that it's just part of the job."

"What's that?" Wiry asked. "All the time away from home?"

"Yeah, but if it wasn't for the secondment she wouldn't be in the house she is."

"You got to see it from her side too," Wiry advised. "It can't be easy all by herself with the three nippers for months on end."

"She's not on her own," Needlepoint spat. "Her mother's staying with her while I'm gone."

"Or is that why you're gone?" Wiry asked and Needlepoint started to guffaw.

"Come on, get the optics lined up," Wiry ordered and his partner placed two metal poles directly in front of Luke. Each one had a trailing wire that led from a small box by Wiry's side and ended at a blunt point in front of Luke's eyes.

"How old are the kids now?" Wiry enquired as he adjusted a couple of dials on the box.

"Ebbly is nine, Shanie is four and -" Needlepoint's words were drowned out by Luke's sudden outburst of agony as the lights were turned on.

That had just been the beginning, now Needlepoint had his face pressed up against Luke's.

"I never known anyone to go for over four hours," he commented.

"Not done humans before, though, eh?" Wiry reminded.

"True, but they're not supposed to be much different to those," he paused in thought and looked at Luke's knee for inspiration. "What were those cribby things two jobs ago?"

"Oh them. The Flamians?"

"That's them. These Humans aren't supposed to be much different to them: technologically retarded, little resistance and fragile." Needlepoint looked back into Luke's eyes and seemed to get hypnotised. "Over four hours he's done. You gotta give that some respect."

"Get on with it," Wiry instructed but Needlepoint was still lost in the zoology of the moment.

"Why have you lasted so long?" he asked and Luke just gasped for breath.

"Why haven't you told us what we want?" Needlepoint continued and Luke stopped for a second. He tried to frown but it hurt too much.

"What?" he ventriloquised? "Watchu wanna know?"

"We want the code," Needlepoint said, surprised that he needed to say anything. "Didn't you know that?" He turned to Wiry. "I don't think he knew what we're after."

"He knows," Wiry said. "He's clever."

"We saw you with her," Needlepoint told Luke.

"Hoo?" Luke sobbed.

Wiry brought forward a small monitor. "There's no point in pretending any more. We got her, we got you. She ain't got the code therefore you got it."

The monitor screen flickered and the girl who had bumped into him came on the screen.

"People of Earth," she announced. "The destruction of your planet has been delayed. The deaths of your countries' towns and cities was meant to be the start of your end but the caretakers are missing a vital part of the viral code -" Her image paused.

"Blah blah blah," Wiry said.

"But we also got this," Needlepoint said and the screen changed to a still image of a corridor. There was a figure further down and when the picture began to play he could see it was the girl running away from the camera which was chasing. She turned a corner then poked her head back round. She had a gun in her hand and she fired it once. The camera shook and a body fell to the floor next to it.

"Was that Goodger?" Needlepoint asked and Wiry nodded solemnly.

The camera picked itself up and continued its pursuit. The screen whited out for a second as it turned the corner and was confronted by an open door to the bright outside. It adjusted, went through the doors, turned and saw the girl running along the street then it paused again and there was Luke, lying on the floor, looking dazed and as if he was about to throw up.

"Don't look so surprised," Wiry told Luke and both the men started to laugh.

"That's cruel," Needlepoint chastened as his chuckles calmed. "Gets me every time though."

"We know it was probably a random exchange," Wiry said. "You just happened to be in the wrong place at the wrong time, but we are certain that an exchange had been made."

"We want the code," Needlepoint told him.

"I goan'k have one," Luke replied.

Both caretakers looked very disappointed.

"Don't be like that," Needlepoint said.

"You've felt what we can do," Wiry added, "and trust me when I say that it's nothing compared to the kit we've got back on the craft."

"She did'n give gne anyfing," Luke implored.

"Why do you think we've gone to all this trouble at your abode?" Needlepoint asked but did not wait for an answer. "Because your friends and family will be back soon and we will dismember them in front of your eyes."

Luke started to sob again. "Gno, clease," he begged.

"What do you reckon?" Needlepoint asked. "Stay with the lights until his girly gets in?"

"Yeah, why not," Wiry replied and went back to the box.

Needlepoint turned back to Luke. "I respect your bravery," he told him, "but will your girlfriend respect it when my partner is scooping her insides out with a blunt spoon?"

Even though all that Luke could do was stare directly in front of him, he still had his peripheral vision so he noticed when the living room door opened. Under normal circumstance it would have been impossible for him to not look at the movement and alert Needlepoint to whomever it was. In fact, it took Wiry a few seconds to realise this new presence but by then it was too late. He flicked a switch and, for Luke, the world evaporated in a white flash and a blast of pain.

Through his screams of anguish he heard someone else yell and then someone was clambering over his body. The optics were extinguished, Luke's vision began to clear and he could see it was Wiry who was crawling helplessly across his lap. In the background he could make out Needlepoint advancing cautiously upon the intruder.

Wiry clambered at the side of Luke's chair and he felt his arm restraints unclip. He lifted his arms to try to free his head and lifted Wiry at the same time. The caretaker had his cane stuck width-ways through his neck; a viscous yellow liquid was bubbling from the wounds and out of his mouth. With a final expulsion of air and mucous his body went limp and Luke dropped him onto his lap. As he landed something hard struck Luke in the crotch. He blindly fumbled in the dead alien's clothes and pulled out a large heavy gun.

Needlepoint had gained the upper hand and pinned the mystery assailant to the floor. Luke pointed the gun over the big man's head and fired a shot. The crack from the barrel created such a sound that caused his ears to ring. The recoil would have sent him flying had he not been securely strapped down but, because he was, the gun butt slammed into his chest. The shot removed a chunk of plaster from the wall next to Needlepoint who had, for the moment, stopped throttling his captive. He stood up very slowly and Luke re-aimed the pistol to cover the man's body.

"What now, son?" Needlepoint asked.

"Fucking kill him," Needlepoint's victim demanded in a female scream.

Needlepoint took a careful step forward and Luke's hand began to shake.

"Just go," Luke ordered. "Leave."

"Can't do that," Needlepoint said.

The intruder pulled herself up but Luke could still only see her as a figure in his peripheral vision. He could make out her definite female figure and his heart raced slightly in anticipation and expectation.

"Kill him," she said. "If you don't, he'll kill you then me then your World."

"I've been looking in your eyes for the past six hours, son," Needlepoint told him but there was something else Luke was trying to remember. "I could see you were brave. Very brave."

"Fucking kill him!"

"Shut up, you self-righteous bitch," Needlepoint screamed.

Something about 'dismemberment,' Luke remembered. Something about insides being scooped out with 'a blunt spoon.'

"But you're no killer, son," Needlepoint said and stepped closer. "I could see that too."

"He *will* kill you," she re-emphasised.

Luke became resolute. "Look again," he told Needlepoint.

"Oh, shit," Needlepoint muttered and went to lunge but Luke pulled the trigger.

He was better prepared for the crack and the recoil this time but not Needlepoint's childlike scream of pain. Luke had missed. Or rather he had missed any point of fatality. Instead he had just managed to rip a mass of flesh from Needlepoint's side. He clutched at the wound and tried to stem the flow of dark yellow blood.

"Kill him," she ordered again but Luke had lapsed into shock.

Needlepoint's agony was turning to rage and he took a large step forward.

Crack.

Luke was not even aware that it had been him who had pulled the trigger this time but realised it must have been as Needlepoint's forearm flew across the room having been shredded from the elbow.

"You stupid little prick," Needlepoint screamed. "I am going to tear you apart."

Crack.

The shot pierced Needlepoint's hip and he fell on top of Luke, their faces only inches away from each other.

"Fucking got you," Needlepoint declared.

"Sorry," Luke hissed and jiggled the gun that had got wedged between their chests. The barrel was pressed firmly against Needlepoint's chin.

"Do it!" she screamed.

Luke knew this man. He had heard all about his family and his home life and he was about to remove him from that life. He was going to deny his children a father; his wife, a loved one; possibly his parents, a son. He was going to be responsible for the eradication of another life and he did not want to do it. He certainly did not want to do it like this.

Comprehension surged through Needlepoint's black eyes and he realised that he was never going to see his family again and this man in front of him was going to be the one to fulfil that. His eyes were imploring.

Then they were not there. Luke did not even hear the crack this time but he did want to have been able to look away so he did not have to see Needlepoint's face dissipate in a spray of yellow mist and shards of bone. For a fleeting moment he saw inside Needlepoint's head: cavities, organs, tubes and bones. He would see it again and again, every time he would close his *eyes and fall to sleep.*

Luke did not jump up screaming from his sleep every time any more, he did not have sweat dripping from his brow and the taste of blood in his mouth from biting his lips. He just opened his eyes and took a second to remind himself that it was not a nightmare, that it had been real and that it was just a memory. For some reason memories did not seem to upset him as much as the thought of a nightmare could.

Kat was sitting in his cell. She was pale and jiggling her leg. She had to double take when she saw that he was awake.

"What's up?" he enquired.

"I got you a sandwich and a coke," she told him.

He took them from her non-proffering, yet unresisting grasp and began to chow down.

"What's up?" he muttered between mouthfuls.

"I thought I was about to die," she said. "I really thought he had come to kill me and there was nothing I could do. I nearly peed myself."

Luke had stopped chewing for a second. "Yeah, that happens," he told her. "And worse sometimes. Who tried to kill you?"

"A man," she said then shook her head. "No one. I just thought."

"So you weren't about to die," Luke deduced. "Some guy just wanted your autograph?"

Kat chuckled. "Sort of but not quite. He wanted to know about my line of questioning and how far I was going to go into the presence of the girl with some of the agency witnesses."

"I was wondering that too," Luke said.

"I told him that I couldn't say anything that might jeopardise our case and the witnesses' testimonies."

"Can you tell me?"

"She's not very relevant to our case, is she?"

"Can we make her relevant?"

"Why?"

"Because she's gone missing and no one wants to say why," Luke said.

"Maybe she's gone home after a job well done," Kat theorised.

"When we came out of The Office," Luke recollected, "she was in a worse state than I was and if I had to go to hospital then she would have too."

"Maybe she died," Kat said.

"Maybe she did," Luke agreed, "but why isn't there a body? Why are there no records of her, or a Jane Doe, being checked in at any hospital in the area? Why is it that the media circus has suddenly forgotten her involvement and only focussed on mine?"

"I," Kat began but realised she did not really have a decent enough answer to give. "I don't know how to make her relevant."

"Impeachment," Luke said. "That weasely fucker Cummings. He's going to say some nasty things about me. Make him out to be a liar and that'll bollocks his entire testimony *and* I might get some answers."

"What about Roberts?" Kat asked.

"He can testify she was there but I bet he's as much in the dark about everything as I am."

Luke's brow furrowed in concentration. "This man who nearly killed you? Was he a reporter?"

"I suppose," Kat said.

"Did he have a notebook or recorder?"

"Er, not that I noticed."

"Who else would care?" Luke wondered.

Kat waited to see if he was going to come to any conclusions but realised that if there were any then he was keeping them to himself for now.

"We've got about twenty minutes until they start again so we had better make a move up when you're ready," she suggested.

"How long did I sleep for?" Luke asked.

"I don't know," she told him, "but I was here for about an hour and you were asleep all that time."

"I think I should sleep in a cage more often," he muttered and rubbed the sleep from his eyes. "You go ahead, I need to freshen up and I'll get brought up in a second."

Kat nodded and left his cell. She wound her way through the corridors and past the witness rooms. Christine and Robin came out to greet her.

"How do you think it's going?" Christine asked.

"It's hard to say, Christine," Kat replied. "The character witnesses are almost just a formality. They can't offer much weight to either side. The important testimonies will come from the examining psychiatrist, physician and maybe Luke's own."

"This is insane," Robin said. "Even if he should go to trial over this, why do they think he might not be able to do so?"

"Something happened to Luke during those five days and he came back a changed man. No one really knows who he is now, nor what the long term affects his ordeal may have on him: physically or mentally," Kat explained.

"So you believe them?" Robin demanded.

"No, Robin, I don't," Kat spat. "I don't believe he should even be here. I think he should be able to go up to anyone on the street and take their life if he wants to. I think he's deserved that but it's not up to me.

"I wouldn't still be here if I wasn't on his side. I would have left with John before we even started."

Robin bowed his head in shame and Christine hugged on his arm. She placed her hand on Kat's and said, "Good luck."

Kat returned a brave smile and continued her way to the courtroom. She took a sneaky glimpse in another of the witness rooms and saw four men with identical haircuts and dark suits in a heated debate. One of them saw her and promptly slammed the door shut.

She entered to the courtroom as the last few spectators were returning to their seats and was welcomed by a barrage of flashes from various places around the building. She could not help but notice one empty seat about a dozen rows back that no one appeared to be interested in reclaiming.

An involuntary shudder rippled down her spine as she remembered how helpless she felt during that 'near death' experience. What was it that she had seen in his eyes to make her so scared? He did not look angry or particularly threatening but there was a look of passion in his eyes. A look that said he wanted something so badly that he would kill for it.

She was probably more scared that she was able to divine something like that just from the way she was being looked at than the actual look itself.

She went through the motions of sorting her papers and tried not to think of those eyes staring at her back. She glanced over to her three rivals who were showing no signs of concern over how events were passing so far. But why would they be concerned? They were not doing this because they believed in their cause, they were doing it either because they were told to or they wanted a bit of exposure. Oh, sure, she had been told she had to do it at first, but the more she got to know Luke and the more she learned of what he had gone through, the more she believed in her cause and her client.

Yeah! She was righteous, and with that on her side there was no way she could lose.

"You keep telling yourself that, girl," she muttered unconvincingly to herself and returned her attention to her paperwork.

The side door opened and Luke, in handcuffs, walked through. He did not pause dramatically this time; he figured every one had had their chance but the camera flashes deposited intermittent bursts of hi-light anyway.

Practically no photo came out right. So many cameras were automatically adjusting their flash for the source of light Luke was in. If the camera thought it was too dark, by the time the flash went off another hundred were going off too and so overexposing the image. If a camera went to take a photo during the barrage then it decided that the ambient light was enough but by the time it went to collect its image the flashes were off and the picture developed underexposed.

Luke was led to his seat and the shackles were removed. He unconsciously rubbed at his wrists and sat down.

"Long time no see," Kat muttered.

"Do you come here often?" he asked and she giggled.

"That's the way," he decided. "We should try to inject a bit more fun into this."

The judges' door opened and the attentive wave was much tighter this time. Less of a wave but more of a geological land movement. They got to their positions and sat down. Henley addressed her microphone whilst scanning her protagonists.

"Everyone ready?" she asked and the lawyers stood.

"Did you remember to pee this time?" Luke asked under his breath and made Kat blush.

"Yes, your honour," the three men chanted and Kat just choked.

"Are you all right, Ms Sabella?" Henley enquired and she nodded her reply.

"Sorry, your honour," she managed at last. "Went down the wrong hole."

"Oo-er," Luke sniggered and Kat could not help herself but smile.

"Something amusing you, Ms Sabella?" Henley demanded.

"No, your honour," she replied. "Or rather, yes, your honour."

"Anything you'd care to share with the court?"

Kat blinked a few times and rolled the possibilities around in her head but then saw her red-cheeked face on the big screen.

"No thank you, your honour," she declared quickly.

"Well, a modicum of decorum, please," Henley chided and the lawyers took their seats.

"You're a naughty girl," Luke mockingly scolded and she punched him on his thigh. He yelped in surprise as his knee jerked up and hit the table which caused the glasses and water jug to clatter together.

Everyone stared at him.

"Cramp," he said and Kat snickered to herself.

"When you two have finally finished," Henley ordered. "Can we please get on? Who is the next witness?"

Umri got to his feet but Henley waved him to sit. Miakoto leaned over and whispered something to her.

"Thank you, Mr Umri for trying to help but you do not need to be quite so eager. It was more of a rhetorical question to order my thought processes again," Henley explained. "Can you call Inspector Henry Roberts?"

The call went along the chain and Roberts walked up to the pulpit carrying a small notebook. He had not changed much in the past month-and-a-half apart from he must have been getting some quality sleep as the dark rings around his eyes had faded considerably. His suit looked new, his shirt was fresh but he still managed to look scruffy.

He raised his right hand and was sworn in.

"Please tell the court your name and relationship to the defendant," Henley instructed.

"My name is Henry Roberts and I was the officer in charge of Luke Robinson's case during the twelfth to seventeenth."

"Are you still in the police force?" Miakoto asked.

"No, sir," Roberts replied. "Retired as soon as I had finished all the paperwork on the case."

"What rank were you at the time?" Miakoto continued.

"Inspector, sir."

"And how many men did you have under your command?"

Roberts cleared his throat. "At the height of the event I was in charge of over five hundred personnel which included officers from several different departments."

"How was it that you had all this authority rather than a higher ranking officer?" Miakoto asked. "Or even someone from the army? Why were the police involved at all?"

"Under the circumstances, sir, no one really knew what the protocol for the situation should be. I became involved from very early on and I, sort of, accumulated the assistance from the other departments as we went along."

"And the army?"

"There was no one for them to fight, sir," Roberts explained. "The caretakers stayed in their ships in a geostationary orbit out of reach of all terrestrial defence systems."

Miakoto shook his head with frustration so Henley leaned over and whispered something to him. He raised a hand in resignation and she leaned forward to the microphone.

"Gentlemen. Your witness, I believe," she said and Singleton stood up.

"Thank you, your honour. Inspector Roberts," Singleton started but Roberts interrupted him.

"Not any more, son," he reminded.

"Quite right," Singleton conceded. "Mr Roberts when was the first time you were made aware of the defendant?"

"Our station received a phone call from his fiancée," he paused to read from his notebook, "a Carolyn Soper. She said she had returned home to find a couple of dead 'people' in her living room. We were approaching a shift change so myself and WPC Phelps went to have a look.

"Upon arriving at the house we could instantly see that it had been the scene of a major struggle: the gate was off its hinges, the garden was in disarray and there were broken flower pots all around. Oh, sorry."

"What is it?" Henley asked.

"I was just reading from my notes and it turns out that there hadn't been any trouble outside. That was actually the condition the tenants had kept their garden in. I'm sorry, I should've rehearsed this a bit better. It has been a while."

"Do go on, In - er - Mr," Singleton urged then added. "Roberts."

There came muffled sniggers from the defence table.

"When we got in the house there was the fiancée and another young man, er," Roberts said and flipped through his book.

"Gary Shepherd?" Singleton suggested.

"That's the chap," Roberts replied. "Anyway, she was very distressed and he was consoling her. In the living room was a man with a walking stick impaled through his neck and another with multiple gunshot wounds and no face. There were signs of a struggle and more large holes in the walls and there was a chair with leg, arm and head restraints."

"Was there any sign that the defendant had been involved with this scene?"

"Yes. Results that came back from DNA testing indicated that he had been held in the chair for approximately 6 hours."

"How was that determined?"

"Blood and tissue samples were taken from the restraints and a time could be back tracked using uniform rates of coagulation."

Judge Jameson seemed to go a bit pale.

"Could it be determined that the defendant had been directly responsible for either of the men's deaths?"

"At some stage we believe that either the defendant got hold of a gun or someone else fired the shots from the position of the seat he was being held in."

"How did you come to the conclusion?"

"The position of the bullet holes in the walls traced back to the one point and the fragmentation, spray and particle trajectory of the man's head indicated that it was a point blank shot to the base of his chin from the position of the chair."

Jameson picked up her glass of water with a shaky hand and sipped delicately at it.

"'Point Blank,' you say? And, 'under the chin'?"

"That's correct," Roberts confirmed.

"So the shooter would have been face-to-face with his target?"

"Well, facing each other, we can't -" Roberts tried to explain but was cut off by Singleton.

"Have you ever shot a person?"

"Objection," Kat screamed. "Mr Roberts is not the one on trial here."

"I want the court to have a relative view of, at the time of a shooting, what goes through an individual's mind," Singleton explained rather irritably.

"The bullet," Luke announced and laughter rippled through audience. Jameson blanched even more. Singleton's jaw tightened and he glared at Luke.

"I'll allow it, Mr Singleton," Henley told him, "but you're treading thin ice. Ms Sabella, talk to your client again about outbursts."

"Yes, your honour," Kat said and sat down.

"Have you ever shot anyone, Mr Roberts?" Singleton continued.

"I have," Roberts replied sombrely.

"Fatally?"

"Yes."

"Was it an unintentional killing?"

"No."

"Can you allow us your thought processes behind this incident?"

They had finally caught up with Robinson and the girl at a storage facility in Walthamstow. The couple had been one step ahead of Roberts from the house onwards but when he had turned up at the sex shop and there were five more caretakers lying dead and mutilated, there had been a business card for this place in the clothes of one of the bodies. At least there were no dead humans that time. It was strange; he had seen dead people of all ages, of both genders and of many races, all presented in various states of demise. He supposed that his exposure to some of the most grotesque bodies had desensitised him to all of them now, but there was something about the caretakers that made his stomach turn. Maybe it was their snot-coloured blood; it just was not natural. Instead of being a neat package of organs wrapped in skin they seemed to be composed of a sponge-like mush wrapped up in opaque cling film. Their skin seemed very flimsy and they tended to break apart if handled too roughly but that might be some sort of bond breakdown after death. They could be easily recycled, unlike humans who had bits of their bodies that would lie around for years.

Robinson and his girl friend had been on a caretaker killing spree. That did not bother him particularly as it was the caretakers that were threatening his life. However, after the mess at Robinson's home, there had been a call from a library the next day and when he got there he found three more caretakers in various states of dismemberment and six dead humans. Now, he had been doing his job for a long time and would be the first not to jump to any conclusions but killing humans was just plain illegal and he needed these two so he could find out what was going on.

Of course, the girl had cropped up on the telly so they kind of knew that she was interested in, and was, stopping the caretakers.

And now it seemed that someone had tipped them off as to where they would be next. His 'squad' arrived in time to see Robinson and the girl disappear into the facility.

He looked around at the collection of officers he had acquired over the past twenty-four hours. There were thirteen of them now: three 'beat' constables in plain clothes, two detectives from CID, two 'special' constables, four armed city officers (two of whom claimed to be ex-SAS), and the odd bloke from MI5 - Agent Cummings - who was there on an advisory role. They had all gotten involved for their own personal reasons and experiences and were acting as an official unofficial investigation. All their superiors had told them to try to sort it out but there was nothing they could do to protect them within their departments if something should go wrong.

Only the armed officers had ever fired weapons before and yet they were all being handed a plethora of guns, shock and smoke grenades, blades and bullet proof vests. All they knew about their targets was that wherever they went, bodies with large chunks of flesh missing kept cropping up.

Roberts was in charge but he had absolutely no experience in storming a building so he handed the direction over to the armed officers. They split into four groups, each being led by one of the experts. They all sidled their way along the rows of adjoining buildings. One group disappeared into the neighbouring building, the second group dipped down a side alley to the back, the third climbed an external staircase and the fourth, containing Roberts, went to the front doors. Each group was in communication with the other via radio units with earpieces.

Roberts played with the weight of the SMG in his hands. It was such a bizarre sensation to know that something so seemingly inconsequential could be so crucial in someone's continued existence. He could remember this nervous sensation from his first call out to a street fight. He felt like he needed to pee. His leader gave the signal to move and he heard three voices in his ear give a similar signal in quick succession.

What was he expecting? The door would get kicked in, warnings would be screamed, each team would be in a vantage point as to keep every angle covered, the end.

The special constable on his team was a big lad. From what Roberts had discerned earlier, he was a rugby forward for The Wasps and got on to the specials because he wanted to try to make the world a better place. He had volunteered for Roberts' squad because he had had family in Gravesend. The man took two steps forward and thumped his foot on the door, which would have crumpled in like balsa if it had not exploded outwards like tooth picks. If it was any consolation, the special did not even get the chance to scream because his body was completely shredded and death was instantaneous.

Roberts was in shock, as was his SAS and CID men. He came to as a hailstorm of cracks began going off in his ear accompanied by a couple of screams. He instinctively ducked, not remembering the sound was coming through his radio, as the wall above his head erupted and showered him with bricks.

He rolled himself up on the floor and wrapped his hands around his head to try to shut out the noise but all it did was shove his earpiece further down his auditory canal and make the sounds that bit more unmistakable.

Someone tapped him on the shoulder and he peered up. There was a hand and index finger pointing excitedly at the sky and as he looked to see who was doing it, he found that there was no arm or body attached and the hand was acting purely on reflex.

The sounds in his ear had quietened and he ventured a look around him then into the warehouse. There was lots of dust and smoke swirling around the room but he could see shadows of people within the gloom. Then over his earpiece he heard.

"There's one still moving at the front."

He did not know where the movement came from but he was on his feet and running before he even realised. Unfortunately when realisation did sink in it was the realisation that he was running into the warehouse instead of away.

Thunderous cracks of kinesis erupted from all around him but he kept running until he plunged headfirst into a stack of boxes. They crumpled at his impact and the top of the tower buckled over to pour their contents over the floor: rubber balls ranging in size from one inch to a dozen. The top ones dropped from twenty feet so bounced back up to ten. As Roberts scrambled to free himself from his cardboard incarceration he dislodged more boxes of balls and soon hundreds were bounding around the building.

"The signal is getting disrupted," he heard in his ear. "I can't isolate him."

"Go in and get him."

Roberts crawled through the spherical turmoil and soon found himself clutching at a pair of shiny black boots. He raised his head and first saw the cannon that man was carrying and, funnily, did not take much note of anything else. He rolled onto his back and pointed his SMG at the man.

"Watchu gonna do with that, little man?" the man asked so Roberts showed him and pulled the trigger.

He presumed that at least the first bullet must have hit its intended target but after that, where the rest of them ended was up to forensics to sort out. The noise that the gun made was one thing, but the recoil was something else and because he happened to be lying on a bed of balls the force sent him flying across the room. He heard the man yell as Roberts whizzed off into the smoke. He collided into some more bodies and soon people were standing, treading on balls then falling over. Then someone else started shooting and, again, all hell began to break loose but it seemed to be concentrating away from him in all directions. More boxes were struck by the random aiming and more balls fell to the floor.

"Multiple targets coming from all angles," a voice in his ear yelled.

Balls bounced, bounded and boinged through the barrage.

A caretaker thudded to the floor with a sticky, smoking, yellow hole in his chest. A table tennis ball ping-ponged off his forehead and 'tatted' across the floor in search of its next target. It disappeared into the gloom and a scream followed.

Roberts wondered if something else was going on or if they really did have a weakness to balls. He started to crawl further away from the main collection of thunderous defence and presumed his last drop of luck had run out when his head clunked against something solid.

He scrambled to bring his gun forward and noticed a pair of feet desperately scrambling away from him. His copper instincts kicked in; when someone tries to run from you for apparently no reason, it means they have got a reason to run. He reached out and grabbed the nearest ankle and had done this too many times before to be surprised that the other foot would return to rescue its partner, so he grabbed that one as well then pulled. There was a meeting of bodies as Roberts yanked himself up onto his escapee and came face to face with Luke.

"Luke Robinson, I presume," Roberts spat.

Luke flailed for a moment, then stopped when he noticed Roberts' eyes. "You're human," he said.

"Inspector Roberts of the Met, my son, and you're fucking nicked."

This made Luke calm right down. "You are joking, right?"

Roberts remembered his place. "When I get you out of here, then you're fucking nicked," he addendumed.

Luke smiled. "Great," he enthused. "Go for it. Are those all your men out there?"

"What men?" Roberts asked.

"Who the caretakers are shooting at."

"Balls, son," Roberts said.

"No, really. I can hear them shooting at someone."

"They're shooting at balls," Roberts explained then added, "and each other. But I think there's only me left."

Luke's enthusiasm waned and a nervous laugh escaped his mouth. "You fucking idiot," he said.

Roberts was lifted off Luke and set on his feet. The person who had done this so effortlessly then bent over and lifted Luke.

"Come on," she said. "We're leaving. Who's this?"

"A policeman," Luke said.

"Why's he here?"

"He's come to arrest me," Luke said.

The girl from the television message looked Roberts up and down.

"Why's he wearing a tank top?" she asked. "Is he cold?"

"It's supposed to be bullet proof," Luke said and the girl laughed.

She tapped Roberts on the chest. "Kevlar?" she asked and Roberts just shrugged. She lifted the SMG and inspected it. "Okay. That makes sense now. I'd get rid of it if I were you; it'll only slow you down. It's no good against their guns."

"Especially when they usually aim for your head," Luke added with a smile.

"Why have you cheered up?" she asked him.

"It's nice to have someone more naive than me around to look scared and clueless," Luke said.

"Why's he staring at me like that?" she asked Luke.

"Your eyes, probably," Luke replied and Roberts suddenly realised that even though they were talking about him like he was not there he actually felt like he was not there. The girl had emerged through the fog and he had recognised her immediately. Then her eyes had transfixed him. There was such a passion there; something that showed she really cared. It was something that did not come through the television screen and something that he had never seen before except during those most personal moments with his wife.

He shook himself to reality. "Can we get out of here?" he asked.

"Yes," she replied. "There's a blast hole in the wall back there we can get through."

Which is exactly what they did do. They got back to Roberts' squad vehicles where he noted that one was missing and a large crowd had gathered to see what all the commotion was about.

"Henry?" a man called from the crowd. Roberts looked up to see one of his neighbours approaching.

"What the hell is going on down there?" the man demanded.

"Caretakers, Mike," Roberts replied.

The man called Mike looked shocked. "Here? On Earth? What are they doing here?" He made a cursory glance at Luke and the girl who had tried to appear inconspicuous.

"Isn't that -?" Mike started.

"Police business," Roberts finished. Again, his experience on the force told him when a bad situation had the potential to turn into a worse one.

"Isn't that the girl off the telly?" Mike asked and a few of the other bystanders mumbled their assent.

"And him," someone else commented. "He was the photo they showed."

This piece of information was new to Roberts and the balance of an internal conflict tipped the other way. He realised Mike was looking at him and his gun.

"Don't do it, Mike," Roberts warned. "Police business, remember?"

"Bullshit," Mike spat. "They want him. They want both of them. Maybe they'll be willing to trade."

"They won't trade," the girl interjected.

There was a mumble of dissidence building up behind Mike and he felt the support.

"Give them to us Henry and you won't get hurt," Mike said.

"See this," Roberts said and lifted the gun slightly. "*This* tells me I won't get hurt, not you."

Mike laughed. "What? You'd shoot me over him? I've known you for over ten years." Mike leaned forward and whispered, "This is our chance to keep our families safe, Henry, and you're going to throw that away over some work ethic?"

Mike was right, of course. The young couple did represent bargaining power and the chance to save himself and his nearest and dearest. But what about the rest of them? His not so nearest? Where could he draw the line? And when he looked at the boy and the girl, what was it that he saw? Two inconsequential pawns who could be sacrificed on the possibility of a trade-off? Or were they more than that? If the caretakers were that desperate to get their hands on them then they must represent a threat to the bad guys which meant, by default, that they were the good guys.

This was the first time in his entire career that he had ever, *ever* been in the company of *real* good guys. Maybe that meant he was a good guy too. Good guys do not sacrifice their pawns; they make the sacrifice to save their pawns. That was what made a good guy definitively good.

"Get out of here," Roberts said to Luke. The youngsters looked surprised and were about to retreat when the crowd became restless.

"Don't be fucking stupid, Henry," Mike yelled. "They could save us."

Roberts raised his gun which caused a few of the less certain to back away.

"I know," Roberts replied.

"Even if you let them go," Mike said, "we'll still catch them."

"You won't," Roberts told him.

Mike smiled. "You're a copper, Henry. You won't shoot me, you can't. I'm unarmed and it'll be murder. I know you and I know you can't do it." He started to advance. Roberts had seen that look before; it was the calm, self-assuredness of a person confident that it would not be them on the receiving end of a pasting. Lads used it when they were in their big groups wandering around town after closing time, and some coppers used it after they had a shit day at home and need to vent some aggression. Mike had it now and it meant trouble was going to follow and he *was* a copper on duty. A copper on duty who had just seen his squad massacred, a copper who just realised he was helping to save the World, a copper with a sub-machine gun in his hand.

What was it they had called him?

"Unofficially official," he muttered. "I'm not a proper copper today."

Again, the noise and reaction the gun made was a shock to his senses but he did not show it and it was not half as shocking as it was for Mike. He danced like a marionette on an unbalanced tumble drier. The crowd scattered and dived for cover as Mike's body flew across the road and hit the ground.

Did Mike deserve it? Probably not. He had kids, he worked hard, he was not a bad man. But this showed that he was a stupid man and was willing to kill his planet on the slender hope that he could save his life. He was a pawn with hopes of knighthood but wanted to get it by sacrificing every other piece on his side.

Roberts did not need to turn around to see if Luke and his girl were still standing there. If they were then they were not the hope for mankind he thought they were.

He got in his car and drove back to his station. When he got there he proceeded to throw up non-stop for three hours *until he was vomiting blood.*

Roberts was staring, glassy eyed across the room. All in the court apart from Luke were in stunned silence.

Singleton came to and checked his papers to recollect where he was supposed to be going.

"So, you, er, shot an unarmed human, did you?" he blurted out.

"That's what I said," Roberts replied.

"And this was the first person you had ever killed?"

"That's correct."

"This man was known to you. He was a neighbour and, perhaps, you might have classed him as a friend. Was it a hard decision to make?"

"Of course it was hard," Roberts spat. "But he was going to jeopardise everything and I couldn't have that."

"You had intended to kill the caretaker that confronted you in the warehouse, had you?"

"I suppose," Roberts shrugged. "I'm not sure, he came out of nowhere and I had the means to protect myself so I fired. I know I didn't kill him though."

"How is that?"

"We met again, later."

"I see. Mr Roberts -"

"Then I killed him."

Someone in the audience 'whooped' their approval and Singleton threw his pencil onto the table.

Kat stood up. "Your honour, I'd like to know what the relevance of all this interrogation is. It is documented that Mr Roberts was discharged with full honours; that all actions outside of his normal course of duty were accepted and praised as, 'conduct employed to ensure the continued safety of the populace.' Mr Roberts is not on trial here and I find it highly disrespectful that my esteemed colleague would make it seem as if he were."

Henley turned to Singleton.

"I have to say, Mr Singleton, that I agree with Ms Sabella although I would not have phrased my complaint quite so self righteously. Where are you going with this?"

"Your honour, I am simply trying to get a first hand view into the mind of a man who finds himself having to kill for the first time," Singleton explained impatiently.

"And what is the relevance to this hearing?" Henley asked slowly and deliberately.

Singleton looked confused and turned to his partners for assistance but they kept their heads down. "To see if it fucks you up or not, your honour," he blurted.

Again there was a stunned silence apart from some sniggering from the defence table.

Singleton was marginally surprised at his own turn of phrase. He had turned red but whether that was from embarrassment or rising anger was uncertain. "Er, whether or not a forced killing would cause any long term side affects that may, er."

"Nice try, Mr Singleton, but you are being found in contempt of this court and will be dealt with accordingly after this hearing is completed," Henley announced.

"Mr Roberts," Singleton continued. "Did you meet with the defendant again before the seventeenth?"

"Not face to face," Roberts replied. "But we talked a couple of times and of course they - the caretakers - had the technology to send signals directly to our televisions so we spoke through that."

Singleton had completely lost his momentum and was shaking his head. "Did the defendant tell you if he had killed any more people during those conversations?"

"Objection!" Kat screamed and Singleton knocked his papers over the floor. Luke burst out laughing.

"Ms Sabella," Henley chided.

"It's not been determined that my client has, in fact, killed anyone, your honour," she announced.

"You go, girl," Luke commended.

"For fuck's sake!" Singleton bellowed. "We all know he fucking killed caretakers. No one really gives a shit that he killed some fucking caretakers. He gets brownie points *for* killing caretakers you stupid fucking bitch."

Luke roared with laughter.

Singleton lost it and threw himself at Luke's table. It seemed that maybe Luke was ready for him or maybe he was just exceptionally quick. He grabbed Kat out of Singleton's path and held out his hand as if to say 'stop.' Keen sighted individuals could have noticed that his fingers were slighted curled so to present the base of his palm which connected with the bridge of Singleton's nose and caused it to burst elaborately across the room. He immediately curled up into a bundle of pain and the nearest guards picked him up. Jameson rested her forehead on her notepad and breathed deeply.

"You fudding bastad," Singleton sobbed as the guards carried him out. "My parents lived in Pittsburgh." Then he was gone.

Umri stood up slowly as Kat and Luke composed themselves.

"Under the circumstances, your honour, may I request a short recess to sort ourselves out?" Umri begged.

"No, you may not," Henley said curtly. "Who the hell screened you guys before you were given this job?" she addressed all of them. "One of you walks out before we get started, another goes ape-shit bonkers. What next?"

The three lawyers looked at each other.

"Nothing," they all said.

"Good," Henley said then Kat raised a tentative arm.

"Yes, Ms Sabella?"

"Can we get a cloth or something to clean this mess up?" she requested and indicated the fine spray of crimson across the floor. "I fear someone could slip and hurt themselves."

A janitor was called out and mopped up the blood as quickly and discretely as possible. With that done, Henley continued.

"Mr Umri, do you have any further questions for Mr Roberts?"

"Yes, your honour," Umri said. "Mr Roberts, during these calls did the defendant offer any information on his progress?"

Roberts sighed. "Yes, Luke Robinson told me that he had killed a few caretakers."

Umri had expected more of a fight to get the fact out so had already prepared the actual question about the killing to come next. Tailor quickly scribbled something on a piece of paper and pushed it into Umri's vision.

"Did he brag about the killings?" Umri read.

"Sometimes," Roberts replied. "When he did give us numbers all the boys in the station cheered. No one would've -"

"Thank you, Mr Roberts," Umri interrupted. "I apologise for my absent colleague, your honours."

Kat stood up.

"Mr Roberts, when you shot your neighbour, Mike Sallis, did you do it because you felt threatened?"

"No, I was not scared at all."

"But did you do it because you thought he was going to kill you?"

"No," Roberts replied, surprised at the line of questioning. "He just wanted me out of the way so he could get to Lu- the defendant and the girl."

"And what did you think would have happened if you had let him through?"

"He would have taken them to the caretakers."

"And then?"

"The caretakers would have destroyed everything like they said."

"So, ultimately you *did* actually think your life was in jeopardy?" Kat reiterated.

"Oh, I see. No. You've got it wrong," Roberts corrected. "Do you know that my life didn't even enter into it? When I saw Mike lurch forward towards those kids I saw him going for my family. He was jeopardising the lives of my wife, kids and grandkids. That's when I pulled the trigger."

"Thank you, Mr Roberts," Kat said. "Just one more thing, to your reckoning, how many caretakers was Luke Robinson responsible for killing?"

Roberts flipped through his notebook. "It's difficult to calculate because we could only hypothesise the crew size of one of their ships but we worked out about six thousand."

There came another rousing 'whoop' from the audience.

"And how many humans?" Kat asked.

Roberts looked at his notebook again. "None," he said.

"Thank you," Kat said and sat down.

"You're too good at this," Luke whispered.

"We're fucking creaming them," she replied as Umri got to his feet.

"Mr Roberts," Umri addressed. "These reports you were given, were they quite detailed?"

"Some were. Some were him simply letting us know that he was still alive."

"Did he ever tell you the context of his killings? What led him to kill?"

"Kill or be killed," Roberts said matter-of-factly.

"Thank you Mr Roberts. We have no more questions, your honour," Umri said and sat.

Roberts was excused and he left the court without fuss.

"Call Agent Emaldine Cummings," Henley ordered and the word went down the lines. "Is that right?" she asked the prosecution. "'Emaldine'?"

Umri stood and shrugged. "That's what we've got, your honour."

Cummings entered the room and took the stand. The only noticeable differences about him from a fortnight earlier were the hearing aids in both ears and his arm in a sling.

"Can you give your name and relationship to the defendant, please," Henley instructed.

"My name is Emaldine Thornton Cummings and I was on secondment from MI5 to assist in the special investigations of Luke Robinson," Cummings said.

"Is that your real name?" Henley asked.

"Yes," Cummings replied, slightly offended.

"Where does that come from?" she enquired.

Cummings looked perplexed and searched the room for some sort of help. "My parents," he told her and there was laughter from the crowd.

Henley tried to work out whether he was attempting to be funny and realised that he was not.

"Can you tell us what your position in MI5 is?" Miakoto asked.

"I am a special field agent in the department of extra terrestrial investigations," Cummings told them. Luke sighed loudly and scribbled something on his pad. He looked up and gave Cummings a tight-lipped smile.

"How long have you been a member of this department?" Miakoto continued.

"Approximately five years," Cummings replied.

"And before that?"

"I was at Oxford University. Which was where I was enrolled because of my academic and aptitude exam results." Cummings looked at Luke as he elaborately scribbled on his pad again. Luke finished and smiled at Cummings.

"And you played an integral part in the events from the twelfth to seventeenth?" Etienne asked.

"That's correct," Cummings replied. "I was seconded to Inspector Roberts' unofficial squad when our paths crossed.

"And so you had some contact with the defendant during that time?" she enquired.

"We were on speaking terms," he replied.

The judges fell silent and the questioning was passed over to the prosecution.

Umri stood. "Had you ever heard of Luke Robinson prior to the aforementioned dates?"

"No, I had not."

"When was the first time you had heard of the defendant?"

"On the twelfth."

"Was that from the television broadcast?"

"No, that was on the thirteenth. We were performing a selection process and his file was brought before the committee."

"What was the selection for?"

"We needed someone to run an interference programme for us and it was deemed necessary to employ a member of the public. Luke Robinson fit most of the profile elements required."

"What was the interference for?"

"We needed to divert the caretakers' attention away from the team of our agents who were stopping them from completing their mission."

Henley interjected. "Excuse me, are you trying to tell the court that Luke Robinson did not stop the caretakers and save the planet?"

Cummings chuckled. "Of course he didn't. The very idea that one person with no field experience whatsoever would be able to defeat a fleet of interstellar aliens is absolutely preposterous. I'm surprised that no one has spotted the ridiculousness of this yet."

Henley slumped back in her seat in shock and indicated to Umri that he could continue.

"Can you go over the details for us?" Umri asked.

"Obviously I cannot mention any names for security reasons but basically we were aware of the approach of the caretakers for some weeks prior to their arrival. However, their intent was unknown.

"We prepared a number of contingencies to allow for various possible eventualities, one being that they were coming to attack our planet. A team of operatives were in place by the time the caretakers' craft established orbit and were able to disrupt their operations by acquiring a code. In the meantime, Luke

Robinson's name and details were leaked to the caretakers as the one responsible and so they went after him."

"Without the defendant's prior knowledge or consent?" Umri asked.

"Absolutely. It was necessary that the individual running the interference was unaware of their role for fear that they may give away valuable information during potential interrogation."

"That's inhumane," Jameson stated.

"It was for the sake of humanity," Cummings replied.

"What was the desired profile you required for the position of interference?" Umri asked.

"We needed a physically fit male who was repressed, who was in a tedious, repetitive occupation, who was on the brink of marital commitment and would be easily convinced of his role within the scenario."

"Why all those things?"

"Psychiatric profiling showed that those combined characteristics would adapt well to the scenario and when put under immense pressure would kick-start a self preservation programme and maintain interference indefinitely if required."

"What if Luke Robinson had died before your department had the chance to complete the mission successfully?"

"We had alternative choices to hand."

"And did your psychiatric profiling indicate any negative side affects that may progressively surface?"

"He would develop an acute persecution complex, paranoia, insomnia, become more aggressive and possibly gain heightened strength and reactions."

"And the success of the mission was worth the cost of that individual?" Umri demanded.

"Absolutely," Cummings replied. "To be perfectly honest we did not think he would survive the final stage so he should consider himself lucky."

"Did you ever inform the defendant of this side of the story?"

"We did, during a debriefing after his release from hospital but he flatly refused to believe it was possible," Cummings said. "Every story he was able to relate to us we were able to explain but he wouldn't have it. But that was a side of the persecution complex."

"Did he become violent during the debriefing?"

"No, just very, very angry. We were advised to back off for fear that he might become aggressive."

"On whose advice was that?"

"The department's psychiatrist."

"Thank you," Umri said and sat.

Henley held up her hand to stop Kat from starting.

"I must say, I do not know what to make of all this," Henley declared. "On the one hand I am disgusted to think that a government body would illegally enrol the life of an innocent to play diversionary target practice but, on the other, I can understand the necessity to do ugly things to ensure the safety of the majority. What I do not understand is why your department has kept this secret for over a month and allowed this poor man to play out this charade of responsibility?"

"We told him what had happened," Cummings explained. "It was then up to him to decide whether he should go ahead with the television interviews and so on. That was his choice. We did not come forward because the less that is known about our department the bigger the element of surprise we will have if this situation arises again."

"So why come forward now?" Henley demanded.

"It has gone too far. We were unaware as to what extent the defendant would continue the role and a human's life has been taken. The department believes it will be better for society, and the defendant, if he were given the appropriate help to enable him to reintegrate into his old lifestyle."

Henley sighed and shook her head. She turned to Kat who was still standing.

"Do you have any questions, Ms Sabella? Or should I just call it now?"

Luke's jaw tightened and he felt his teeth grind together.

There had been a general murmuring of shock and disbelief throughout the audience as Cummings had delivered his testimony, but now there was something else that surfaced from the very back of the room. There were loud voices and Luke was already sliding to the floor under the table.

It all seemed to happen so slowly. Kat was about to tell Henley that she did indeed have questions when she felt Luke slip by her legs. She started to lean down to find out what he was doing while, at the same time, Henley was rising from her seat to get a better look. Luke grabbed Kat by her collar as she heard a noise that sounded like a loud handclap and something whistled past over her head. Someone screamed, she was on the floor and Luke had pulled the table over so the top faced the crowd. Something clattered against Kat's foot and she looked down to see half a pair of glasses that had been snapped neatly at the bridge. It looked like Henley's glasses.

She turned her attention to the judges' podium in time to see Henley's arched body fall backwards out of site. There was a crimson starburst across the wall where she had been standing. The other judges were getting out of their seats in confusion and Kat noticed a small red dot appear on Miakoto's forehead and then he no longer had one. His half-headed body did not seem to know what to do as it dithered on the spot and then slipped behind the podium.

Kat looked to Luke for some sort of comfort and he was sat with his back against the bottom of the table-top just watching the panic and confusion on the court floor. All he needed was a box of popcorn and he would have been set.

The shooter had now lost his (or her) element of surprise and so was just cracking off shots here and there, supposedly not concerned if anyone else actually got hit or not. Everyone on the court floor was scrabbling behind their table and, or, each other. Eventually an air of calm swept forward and no further gunfire was heard for a few seconds.

"What happened?" Kat demanded.

"It looks like I had a fan in the audience," Luke commented.

"What?"

"Whoever it was, they seemed to think that by getting rid of my judges they might help me go free," he theorised.

"That's stupid," she told him. "They might postpone for a day or so but -"

"An hour, max," Luke interrupted. "To clean the mess. This is why they got five of them."

"They needed a fair representation of the World," Kat said and Luke turned to her with a smile.

"If they wanted a fair representation then shouldn't they have a representative from every nation? No, they want this over as quickly as possible so needed to cover the odds. That's why she didn't want to be a part of this hearing because she knew the danger she was in. Just like you."

"How do you know the shooter was on your side?" she asked and Luke replied by tapping the tabletop.

"This would not have stopped those bullets," he told her.

Some armed guards trooped onto the floor. "It's all okay now," one of the guards told them.

"Thanks for all your help," Luke said and stood up. He assisted Kat to her shaky legs and they looked out across the audience. Some sort of set of emergency instructions must have been in the audiences' packs because everyone had their head tucked between their knees. They could see right to the back door where a collection of guards had dogpiled the gunperson and were roughly bundling him, or her, out of the building.

"We're going to have to take you back down to the cell for the moment," the guard informed Luke.

"Fair enough," he replied and held out his wrists for the cuffs to be applied but the guard just grabbed Luke's shoulder and escorted him quickly through the door. Another guard grabbed Kat, followed suit and then she noticed that a number of other guards were leading the prosecution lawyers and surviving judges out the other door.

She was ushered past the witness rooms where doors had been opened and the occupants were looking out, much to the chagrin of their respective protectors.

"What happened?" Robin yelled.

"Assassination," was all Kat managed before she was led down the staircase to the cells below.

Luke was already sitting comfortably on his bed as she entered.

"We'll let you know any news as it comes," her guard said and returned up the stairs.

She fell down onto the spare chair.

"What the fuck's happening?" she despaired.

"Welcome to my world," Luke told her.

"What world?" she sneered. "It sounds like you got played."

"By the agency?" Luke chortled. "You didn't seriously believe his story, did you? He's a fucking idiot. He probably doesn't even know what contingency means."

"Even for a paranoid schizophrenic, you have to admit it is a pretty convincing alternative version," Kat suggested.

"I'm not schizo," Luke complained.

"Whatever," she sighed.

"And someone has to prove that the World is *not* out to get me before you can call me paranoid," he added.

Kat tried to sort it all out in her head but could not. She looked at this man again for some sort of answer but just found more confusion. How *could* one man save the World? That was done in movies. The real saving was always done by armies, agencies, departments and, on the odd occasion, spies. That was why Cummings' story was convincing, it *did* make sense. It was Cummings' side that did put the pieces together neatly: a trained group, who were paid to save the World, snuck in the back and did all the real damage. Not this ... nobody who had no experience, no training and no real reason to put up with the things he had.

But then, really, in life, what ever did add up neatly? Was it not the movies, again, that always provided the exact answers? In life you had two and two but still ended up with five and one-third and had to just pocket the remainder in the hope that it would work itself out later.

There was Luke; a huge remainder. Saviour of the human race or paranoid delusional? Or both?

Kat did not know any more.

"Look, it's simple," Luke said. "All you have to do is ask him about Tasya."

"Who?" Kat asked as she was yanked from her contemplative state. "Oh, the girl."

"All the way through his testimony he didn't once refer to her as even being involved," he continued. "She's their weak spot."

"I need the toilet," she announced. "I'll be back." She walked out and left Luke alone in his cell.

She *had* been the caretakers' weak spot. For some reason none of them were able to consider her in the equation; they always concentrated on him. He would take the bruises and she would eventually drag him out.

He smiled to himself because he remembered that, of course, there had been the dragging in as well.

Tasya's head was chewing at his thigh and he was desperately trying not to scream out. They had both suffered terrible ordeals in the last twenty-four hours and this was not the worse pain he had felt so far but at least he had been allowed to cry, wail and holler at the other times. He was fighting back a desire to smash her in the back of her skull with the butt of his rifle when she stopped and lifted her head. She wiped his blood from her chin and nodded in approval.

"That'll hold for a while," she told him and he looked down at his leg. She had ripped his trousers too daringly high as far as he was concerned but then the gash did start only a few inches away from his crotch and stretched halfway down his thigh. It had been very deep as well and he had lost a lot of blood. There was a moment when Tasya pulled the blade out and there was a release of pent up red that caused him to pass out and, when he had come around, she had managed to drag him out of the operating theatre and into this ... what was it? An interstellar broom cupboard, he supposed. She had brought the thread and needle with her and got started putting him back together but it had been the biting off of the loose end that had really hurt.

"Can I walk on it?" he asked and tested the seam with his finger. As he pressed down it oozed at the edges and he felt a bit dizzy again.

"Normally I'd say no," Tasya said, "but we have to move or they'll find us very quickly. I filled you up with a blood substitute. It'll maintain your pressure level and keep all your organs functioning properly but you will feel a bit weak for a while."

"But you still want me to move?" he demanded.

"Worse than that," she said. "We've got to hit the bridge now."

Luke's eyes drooped. "I can't," he moaned. "Really, I can't go on."

"You've got to," she urged. "For your people's sake, for my sake and for your sake. We can't stay here, and the only way to get safe is to get on to the bridge. That's where the escape shuttles are."

"What? All of them?" Luke demanded. "Something this big has only got life boats for the captain and his best mates?"

"No, there are pods all over the ship but if we take any other one it has automatic controls and can be piloted by the mothership's mainframe. The pods on the bridge are manually controlled which will mean we decide where we go."

"You've got an answer for everything, don't you," he sneered.

"Only when it comes to the best way to save lives," she replied. "Starting with ours."

With Tasya's arms under one shoulder, he used the three-foot rifle barrel to ease himself up. He tested his wounded leg by applying some weight to his foot and then quickly lifted it when the pain coursed through his thigh and into the base of his spine.

"I don't think I can walk on it," he confessed. "It feels like it'll rip open if a try to stand on it."

Tasya thought for a second. "Wait here," she said and left the cupboard. Luke eased himself back onto his seat and, for a second, thought that she had just left him there and that was it, all over. The next time that door opened there would be a caretaker standing over him with a big smile and an even bigger gun.

The door slid open and there was a caretaker. He was surprised to see Luke just sitting there but it did not take long for a smile to spread across his face. Luke did not even have the chance to level his gun before, what looked like a chair leg erupted through his chest and showered Luke with the caretaker's life sauce. The guard dropped to his knees to reveal Tasya, grim determination set on her face, standing behind. The caretaker fell on his face and thrust the chair leg out his back.

"I got some of this," she declared and showed Luke a spray can. "It's a bonding agent used in temporary spacesuit repairs. It should work okay on your skin and suffice for now."

Before he had a chance to ask any questions, or even agree to the process she had popped the cap and began spraying liberally over the foot long laceration.

Everything turned red and then black as Luke passed out again. When he opened his eyes Tasya was leaning over him awe-struck.

"Wow," she said slightly muffled. "You're still alive."

Luke found it hard to breathe and he had to cough to clear his airways. He doubled over and exhaled a mass of rust coloured liquid. He blew out of his nose and cleared a gobbet of the same stuff.

"What the fuck?" he asked woozily and wiped at his aching eyes. His hands smeared against moistness and he found the same deep red substance all over them.

"I think the bonding agent must have swept through your system and caused some sort of instant repairing mass haemorrhage," Tasya explained in wonderment. "Your body reacted explosively to the agent but it was able to put everything back together the instant it burst."

"Fuck," was all Luke could manage.

"It was extraordinary," she told him. "It was like watching an explosion and implosion happen at the same time."

"I feel all fucked up," Luke commented.

"You use that word a lot," she said.

"You use it too," he argued.

"Yes, but in the proper context."

"Why do you always have to be right?" he demanded and started pulling himself up.

She offered him her arm to lean on. "I don't 'have' to be, I just tend to be when *you* argue with me."

"And you always have to have the last word," he said. "Even when I ask a rhetorical question."

"That's because -"

"Stop it!"

"What?"

"Talking."

"Okay."

"You can't."

"Can."

"See?"

"What?"

"The last word. Always!"

She said nothing. They both noticed he was standing under his own strength. He took a tentative step forward and winced as his damaged leg bore his full weight. He limped out into the bright corridor and started along its length.

"You had it that time," she muttered.

"I heard that," he told her.

"And that one."

"How can I be having the last word when you insist on saying something after me?"

"I'm having the first word this time," she said.

Their progress through the upper levels went reasonably unhindered considering there were very few caretakers who actually knew they were on their craft. The majority of staff were asleep, and those on night shift were not paid enough to be concerned by odd looking people mooching around. It was one of those 'Titanic' syndromes that stated the ship was impenetrable so there was never any need for security and anyone on the space ship was obviously meant to be there.

They edged their way closer to the door to the bridge. These door sensors were a pain in the arse and made it practically impossible to burst in on a room. It was hard to kick a door down if it disappeared before your boot connected with it as Luke had discovered earlier. It was probably more shocking and disturbing for the people in the room to watch a man enter foot in the air and to fall into the splits.

"There will be about half a dozen caretakers in there, but none of them will be expecting us," Tasya told him. "We'll do this as we rehearsed, okay?"

Luke nodded.

"I activate the sensor, you slide in low and I'll enter high," she reminded.

"I know," he hissed and took a step back ready for the off.

"On three," she said. "One. Whatever happens in there -" she added, "two - I *will* be right behind you."

"What the hell is that supposed -"

"Three."

The door hushed open and his legs carried him in before his brain had the chance to register the fact. It was not until he got in there that he realised he was totally and utterly alone. In the sense that the door closed behind him and she was not there. It was probably the only time that she had *actually, really lied to him.*

There was a guard at his cell door. "Robinson," he called.

Luke blinked at his surroundings and was fairly sure that he had not fallen asleep that time. "Has Kat Sabella been back down?" he asked.

"No," the guard replied and opened the cell door.

"How long have they been?"

"About twenty minutes just clearing up," the guard answered. "Now they're going through some more security checks. You've got a visitor," he informed Luke.

"Who?" Luke demanded.

"Me," announced Roberts as he stepped into view.

"Entrez vous, mon mal du tete, s'il vous plait," Luke declared and Roberts walked in eyeing him suspiciously.

"I don't know what you just said," Roberts confessed, "but I bet it wasn't polite."

"You know me too well," Luke retorted with a grin. "What do you want?"

"I want to know what happened up there," Roberts told him.

"Well," Luke pondered, "rumour has it that there was this big bang that created all life."

"Oh yeah," Roberts said. "I forgot how funny you were."

"There was a disturbance, I took cover, two judges got waxed before the security could do what they've been so ineptly employed to do."

"And you know nothing more than that?" Roberts asked suspiciously.

"I thought you had retired?" Luke returned.

"You can take the man out of the police," Roberts started.

"But you can't take the nosy, fascistic, sadist out of the man, right?"

"There's that humour again," Roberts said.

"Who's laughing?" Luke asked.

"I want to know if there are any caretakers still hanging around?" Roberts demanded.

"Ah, so you've retired from the force and just gone freelance, have you?"

"Just keeping an ear to the ground," Roberts explained.

"Trust me," Luke said in all seriousness, "they've gone and it'll be after your lifetime before they get back here."

"So who was doing the shooting up there?"

Luke was beginning to get agitated. "Why don't you ask him?"

"'He' has been taken into 'special' custody," Roberts explained.

Luke sighed with resignation. "He was professional. Possibly acting on behalf of someone else."

"What makes you say that?"

"The weapon: sniper rifle, laser sighted, multiple round, quick loading. That's not something your average psycho can pick up on the high street. On top of that he made sure he got a back row seat so as draw less immediate attention *and* he didn't shout out as he fired."

"What's the shouting got to do with anything?"

"Passion and personal motivation," Luke replied. "This was potentially a suicide job so an employee won't waste time announcing the deity who told him to do it, nor the cause he's doing it for, nor to make sure the victims know what infidels they are before they're about to die. That's what amateurs do to bolster their confidence to get the job done."

"Someone hired an assassin to stop your hearing," Roberts surmised.

"Or an assassin had some pretty strong feelings on the matter and was doing a freebie," Luke added.

"What was Cummings up to?" Roberts asked.

"I don't know what the fuck they're playing at," Luke spat. "He just announced his whole, 'We Saved The World Really. No, Really,' version of events."

"And?" Roberts asked.

"Well, he's under oath isn't he? *And* he's a Government official so of course everyone bloody believed him," Luke exclaimed.

Roberts watched him carefully. "I recognise that look. You've still got to cross examine, right?"

"Oh yeah, it's our turn next," Luke enthused.

The guard returned to his cell door. "They're ready to get started again," he told Luke.

"And still no sign of Kat Sabella?" Luke asked and the guard shook his head.

"I'd wish you good luck but I think Cummings is going to need it," Roberts said as Luke got to his feet.

"Damn straight," Luke agreed and allowed the guard to escort him back up the staircase.

He was going back in alone. Kat had lied to him about coming back. Was it all falling apart again? And just because of that skinny twat, Cummings. If the dozy fucker had not been damaged after the climax Luke might have considered that he needed paying back. He was going to get it now and Luke *was* going to get the answers he had been after since that return to consciousness in the hospital.

As soon he stepped through into the courtroom he noticed the change in the atmosphere. There was a definite air of fear. All heads that turned to him as he entered looked at him with eyes full of blame. The room was now only half full with audience as the ones who had departed must have decided that things were going a bit too far or were just plain scared for their own safety. Even the camera flashes seemed to be half-hearted.

Kat seemed to be the only person who did not look up. She kept her head down and continued to sort her paperwork. She looked at the piece of paper Luke had been writing on:

Cummings = arse!
Before agent?
Just because of uni results?
Contingency?

Luke took his seat and Kat looked up. "You okay?" she asked.

"Fine," he replied. "Why didn't you come back?"

"I didn't have time," she said. "I was about to when they announced we were about to start again."

It sounded reasonable but Cummings had put doubt in her mind, doubt in everyone's mind, and that meant he had to second-guess her now.

"It'd be okay if you wanted to leave?" Luke suggested.

"I'd get disbarred," she said.

"Okay with me, I meant," he reiterated.

"I don't quit."

"Look, it doesn't matter if Cummings is right or not," Luke said. "It doesn't matter who it was that saved the World in the end. I still went through everything I did. Can't you see? Nothing has changed. If he's right then I'm a poor, deluded shmoe who got fucked by the authorities. But if I'm right then he's a lying fuck-bag and you get to uncover that before the entire World."

"If he's right, though," she mused, "it means that you carried on a pretence after the event and suckered the World into believing in you."

Luke shook his head. "No, I never. You lot were doing that all ready. All I did was go on the telly and tell you what happened and what's going to happen next time."

"You didn't tell anyone about this alternate version," she said.

"Because it is a lie."

Before Kat had the chance to voice any further confusion the side door opened and everyone got to their feet in lieu of the arrival of the elected judiciaries. Or at least, what was left of them: Jameson, Farthing and Etienne.

It had been made quite apparent that Jameson was quite squeamish anyway but now she carried an almost green hint to her complexion. She tried not to look at the spots that had recently been wiped down, or at the seats where her compatriots had been sitting.

Her heel stepped in something and she lost her footing. She looked down then had to turn and run out of the court for fear of making more of a mess. The last two judges pondered their next move and decided to take their seats. Farthing took Henley's old position and Etienne had shuffled along one space to take his.

"It has been decided to continue with today's hearing," Farthing announced.

"Decided by who?" Luke wondered aloud.

"Despite the tragic events that have occurred we believe that it is imperative that this case be heard as cohesively and quickly as possible," Farthing continued. "We owe it to the defendant and to the citizens of this planet."

He turned to Etienne and they whispered to each other. He returned to his microphone.

"While we await the return of Judge Jameson we shall call the previous witness, Agent Cummings, please."

The call went out and Cummings appeared once more. This time he was more hesitant to step from the protection of the door and quicker to cover the open distance between it and the witness stand.

"You understand that you are still under oath," the man beside him stated.

"I do," Cummings replied.

At that point, Jameson marched back in. There was a half-hearted attempt at people standing but Jameson waved them all to their seats.

"Sorry about that," she apologised and delicately placed herself in Miakoto's old place. She did not look happy at all.

"We were just about to continue with the defence's cross-examination," Farthing told her. "Ms Sabella?"

Kat stood up.

"I have to say that you've totally thrown me off balance, Agent Cummings," Kat confessed. "So you'll excuse me if my line of questions seems a little quirky."

Agent Cummings just smiled patronisingly at her.

"You said that you were aware of the caretakers' arrival long before they got here," he read from her notes.

"That's correct."

"Are you able to tell us how that is possible?" Kat asked.

"We have long range sensory equipment."

"Why?" Kat asked and Cummings frowned in confusion.

"It's an early warning system that tells us when the Earth is being approached by alien craft," Cummings told her.

"Is it used much?" Kat asked.

"It's always on," Cummings replied, "if that's what you mean."

"I mean have you had many results from it?"

Cummings face dropped. "Not to my knowledge, no."

"This was the first."

"I suppose."

"Before the caretakers' arrival did your department have any proof that there is other life beyond our World?"

Cummings eyes flittered around the courtroom. "Erm, I don't know."

"But not within the five years you've been with the agency."

"I don't know."

Kat raised her eyebrows. "Really? Are you saying that it's possible that your department has kept information from you, a 'special field agent'?"

"Well, no. Of course not," Cummings said.

"But you don't know if the agency knew about extraterrestrial life before the caretakers."

"Erm yes."

"During your employment in the agency, have you always been a special field agent?" Kat asked.

"No," Cummings replied with a twinge of dejectedness in his voice.

"What position did you hold prior to special field agent?"

Umri jumped to his feet. "I object, your honour. I really do not see the relevance in this line of questioning."

"Would you care to explain yourself, Ms Sabella?" Farthing offered.

"Yes, your honour," Kat replied. "My aim is to impeach Agent Cummings to within an inch of his life to prove that he is a lying little shit and none of his testimony is credible."

"Your honour," Umri declared.

"Sounds fair enough," Farthing replied. "Objection overruled."

Luke gave her a sideways glance and a look of 'thank you.' She leaned down to him.

"I'm doing this for me," she whispered in his ear. "I need to know for sure."

She stood up again. "You can answer the question now, Agent Cummings. What was your position of employment within the agency prior to being a special field agent?"

"I was in the post room," he confessed. "But -"

"And how was it that you got that job?"

"I told you," he whined, "I was at Oxford."

"And it was just because of your grades?"

"Yes!"

Kat dropped her head, picked up her pen and wrote, *?*, next to Luke's, *Just because of uni results.*

Luke wrote, *uncle*.

"Who is your uncle?" Kat demanded quickly.

Umri jumped up. "Your honour, really."

Why are they trying to protect him so much? She thought. *Unless it is a mass conspiracy.*

"Sit down, Mr Umri," Farthing ordered. "Ms Sabella knows what she is doing."

"You're uncle is?" Kat reminded.

Cummings was sweating now and his eyes were more imploring than ever.

"Albert Herald," he announced.

There was a stunned silence in the court as everyone realised that no one had ever heard the name before.

"Who?" the judges and Kat asked.

Cummings was almost insulted by the wrong reaction. "Director of the department of extraterrestrial investigation."

"Oh," Kat said. "So he got you the job?"

Cummings' head fell again.

"Yes."

"So how did you get involved with Inspector Roberts' unofficial squad?" Kat asked.

It was the Thursday morning after the first television announcements about the caretakers' arrival and he knew as much about them as did every other normal person, from what had been revealed in the media. Despite working within the most secret corridors of the most secret department of the country's secrecy agency, he was unable to divine the slightest clue as to what was happening in Office Four. Sorry, 'The War Room,' as everyone had to call it now.

Office Four had become The War Room because all the other offices were being used for meetings. Apart from Office Two which was being used as a temporary stationery cupboard but they could not use that because the stationery manager had been called away to Delhi for two weeks and had taken the key with her and no one could find the spare.

He had heard on the news before he had left his flat that the population of Gravesend had died overnight and that could signify the beginning of the termination of everything but everyone seemed be reacting amazingly British about it all; 'Bwa! Still time for another game of bowls before the big off, what?'

He had thrown up twice before he had left the house.

He had nothing else to do. He had sat down and seriously thought that this might be his last day alive so what were all the things that he always wanted to do? Who were all those people he needed to talk to? Should he call his parents to say he loved them? Should he phone Marcy the receptionist and declare his secret love for her? Tell his boss what he thought of him?

Cummings cleaned himself up and walked to work as per normal. He was in no particular rush because he was on the late shift but, as per normal, he had nothing better to do so tended to turn up early, try to make idle chat with Marcy, and then talk to the other boys in the post room about how the department would be run if they were in charge. At least they could talk about the real aliens today.

At that thought he raised his head to inspect the black blobs in the sky. It was like looking at a negative image of a clear night sky; you could see the dots but they were hard to keep focus on and count accurately. He wondered if any of them were focussing on him at that moment. Whether they knew that he was the only person standing between the Earth and their successful mission. Or maybe *they* had come for him at last. He had been identified from across the universe as a potential asset in their civilisation and needed his brilliance. Maybe they were aiming their laser gun at him and had one of their scaly, green, mucous covered phalanges hovering languidly over that red button.

He actually shat himself. He had that thought in his head and had managed to convince himself that that was the very moment he was about to die when he was struck in the chest by something very hard and very fast.

Sometimes we have these, 'What if,' moments and the mind is so powerful that it can conjure images and scenarios that can temporarily persuade the conscious that they are real. Then a millisecond later our conscious remembers where it is and says, 'Don't be stupid.' Cummings conscious had not had that chance to remember and so it caused his bowels to clear.

He landed on the floor and rolled over a few times screaming like a little child who had just touched a hot radiator for the first time. As he lay on his back he was too scared to peer at the mess that might remain of his displayed internal organs. That was when a girl appeared into his vision. There was nothing remarkable about her but everything seemed to be plainly perfect. As he looked into her eyes he saw something that he could only describe as pure devotion. Was she an angel?

"Am I dead?" he asked.

She seemed to be swilling something in her mouth. Then she spat at him.

He was repulsed and turned his head away. Her saliva smacked him on his cheek and he started squealing again.

"You stupid idiot," she said, stood up and started running along the street.

For some reason the horror of the spit had superseded his potentially flailing internals so he jumped to his feet and wiped his cheek with his coat sleeve.

"You're disgusting," he shouted but she was still running.

He started after her and he was not sure why. He was never the type to get involved in a confrontation but something just happened and he wanted to know what. Was it the collision? Her eyes? The spitting? He needed to catch up with her but she was very fast and he was becoming more increasingly aware of the lumps dancing around in his shorts and sliding down his trouser legs.

She rounded a corner and he followed.

He screamed again as she grabbed him by the throat and slammed him against a wall.

"Do you have any idea what you've just done?" she demanded then shook her head. "Of course you don't. None of you have any idea about anything. I don't know why I bother."

"What are you doing?" he croaked.

"Trying to save you people," she huffed, dropped him and took off again.

"Wait," he called and started running after her, rubbing at his throat as he went.

She stopped before the end of the alley.

"Stop following me," she ordered.

"I can help," he pleaded.

"You could've," she said, "but you didn't." She looked up and down the cross street. When she was happy that it was clear she sprinted on her way again.

"I don't understand," Cummings shouted. "What did I do wrong?"

This was the first time that something had actually happened to him, somehow he had managed to mess it up and now that was it; all over.

"No," he growled through gritted teeth. "It won't end like this. Not when I'm so close to dying. This is what I've always wanted to do and she's the one I want to tell I love."

He started running but soon realised that there was nowhere to run to any more. His pep talk had taken that little bit too long and she had slipped from his sight. He tried running just to see if he might bump into her again but it was to no avail.

He started to walk to work again. One of his chores was to pick up coffee on his way in so he popped into the men's toilets quickly to see if he could salvage some dignity from this day. He wiped, dabbed and blow dried his trousers but just had to throw his underwear away. He went back to the coffee shop, got his four cappuccinos of varying ingredients, turned to leave and dropped them because he saw the girl run past the window.

Without hesitation he ran out and collided with two men who must have been chasing her. He did not even think about it, he just jumped up and carried on running. He was not even totally aware of the sound of distant 'cracks' and the exploding masonry next to his ears. He just kept his eye on where the girl was going.

He never ran. He did not do any exercise and, had he thought about it, he should have been throwing half his guts up from the exertion but he *had* to keep up with her.

Corner after corner, through doors, rooms, up and down stairs and back on to the street. He was catching up, so he jumped.

They both tumbled to the floor in a tangle of limbs. As he composed himself he found he had a gun barrel pressed into his neck.

"What are you doing?" she demanded.

"Helping?" he suggested.

The door they had just exited exploded into the street. She pushed Cummings off her and aimed the gun at the entrance. A head poked out and she fired three shots at it. What was left of the doorframe atomised as the head whipped itself back in.

"Stop foll-" she started then stared in horror at the fist sized, chrome ball that rolled towards them. She swung her body round and kicked it off the curb. It rolled under a parked car and into the road.

The grenade detonated just as a double-decker bus drove past. All sound in the immediate vicinity was sucked into the blast then expelled again in an almighty shock wave that shredded the bus like a sandcastle in a hurricane.

The parked car next to the couple was lifted effortlessly in the blast and thrown into the shop behind them.

The two men had emerged from their hidey-hole and were shooting carefully aimed shots at the path around the cowering pair.

"Now's your chance," she muttered at the trembling Cummings. "Help now."

He raised his hands.

One of the men picked him up and tossed him through the shop window onto the bonnet of the car.

When consciousness returned, he stepped back into the street in time to see the police turn up. They asked him questions and he showed them his agency pass. Then they drove him down to the local police station where he was introduced to Inspector Roberts.

"I've been given unofficial permission from the Prime Minister to put together a squad of personnel to try to sort these alien bastards," Roberts had told him. "With your experience in the agency and your first hand encounter I think you'd make a valuable member."

Cummings was still in a state of shock so he just nodded. His agency pass is not widely recognised and the layman certainly would not be able to determine which area of the department he was from by the colour coding. Maybe this way he would get to meet the girl again.

"Excellent," Roberts said. "I'll get a PC to get you some clean clothes then come to the briefing room down the hall. You smell like you must have rolled *in something nasty out there."*

"So when was it that you were promoted to a field agent?" Kat asked.

"Two days later."

"So Luke Robinson was not selected to be diversionary tactics?"

"No."

"'No', he wasn't?"

"No. 'No,' he was."

Kat sighed. "Please explain."

"I found out later that the girl was a field agent in charge of the team who were working against the caretakers. She had recognised me as a fellow agent but, because of my lower position, I did not, er, recognise the 'secret handshake', if you want."

"Was this the same girl who appeared on the World's television sets and later teamed with Luke Robinson and was known as Tasya?" Kat demanded.

"Yes."

"Why was the head of your elite team running around looking after your diversion?"

"He was needed to survive for as long as possible so while her team were thwarting the caretakers' plans she was ensuring that Luke Robinson did not get in their way and stayed alive long enough for the real job to get done."

"That makes sense," Kat commented. "What's a contingency?"

"Pardon me?"

"A contingency, Agent Cummings. You stated earlier that," she flipped through her notes again, "'we prepared a number of contingencies to allow for various possible eventualities,' and I just wondered what 'contingency' meant."

"I, er," Cummings stuttered and looked to the prosecution.

"Your honours, this has gone too far," Umri declared. "I beseech one of you to end this insane line of questioning."

Farthing had a sideways exchange with his colleagues and then he returned to his microphone. "Maybe after Agent Cummings has told the court what 'contingency' means, Mr Umri will do the same with 'beseech.'"

There was a tittering through the audience and Umri, dejected, took his seat again.

"It's a -" Cummings started. "It's difficult to explain. When you get a set of things that could or could not happen in the way that you want them to, you need to instigate a series of contingencies to make sure you get the right answer."

"But what is a contingency?" Kat asked.

"I just told you," Cummings said.

"No, you just used the word contingency in a sentence. You haven't said what it means yet."

"If you -"

"No," Kat interrupted. "You start with, 'It means.'"

Cummings had turned red and looked as if he was about to cry.

"I don't know," he blurted.

"Agent Cummings, is it true that you have been rehearsing your testimony?"

"Yes."

"And is it true that your testimony was given to you by your superiors?"

"Yes."

"And as far as you know the information given to you may actually be false?"

"I suppose."

"Where's the girl now?" Kat asked.

"She's -" he started then stopped. "I can't tell you because it might jeopardise her current covert mission."

"Did you superiors tell you to say that too?"

Cummings hung his head. "Yes."

"So you don't know where she is?"

"No."

"When was the last time you did see her?"

"After the climax," he said. "I saw her get lifted on an ambulance before it left."

"Was she alive?"

"I don't know."

"So you don't really know who saved the World."

"No."

"And did you ever see this agency team of operatives?"

"No."

"The only people you saw trying to save the World were the girl and my client. Correct?"

"Yes."

"No more questions, your honour," Kat said and rested.

Umri and Tailor were whispering between themselves.

"Why didn't you press him on where Tasya is?" Luke demanded.

"Look at him," Kat said. "He's an idiot. Everyone knows he's an idiot. He knows he's an idiot. His bosses aren't going to risk giving him any useful information."

Tailor stood up. "Agent Cummings, how much project and mission information are you privy to in your new position?"

"Whatever information I am given," Cummings replied.

"So you're job is to act on whatever information you are given by your superiors and take it for granted that this information is correct and accurate."

"Yes."

"So your testimony here has been based on that presumptive information that has been given to you?"

"Yes."

"Thank you, Agent Cummings. No more questions, your honour." Tailor sat down again.

Cummings was excused and returned to the safety of the witness rooms.

"Call Doctor Halfenshaw, please," Farthing requested.

Luke had his forehead resting in the palms of his hands.

"What's the matter?" Kat demanded. "I thought that went quite well."

Luke shook his head. "He was the only reason I agreed to sit through this charade," he hissed. "I need to know where they've got Tasya and he was the only link coming up here who has any inside info."

"He didn't have any information," Kat told him. "He knows nothing but what he has been told.

"This guy is going to be trouble," she commented. "I hate questioning psychiatrists."

"You should've been there when he was talking to me," Luke muttered. "He nearly drove me mad."

A short man entered the courtroom. He could not have been taller than five foot but he wore his hair gelled up to give him an extra inch. He walked up to the pulpit and the man next to it was about to swear him in.

"Please stand while you take your oath," he told Halfenshaw.

"Ha!" Luke barked.

"I am," growled Halfenshaw.

The man turned red and swore the doctor in.

"Please state your name and relationship to the defendant," Farthing requested.

"My name is Doctor Phillip Halfenshaw and I was Luke Robinson's psychiatric counsellor for a week after the invasion."

"Did the defendant request your services, Doctor?" Etienne asked.

"No, I was called in to check Luke while he was still in hospital," he replied.

"On whose authority?" Etienne continued.

"It is standard hospital practice for a psych consult to be called in to talk to trauma victims."

"And you have dealt with many different traumas?"

"My word, yes," he bragged. "I have helped victims of rape, attack, burns, shootings and even the families of the victims."

"And what would you say the purpose of your consultation would be?"

"Many victims try to step back into their old lives treating the trauma as something that 'just happened.' In most cases, however, the trauma becomes a day to day factor of their lives and it is my task to get the victim to concede that they have become a slightly different person and to try to accept these changes. That way, they will be able to reintegrate more effectively."

"Would you say you have a high success rate?" Jameson asked.

"It is widely regarded in the field that I am very good at what I do," Halfenshaw replied.

"What about the failures?" Farthing asked. "What happens to those people who are not able to accept and reintegrate?"

"General psychoses permeate because of denial and an internal struggle. If a trauma victim tries to deny that the events could change them or have any lasting affect then they may become anti-social to the extreme of psychotic."

"Have any of your victims gone that far?" Farthing asked.

Halfenshaw laughed. "My 'patients', you mean?"

"He knows what he means," Luke blurted.

Halfenshaw scowled at Luke. "Most of my patients are able to carry on with their lives with a seminal acceptance of the trauma. A few are unable to accept, reintegrate and find that their lives revolve around the trauma rather than the trauma becoming part of the lives. These people tend to find their lives fall apart around them and, in some drastic cases, may end up requiring further psychiatric treatment or institutionalisation. Some can be belligerent, deliberately unwilling to accept the events surrounding the trauma, and it is those people who need to be watched as the potential psychotics."

"Objection, your honour," Kat called.

"On what grounds?" Farthing enquired

"I didn't like the way the Doctor was staring at my client while he made his last statement."

"Strike the witnesses 'look' from the record," Farthing announced and the two typists looked at each other quizzically. Kat took her seat looking rather embarrassed.

"Over to you, Mr Umri," Farthing said after a quick exchange with his colleagues.

Tailor got to his feet. "Doctor Halfenshaw, can you tell us how many hours you spent with the defendant?"

Halfenshaw pulled a small notebook from his inside jacket pocket and flipped a few pages. "Over the course of seven days we spent approximately fifty hours together."

"And you stated that it was not a voluntary series of consultations."

"That's correct. The first is a standard examination executed as an informal chat. From that it was easy to determine that he be assigned to my care for the duration of his recovery in hospital."

"What was it about that first 'chat' that made you so sure he needed that much help?"

"He was delusional, incoherent, suffering from bouts of paranoiac misconceptions and severe flashbacks."

"Did these conditions improve over the course of your consultations?"

"Generally, yes, but I did find that he had learned to hide the symptoms of the flashbacks."

"Do you believe that Luke Robinson discharged himself from your care too early?"

"Absolutely. It is my professional opinion that Luke Robinson is in no state to return to the life as he knew it prior to the invasion."

"What was the defendant's condition after he left you?"

"He was still suffering the flashbacks, as I stated, but the paranoid delusions had worsened and he had taken on an almost nihilistic outlook on life itself."

"Could you explain that further for the court?"

"Apparently, when he had been taken by the caretakers, part of the torture he underwent was to, somehow, personally witness the deaths of everyone and everything on the planet as was the caretakers' original intention. On top of that, he believes that the invasion was not stopped but simply delayed. There was a slight dichotomy of, 'All life *was* dead,' against, 'All life *will* die.' Living with that concept would make anyone think, 'What's the point?'"

"So he gave no value to life any more?"

"Certainly he gave no value to the life around him," Halfenshaw remembered, "but I did ask him if he was suicidal and he was emphatic that he was not. This could be interpreted as part of the nihilism in that to take one's own life would be a display of a degree of passion and he did not even have that."

"Could you determine whether there was anything that he did care about?"

"The girl," Halfenshaw replied. "The one he called Tasya. She had been involved on his side of his adventure and a strong emotional bond had been built between them."

"Mutually?"

"I couldn't determine that unless I could speak to her."

"Thank you, Doctor," Tailor said and before he could take his seat, Kat had leapt up.

"Doctor Halfenshaw, are you published?" she asked.

"Yes," he replied.

"How many books have you had published?"

"Two so far."

"'So far'? You have a book in the making?"

"Yes," he replied.

"What are your books about?"

"Case studies."

"So you have written books about the psychological disorders of some of your patients?"

"That's correct."

"How does that equate with the patients' privacy privileges?"

"I never give the real names of the patients involved and so it is acceptable. It is common practice in the realms of psychiatry, psychology, surgery and so on."

"Can you tell us the subject of your new book?"

"I can't tell you the patient's name, no," Halfenshaw told her.

"Could you give us a synopsis of the work in progress instead?"

Tailor jumped to his feet. "Your honour," he complained, "she's at it again. What is the relevance?"

Farthing set him a steely gaze. "Mr Tailor, if you really don't know where this is going then you should just pack your things and leave now. Sit down."

He did so.

"A synopsis, Doctor," Kat reminded.

"Well it's still a bit sketchy at the moment," Halfenshaw stuttered, "and I am waiting for some reference data."

"Have you already been paid an advance for this book?"

"Yes I have," he confessed.

"And your publisher is currently waiting for the finished manuscript?"

"Yes."

"Are you behind schedule?"

"Yes."

"Is the book supposed to be about Luke Robinson?"

Halfenshaw hesitated and looked at the judges for support.

"We all know the answer anyway," Jameson told him.

"Yes," he said.

"And you can't finish the book unless Luke Robinson becomes your patient again. If you don't finish the book you will have to give the advances back."

"Yes."

"How much?"

"Two hundred and fifty thousand dollars."

"That's quite an ulterior motive you have for wanting my client institutionalised."

"Objection," Umri and Tailor bellowed but Kat had already sat down.

The two prosecutors stared at the judges and they stared back.

"Well?" Farthing asked.

"We were objecting, your honour," Umri said.

"I don't see anyone to object to anymore, Mr Umri," Farthing responded. "Is there anything else *one* of you gentlemen would like to ask the doctor?"

Umri took his seat again and Tailor remained standing.

"Doctor Halfenshaw, in your professional opinion, could Luke Robinson be a danger to himself and, or, others around him?" Tailor demanded.

"He certainly has the correct mindset to be," Halfenshaw replied.

"No more questions, your honour," Tailor finished and sat down.

"Well that went quicker than expected," Farthing commented. "Let's not stop this roll. Call Doctor Gregg, please."

The woman who stepped through the door was, like Halfenshaw, quite short but it did not seem to be as obvious. She was wearing a deep red skirt suit and cream blouse. She had auburn hair that bounced just below her shoulders.

She was sworn in.

"Please state your name and relationship to the defendant," Farthing instructed.

"I am Doctor Helen Gregg. I was Luke Robinson's physician during his recovery in hospital from the eighteenth to twenty second of February."

"Had you known the defendant prior to this period?" Jameson asked.

"I did not," Gregg replied. "Apart from the stuff I had seen on the telly."

"So when he came in you knew who he was," Jameson continued.

"The ambulance had radioed ahead so the entire hospital knew he was coming."

"How did you get his case?"

"It was early Tuesday morning and we were short staffed," she explained. "There was no one else."

The judges fell silent and Jameson whispered something to Farthing.

"No, no," he replied. "Let them get on with it."

Tailor stood up.

"Doctor Gregg, what condition was the defendant in when you first examined him?"

"I don't think I had ever seen anyone as badly beaten as him," she commented. "I have seen people arrive in a real mess from car wrecks, burns and industrial accidents but they all tend to be instant wounds. Luke Robinson had bruises on top of bruises, cuts within cuts and -"

"Breaks within breaks," Tailor interrupted. "Please, Doctor, just a run down of the type of injuries the defendant had sustained."

"Multiple lacerations and bruising across his entire body, heavy burns on his legs and forearms, bullet wounds through his left shoulder and right thigh, extensive blistering across the soles of his feet, capillary haemorrhage in his eyes, eight missing teeth, three loose, four missing nails from his fingers and three from his toes," she recited. "They were just the injuries we could diagnose from looking. Further examination and x-rays showed shin splints, micro fractures in his tibias, fibulas, humeri, and femurs, widespread internal haemorrhaging (although we could not find a source), scarred eardrums and retinas, evidence of dislocations in both shoulders, his left knee, sixty-five per cent of his phalanges and his coccyx."

A sharp intake of breath could be heard from many places around the room at this last revelation.

"Evidence of broken ribs, scar tissue on his lungs, kidneys and liver, and severe burning to his wind pipe and oesophagus."

She didn't mention his earlobe, Kat thought.

Tailor seemed at a loss for words. This was purely theatrics, however, as each lawyer there had already been aware of the full extent of Luke's injuries. He just wanted to give the judges time for the information to filter through.

"You said a few times then that you found 'evidence' of certain injuries," Tailor said.

"Yes, that's right."

"Do you mean that you could recognise an injury from the way it had healed?"

"Yes."

"Considering the time frame involved here wouldn't most evidence imply that the injury would have taken place before the defendant's ordeal?"

"Normally, yes," Gregg agreed. "But you can read scar tissue also and what we concluded from the state of Mr Robinson's body was that it had healed a lot quicker than human tissue normally would."

"Hence why you could not locate a source for the internal haemorrhaging," Tailor deduced.

"Yes. Whatever it was that had been bleeding had healed."

"Is that possible?" Tailor enquired.

"It happens," Gregg replied. "It entirely depends on the extent of the ruptured internal organ."

Jameson seemed to be turning pale again.

"What did the 'evidence' of the defendant's rupture show?"

"Multiple organs and massive internal bleeding."

"Is it possible for that sort of injury to resolve itself?"

"No. Something like that would signify immediate, painful death."

"Did you run the defendant through any fitness tests?" Tailor asked.

"Yes, after such a while of being bed ridden he was given basic stamina and respiration exercises."

"And the results?"

"Remarkable. We had to stop the tests because we ran out of time. Mr Robinson showed no major signs of stress throughout any of them."

"This is normal?"

"No," she laughed. "There should've been some sort of fluctuation in his heart rate but it did not alter at all."

"Did you get the chance to compare your results with any medical records from before the caretakers' arrival?"

"Yes and there showed a dramatic change in his fitness levels, some of his health complaints and his basic records."

"Including?" Tailor urged.

"His blood group had changed, a mild asthma had cleared up, an astigmatism had gone, his audio range had heightened, his site was beyond perfect twenty-twenty."

"Did you do a DNA test?"

"Yes. It had changed."

"Please Doctor, don't be coy," Tailor said.

"Human DNA is helix comprised of two intertwined sugar-phosphate backbones with attached paired bases of adenine with thymine and guanine with cytosine all connected by non-covalent hydrogen bonds. Mr Robinson's was, is, five backbones with additional pairing structures within."

This caused a gasp of amazement to flow through the room.

Tailor gave everyone a moment for this to sink in.

"Are you saying that Luke Robinson is no longer human?" he finally asked.

"I don't know," Gregg faltered. "I'm saying he's beyond human."

"Beyond human with increased strength, stamina, hearing, eyesight and recuperative abilities," Tailor summarised.

"Yes," Gregg answered.

"Thank you," Tailor said smugly and dropped to his seat.

Kat got up and asked, "Do you know how the injuries that my client sustained were caused?"

"No, not exactly," Gregg replied.

"Then why do you presume to know exactly how some of them healed?"

"I don't understand," Gregg said.

"Do you know for a fact that Luke Robinson's healed injuries were done so by his body's natural workings?"

"No."

"It is possible that they were healed by a technological process."

"Not one I've ever heard of," Gregg scoffed.

"Do you know how the caretakers' space craft maintained a geostationary orbit so far within the Earth's atmosphere without expelling any kind of detectable energy exhausts?"

"Of course not."

"Do you know what medical equipment the caretakers had on their craft?"

"No."

"So Luke Robinson's wounds *could* have been healed by a technological process that you *have* never heard of?"

Gregg was stumped. "I, er, well, yes."

"Did you have a record of Luke Robinson's DNA from before his ordeal?"

"No, I did not," Gregg replied.

"So for all you know his DNA strand may always have been this way," Kat suggested.

"Possibly."

"And it's possible that there are other humans on this planet with the same DNA pattern as Luke Robinson," Kat hypothesised.

"I'm sure if that were the case then science would have come across it by now," Gregg argued.

"But if this quintuple-helix is responsible for faster recuperation don't you think that would mean those individuals would not need to see a doctor as often as us normal doublers?"

"Possibly," Gregg conceded.

"So Luke Robinson may just be the first example of the next step in human evolution," Kat theorised.

"If you want," Gregg huffed.

"You don't make it sound like this is a good thing," Kat commented with a frown. "You seem to think the progression of the human race to a higher level is something to be feared than praised."

"In light of recent events," Gregg retorted, "you'll excuse me if I become a little paranoid by what could be a wolf in sheep's clothing."

"Why would the wolf save the sheep from his fellow wolves?" Kat wondered.

"So he could have all the sheep to himself, perhaps?" Gregg spat.

Luke started scribbling something on his pad and he thrust it under Kat's attention.

"You're not getting a book published based on your research and results are you?" she read.

Gregg's eyes widened in shock and Luke started to scribble something else.

"No!" Gregg barked and Luke thrust his pad across the table again.

"What about an industry dissertation?" Kat read.

"I, er," Gregg stuttered and Luke continued scribbling.

"How much will you get paid for it?" Kat asked while she waited for Luke's next question.

"That's none of your business," Gregg said.

"Your honour, please?" Kat pleaded.

"You will answer the question," Farthing instructed.

"Fifty thousand pounds," Gregg said and Luke shoved his pad over.

"What is the most unusual foreign object you have ever removed from a man's -" she stopped and looked down at Luke. He was biting his bottom lip and his eyes were watering.

"Ms Sabella?" Farthing called.

"I need to, er, rephrase the question, your honour," Kat said. She dropped her chin to her chest and whispered, "Bastard."

Luke made a choking noise at the back of his throat as he fought back the laughter.

"Doctor Gregg," Kat declared resolutely. "No more questions, thank you." She sat down with everyone staring at her.

Tailor stood up slowly, not sure whether she had really finished or not. He looked at Farthing for approval to continue and the judge waved him on.

"Doctor Gregg, apart from this unusual discovery in the defendant's DNA being caused by natural development, in your expert opinion, what other reasons could it be down to."

"Either he is not of human origin, one of his biological parents weren't human, or he had something done to him at a cellular level."

"Thank you Doctor Gregg," Tailor said. "I have no more questions, your honour." He sat down.

Gregg was excused and she left the courtroom.

The judges looked at the witness sheet and started to mutter between themselves. Eventually Farthing came closer to his microphone.

"Mr Umri? Ms Sabella?" he called and they both stood up.

"We are a bit confused as to what witness we are suppose to be calling next," Farthing explained. "There *is* supposed to be another witness now, correct?"

Umri looked at Kat and she nodded to him.

"Your honour, this next witness is somewhat beyond the convention of normal hearing procedures," Umri said.

"Well, what has been normal today?" Farthing asked rhetorically.

"Ourselves and the defence have agreed that some light might be shed on the proceeding if a complete outsider were selected to testify their feelings on the matter," Umri continued.

"And what would be the purpose of that?" Jameson demanded. "Who cares what someone outside of these events really thinks? Surely it's the people inside who only matter?"

"The prosecution seem to think that by parading a complete stranger in the witness stand we might see a re-enactment of the night in question as was the situation then," Kat interjected. "I think it's silly but I don't have any objections to doing it."

The judges conferred again and Farthing raised his hands in resignation. "Like I said," he muttered, "what's been normal today, anyway?"

The other two judges nodded.

"Go on then, Mr Umri," Farthing instructed. "We are all extremely intrigued as to who your stranger witness is going to be. I hope you are not playing some crafty trick here."

Umri looked shocked. "Absolutely not, your honour. In fact I think it should be your honours who select the witness."

"How do we do that?" Farthing demanded. "Have you got the names of everyone in the world in a hat there?"

Umri looked confused. "No," he replied.

"Well?"

"We believe we have a fair representation of the nations in our spectators gallery," Umri declared and the audience became slightly self conscious that the hearing had developed an 'audience participation' segment.

"So if your honours would select a letter to represent the seating row and then a chair number we will have a random witness."

"Makes sense," Farthing muttered. "Of sorts."

They chatted for a second then Farthing announced, "Row A J. Seat forty-four."

Heads turned in the general direction of a commotion building in one particular section. A man with a large camera hanging around his neck stood up.

"Are you a journalist?" Farthing demanded.

"Er, yes," the man shouted back.

"Then sit down," Farthing ordered. "I don't think a journalist can give the kind of objective testimony I think you are after, Mr Umri."

"Quite, your honour," Umri agreed.

"You, in front of the journalist," Farthing called. "No, not you. In front. Directly in front. Yes, you madam. Would you stand please? Are you a journalist?"

"No," the woman squeaked.

"Bailiff, escort that lady up here please," Farthing instructed the guard at the rail.

Camera flashes were popping all around again as the guard wandered up the aisle to meet an overweight woman who was edging her way along the row of seats and apologising to those owners of feet she trod on.

The guard took her arm and led her back down to the front of the room. She was obviously a bit anxious at having been selected so ruthlessly. Her eyes darted around the room and tried to pinpoint the source of each camera flash. Her hands shook as if suffering the worst delirium tremens ever and her legs looked unable to carry her body to the witness stand unaided.

With the guard's help - and the intervention of another - she was carefully placed in the pulpit. She was now sweating slightly and out of breath. She was about fifty years old and had stringy, blue rinsed grey hair that had recently been tightly permed. Probably for this special occasion.

Jameson leaned over, placed a calming hand on the woman's arm and she jumped at the contact.

"Can I get you a glass of water?" Jameson asked.

"Please," the woman replied. She was English.

The drink was passed along the judges and handed to the woman. It trembled in her hands but she managed to sip some without it spilling everywhere. She was also handed a paper towel with which she dabbed at the corners of her mouth and across her brow.

"Okay?" Jameson asked and the woman nodded. "There is no need to be nervous, you're not on trial here."

The woman forced a chuckle but looked like she was going to throw up.

"I'm okay," she managed.

"Can you give your name and relationship to the defendant, please," Farthing parroted and got a nudge from Etienne. "What? Oh yes. Your name and if you have a relationship with the defendant, please."

"My name is Rosemary Fletcher and I have never met or spoken to Luke Robinson ever in my life," she said.

"Do you know any of Luke's family or immediate friends?" Jameson asked.

"I don't think so," Rosemary replied.

"What do you do for a living?" Etienne asked.

"I'm a housewife," she said.

"And your husband?"

"George? He's retired now."

"Any children?" Etienne continued.

"Yes, three children and four grandchildren so far," Rosemary said proudly.

The judges handed the witness over to the prosecutors and Umri stood up.

"Mrs Fletcher, many thanks for doing this," he said.

"Oh. I didn't realise I had a choice," she interrupted. "I don't think I would have done it if I realised I had a choice," she said to Jameson.

"Well, thank you anyway," Umri continued. "Mrs Fletcher, could you take us through the events of the twelfth to seventeenth of February as they happened for you?"

"Okay. Well, I first heard about the aliens when we got an email sent to us from my eldest daughter, Sandra. She works in the BBC, don't you know, and is always sending us these silly jokes and pictures and things. Sometimes they can be quite amusing but most of the time they're just vulgar and tasteless and of course you never know what sort of viruses they might be carrying. I prefer those ones that come by with little words of comfort and joy. You know, 'Send this on to at least eight people and your dreams will come true.' Of course it never happens but at least you know your spreading a bit of happiness rather than some of the hateful stuff."

As she paused for a breath, Jameson turned to Rosemary. "You do know that it is usually those ones that are considered to be the virus?"

"Oh no, we have a virus checker and there's never anything nasty in them," Rosemary replied.

"No," Jameson corrected. "It's the actual email that is the virus. Everybody sends it on to eight people, they each send it to eight and so on and servers get clogged up with sycophantic rubbish."

"Well, I think it's nice."

"You received an email," Umri interjected.

"That's right. From Sandra. It was this warning from a website saying that everyone was going to die. At the time I just thought it was tasteless and just deleted immediately. Then that evening there was a piece on the news about how far this email had travelled and that the culprit had put similar warnings on sites all around the world."

"But you still didn't think anything of it?"

"Of course not. There was more about it on the news the next morning and then we saw the blobs in the sky."

"What did you think they were?"

"I was hanging my washing out at the time. It was an unusually warm day for February so I thought I would make the most of it and get a load done and aired properly. I was just pegging out some sheets and I thought my eyes were packing up on me; all these black dots appeared across the sky and I thought my retina must be detaching or something." Rosemary hunched her shoulders up and rolled her eyes skyward in mock embarrassment.

"So after I'd rubbed them a few times and stared at the ground to see if the dots were still there, I looked up again and there they were. I called to George to come see and he did."

"What did you think then?" Umri asked.

"Well, nothing actually," Rosemary confessed. "There's so much that goes on these days that we don't have the faintest idea about that we just accept and leave it at that. George helped me with the rest of the washing and then we went in for a cup of tea and a cake."

"You weren't scared?" Umri demanded incredulously.

"No," she said. "They were just dots in the sky."

"But surely you had never seen anything like that before in your life?" Umri asked.

"Young man, there have been plenty of things in my life that I had never seen before until the day I saw it for the first time. Had I gone around all scared and panicky every time, I don't think I would be sitting here now."

"When did you hear about the deaths of the first cities?" Umri asked.

"The next morning on the news. That was a bit unnerving, I must say."

"'Unnerving'? Thousands of people died overnight and you were 'unnerved'?"

Rosemary sighed and looked pityingly at Umri. "Thousands of people die around the world every night. Did that ever scare you?"

"But some of these people were in your own country," Umri explained near to exasperation.

"And that was unnerving."

Umri was speechless.

"Now, when that man, Evershine, came on we thought it must be a big prank. Someone was trying to have a joke with us."

"What about the girl's transmission?" Umri asked. "The girl called Tasya?"

"Well, we missed that at the time because Thursday is market day in the village but we caught it later that evening and I thought she was a bit plain looking for a presenter and should have had a touch of make-up on but George was quite taken by her."

Umri was wide eyed. "You do know that she wasn't a television presenter?"

"Well I do now, obviously," she huffed. "But at the time we thought she was doing an advert for a new show or something."

"Okay," Umri tried to get the chronology straight. "So then you saw the transmission with Evershine and the defendant's name and photo?"

"That's right," she said. "But we were starting to get a bit bored of it all. Every news programme was showing the same clip so when he came on George nearly switched off until I told him it was a different one. George said he didn't care as it was nearly time for *Top Gear* on BBC 2 but when he turned it over of course the man was there too. George tried the other two channels and even asked if I'd been fiddling with the tuner. I just laughed at him and he laughed back because he knows how useless I am with electronic gadgetry."

Umri stopped her. "Sorry, the other 'two' channels?"

"Oh yes, we don't believe in Four and Five."

"I'm sorry, you've still lost me."

"BBC 1, BBC 2 and ITV for Coronation Street, Emmerdale and Millionaire. Those are the channels we watch and not the other two."

"So what did you think when you saw the defendant's photo and heard his name?"

"Not much, I had never heard of him so presumed he must have been a celebrity from that *Big Brother* show and then George just turned the telly off and got the cards out."

"'Cards'?"

"We had an hour of playing Gin before bedtime."

"Mrs Fletcher," Umri appealed, "you do know that Luke Robinson had not been from any television show and that Evershine was a real alien intent on destroying all life on Earth?"

"I find your manner most disagreeable," Rosemary told him. "I am not a stupid person. I am telling you how it was at the time like you asked me to."

Umri's demeanour changed instantly.

"Please accept my humble apologies, Mrs Fletcher," he said and bowed his head. "Do go on."

"We live in a small village where television does not play a large part of our lives. Of course we started to get a bit concerned when our Sandra called to say how much she loved us and how sorry she was for anything she might have ever done to be naughty when she was little but couldn't remember it herself."

"I'm sorry, I don't -" Umri started.

"She was making her peace," Rosemary said. "It was then that we started to pay a bit more attention to what was going on."

"And how did you feel to know that everyone's lives were in real danger of being extinguished?"

"We couldn't quite believe it," she said. "I suppose it must be one thing to have a mugger come up to you with a knife in his hand and threaten to kill you but to have someone make this sweeping statement that everyone is going to die seemed a bit impersonal and it was difficult to comprehend. It was rather rude, really."

"So, you didn't think much of it at all, then?"

"We sat down with a pot of tea and a cherry bakewell, I believe, to chat it over and then George jumped up and said, 'To hell with it! I'm opening the Laphroaig.' He had been saving it for a special occasion and he was right at the time but in retrospect we think he might have been a bit hasty. It was very smooth and would've been nice to have been able to share it with some friends but the Applebys next door had decided to go down to spend a couple of weeks with their children in Gravesend which turned out to be a *big* mistake.

"Anyway, we had a few drinks and forwent the cake. I didn't think they went together really and we came to the conclusion that there didn't seem to be anything we could do to stop anything and there wasn't anything we needed to clear up so we might as well just get on with things as per normal and hope the end wouldn't be painful."

Umri just stood there in silence for a moment.

"You had just realised that you were about to die and you didn't change your lifestyles at all?" he finally demanded.

"We started to say how much we loved each other more often," Rosemary replied.

"You didn't feel obliged to settle any outstanding debts? Financial or emotional?"

"We don't have any," Rosemary told him. "'Never a lender nor a borrower be,'" she cited.

"You weren't scared, angry or upset at all?"

"Young man, we are in our twilight years as it is and have had the prospect of our end of everything ever since George's bypass six years ago. This was almost a blessing because at least it meant we were going to go together and not leave the other all alone."

Umri's eyes moistened slightly. "For the first time in my life I was truly scared," he confessed. "I don't think I had felt as alone and vulnerable since I had been a child. I remember sitting in my bed crying for my mother. I envy you Mrs Fletcher."

Rosemary had a tear in her eye. "You have learned an important lesson in life," she told him. "But what have you done with it?"

Umri blinked away the tears and came to his senses. "What do you mean?"

"You had a moment of reflection and found that there was no substance in your life. You were going to die without having left a mark in this life, without having truly touched another's soul or have your soul touched by another. You lacked love and life and when the threat had passed what did you do with this revelation?

"You did nothing. You bottled it away as a bad experience, maybe as even a sign of weakness and have carried on regardless. This hearing has already revealed two people who allowed this experience to alter their lives and they were Luke Robinson's lawyer and the poor soul with the gun. There are those of us who have had no reason to change and there are those who won't allow it to change them."

The entire room looked at Umri to see if he would break down in tears or maybe strip off his clothes and run from the court. He pursed his lips and lowered his head to inspect the papers on his table.

"You are quite correct, Mrs Fletcher," he said and lifted his head. "I do have some introspection ahead of me but that shall wait until after the hearing.

"Mrs Fletcher, how did you feel on Tuesday morning when you heard that the invasion had been stopped?"

"I won't deny that I was relieved," she said. "Both of us were happy that our grandchildren may have the chance for a long life and we were going to continue to enjoy our last years together."

"And what were your thoughts when you found out that it was Luke Robinson who had, supposedly, saved your life?"

"I didn't really think of it that *my* life had been saved by *that* man," she said. "I suppose it was much the same as when the caretakers had said we were all going to die. I couldn't take it personally. That was the same as hearing about Luke. He hadn't saved *my* life, he had saved everyone."

"How do you feel about seeing him today?"

She gave Luke a quick glance; he waved at her and she blushed.

"It's a bit strange, really," she spluttered. "I've never seen anyone famous before except for the Queen when she was at the Ilkley Moor garden show and she only drove past in her car so I don't think that really counts. Mind you, there was the time that Ken Barlow came to open the new Woolworths but that was nearly twenty years ago now."

"You think Luke Robinson is famous? Like a film star?"

"I suppose," she said. "But more so. He saved the World, didn't he? There has never been anyone like that ever. One person who everyone in the World accepts as their saviour. Not even Jesus is accepted by everyone."

"You compare him to Jesus? Have you deified Luke Robinson?"

"I beg your pardon?"

"Have you put Luke Robinson in the same social position as a god?"

"Of course not," Rosemary spat. "Luke Robinson is real and has obviously done something good for the people of this planet unlike any god who only ever seems to look out for their own."

"Do you feel like you owe Luke Robinson anything?"

"I owe him my life."

"That's quite a dept, don't you think?"

Rosemary shrugged. "It's the biggest ever."

"How are you ever going to repay that?"

"I don't think I can."

Tailor slid a piece of paper across the table in anticipation of the next question.

"What was the adage you used?" Umri asked and looked down at the note he had passed to him. "'Never a borrower nor a lender be,'" he read. "How does that fit in?"

Rosemary became flustered. "I didn't borrow anything."

"But you do owe him," Umri stated. "And *you* don't owe any debts to *anyone*. How does that make you feel?"

Rosemary was taken aback and she looked at Luke without any trace of awe. He waved at her again but she did not avert her gaze; she only frowned at him.

"Mrs Fletcher?" Umri prompted.

"I don't know," she said. "I don't like the idea of having to owe him something I can never repay, nor owe him for something I never got."

"You and your husband had, in fact, prepared yourself for the end only to have that peace of mind taken away from you," Umri stated and Kat pulled herself to her feet.

"Objection, your honours," she moaned. "Is the prosecution trying to make out that Luke Robinson should now be punished for not allowing everyone to die?"

"Mr Umri?" Farthing addressed.

"Your honours, I am simply trying to get an overview of the emotions of this random member of the public."

"You're leading the witness to testify false feelings," Kat spat.

"I am uncovering subconscious sentiments," Umri declared.

"Neither you or the witness has any background in psychological determination and you are trying to get her to hate my client when she has already stated that she holds him in high regard," Kat bellowed.

"How do you know how she really feels about this when you don't know how you really feel," Umri shouted.

"How would you like me to come over there and show you how I really feel about all this," Kat threatened and brandished her clenched fist at him.

Umri's eyes widened and he turned back to the judges for help.

"Your honours," he cried, "I beseech you. The defence is threatening to hit me."

"I'm going to kick your arse all the way back to the Hamptons," Kat interjected.

"Ms Sabella," Farthing calmed. "I have no idea what that means but I do believe you two need to 'get a room.'"

"Ew!" Kat blurted.

"I don't -" Umri started in confusion.

"Mr Umri," Farthing interrupted, "please restrict your line of questioning to what lies on the surface and not what you might presume may be repressed below."

The court suffered an embarrassed silence while Kat took her seat and Umri, self consciously, shuffled his papers with his head hung low.

He cleared his throat and returned his attention to Rosemary.

"Mrs Fletcher, can you tell us exactly how you feel about Luke Robinson?" Umri asked and tried to ignore the burning glower from Kat.

"I suppose, now I really think about it," Rosemary started and gave Kat a wary glance, "I'm a little bit put out that all this stuff has gone on completely out of my control. I am a bit angry about that."

"And this anger has to be targeted at Luke Robinson," Umri stated.

"Yes," she replied solemnly. "There isn't anyone else."

"Thank you, Mrs Fletcher," Umri said and lowered himself into his seat making sure he did not catch eye contact with anyone.

Kat composed herself and straightened her suit jacket as she got to her feet. "Do you mind if I call you Rosemary?" she asked.

"Not at all," Rosemary replied. "You can even call me 'Rose' if you like."

"Thank you, Rose," Kat said. "Now, you say that you are feeling a bit annoyed about the whole situation. What with it being totally out of your control, having to face your own mortality, the imminent deaths of your children and grandchildren, the futility of existence, the pointlessness of the struggles of life, et cetera."

The court fell silent and Rosemary's eyebrows had crept up her forehead.

"Er, yes?" she said, unsure as to whether she had actually been asked a question or not.

"That's understandable," Kat commented. "You made your peace, accepted your lot, came to terms with the inevitable?"

"Er, yes," Rosemary said.

"Gave up?" Kat suggested.

"What?"

"Is it fair to say that you gave up?" Kat reiterated. "You decided that there was nothing you could do to save yourself or your family so gave up any notion of fighting or surviving?"

"I wouldn't go that far," Rosemary argued.

"Then what would you call it?" Kat asked.

"Like you said, it was accepting the inevitable."

"But that's only what I said," Kat responded, "because it wasn't, was it?"

"What?"

"The inevitable," Kat told her. "I mean, death is, obviously inevitable but it wasn't then. Was it? So when the inevitable didn't happen, you - like everyone else who had 'made their peace' - must have felt a bit embarrassed. Perhaps ashamed? Especially when we all discovered that this man," she waved her arm to her side to indicate Luke, "this nobody -"

"Thanks," Luke muttered.

"- did not give up but *did* do something to save his, and everyone else's, lives."

Kat allowed a moment of silence for her words to sink in.

"Rose?" she asked. "Do you really think you are angry at Luke Robinson or maybe someone else?"

"Yes, you're right," Rosemary said. "At the time we were only thinking of ourselves and then, after, I thought about it all again and had to have a cry when I thought of all my little ones being killed."

Rosemary's throat dried up and she tried to blink away the welling moistness in her eyes.

"I'm their mother and I should've done something to try to protect them," she declared.

The court fell silent again and Rosemary dabbed at her eyes with a handkerchief she pulled from her sleeve.

"There was nothing you could've done," Luke announced.

"Why?" Rosemary demanded. "Why could I have done nothing but you could?"

"Thirty-seven," the voice continued. "Thirty-six."

Luke stared at the computer console; there were so many buttons and so many symbols that meant absolutely nothing to him.

"Can't you stop it?" he asked.

"Thirty-five."

Tasya pulled herself out from the machine banks below him.

"I'm not sure," she muttered as she untangled a collection of wires through her fingers.

"Thirty-four."

"I should be able to but I need more time."

"Thirty-three."

"Can you slow the countdown?" he asked.

"Thirty-two."

"There's a port socket over there," she said and pointed to the side of the console.

"Thirty-one."

"You need to find something that will inhibit the electron flow across it."

"Thirty."

"I don't know what that means," he yelled desperately.

"Twenty-nine."

"Get something that is a couple of inches thick and a few inches long and shove it in the hole," she screamed at him.

"Twenty-eight."

Luke's eyes widened.

"Twenty-seven."

"Hurry!"

Tasya hauled herself back into the web of electronics whilst Luke's conscience battled with his libido.

"Twenty-six."

He shuffled over to the hole to discover it was at waist height.

"Twenty-five."

He dropped his trousers.

"Twenty-four."

Tasya pulled her head out from the mesh. "Do something quickly otherwise we're both dead."

"Twenty-three."

She heard the crackle of electricity and a drawn out scream from Luke.

"Twe."

"Good job," she commended. "Keep whatever it is in there until I say, okay?"

"Graagh!" Luke replied.

"Ent."

Tasya wriggled back in and continued with her machinations.

Luke clamped his jaw shut, closed his eyes and tried to ignore the *smell of burning hair*.

"*Ty.*"

"Just because," Luke told Rosemary and squeezed his thighs together.

"Mr Robinson," Farthing called, "you will get your chance to talk later. Please refrain from speaking directly to the witnesses. Do you have any more questions, Ms Sabella?"

"No," Kat replied. "I'm finished. Thank you Rose."

As Kat sat, Umri got up.

"I have nothing more, your honours," he said and sat down again.

"Very well," Farthing muttered, made a couple of notes on his pad then turned to Rosemary. "Thank you very much, Mrs Fletcher, your testimony has been enlightening to say the least. Please escort Mrs Fletcher back to her seat," he told one of the guards and the court watched as she was led back up the aisle to her row and then as she sidled her way back to her seat. As she sat, the man next to her took her hand and gave it an encouraging squeeze.

ACT 4: Who He Might Be

Farthing had a quick chat with his two associates and returned his attention to his microphone.

"We have decided to forgo another recess at this time," he said. "We still have another half-dozen witnesses to get through and the day seems to be passing quickly. So, if there are no objections?"

All three lawyers shook their heads.

"Very well, please call police constable Bambury," Farthing instructed and the call went down the chain of communication.

A blond, uniformed British policeman stepped through the door and marched up to the witness stand. He was sworn in and stood rigidly to attention. His line of vision was set above the heads of the audience and fixed squarely on the back wall.

"Now, Constable Bambury," Farthing addressed.

"Yes sir, your honour," he spluttered nervously. "Sir."

"Calm down, Constable," Farthing soothed. "We're not in the army and it's not you on trial. Is this your first court appearance?"

"Yes your honour, sir," Bambury replied.

"Well, just relax, young man," Farthing soothed, "and speak slowly."

"Thank you, your honour," Bambury said.

"Not the ideal case for your first hearing, huh?" Farthing said aside.

Bambury's demeanour altered slightly and his shoulders dropped. "No, not really," he said.

"How long have you been a constable?" Jameson asked and he stiffened up again.

"Just over four years, ma'am, your honour," he replied.

"That seems like a long time to go without ever having to testify in court," Etienne commented.

"Yes, your honour," Bambury replied. "That would be because I have never made an arrest or been present at the scene of a crime."

The three judges exchanged glances.

"Never?" Etienne asked.

"That's right ma'am, your honour. For some reason I have always been in the wrong place at the wrong time."

"Maybe that should be, 'In the right place,'" Farthing commented.

"Not when your job is to nick people, sir," Bambury replied with a hint of agitation in his voice.

"'Nick'?" Etienne enquired.

Bambury cleared his throat in embarrassment. "Beg your pardon, ma'am. I meant to say when your job is to maintain the peace."

"Maybe you do that too well, young man," Farthing stated. "Hence why you have never seen any 'action.'"

"That's not how the boys down the station think on it, sir," Bambury replied sullenly.

"I suppose not," Farthing concurred. "If you would like to go ahead and deliver your report, PC Bambury."

"Very good, your honour." Bambury slipped his right hand inside his jacket, pulled out a small notebook then cleared his throat again.

On the evening of the twenty-eighth I was walking my usual beat when at approximately eleven forty-five I received a call from the station to check out a D&D (which in layman's terms is a drunk and disorderly call). This is quite usual at that time of night what with it being shortly after kicking-out time but normally by the time you get to where the call has been reported the individuals involved have either moved on, it's calmed down or there are no clearly identifiable offenders.

"However, on this particular occasion I arrived on the scene at the top of Hurstpier Road about five minutes after the call to find four young men in various states of consciousness on the path, the body of a fifth male in the road and a stationary metallic-blue, Vauxhall Astra - with driver still inside - was situated slightly further up the road.

"The young men were all aged in their mid-to-late-twenties (very common) and eventually identified themselves as Alec King, Jamie Argento and Anthony Hamilton. They identified the dead boy in the road as David Wilkinson and that was later confirmed by identification found on his person. The fifth male was the defendant, Luke Robinson. The driver identified herself as Mrs Mary Hopkins.

"I received statements from all present as well as a passer-by, Malcolm Ingrams. Mrs Hopkins said that she could see a commotion on the path as she drove towards them. Then, as she was about to pass, David Wilkinson seemed to jump into the road and she was unable to avoid him.

"The statements from the three boys were slightly varied and incoherent as each seemed to have taken quite a beating and may have been suffering from concussion. Needless to say, none of them had seen how David Wilkinson ended up in the road.

"Mr Robinson stated that he was attacked by the four boys. He defended himself and pushed Wilkinson away from him. Wilkinson backed into the road and was then hit by Mrs Hopkins.

"Mr Ingrams stated that he had watched the altercation from its beginning and confirmed Robinson's claim that he was indeed the initial victim. However, after the first blows had landed, Robinson was fully in control of the situation and despatched each of his attackers one-by-one. It was as he was about to send Wilkinson packing that he seemed to hesitate before giving him a little shove. Wilkinson appeared to leap backwards directly into the path of Mrs Hopkins' car. It was then that Mr Ingrams called the police from his mobile phone."

Bambury flipped his notebook closed and looked up to the judges. They were furiously scribbling notes down on their paper.

"PC Bambury?" Etienne asked as her writing came to a close.

"Yes, ma'am?"

"At what point were the charges for murder brought against Luke Robinson?"

"We called all the witnesses back to the station and gave them individual interviews. It became apparent that with Mr Robinson's background and experience that it was highly likely that Mr Wilkinson's death was not an accident but intentional. It was then that he was charged with murder."

Bambury looked to the judges for approval of his delivery but they still had their heads down making notes.

"Do you have anything to ask, Mr Umri?" Farthing finally questioned and Tailor got to his feet. Bambury's face fell slightly as he looked expectantly at the prosecution.

"Yes, thank you, your honour. PC Bambury, you mentioned that the four living males were in various states of consciousness. Could you elaborate, please?" Tailor requested.

"Yessir," Bambury spat, pulled his notebook out again, flipped it to the appropriate page and read. "Alec King was unconscious on the path, Jamie Argento was unconscious in a ditch to the side of the path, Anthony Hamilton was conscious and sitting on the curb but apparently in shock, Luke Robinson was fully conscious and sitting on a bench at a bus stop."

Tailor checked his notes. "That's four. You said there were five?" Umri tugged at his jacket sleeve.

"Five?" Bambury looked confused but continued his delivery none-the-less. "The state of consciousness of the fifth lad, David Wilkinson, was non-existent because he was dead."

Tailor blushed and cleared his throat. "Of course, my apologies. Was there any obvious physical damage to any of the males?"

"Oh yes, the three who had been knocked about had bruises and cuts all over the faces and hands. Robinson had a nice shiner over his right eye and bruising around his neck."

"And how was the defendant's demeanour?"

"Demeanour?"

Farthing slapped his pen down in front of him. "Why do you people keep using that word?" he demanded and then turned to Bambury. "How was Robinson behaving when you got there?"

"Oh right. Yes," Bambury comprehended and looked at his notes again. "Robinson was quite calm and very co-operative. He offered a full statement at the incident site that did not alter in details when he was later interviewed at the station." Bambury looked up to the judges. "His statement was actually taken to be the true account of events over the three statements given by the other boys due to their inconsistency over the details."

"Was he at all concerned about Wilkinson's death?"

"He didn't seem to be."

"Not even when he was charged with murder?"

"No, sir."

"No emotion at all?"

"None. He just sat there and nodded."

"And throughout the entire interview session, had he accepted *any* responsibility for Wilkinson's death?"

"He just said that he had pushed Wilkinson away and that he did not kill him."

"Thank you, PC Bambury," Tailor said and took his seat.

There was a moment of silence. Kat had leaned over to Luke and was whispering in his ear.

"Ms Sabella?" Farthing asked and she held up her index finger to give her a moment. She turned her head and Luke whispered something in her ear then she stood.

"PC Bambury," she addressed.

"Yes, ma'am," he replied.

"So this was your first arrest, is that correct?"

"It is," he said.

"No arrests at all? Ever?"

"None."

"Wow!" she exclaimed. "This was a biggy then, huh?"

"Er," Bambury looked to the judges for any sign of support but they just looked at him. "Well, yes. Very much so."

"I presume you knew about Luke Robinson prior to this incident?"

"Yes. Yes, I had followed the events closely," he said. "As had every member of the force who had to go out and quell outbreaks of public insurrection."

"Well recited," Kat commended. "What was your reaction upon first realising that Luke Robinson was one of the individuals involved?"

"I knew that he lived in the town but I never thought I'd get to meet him," Bambury replied.

"'Meet him'?" Kat questioned. "Did you get his autograph?"

Bambury flipped his notebook open. "Just here," he said and the audience stifled a laugh.

"So regardless of the fact that this was your first ever arrest, this must have been the biggest arrest in the history of the British Police Force as we know it," Kat stated.

"I suppose," Bambury replied.

"What a catch, huh? An incident involving the saviour of the planet? That must've gone down well on the record sheet. Even better if it resulted in a charge, yes?"

Bambury was about to reply when Tailor leapt to his feet.

"Objection, your honour," he screamed. "She's badgering the witness."

"Oh shut up," Kat shouted and Tailor's eyes widened.

"She's doing it again," he exclaimed to the judges.

"Ms Sabella," Farthing soothed. "Please calm yourself."

"Well, really," she muttered.

"Your honour?" Tailor pleaded and Farthing sighed.

"Please play nicely children," he demanded.

"What about my objection?" Tailor asked.

"Overruled," Farthing said.

Kat scowled at Tailor until he sat down. She then turned her attention back to the officer.

"Such an arrest would look exceptionally good on your records which have otherwise been devoid of any sort of result," Kat stated.

"Well, yes," Bambury replied. "It would look good on anyone's records regardless of how many arrests they had made."

"I'll be blunt, PC Bambury, was your job on the line at all because of you appalling ability to do your job?"

"Objection!" Tailor screamed. "Who the hell is she to state whether PC Bambury was good at his job or not? Arrests are only a part of the role, keeping the peace is the major part and maybe that's why he hadn't made any arrests because there was nobody committing any crimes while he was on duty!"

Tailor inhaled heavily. His face had turned bright red and beads of sweat had appeared across his forehead.

"I'd suggest you took your seat, Mr Tailor, before you pass out," Farthing advised and he did so. Umri passed him a glass of water, which he took in a very shaky hand. Kat tried not to smile.

"I'll withdraw the question, your honour," she stated.

"Very humble of you," Farthing commented.

"PC Bambury? Are you aware of your superiors' opinion as to whether you were good at your job or not?"

Bambury shuffled in his seat. "I'm a good copper, miss," he said.

"That wasn't the question," Kat replied. "Would you like me to repeat what the question was?"

"That won't be necessary," Bambury said. "I was aware that some of my superiors were not too approving of my abilities as an officer of the law."

"They thought you were shit," Kat paraphrased.

"OBJE-"

"You could put it like that," Bambury said.

"Oh, sweet Jesus," Tailor mumbled and he doubled over onto the table.

"Is he all right?" Jameson asked Umri.

"Theatrics," Kat spat.

Umri leaned over his colleague who then grabbed his tie and pulled him in close.

"Heart attack," Umri announced at which two of the court guards ran forward, lifted Tailor on to the table and loosened his tie and shirt collar.

Kat slumped into her seat.

"Shit. Did I do that?" she muttered to Luke.

"I never realised this was part of the plan," he replied. "Bumping off the opposition one by one. It's unconventional but that's why I like it."

"Shut up, Luke," Kat reprimanded in all seriousness. "He might die."

She looked over to where one of the guards was rhythmically pushing on Tailor's chest.

"Oh, I can guarantee that he's going to die," Luke said.

Kat's eyes widened. "How do you know?"

Luke tutted and rolled his eyes to the ceiling. "Even I'm getting bored of repeating it," he said. "But you're all going to die eventually."

Kat shook her head. "You're right, you are getting boring."

Tailor inhaled sharply and began coughing. Two paramedics entered the court from the side door pushing a gurney between them. They lifted Tailor and trundled him out. He stared at Kat as they passed her table.

"Your honour," Umri started.

"No recess," Farthing barked. "I want to get through this and retire to Antigua before next weekend please."

Umri took his seat and started to reorganise the muddle of papers over his desk.

"Come on, Ms Sabella," Farthing ordered. "Let's see you crush this hapless soul too."

Kat got to her feet and pulled a face which she presumed indicated that she was hurt by the judge's remark; that she was, in fact, being totally misunderstood and that she was a really nice, sensitive and caring person. This was just a job and she was doing what she felt necessary to get the job done right.

Farthing saw her pout and scowl at him and presumed he was next on her list. Antigua seemed like such a long way away.

"PC Bambury, it's true that the routine evaluations you were getting throughout your career were not very good ones, isn't it."

"There were worse," Bambury responded.

"Let's face it, this arrest has probably saved your job on the force, hasn't it."

"I wouldn't go that far."

"Okay, it's delayed a potential dismissal, then?"

"Probably."

"So you have a major personal interest in this arrest arriving at a successful trial and prosecution."

"Not at all, miss," Bambury exclaimed. "It wasn't me who actually charged him with the murder nor read him his rights. I'm simply the incident officer."

"Who charged him with murder?"

"The DI got involved the moment she heard it was Robinson."

"Is that unusual?"

"I'll say," Bambury chuckled. "She barely lifts a finger apart from when someone needs taking down a peg or two."

Kat stood there and stared beyond the officer for a moment. It disconcerted him more than where the line of questioning may have been leading.

"Do you think she might have gotten involved purely because of the media attention?" Kat thought out loud.

Umri jumped up. "Your honour, I'm not sure where Ms Sabella is going with this but I don't think Officer Bambury is in a position to interpret the motivations of his superiors."

"You're quite right Mr Umri," Farthing agreed. "Ms Sabella, anything the officer had to say on this subject would be pure conjecture and inadmissible."

"Word gets round the work place, your honour," Kat replied. "I am trying to disclose that there are ulterior motives present that would like to see Luke Robinson put away out of the public eye."

"I understand that, Ms Sabella, but you know as well as I do that you would need to get those answers from the individuals directly involved."

"Yes, your honour."

"Would you like to continue?" Farthing asked and Kat stared some more.

"PC Bambury?"

"Yes, miss."

"As incident officer for this case, you must have seen the majority of paperwork that passed through the files."

"Yes, I was present at the interviews and had to sign off on all the transcripts and arrest documentation."

"Was there anything unusual in that procedure?"

"Couldn't say, miss. It was my first time remember? I simply did what I was told."

"Told by?"

"Well, the DI of course."

"But you must have known of the paperwork procedure involved prior to exercising it? That's a part of basic training, no?"

"True, but that was a long time ago and this was special circumstances."

"How so 'special'?"

"It was Luke Robinson."

"So?"

Bambury looked perplexed and tried to say something but no words emerged from his open mouth.

"I realise the social importance my client has but surely the procedures behind his arrest should have been the same as for any John Doe off the street," Kat explained. "What was so 'special'?"

Bambury swallowed and looked around the courtroom for help. His search fell upon Luke who was smiling at him.

"There was external involvement," he finally blurted.

"Is there a reason why I've had to try to pry this information from you?" Kat enquired sweetly.

"The witness is simply answering the questions as they've been presented," Umri declared.

"Bollocks, you're all in on something," Kat shouted back.

"I resent the implication that I might-" Umri squealed.

"'Might'?" Kat laughed.

"Your honour! She's harassing me!"

"I'm not getting involved this time," Farthing sighed and slumped back in his seat.

"What?"

"Come on you devious bastard, who's paying you to send Luke down?"

"Oh, 'Luke' is it?" Umri laughed. "I think you might be taking all this a little too personally. You might want to take a step back."

"I'll take a step back all right," Kat hissed. "Just so I could get a better run-up."

"She's threatening me again," Umri cried.

"All right people," Jameson interjected. "Everyone is getting a bit emotional over this."

"I'm not," Umri muttered.

"What ever, Mr Umri," she said. "I think we should go for a recess."

"Oh, not another," Farthing complained.

"You just passed over your control just now," Jameson told him.

"Your honour, would it be possible to finish with this witness first?" Kat asked.

Jameson hesitated.

"Please try to be nice, Miss Sabella," she finally said and Umri slumped into his seat with a huff.

"Thank you, your honour," Kat said.

Farthing mumbled something out of the range of the microphone.

"Well, you said you needed to go again anyway," Jameson responded.

"PC Bambury, do you know who the external involvement was from?" Kat asked civilly.

"No," he replied. "They were a governmental department who I had no direct contact with."

"Thank you," Kat said and sat down.

"Mr Umri? Anything else?" Jameson asked.

"Most definitely," Umri replied.

"Don't get stroppy with me, young man," Jameson warned.

"My apologies, your honour. PC Bambury."

"Yes sir?"

"Does it matter?"

"What's that?"

"The external interest in this case."

"I'm not sure I understand, sir."

"Well, if you would not mind indulging me by going over the facts of the incident?"

"Okay." Bambury flipped open his notebook again. "I was called to the scene where I discovered one dead male, three beaten males and Luke Robinson who had taken a bit of a pummelling himself. The evidence given by all present indicated that Mr Robinson had been set upon by the other four males who had then been slapped about by Mr Robinson which had then led to the death of David Wilkinson. After careful questioning it was deemed that the cause of his death was more than likely intentional on the part of Mr Robinson at which point he was charged."

Umri waited for a moment. "That's it?"

"Er." Bambury flipped through his notes again. "Aside from the eyes and tees, sir."

"I didn't hear where the external interest played a part?"

"Well, they didn't seem to, sir. They were just interested."

"As their name states," Umri said.

"I didn't know their names, sir," Bambury replied.

"I wasn't-" Umri started and then noticed a discouraging shake of Jameson's head directed at him.

"That's all, your honour," he said.

"Thank you, PC Bambury. You may step down now," Jameson informed the constable. He bowed his head respectfully to the panel of judges and left the room.

"Fifteen minutes, people," Jameson told the room and stood. Etienne and Farthing got to their feet and the rest of the room followed suit. The judges marched from the room and everyone took their seats again. The audience started chatting amongst themselves.

"Looks like you're uncovering a major conspiracy here," Luke commented and Kat turned sharply to him.

"Am I?" she demanded. "Am I really? I don't know what I'm doing here. At every turn there seems to be something else going on but with each new witness I've got myself doubting everything that I believe in. Or rather everything that I believe in you." She turned back to her paperwork.

"You think I killed that guy?" Luke asked.

"I don't know."

"I didn't."

"So you keep saying."

"The car did."

Kat chewed on her bottom lip then she turned to him again and peered at him over the rim of her glasses. What did that mean? She was not sure she wanted him to answer her question now.

"Was the Agency at the police station?" she asked instead and she would have sworn that a look of disappointment crossed his face.

"More than likely," he sighed. "They've been watching me, my family and friends since it all ended."

"What do they want?"

"What the caretakers wanted."

"To destroy all life on Earth?"

"Bizarre isn't it," Luke commented.

"I don't believe it," Kat scoffed and got back to reviewing her notes on the next witnesses.

"Doesn't matter what you believe, Kat," Luke said. "There was that time when people didn't believe that the World was round. People didn't believe that there was life on other planets. People didn't believe that a fabric conditioner would kill oxygen-emitting bacteria in the Atlantic that fed a third of the ocean's life. Never stopped it from being true."

She was staring at him looking into space.

"What did they do to show you everyone dying?" she asked before her brain could determine whether it was a sensible thing to ask and whether she actually wanted to know the answer.

"It was the strangest sensation," Luke murmured. "I don't know what or how they did it but I could see and feel everything. It was like I was the planet and they speeded time but I could still make out every living body on me. It was like when you look at a spinning disk of colours and they all merge to make one overall colour. The movements of the human race merged into one theme and that was death. People died, people killed each other and then I noticed that they were killing themselves. An action here mushroomed to something dying over there, or maybe a lot later.

"And then they showed me the end. They took it beyond now and showed me how life on Earth was choking on its own refuse and it was then that I saw the people I know die. It's all still in my head and I still wake at night seeing you all gasping for your last breaths like an expelled goldfish."

He blinked and tried to force a smile. "I recognise everyone I see now as another person I saw die in one way or another."

"You saw me?" Kat asked.

"Yup."

"How," her voice cracked and she had to swallow to strengthen her resolve. "How did I die?"

"Kat, I don't know if they showed me the future or managed to get an imprint of everyone and extrapolate a likely scenario."

"So you don't know."

"You died in this room," he said bluntly.

She tried to say something but an irrational fear had gripped her. While he was saying everything, she knew it was ridiculous to think he had seen the future of everyone on the planet, and yet it was as ridiculous to think he could have single-handedly battled an armada of invading aliens.

"Today?" she managed.

"Could be," he replied and swivelled around in his chair. "I recognise a few other faces here too."

"What are you going to do?" she enquired.

"Live, probably," he said. "If it's any consolation I wasn't sitting next to you when it happened."

"Won't you try to save everyone?"

"Look what happened the last time I saved everyone."

"That's not funny."

"Who's laughing?"

"Seriously, Luke, are you not going to do anything?"

"Let me ask you one simple question," he said and she nodded. "Do you believe you are going to die soon? In this room? Perhaps in the next few hours? Just because I said you will?"

"No," she replied. "Not really."

"And why would you? The only time any of us truly believe we are going to die is when we're right on the brink. You don't believe it and they won't believe it so there isn't anything I could do even if I tried. None of you will ever believe it until it's too late."

"And then?" she asked hopefully.

"Well, 'too late' by definition is too late, isn't it?" he told her.

Kat stared into the distance again for a moment.

"It's not too late to get up and walk out, you know," he told her.

"Yes it is," she muttered back. "You wouldn't understand."

Luke blurted a laugh that made Kat jump back to reality.

"Oh sure, because I didn't have plenty of opportunities to back out," he laughed.

"But you didn't. Why?"

The smile and laughter went as quickly as it had come and the serious, melancholic Luke was back again. He sighed, slouched his shoulders and looked tired.

"Nine times out of ten was because I knew I would get killed if I continued *or* turned around."

"What stopped you from curling up into a ball and going mad?"

"Tasya," he said dreamily. "She would either pick me up or kick me in the side of the head until I kept going."

"Feisty girl," Kat commented.

"Like you wouldn't believe," Luke replied and a slight spark returned to his eye. He turned to Kat with a grim smile. "Or perhaps you would," he said.

Kat cocked her head in puzzlement just as the judges' door swung open again and everyone pulled themselves to their feet.

Etienne entered first this time, followed by Jameson then Farthing. Jameson took the middle seat, inspected the notes in front of her then leant into her microphone.

"Let's get on with this then. We're calling the three boys in turn, a character witness, the driver and then the eyewitness. Is that correct?"

Kat and Umri lifted themselves slightly and assented.

Jameson sat back and turned to Farthing. "Christ, this could still take hours." Farthing shrugged his shoulders and she seemed to ponder a couple of scenarios in her head. Finally she leant forward again.

"Call Alec King, please."

The call went down the chain and a young man in his mid-twenties entered the court. He immediately stared at Luke who winked in return.

Alec had short fair hair with an upward spiky fringe that glistened from over enthusiastic gel application. Apart from that, there was nothing striking about him at all. He wore a simple blue suit and open collar white shirt. Under the shirt could been seen the sparkle of a gold necklace.

He took to the stand and was sworn in.

"Tell the court your name and relationship to the defendant, please," Jameson instructed.

"I'm Alec King and the defendant killed my best mate," Alec said and sniffed.

"Oh, come on," Kat called.

"Ms Sabella," Jameson barked. "I realise things have gotten a bit strained but this is still a courtroom and you will please dignify a respectful tone when addressing it thusly."

Kat stood up.

"Sorry, your honour," she said. "I will."

"Good," Jameson said and instructed her to sit down. "Young man, that goes for you too."

Alec just glared at Luke and sniffed.

"Are you employed?"

Alec sniffed. "I'm a tradesman."

"What does that mean?"

"I do plastering, plumbing, carpentry. A little bit of everything."

"Right, your story. From the start," Jameson ordered.

Alec sniffed. "It was Friday night and we was down the pub as usual. We were having a laugh when-"

"Mr King," Farthing interrupted. "Could you give us a bit more detail? The date in question, the pub in question, and the members of your party."

"It was Friday twenty-eighth of February and I was down the Wack 'n' Fank with-"

"The what?" Jameson demanded.

"The Wack 'n' Fank. The pub we was in."

"The whacking what?" Etienne asked Jameson.

"It's a franchise of pubs in England," Farthing said. "They are owned by one brewery and are called 'The Wack *n* Something'. Rather than 'The Fox and Hounds' or such like. It has the intonation of swearing which is supposed to be humorous and appealing to the youth of today."

"How so?" Etienne asked.

"It's spoonerism," Farthing explained. "Swap the first letter of the two words and you get swearing."

"The fack 'n' wank?" Etienne asked and a ripple of laughter went through the audience.

Jameson cleared her throat loudly. "Anyway, carry on please Mr King."

Alec sniffed. "So there was me, Jimbo, Tone, Dee-Double-You, Finkle-"

"Mr King," Jameson snapped. "Are you deliberately attempting to antagonise this court?"

"No," Alec spat defensively.

"Dates, times, places and *real* names, please, Mr King."

Alec sniffed.

"And *please* blow your nose," she ordered.

"I don't need to," he said.

"Then why do you keep sniffing all the time?"

"I'm not."

He sniffed. And Jameson glared at him to see if he was goading her.

"Get on with it," she muttered. "You 'was dahn' the pub," she mimicked, "with?"

Alec sniffed. "There was me," he leant into the microphone, "Alec King," he leaned back again, "with," he leaned forward again, "Jamie Argento, Anthony Hamilton, David Wilkinson, Barry Finks and Rob the Scot."

Jameson slammed her hand down on her desk. "Mr King!"

"No, honestly," he whined. "That's his name. No one knows him by anything else."

She turned her attention to the prosecution. "Mr Umri, did you prep this witness in any way whatsoever?"

Umri raised himself and tried to look Jameson in the eye but could not. "I tried," he confessed.

"And this, 'Rob the Scot'?"

Umri shrugged his shoulders. "He did not seem to be essential to this hearing. That *was* the name that he went by. Apparently he carried identification with that name on it. And then we were unable to contact him or Barry Finks anyway."

Jameson unlocked her jaw then turned to Alec.

"Right. You. Get to the point, quickly."

Alec sniffed and Jameson's lips tightened.

"We was all down the pub as per usual, just having a few beers and a laugh when one of the boys noticed him in the room." Alec nodded at Luke.

"Name!" Jameson barked.

"Luke Robinson," Alec bit back then sniffed. "He was there with someone."

"Do you know who it was?" Farthing asked.

"No. Just some bloke. Never seen him before nor after."

"Go on," Jameson urged.

"Anyway, I noticed that they kept looking over at us. Kept staring and giving us dirty looks."

"How did you notice this?" Etienne enquired.

"I was standing facing them and I kept seeing his mate swivel round to look at us. Then every time they looked they started laughing. I told the others and they all turned to have a look and that's when we decided that they were fucking with us."

"Mr King!" Jameson snapped.

"Sorry, but I don't know how else to describe it," Alec whined. Then sniffed.

"Then try to explain it in more detail," Jameson suggested.

Alec sighed then sniffed again. "It's the look when someone is after a fight but don't use any words. It's like they're staring at you nastily."

"Intimidating," Jameson offered.

"I weren't intimidated, no," Alec protested.

"But that's what the staring was supposed to do, yes?"

"I suppose. It was then that Fink - I mean, Barry Finks and Rob the Scot left us. It was getting close to closing time when him and his mate left too. And we followed."

"So you went specifically with the intention of causing a fight," Jameson suggested.

"No, we just wanted to teach them a lesson."

"Carry on."

"Eventually his mate left him and we carried on following."

"Who?" Farthing asked with a sigh.

"We did."

"You followed who?" Farthing reiterated.

"We followed him. Robinson," Alec said slowly and carefully. He sniffed. "A little way up the road we called to him and he stopped. We caught up and Dave started talking to him."

"And said what?" Jameson demanded.

"I can't remember exactly. I was pretty hammered and the doctors said that I was probably suffering from concussion which was why I can't remember properly."

"So what do you remember?" Jameson asked.

"Robinson said something, Dave took a swing and lamped him on the side of the head. He then gave Dave a belt and sent him into the bushes. Jamie got round behind him and grabbed him round the neck, I stepped forward and -"

The silence took a second to register and everyone watched him with expectation.

"And?" Jameson pressed.

"I don't remember anything else until I was sitting up and an ambulance man had a cold cloth at my head."

Jameson sat back in her seat and turned her attention to the lawyers.

"Do you two have any questions? Mr Umri?"

Umri raised himself slightly. "No, your honour," he said and sat back down.

"Ms Sabella?"

Kat lifted herself up. "Yes, your honour. Mr King, when you first saw Luke Robinson in the pub did you recognise him?"

"We knew that we'd seen him somewhere before but-"

"Did you recognise him, Mr King?" Kat interrupted. "Not, 'Did your Borg collective recognise him?' but did *you* recognise him?"

Alec sniffed. "I did. But I didn't know where from to start."

"But eventually the six of you discussed it and realised who he was?"

"Yeah, it was Barry who got it straight away."

"Then what happened?"

He sniffed. "I told you already, he started staring at us."

"But this was after you had drawn your group's attention toward him and had started talking amongst yourselves about him?"

"I suppose," Alec replied testily.

"And what was your opinion about Luke Robinson?"

Alec sniffed and shrugged his shoulders.

"You must have formed an opinion towards this person as you became more aware of the events during the twelfth to seventeenth of February?" Kat reiterated.

"Not really," Alec said.

"You do know that if it wasn't for Luke Robinson's intervention then you would be dead?"

"Yeah."

"And that doesn't make you have any feelings toward your state of mortality or Luke Robinson?"

"Not really."

"I don't believe it," Kat muttered and Umri lifted himself to his feet.

"I object, your honours. The defence is bullying the witness."

"Sustained," Jameson concurred. "He's already given you the same answer three times, Ms Sabella."

"But he's obviously lying," Kat argued.

"Your honour!" Umri pleaded.

"That's enough, Ms Sabella. Mr King cannot help being emotionally retarded and intellectually dysfunctional," Jameson said. "So you will have to accept his testimony at face value."

"Yes, your honour," Kat grumbled and rapped her fingers on her table in frustration.

She took a moment to compose herself whilst Umri sat down.

"Mr King, if, as you testified, you had no opinion as to the defendant prior to the twenty-eighth why was it that he made such an immediate negative impression on you?"

"I told you, he was fucking with us."

"It sounds, to me like you were fucking with him first."

Umri jumped up.

"Don't push your luck, Mr Umri," Jameson warned and he lowered himself again.

"He thinks he's so fucking hard," Alec blurted.

"I beg your pardon?" Kat asked.

"I said, 'He thinks he's so hard.' He was asking for trouble."

"Ah, I see. So Luke Robinson told you he was stronger than you did he?"

"No."

"Okay, but he did state that he could beat you at some physical level though?"

"No."

"Then how do you know that he thought he was 'hard'?"

Alec's eyes flittered around the room. He sniffed. "You could tell."

Kat smiled. "Could you?" she asked. "No more questions." She sat down.

"Do you have anything to ask now, Mr Umri?" Jameson asked.

Umri rose. "Mr King, when you were at the pub, did you notice if the defendant was attracting the attention of any of the other patrons?"

"Other what?" Alec demanded.

"The other customers."

"Yeah, practically everyone was talking about him at some stage."

"Thank you. No more, your honour," Umri stated and took his seat.

"What has that got to do with anything?" Kat murmured.

"You can step down now Mr King, thank you," Jameson said and Alec left the room.

"This is pointless," Kat whispered to Luke. "Each one is going to come out here say you were acting boisterous but ultimately each of them will have to admit that they hit out first. I don't get it."

"Maybe he thinks he can find a reason for them to have attacked me," Luke said. "Maybe I spilled one of their pints or stared at their birds."

"It's all so stupid," she said to herself.

"That's only just occurred to you?"

"Call Jamie Argento, please," Jameson announced and eventually another young man entered and made his way to the witness stand. He had short black hair flattened evenly over his head. His hair glistened as if he had just received a good soaking but had actually been doused in gel like his compatriot's before him. He was wearing a black pair of light trousers and a white shirt. He unashamedly brandished a thick gold chain necklace outside of his collar and a couple of matching rings on his right hand. His face was marred with acne scars and it looked like he was trying to grow a moustache.

He made his way to the witness stand and was sworn in.

"Please state your full name and relationship to the defendant," Jameson instructed.

"My name is Jamie Phillipe Argento and I know the defendant from a fight we had on the twenty-eighth of February of this year," Jamie announced.

"Are you currently in employment?" Jameson asked.

"Yes, your honour. I'm a sales executive at KVN Financial Services."

"Very good," Jameson commended. "Please could you tell us the events that took place leading up to and including the altercation on the date in question?" Jameson requested.

"It was a Friday night so I had gone down to our local pub, The Wack 'n' Fank, to meet with a couple of friends: Barry Finks and Dave Wilkinson. I got there at about eight o'clock in the evening and they were already there with another bloke who just calls himself 'Rob The Scot'. After about an hour Alec King and Tony Hamilton turned up. It was sometime after that when Alec pointed out that Luke Robinson was also there so we all turned to have a look.

"We started having a chat about him, the invasion and what we had all been doing during that week. Alec then said that Robinson and his friend had been staring at us so I went over to him."

Jameson sat up to attention. "You did what?"

"I said, 'I went over to him'."

"You talked to him? When he was sitting in the pub?" she asked.

"That's correct," he replied. "I just wanted to find out if he had a problem."

"What kind of problem?" Etienne enquired.

"You know, if he had a problem with us."

"No, I do not understand," she told him.

Jamie became a bit flustered. "A problem! If he was - I don't know - after a fight."

"I see, thank you," Etienne said.

"Do you have any idea why your friend, Alec King, did not mention that you had approached the defendant?" Farthing asked.

Jamie shook his head. "I don't. Like I said, it was him who pointed out that Robinson had been looking over and I went over pretty much straight after."

"Carry on please," Jameson instructed.

"Anyway, as I got closer I noticed Robinson roll his eyes. He then dropped his head so as not to look at me. I told him that I'd seen him staring at us and he denied it. I then told him again that we had all seen him looking at us and he said he said that he hadn't been. It was then that his mate piped up and said something like, 'Do you know who he is?' and I said I didn't care who he was, if he carried on eyeballing us then there was going to be trouble. It was then that he lifted his head and looked at me. I just turned round and walked back.

"Over the next hour or so, Robinson carried on looking over and as last orders were called him and his mate left. We decided to follow."

"All of you?" Farthing asked.

"Sorry, no. All of us except for Rob the Scot and Barry Finks. I think they must have wandered off a bit earlier."

Jamie stood there for a moment, deep in thought as if something was nagging at his memory.

"Yeah," he finally said. "They wandered off a bit earlier."

"Do go on," Jameson said.

"We followed them from a way back and just as they got out of the town centre his mate wandered off. We followed Robinson a bit further up the road and eventually caught up with him. Dave started talking to him and then Robinson gave him some lip so he hit him."

"Who hit who?" Jameson asked.

"Dave hit Robinson. But he was provoked."

"How so?" Jameson demanded.

"Robinson was being mouthy."

"What was it that the defendant said?" Jameson asked.

"Piss off you whiny little shit," Jamie told her.

"I hope that was a quote," Farthing muttered and Jamie's eyes widened.

"Oh yeah," he spluttered. "That's what Robinson said to Dave. I wasn't saying it."

Jameson continued unabashed. "What did David Wilkinson say to the defendant?"

"Nothing, he hit him," Jamie replied.

"You told us that David Wilkinson addressed the defendant prior to the cited outburst," Jameson explained. "What did he say?"

"I don't know," Jamie replied. "I couldn't hear him."

"What happened after the defendant was struck, please?" Jameson asked.

"I noticed that he didn't move at all. Dave was a big bloke and he caught Robinson right on the side of the jaw but he didn't even wobble. I think I saw him smile. Anyway, Robinson swung back at Dave and sent him into the bushes. At this stage I had moved round behind him and grabbed him to try to restrain him but he managed to lift me over his head. I landed on Alec and must have knocked him out. Tony was moving in as I tried to pick myself up. As I got up and turned around I found Robinson standing directly in front of me. He head-butted me in the face and then kicked me in the boll- in my testicles.

"I fell over and must have passed out because the next thing I know is there are a couple of paramedics over me and a policeman."

"When did you discover that David Wilkinson was dead?" Farthing asked.

Jamie pursed his lips and swallowed. "After I got discharged from the hospital."

The judges fell into their customary silence and then had a whispered discussion. Jameson then returned to her microphone.

"Mr Umri? Your witness."

Umri prised himself up. "No questions at this time, your honour." He lowered himself back into his seat.

"Ms Sabella?"

Kat raised herself. "Would you say your lifestyle displays a distinct propensity for violence?"

"Not at all," Jamie replied.

She pushed a piece of paper to one side as if uncovering a note beneath. "You work in financial sales, is that correct?"

"That's right. I'm a sales executive," Jamie told her.

"Are you on a decent salary?"

"Yeah, not bad."

"Your honour?" Umri called and raised his hands as if pleading to the gods.

Jameson sighed. "Mr Umri, she's nearly always got a reason for this line of questioning. Please let it ride for a while."

"But-"

"Mr Umri," Jameson interrupted, "we know how to do our job. If we think the line of questioning is irrelevant then we will intercede. Okay?"

"Yes, your honour."

"Carry on, Ms Sabella," Jameson instructed. "And this had better be good."

"Thank you," Kat said. "So you are on a good salary, then?"

"Yeah," Jamie said. "I can take home up to five grand a month sometimes."

"Sometimes?"

"Well, depending on how sales go that month."

"Ah, so you get a commission too," Kat said.

"Just commission," Jamie corrected.

"But you just said you took home a salary," Kat told him.

"Is this semantics, Ms Sabella?" Jameson asked.

Kat paused before her mouth said something her brain would regret a second after. Then she said, "Quite possibly, your honour."

"Mr Argento, your monthly income is dependant on what sales you make each month. Is that correct?"

"To a certain extent," Jamie replied. "I do have rolling commission which comes from regular customer contributions to existent policies but the big money comes from bagging a new sale."

"So it's quite competitive?"

"There's a friendly rivalry in the office, yes."

"And you have to make quite a few cold calls?"

"Pardon me?" Etienne requested.

"Cold calls, your honour, are when sales people make impromptu telephone calls searching for potential clients," Kat explained.

"Ah, those," Etienne responded with an air of indignation.

"Do you need me to repeat the question, Mr Argento?" Kat asked.

"No," Jamie replied. "I have to cold call, yes."

"How long have you been making cold calls?"

"About six years."

"And you're obviously very good at it."

"Better than a lot of the blokes in the office, yeah," Jamie bragged.

"Does it take a certain skill, then?"

"Well, yeah. Not everyone can do it. You have to have ba-" he stopped himself and blanched slightly. "A certain degree of confidence to do it well."

"Do you think that was why you went to approach Luke Robinson that night rather than any one else?"

"Could've been."

"And you did so specifically to impress your friends?"

"No," Jamie replied incredulously.

"Then why did you?"

"Because he was staring at us?"

"And?"

"He was challenging me."

"How so?"

"That's just the way it works."

"How did you know that he knew that was the way it works?"

"Eh?"

"Would you like me to rephrase the question?" Kat asked.

"Yes please," Etienne butted in.

"You seem to claim that it is an unwritten law that everyone knows that if you stare at someone you are obviously challenging them in some way."

"Yeah?"

"I didn't know that and I'm sure there are many other people in this room who didn't know that so I'm asking you, Mr Argento, how did you know that Luke Robinson knew that and that was his specific intention?"

"Well, what else could it have been?" Jamie blurted.

"Maybe he found you attractive," Kat suggested.

"I'm not gay," Jamie told her.

"I didn't say you were, I simply offered an hypothesis as to why Luke Robinson might have been staring at you."

"Your honour, this is all pure conjecture," Umri declared.

"Where are you trying to get to with this, Ms Sabella?" Jameson demanded.

"I just want to try to find out why Mr Argento presumed he was receiving threatening behaviour from Luke Robinson when he knew that Luke had put his life on the line for the safety of Mr Argento's."

"Well, why didn't you just ask that?" Jameson enquired wearily.

"Because I'm concerned that he might be a lying little shit-bag like the rest of his mates," Kat said.

"Oi!"

"Your honour!"

Jameson buried her head in her hands and groaned. "You were doing so well, too," she mumbled. She raised her head.

"Ms Sabella, I've got no choice but to find you in contempt of this court and hereby fine you -" Jameson stopped and turned to her companions.

"What currency should I use?" she asked.

"Use hers," Etienne suggested.

"One thousand pounds sterling," Jameson said. "And I want you before a review board to answer to your conduct here today."

Kat looked remorselessly over the frame of her glasses at Jameson. She rolled her eyes and said, "Whatever, your honour."

"Don't push your luck, young lady," Jameson warned.

Kat stared at a blank wall for a couple of seconds and clenched her teeth a few times. She then turned her attention to Luke and his missing lobe caught her attention.

"It doesn't make any sense at all, Mr Argento," she said still staring at the side of Luke's head. "There sat a man who you, firstly, had no way of knowing what his intentions were when he stared at you. Secondly, he saved people's lives so I don't understand why you would think he might want to threaten those he protected. Thirdly, he went one-on-one with aliens who were stronger, faster than any human and had access to advance weaponry so, by all accounts, anyone would put their money on him being able to kick your scrawny arse without breaking a sweat."

Jamie just stared at her.

"Is there a question in there, Ms Sabella?" Jameson demanded.

"I just want to know what you have got against my client?" Kat asked.

Jamie's eyes clenched. "You know nothing. You've already admitted that. There *are* unwritten laws that you know nothing about and there are actions you have to take if you want to have any self-esteem in your life. I know Robinson knew what he was doing and someone had to do something about it. The only thing everybody knows about him is that he saved the World. That's it. No one knows who is really is and what he's really like. Well I saw it that night. He's a calculating murderer."

"But you didn't even see David Wilkinson die!" Kat exclaimed. "You had fainted on the side of the path."

"I didn't fucking faint!" Jamie screamed. "I passed out."

"Whatever," Kat dismissed.

"No! Not, 'Whatever'. He kicked me so hard I couldn't even scream in pain!"

"Oh, he kicked you."

"I already said that he kicked me right in me nuts," Jamie bellowed. His face had turned red and tears were welling up in his eyes. "Kicked me so hard there were," his voice broke and he swallowed back his faltering resolve, "complications."

"Sang a bit higher for a week, did you?" Kat asked.

"Your honour!" Umri bellowed form his seat.

"No, you stupid bitch, I had to have an operation," Jamie screamed. Little tracks of spittle had formed in the corners of his mouth and a tear was rolling down his cheek.

Kat was slightly taken aback and her callous attitude slipped but it was too late. Whatever pent-up emotion had been keeping Jamie Argento rational for the past month had now been unleashed.

"They swelled up like fucking footballs," he cried. "I couldn't walk for a week." He reached inside his jacket, pulled out an envelope and threw it across the room at Kat. As it sailed through the air, the envelope opened and a handful of photographs fluttered out in its wake.

"Look at them, you bitch," Jamie ordered and Kat pulled out the last photograph that had managed to stay in the envelope that had landed on her desk in front of her. One of the bailiffs had scurried from his post and collected the others from the floor and handed them to Jameson.

"I couldn't even sit down to take a shit," Jamie continued.

The photograph in Kat's hand was an image of a man's naked thighs and midriff straight on and, indeed, his testicles had swollen so grotesquely that they came down to his knees. The penis seemed to have shrunk back into the pelvis so only the crown was visible.

"I couldn't piss properly, I couldn't lie down, I didn't sleep for four days straight and then when they started going down the doctors told me there was a ninety per cent chance of them turning cancerous so I would have to have them removed."

The entire room let out a sympathetic 'ooh' and Jamie was brought back to the level of his reality and exactly how many people he was making his confessions to. It was too late to stop now, though, and he did seem to gain some sort of relief from unburdening the horror. Kat stopped staring at the photograph and placed it on the table.

"I don't have any natural testosterone in my body any more," he said. "If I slip up on my medication I could grow tits for Christ sakes."

"Fuck me," Luke blurted as he looked at the discarded photograph.

"And he's the one who did this to me," Jamie accused. "'Life saver'? He's destroyed mine. I can't have kids, I can't grow facial hair any more-"

The audience let out a louder 'ooh' in unison and Jamie searched their faces to try to ascertain what it was in relation to. Every face was staring at the huge screen above his head. He turned to see what it was and saw a wavering hand holding the photograph of his elephantised gonads. Which meant every nation on the planet was now looking at them too.

Jamie's faced changed to sheer panic and he searched each camera to find out what was going on. Then he noticed, to his left, the camera with a red light on, pointing down, aimed at Luke's back with him angled so the camera had a clear shot of the photograph over his shoulder.

"You bastard!" Jamie screamed.

"At least you haven't got any masculinity left to challenge," Luke roared with mirth.

"You fucking bastard!" Jamie bellowed again.

Jameson picked up her gavel and slammed it on the desk.

"Can we have some order!" she demanded. "Bailiff, remove Mr Argento immediately."

"Miss Argento," Luke corrected.

"Mr Robinson!" Jameson barked.

"I'm going to fucking kill you!" Jamie screamed as two bailiffs restrained him by his arms and started dragging him towards the door.

"You got your blob on or something?" Luke asked him.

"Bastard!" Jamie bellowed as the door slammed shut behind him.

Jameson was furious. "What the hell is the matter with you two?" she demanded. "Can't you go an hour without upsetting or killing someone?"

"He was my first," Luke said.

"Mr Robinson," she shouted again, "you shouldn't be saying anything let alone badgering the afflicted with such infantile and sexist insults."

She collapsed back in her seat.

"I want to go home," she muttered then turned to Etienne. "Do you want to chair for the last run?"

"No, thank you," Etienne replied so Jameson turned to Farthing who already had his hand turned up in declination.

Jameson sighed. "Call Anthony Hamilton, please."

Kat slowly lowered herself into her seat as if trying not to draw attention to herself.

"That went well," Luke muttered.

"Not really," Kat hissed through gritted teeth. "We didn't get a chance to rebuttal."

"Did you need to?"

"Yes!" Kat spat. "He had the last word that you maimed him and your last word was that you don't give a toss."

"I don't."

"That's not the point. The point is to make everyone know that whatever happened to him is a result of his own erroneous actions."

"Kat, you're starting to take this a bit too seriously again," Luke commented.

"I'm mixed up, Luke," she confessed. "I don't know what the hell is going on any more. This should be serious. This is the most important case I'll ever have in my life but you keep convincing me that nothing that happens here is consequential in the grand scheme of things."

"There's hope for you yet," Luke commended.

The bailiffs returned to their posts as Anthony Hamilton entered the court.

Anthony was dressed in a dark blue, pinstriped suit, white shirt and matching blue tie. He had a gold tie pin that pierced through the knot and a delicate chain that hung between the two studs. He was probably only in his late twenties but premature recession of his hairline had encouraged him to have his hair shaved back to a bare stubble.

He took the stand and was sworn in.

"Can you please tell the court your full name and relationship to the defendant," Jameson instructed.

"My name is Anthony Hamilton and I was involved in a fight with the defendant on the twenty-eighth of last month."

"Please tell us the details of events of the evening in question that led up to the altercation," Jameson told him.

"Me and Alec King had met up at about eight at a pub in town."

"The Wack 'n' Fank?" Etienne asked.

"No, that was later," Anthony said. "Me and Alec met at The Runting Cat a bit further up the High Street. Alec wanted to have a chat about him and his girlfriend, Juliet Stevens, before we met up with the rest of the boys."

"The 'rest' being?" Farthing prompted.

"Well, we had arranged to just meet with David Wilkinson, Barry Finks and Jamie Argento but when we got there this ligger called Rob was hanging around too."

"'Ligger'?" Etienne asked.

"Erm, someone who hangs around and tries to get drinks for free off you," Anthony explained.

"And that would be the enigma who is Rob the Scot, correct?" Jameson asked.

"That's right," Anthony concurred. "So, we were all at the Wack 'n' Fack and Alec told us that there was some blokes chatting up Juliet and we eventually worked out that they were Luke Robinson and a mate of his."

"What were your relative positions in the pub?" Farthing asked.

"Him and his mate were sitting in a booth in the corner of the room and we were standing up by the bar," Anthony told him.

"Anyway, Alec had already had quite a few and he was getting upset so went off to have a word with his girlfriend and Jamie went over to Robinson to warn him off."

"Do you know what Mr Argento said to the defendant?" Jameson asked.

"No, but I presume it was to tell him that Juliet was taken."

Kat started to get to her feet but Jameson held out a hand to keep her at bay.

"Strike that last statement, please," she instructed the transcribers. "Mr Hamilton, please restrict your testimony to the things you do know. Don't guess, presume or speculate, please. You're not on trial, so if you don't know the facts then you can just say, 'No'. Okay?"

"Okay. Sorry," Anthony said.

"Carry on, please," Jameson instructed.

"So, Alec got back and he was really angry. Said that Robinson had tried to cop a feel of Juliet, then Jamie came back and said he'd sorted it all out.

"We carried on the night although Barry and Rob took off at some stage. I'm not sure what time that was. Then, just as last orders were called, Alec noted that Robinson was leaving so he and Jamie necked their pints and followed. David was already waiting to go anyway so I just left my drink and we went too. It was then that I found out that Robinson and his friend hadn't stopped eyeballing us all night."

"Why was it that you hadn't noticed this behaviour?" Farthing demanded.

"I'd been talking to Barry and Rob for most of the night so hadn't noticed anything out of sorts. When the boys told me what was going on then I agreed to go with them and try to sort things out.

"We followed the pair of them for a while until Robinson's friend went his own way then we caught up with Robinson."

"Did you deliberately wait for the defendant to be on his own?" Etienne asked.

"That wasn't my intention. There wasn't really any way we could know how long the two of them were going to walk together. They could've been going to the same place for all we knew. Him ending up on his own and us catching up then was just coincidence."

"And then the altercation took place," Jameson prompted.

"Yeah. David went straight up to Robinson and asked him who he thought he was, going around trying to nick other blokes' girlfriends."

"You heard him say that?" Farthing demanded.

"That's right. I was standing just behind David when he spoke to him."

"And the defendant's reply was?" Jameson asked.

"He said that he thought he was the person that saved David's 'miserable' life and that it was possibly the biggest mistake he ever made."

"Then David lamped him."

"That means 'hit'," Farthing said to Etienne.

"Thank you, I did work that one out for myself, though," she replied.

"Please go on," Jameson instructed.

"Robinson barely wobbled on the spot. He looked back at Dave and licked a spot of blood from his lip then smiled. Dave was about to take another pop but Robinson slapped him across the side of the head and sent him into the bushes. Jamie grabbed Robinson around the neck but he was hauled right over his head and fell right on top of Alec. At this stage I moved forward. I didn't really know what I was going to do but figured I had to try something to calm him down before he killed someone."

"Objection, your honour," Kat hollered.

"On what grounds?" Jameson demanded.

"At that stage in the proceedings it was purely speculation as to whether my client's actions would result in the death of someone. Mr Hamilton has used an inappropriate colloquialism."

"How do you know?" Jameson asked.

"I beg your pardon?" Kat asked.

"How do you know if Mr Hamilton does not have the experience to know when a fight is going too far or whether that was his genuine fear at the time?"

"I don't," Kat muttered.

"Well then, it's up to you to find that out when it's your turn then, isn't it? Objection overruled." Jameson said and Kat took her seat. "Carry on, Mr Hamilton."

"Right. So I steps forward and, without hesitation, Robinson grabs me and chucks me on top of Dave in the bushes. We scrabble to get up and I see Jamie fall to the floor. Robinson then turns round to face us and we both move forward together but he just zips right between us and catches me on the bridge of my nose. I can taste blood down the back of my throat and there are tears pouring out of my eyes but I hear Robinson say something like, 'I hope you boys have learnt a lesson tonight,' then there was a car screech and an almighty thump. When I cleared my eyes, I see Dave lying in the road right in front of me. I don't really know what happened next. I just sat down and looked at him."

Tony stared into the distance for a moment and the courtroom fell silent. He remembered where he was and came back to attention.

"Dave was lying on his side with his eyes open and staring right at me. He had a trickle of blood running from his temple right across one of his eyeballs and dropping off his nose like tears."

"Mr Umri?" Jameson invited solemnly.

Umri stood up. "No questions, your honour," he stated and sat down again.

"What is he doing?" Kat demanded quietly. "Why isn't he asking any of his own witnesses any questions?"

"Maybe he doesn't need to," Luke replied. "They're not denying that they started it and that they were looking for trouble."

"Ms Sabella?" Jameson said.

Kat stood up. "Mr Hamilton, would you say that you were relatively sober compared to your friends?"

"I wasn't sober but I hadn't had as much as Alec and Jamie, but I don't think Dave was particularly drunk," Tony said.

"And Alec King was particularly upset because of the situation with his girlfriend," Kat said.

"Yeah."

"Was he looking for trouble then?"

"I don't know what he was after."

"But when he saw his girlfriend - Juliet Stevens - talking with Luke Robinson he became particularly agitated."

"Yeah."

"And it was Jamie who first confronted Luke Robinson with the group's displeasure."

"I suppose you could put it like that."

"And it was David Wilkinson who challenged Luke Robinson both verbally and physically."

"Yes it was."

"And then my client was attacked from behind by Jamie Argento."

"Yes."

"Who happened to collide with Alec King."

"I dunno about 'just happened'-"

"And *then* you marched in to try to calm the situation."

"Yeah, that's right."

"You don't suppose that after all of the previous unprovoked hostility, my client presumed that you were going to deliver some of the same and hence why you were so hastily despatched?"

"Whatever," Tony dismissed, "but that doesn't give him the right to kill Dave, does it?"

"How *are* you such an expert on street scuffles?" Kat asked.

"Pardon me?" Tony shot back.

"Well, when you were delivering your testimony I was admonished for questioning your authority on reading fight scenarios. I was then told to dispute your expertise when it was my turn to question you. So here we are, my turn. What made you think that the scuffle required your intervention to prevent the potential death of someone?"

Tony shook his head and frowned. "I don't understand what you're asking."

"David Wilkinson was in the bushes!" Kat bellowed. "Alec King was unconscious and Jamie Argento was on top of him. Why, at that point, did you think it was Luke Robinson that needed calming down and not any of your three friends who had initiated each stage of the offence?"

"They were my mates," Tony responded.

"So you went forward to stop Luke Robinson from defending his self from your three incapacitated friends?"

"No," Tony spat defiantly.

"You went forward to stop Luke Robinson from defending himself against you, then?" Kat suggested.

"Eh?"

"The best defence is a good offence," Kat cited.

"Yeah. I suppose."

"Thank you," Kat sighed.

"What?" Tony demanded.

"Have you ever seen someone get killed before?" Kat asked.

"No," Tony replied.

"But you do know of someone - other than David Wilkinson - who died as a result of a street fight," she said.

"No."

Kat frowned at him and looked at the wall over his shoulder.

"What the fuck made you think the fight was going to end up with the death of someone?" Kat demanded incredulously.

"Because he's a dangerous son of a bitch," Tony bellowed back and pointed at Luke.

"In what capacity?"

"We added it up. He must have killed thousands of those aliens."

"'We'?"

"Me and Jamie and Dave and Alec and Barry and Rob," Tony staccatoed as if talking to a child.

"So you all decided he was dangerous," Kat clarified.

"Yes," Tony spat.

"And yet you all still picked a fight with him."

Tony was speechless.

"Okay, if you can't respond to that then answer me this: What sort of a masochistic idiot would go up against someone who was known to have a lethal history?"

"Objection, your honour," Umri called. "Mr Hamilton does not have the professional psychotherapeutic experience to answer that sort of question."

"Of course he does," Kat scoffed. "He *is* that masochistic idiot so can give us a first hand account."

Umri raised his hands pleadingly at the judges.

"Once again, Ms Sabella, you need to select your turn of phrase a bit more carefully but we would like the question answered," Jameson stated. "Young man, if you had all discussed and agreed upon the violent side of Luke Robinson's reputation, then why consider yourselves capable of matching your strengths against his?"

Tony took a moment to calm his raising anger. He looked around the courtroom at all his accusers: the judges were staring at him, that bloody useless Umri had given up and was sitting down again, Kat had a self-satisfied grin across her face and Luke raised his eyebrows in a 'come on then' way.

How could Tony tell them? How could he describe the emotions that were triggered amongst their tight-knit group of utterly heterosexual mates? They drank beer, they snogged birds and they watched footie. They did not get scared, they did not cry on each others' shoulders and they did not go around asking things like, 'How are you feeling today? Would you like to share?'

He was only a man. He did not emote in any form except for when he was angry or when Palace had a good game.

"He's nothing special," he stated. "Just some lucky wanker who was in the wrong place at the wrong time. You can see that in him. I see them all the time; little boys acting hard around their mates and girlfriends. Pretending to be something they're not. He's got that shitty haircut and stupid smug grin but everybody loves him. He comes down to *our* local and everyone's staring at him: cooing and oohing and ahing and wanting his autograph? Who the fuck *does* he think he is?"

"So you felt it necessary to bring him down a peg or two?" Kat asked.

"You could call it that," Tony agreed.

"Does it make you feel a bit more confident in your own masculinity to quash someone else's?"

"What's that supposed to mean?"

"You still haven't really given a reason as to why you wanted to fight Luke Robinson?"

"It doesn't matter!" Tony shouted at her. "We may have started the fight but the fact still remains that he killed Dave. That's it. End of story. And all this round-the-houses questioning, trying to uncover some seedy conspiracy isn't going to change that fact. He killed Dave Wilkinson."

Kat looked over to Jameson who rolled her eyes. The judge leaned over to the transcribers.

"Can you strike Mr Hamilton's last statement please," she instructed with a sigh.

"From, 'It doesn't matter'?" the typist asked.

"Yes."

"What's that for?" Tony demanded.

"Mr Hamilton," Jameson said deliberately, "did you actually see David Wilkinson's death?"

"No," he replied.

"You seem to be an intelligent and articulate young man so you will understand that your testimony should be grounded in what you know and not in speculation."

"This is bullshit," Tony muttered.

"That has been suggested many times before today," Jameson added despondently. "Ms Sabella? Do you wish to continue?"

"Well, only if Mr Hamilton is able to come up with a coherent answer to the previous question, your honour."

Jameson turned her attention back to Tony. "Well?"

"What?"

"Do you have a better answer for why you and your friends wanted to pick a fight with potentially the most lethal man on the planet other than 'because he seemed to be enjoying himself'."

Tony scowled and dropped his head slightly. "We don't like show-offs."

Jameson shrugged to Kat who then sat down and said, "That'll have to do, thank you."

"You can step down now Mr Hamilton," Jameson instructed and Tony walked from the room.

There was a moment of silence as lawyers and judges made notes and reorganised their papers. From somewhere in the audience a slight disturbance caught the attention of a couple of the guards. Everyone looked to see what was going on and saw a shabbily dressed, hirsute man shuffling his way along his row towards the aisle, quietly excusing himself as he nudged and bumped each pair of legs in his way.

One of the guards got a bit closer and asked, "Is there a problem, sir?" and placed his hands in an easily accessible position towards his firearm. Then panic broke out as everyone seemed to remember the events of earlier.

The man threw his hands up in the air so quickly that the guard instinctively drew his weapon which made six of his associates do the same which made everyone around the man try to break for cover which caused the guards to start waving their weapons at every point of commotion to assess each for their level of potential danger which, of course, made everyone that their guns pass across dive for cover.

More guards burst into the room from every door with weapons raised and ready to unleash a hail of lethal screaming lead into anyone may appear as a threat. At that precise time, that implied everyone.

The guards at the front of the hall bustled the judges, lawyers and defendant out to the relative safety of the corridors beyond and into the allotted rooms. Luke and Kat were left in his cell with an armed guard standing on duty.

Luke slumped down onto his bed and 'hurrumphed' his disapproval. He looked up at Kat who was wide-eyed and breathing heavily.

"Sit down," Luke instructed but she did not react.

"Sit. Down," he ordered and she came slightly to her senses and lowered herself onto the nearby seat.

"What the fuck was it this time?" she managed to pant.

"Probably some poor sod had too much to drink at half-time and needed to go piss," Luke suggested and chuckled silently.

"Or another assassin?" Kat said.

"An assassin who excuses himself politely and slowly edges his way to the centre aisle to get a decent shot?"

"Oh yeah, I forgot, you're an expert, right?" Kat said with disdain as her breathing became more regulated.

"I could get us out of here if you want," he told her.

Kat essayed their surroundings: the locked cell door, the one armed guard just beyond and in full view of them. Then there were the countless others just itching to come running and start drilling holes in someone just so they could say they earned their money for today.

"Can I put the telly on, please?" she asked just to change the subject.

"Sure," he replied and nodded to a remote control on the table next to her.

She picked the device up, studied it for a second then raised it, pointed it at the television screen and very deliberately pressed one of the buttons.

"Did you not set the video up to tape *Eastenders*, then?" Luke asked and watched as the screen flared into life.

"I want to see if we can find out what's going on out there," she sneered.

The television showed a newsroom studio with three smartly dressed presenters seated behind a long desk. In the top right corner of the picture was a superimposed shot of an 'on the scene' reporter. The three presenters were firing multiple questions at the man whose face was screwed up in concentration with his finger in his ear.

"We're not entirely sure at this moment, but the man in question did not seem to be posing any particular threat," the reporter said.

"Jack, have any of the audience been allowed to leave the auditorium?" a tanned, slick-haired presenter asked.

"Yes. The courtroom was totally cleared as soon as security was able to determine the only threat at that time was the man."

"Have you managed to speak any of the witnesses?" a black haired woman in a sun-yellow suit asked.

"I did, but to be totally honest, no one really knows what was going on nor the intentions of the-" The reporter stopped mid-sentence and shoved his finger further in his ear as did the three presenters. "The police have just released the man's name," the reporter said. "Apparently he is one Robert Sescott and he was totally unarmed. He just," the reporter paused as the breaking news was filtered through. His face cleared of all confusion and his finger came out of his ear. "He just wanted to say something to the court," the reporter said.

The screen focussed on the slick-haired man; his mouth was opening and closing but no words were coming out. The screen panned to the woman who had a quizzical look on her face.

"Well, we can't deny that this is a most unusual hearing anyway," she said.

"And remember that one randomly selected member of the audience has already been called forward to testify," said the other presenter who was an older, white haired man.

"Maybe this Robert Sescott thought it was an open question and answer session," the woman suggested.

"Perhaps he wanted an autograph before it was too late," the old man chuckled.

"Is there anything else, Jack?" the slick-haired man asked and the screen switched to the reporter.

"Apparently the man has been granted access to the Judges' chambers," Jack announced. "But that's just a piece of information that's floating around out here." His camera took that moment to scan around his immediate surroundings and showed about thirty similar reporters with their crews all feeding back any information they could gather - even if it was misinformation. At least that way they could create another story that could denounce the previous item they had invented when real news still refused to come to light.

"Whoa," the woman called. "Don't tell me you're collaborating with the competition, Jack," she joked.

Jack mustered a fake laugh. "We don't get much choice, Sal. With the identical images being broadcast globally and all press releases being despatched simultaneously. It's nigh-on impossible for anyone to grab an exclusive on this one."

"What are you saying, Jack?" slick-hair asked with a wry smile at the camera. "Do you think you're wasting your time out there?"

"Yes, Jeff, I do," Jack replied bluntly. "Let's face it, we've all been here for god-knows how many hours and all we've been doing is going over the same old crap time and time again. This is totally pointless. No network is allowed to place advertising breaks so we're not even making any money out of it. The World is glued to billions of little glowing boxes awaiting a verdict of something that they could find out in retrospect and it still wouldn't make any difference to the outcome.

"If the recent invasion has proved anything it's that life *is* too short yet here we all are, 'blah blah blah,' wasting a few more precious moments of our endangered existence.

"Inside that courtroom is a man who ended up doing something about a situation and all we did was watch. Now that man is on trial on highly contentious charges and what are we doing? Still watching.

"Now, I'm not saying that we *can* do anything about it or that even we should. After all, a charge has been placed and the law should be allowed to progress. What I am saying is maybe we should all stop watching and do something. Anything. Go play ball, paint a picture, wash the car or take the dog for a walk. Just do something with our lives while we still have them."

There followed another silence.

"Wow, Jack," slick-hair said, "how long have you been thinking about that one?"

"Ever since my grandparents died during their holiday in Alsace. Dick," Jack replied. "I'm outta here."

He pulled his earpiece out and dropped his microphone on to the floor. The camera followed him as he wandered past some of his counterparts. Maybe some members of the closer crews had managed to overhear, or perhaps they had been feeling the same way but just lacked the resolve or spontaneity to have made the move. But Jack started something and people began to drop what they were doing and head of in the direction they needed to, which would get them to somewhere better in the quickest possible time.

The screen came back to the studio where the presenters were all transfixed with their monitors and the exodus thereon.

"It looks like Jack has started a revolution," slick-hair said but received no response.

He looked up to see the older man with tears in his eyes and the woman was removing her earpiece and clip-on microphone.

"What?" was all slick-hair could manage.

"I've got a marriage I need to rebuild," the woman said and started her way off the set.

The older man was removing his communicative devices whilst wiping his eyes and nose on his suit sleeve.

"I've got grandchildren I haven't seen properly in three years," he confessed and started crying again.

"Jesse, baby. Daddy's on his way," he bawled and ran off camera.

Slick-hair stared at the camera with his mouth opening and closing.

The screen went black.

"Well, some good has come out of all this, I suppose," Luke muttered.

"Why do I know that name?" Kat asked herself.

"Never heard of him," Luke told her.

"Something familiar," she mused.

"An ex-boyfriend, maybe," he said but she didn't seem to hear.

Luke sighed loudly, slumped onto his bed and stared at the ceiling.

"I remember this one time at school when I was about eight or nine years old," he said. "We had all come in from playtime and our form teacher came in. Man, she was pissed off about something, which put everyone on edge. I mean, she was nice, everyone liked her and most of us boys had a crush on her."

"At 'nine'?" Kat demanded.

"Oh, are you still here?" he asked and she gave him a humourless grin. "Yes I had a crush on my form teacher at nine. It wasn't sexual or anything. God, we couldn't even spell erection let alone get one at that age."

"What constitutes a 'crush' for a nine-year-old boy then?" she asked with conspiratorial amusement.

"Well, I can't speak for *all* boys but with my mates we played a game called, 'Oodya'"

"I'm frightened to hear any more," Kat said. "I remember some of the boys when I was little."

"Basically it works like this; if your life depended on it, between Judge Farthing and Jameson, 'oodya' give a French kiss to?"

Kat rolled her eyes. "That is sooooo typical."

"So as it all turned out, our form teacher always came out on tops hence why I consider it to be a crush."

"That's so romantic," Kat commented sarcastically.

"So she comes in at registration period and she is looking absolutely mad and she sits down and no one makes a fucking sound. We're all kids, you know? We've all got guilty consciences so we're all probably thinking, 'What the fuck have I done now?'

"Then she tells us this story. A kid had come up to her during the break to tell her that someone had been catching these little frogs that lived under the huts and were pulling their legs off."

"What?"

"Exactly. I was thinking, 'That's the sort of stuff from kiddies books and fairy tales, not real life.' So at first I was sickened but then I remembered all these other moral bound stories that she used to come up with. The stuff that had the kid leaning too far back on his chair or running across the desks or throwing rubbers. Schoolroom urban myths, that sort of thing. So I presumed it was one of those.

"But then she asked for whoever it was who had been doing it to own up and two of my best mates stuck their hands up. I was absolutely gobsmacked that I knew two people who were capable of such unadulterated barbarity."

Kat watched him staring at the ceiling for a moment to see if he had finished or was just employing his dramatic pause technique.

"So what's the moral?" she finally asked. "Kids are bastards?"

He closed his eyes and pursed his lips.

"There isn't a moral," he whispered. "Kids just get bigger, that's all."

"Are you going to sleep again?" Kat demanded but received no obvious response.

"Great," she muttered. "I'll just sit here all by myself then will I?"

"Can you arrange for my parents to go home, please?" he asked and made her jump.

"Why's that?" she asked.

"I don't want them around here any more," he said with his eyes still closed. "There's too much going on and they'll be getting confused and upset. Get Gary to take them home."

"Are you sleeping or not then?" she asked again.

"Gonna try," he mumbled.

"I'll see if they'll let me out and-" She stopped mid-sentence because she could see his eyes flickering manically under their lids as his dreamlike flashbacks kicked in. An inquisitive and naive part of her wanted to know what he was seeing, whereas a bigger and more experienced part told her to get out before he woke up.

He had woken up with such a scare. His heart was racing and sweat was pouring off his forehead. He panted and searched around him to try to work out where he was but it was too dark to make anything out. He wanted to have woken in his room with the aliens dissipated as a bad dream. He wanted to be able to talk to Gary later about the strangely beautiful girl he had had a dream about. He wanted to know that the librarian was just a figment of his imagination although he would have to have been a pretty sick individual to have imagined something like that happening to anyone.

He had woken up with her face in his mind and her hands still clutching at his chest.

But that was all yesterday and the panic now was wondering what new nightmares he might suffer.

He wanted to cry, or maybe throw up, but knew the girl would give him a row for making too much noise and she was the only person who knew what was going on and seemed capable of keeping him alive.

"Good, you're awake," she muttered from the darkness and he nearly added another bodily expulsion to the list of things he wanted to do.

"Tasya, are we safe?" he managed.

"For the moment," she replied, "but we've got to get moving. Did you have a bad dream?"

Luke lowered his chin on to his chest and covered his face with his hands. "The library," he said.

"I'm not surprised," she sympathised and edged forward so he could just see the shape of her face through the gloom. "I am sorry," she said, "but I really had no choice. I was running out of options and I happened to bump into you."

"What is this 'code' that you were supposed to have given me?" he asked.

"'Supposed'?" she questioned. "I did pass it to you."

"But they searched me and never found anything," he said.

She stared at him for a moment and ran a few 'what if' scenarios through her mind to see how much information he might be able to handle or even comprehend. Luke could only see the slightest glint in her eyes that was reflected from the minimal light that entered the room. He could not divine her thought processes but pondered whether he was falling in love with her or it was simply a crush he was developing because she had saved his life so many times. Although technically, he supposed, if that was the case then surely it should work for the opposite too; that he should hate her that little bit more every time his life was put in jeopardy considering it was all her fault.

"I'll explain it all to you later," she said. "I promise."

"So what do we do know?" he asked.

"I need to get a message back to my office," she said.

"What, tell them you're pulling a sicky or something?" he suggested.

"A 'what'?"

"Doesn't matter. Shall I just wait here?" he hoped.

"No, you'd better stick with me," she told him. "There's no telling what level of security they are scanning the planet with," she said. "As soon as I pop my head out, they might be able to pick it up and then they'd just evaporate this building to be on the safe side."

Luke desperately needed to purge his bowels now.

Why was it, that yesterday morning, he was so not bothered about the orbiting threat of imminent death and yet this set-up seemed so much worse? Was it because now he had some input into the outcome of his existence? Whereas before he was as insignificant as the next guy and there really was nothing he could do about his life but now, it *did* matter. His actions, or lack of, could lead to the direct reaction of his demise. In his last work appraisal, Sanj had said that he was not proactive enough. Luke had come back with a quip that he saw what proactive turned people into and he was quite happy not being a wanker. That had not gone down well.

He could no longer afford to be reactive all the time because, eventually, his luck was going to run out and he wouldn't be able to react quickly enough.

"What do you need to send a message?" he asked. "Telephone? Email? Speak and Spell?"

"An internet connection might be sufficient," she said. "I should be able to hack into NASA from there."

"You work for NASA?" Luke gasped.

"Don't be daft," she replied. "They've got a powerful enough communications network that should get a message back."

Luke was silent.

"You're an alien, too?" he asked.

"I'm not human, if that's what you mean," she said.

Luke suddenly re-evaluated the whole 'love' thing.

"I can get you on-line," he said by way of avoiding that topic. "I can get us into my work."

"That'll be too dangerous," she said. "They're bound to be looking there. One of the buildings around here must be connected, no?"

Luke shuffled himself around and crawled towards the pinprick of light. He gently rubbed his finger over the blackened window and made the hole slightly bigger. He placed his eye to the clearer glass and scanned the street outside.

"What time is it?" he asked.

"About five in the morning," Tasya replied.

"That means we'll have to break in to somewhere. There."

He crawled back to Tasya.

"There's a, er, specialist adult emporium across the road," he told her. "Internet access and no security alarms."

"How do you know that?" she asked suspiciously.

He remembered her uncanny ability to know when he was lying. "I, er, know the manager quite well," he embellished. "And he drinks down at my local pub sometimes too."

"Riiiiight," she said sarcastically. "Luke, I may not be a native to your society or culture but I do know what a sex shop is."

Luke blushed in the darkness and said nothing.

They emerged from the basement of the derelict house and tried not to look too suspicious as they legged it across the road performing an overactive rendition of the Green Cross Code.

Luke directed Tasya to a narrow side street that ran along the right side of the *Pleasure Hut* and the came to a fairly solid looking wooden door. Tasya braced herself to kick it down but Luke held her back and gently thumped twice on the door under the handle. On the third knock there came a subtle noise of two bits of metal sliding against each other and a gentle 'click'. Luke turned the handle and pushed the door open for her to enter. She passed and bowed her head graciously to him.

Luke followed, peeked down the street to ensure no one had seen them, then closed the door behind him. They turned left and wandered along a narrow corridor to another door that opened into the shop.

Tasya stumbled around the darkness and yelped in fear as something brushed against her face. She tried to push it away but it bounced back, grabbed her around the neck and started moaning at her.

"I got you now, baby," a female said from above her.

Luke turned the shop light on to see Tasya carrying an inflated sex doll on her shoulders but with the passenger facing the wrong way.

"If you two would like to be left alone," Luke suggested and Tasya wrestled the surprised looking plastic girl to the floor who gave out another groan of satisfaction.

"Oh yeah, baby," the doll said. "You're the best."

"Turn the light off," she scolded in an attempt to hide her embarrassment.

"It's okay," Luke calmed, "it's the law that the window has to be blacked out so innocent children can't find out what their parents get up to."

Tasya frowned at the doll with her welcoming arms, legs and two 'life-like' holes. She tentatively rolled it over and found a third.

"How can they call them 'life-like'?" she questioned. "She doesn't even have buttocks."

"But that's half the battle out of the way, then," Luke commented.

He made his way over to the pay desk in the immediate right corner of the store and turned on a computer that was positioned on the counter.

Tasya took the opportunity to browse the rest of the store. Not simply looking at the multitude of products but, on occasion, studying the object's shape and form. Beyond the inflatable females, males and animals of varying quality, colour, diverse hole actions and sound effects came an entire display cabinet of prosthetic penises and phalluses in a plethora of sizes, material, shapes and multifunctional extras. Made for his and her pleasure: to make him bigger, to make her tighter, to make her a him, to make him a her, to score two holes-in-one, to pinch while it twitched, to twist, wind, wriggle, pump and oscillate. From one that would fit discreetly in a purse to another you would not give a second glance had it been placed on an oversized chessboard.

"You people take your sexual recreation seriously, huh?" Tasya commented but Luke either did not hear her properly or did not have anything to say about it. He kept his head down to ensure he did not look at anything else around him.

"This machine needs upgrading," was all he said.

The next section could have been mistaken for a jewellery display. Strings of beads were on show of different colours and material but were designed *not* to accessorise with ear-rings. But there were rings - too big for fingers - with fronds, frills, flaps, bumps and a few with ac adapter sockets. Frictionless, plastic balls, attached with string looked more like a child's toy or boluses for hunting antelope but the directions on the packaging insured the gazelles should remain unharmed.

Next was what Tasya considered to be the amputees section where it seemed many humans had simply been cut into pieces and specific bits packaged. Tongues, fingers, mouths on the ends of tubes, carefully crafted vaginas and anuses and an entire forearm with clenched fist. Tasya picked it up and was staggered by the weight of it. It was covered with a synthetic skin and, again, crafted to the finest detail. She tipped it up and found a switch on the underside which she could not stop herself from flicking it on. The limb silently thrummed in her hands and as she uprighted it she discovered that the fist was gently pivoting at the wrist. She stared, totally hypnotised by the motion and mesmerised by the notion of its use.

"It's a coffee grinder," Luke joked and brought her back to her senses.

"You people are so weird," she said, switched the arm off and placed it back on its pedestal.

"Don't tar me with their brush," Luke complained. "I don't use stuff like that."

"Whatever," she dismissed. "Have you got that working yet?"

"Ready when you are," he said.

She walked past the front door and idly skimmed over the wracks of glossy, flesh-ridden magazines that were shelved directly in front of the windows. As she made her way around a section in the centre of the room of videos, DVDs and computer games she came to the opposite side of the shop where mannequins were of varying stages of undress. An androgynous one was completely covered from head to toe in black rubber with zips in place for eyeholes and breathing orifices. It had velcro nipple patches, chain links at various points and a towel hanging accessory protruding proudly from the crotch.

The next mannequin was overtly female and was wrapped in a couple of pieces of string that would barely cover her sensitive parts if she had any. In fact she seemed to be the only man-made representative of human form that was actually devoid of any genitalia.

Tasya looked closer at the 'knickers' and noticed that the string was in fact a fine silver chain encrusted with diamonds.

The walls were adorned with whips, batons, handcuffs, leads, collars, belts, straps, tassels, studs, leather, lace, rubber, spandex and sheet steel.

She decided that she had wasted too much time so skipped the flavoured lubricants, dietary supplements and novelty shaped chocolates and went straight to the computer.

"Isn't it password protected?" she asked as the pair swapped places.

"They don't need security in this place," Luke told her. "They provide security to others."

"I don't understand," she said.

"No one would dare break into this place," he said. "It's a cover for money laundering, extortion, prostitution and drugs."

"What nice people you know," she commented as she produced a purple device that looked like a mobile phone. She pulled a wire from it and plugged it into the USB port of the hard drive.

"What's that?" Luke asked.

"Technical," Tasya replied and started tapping at the buttons on the device. "It's sort of like the upgrade you said this machine would need."

A couple of windows popped open in the computer's monitor then the terminal let out an alarming beep and a message appeared on the screen.

'Your session has been unexpectedly terminated. Please save all open documents and restart your computer.'

"Oh! Stupid machines," Tasya spat. "They're just so incompatible with any other hardware."

"That's good business sense," Luke said.

"No, that's plain selfishness," she retorted.

"Same difference," he muttered.

"Why doesn't anyone on this planet use a Mac?" she asked rhetorically as she rebooted the pc.

"I thought your alien technology would be advanced enough to interface with any software," Luke said sarcastically.

"Mine is, yours isn't," she huffed back and impatiently tapped her fingers on the desk while the computer did a system scan because she did not close down properly and she should always turn it off using the start menu. "Apart from the American translator," she mumbled. "It seemed to just take the 'u's out of every word."

"Of course, I forgot," he said. "You people are perfect and do everything right whereas everything we do is wrong and utterly shit."

"You're fifty per cent right there," she told him.

"Yeah?"

"Nobody's perfect," she said and the front door and half of the magazine rack exploded.

Luke thought it had been the blast that knocked him to the floor but then he realised Tasya was lying on top of him and remembered how quick her reactions were and how inconsiderate she could be with her strength.

"Stay down," she hissed at him. As she jumped to her feet she flipped the multimedia display over towards the front of the shop. Luke wished his eyes could work in *Bullet Time* and witness these super-beings thrash it out amongst the delicate snowfall of porn-covered entertainment cases and ripped, flesh glossy pages. But reality is always disappointing because the whole lot just came crashing down in an ungraceful clatter and left Tasya standing there ready to square off to an empty doorway.

Luke pulled himself up on to his elbows to get a better look at the ominous entrance and was grabbed around the neck and dragged to his feet.

"Tasya," a caretaker in front of Luke called.

She spun on her heels to face her aggressors: there were five of them standing in the rear doorway, big ones too, all suited in their familiar beige overalls but these had the bonus freakishness of being facially identical. The front man was the one who spoke, behind him was the one holding Luke, the next two were trying to squeeze through the door and the fifth could just be seen still in the corridor beyond.

She sidled across the shop floor to face the one who had addressed her.

"It's over," Hwun said.

"It's wrong," Tasya told him.

"Jus' following orders," he said.

"Wrong orders," she urged.

The caretaker rolled his eyes. "Whatever, Tasya. We've got him and if you don't come along nicely then we'll just kill him here."

The caretaker holding Luke tightened his neck-lock which made him gargle for breath.

Tasya looked between the two of them.

"You wouldn't," she dared.

"I think they would," Luke croaked.

Tasya looked at Luke and her frown disappeared. She shrugged her eyebrows at him which the caretakers took for a sign of resignation. Tou relaxed his grip around Luke's throat. The caretakers could not see Luke's expression which had changed from intense discomfort to wide-eyed panic.

"You're coming with us," Hwun instructed again and Tasya bowed her head in mock subservience.

"You're just going to have to," she paused, "suck my big, puce penis."

She raised her head and smiled. The caretakers peered down to Tasya's crotch in confusion and saw that she had picked up a foot long, three inch thick, heavy, purple dildo and was holding it by the head. Without hesitation, she swung the mighty testicles up and cracked Hwun across the jaw who then flew back through the door and sent Vree, Phor and Phyve reeling with him.

Tou threw Luke to the side and into the inflatables shelving. The racks and boxes poured down on him. The caretaker then pulled a pistol out of his overalls and pointed it at Tasya. She felt a bit impotent with only a 12 inch erection to hand and desperately searched for an out.

Luke burst from the boxes and swung Tasya's plastic piggy-back pal at Tou. It stopped when it hit him. Luke was not entirely sure what sort of reaction he was hoping to happen when he tried to hit a three hundred pound man with a one pound sex balloon but figured that 'absolutely nothing' would not have been a bad guess.

Tou was less than impressed and levelled his gun again only to find Polly was giving the barrel a good oral seeing to.

"Do it in my mouth," Polly ventriloquised. "Let me have it."

Luke yanked at her legs just as Tou fired. The back of Polly's head shredded and the shot detonated on the display of surrogate man-sausage.

Tasya dived behind the upturned video display cabinet as Luke fell back into the mess from whence he had come. But as he fell, the remains of Polly's skull yanked the gun from Tou's hand and into the mounting confusion of sexual aids that was spreading across the floor.

Tou let out a scream of frustration and waded through the clutter to get to Tasya as his brothers were getting their act together and returning to the fray. Phor helped Hwun get to his feet as Vree stepped over Luke to assist Tou.

Luke scrabbled amongst the boxes, trying to find a piece of stability from which he could safely lift himself but all he found was Tou's gun.

"Oh, bugger," he muttered.

Tasya was back on her feet and she launched herself at Tou, only to be battered away with the same disinterest that Polly had received. She clattered awkwardly into the mannequins and became tangled in a fetishist game of *Twister*.

Tou grabbed her by the back of her neck and hauled her out.

"Freeze," Luke commanded, shakily pointing the pistol at Tou and Vree.

"Let her go," he ordered and Tou did so, unceremoniously and with a smile on his face.

"Behind-" was all the warning Tasya could give to Luke before he was tackled into the remaining displays by Phor and Phyve.

Luke panicked, indiscriminately pulling on the trigger in all directions. He managed to take out two of the four fluorescent light tubes in the ceiling and destabilised a third, making it flicker aggravatingly. Tasya leapt up from her position on the floor onto Tou's back as wall, ceiling and tubs of flavoured lubricant detonated around them. She wrapped the diamante g-string around his throat and pulled back, hard.

Phor and Phyve swung random punches into the pile of phalluses, boxes and Luke hoping the cease his barrage.

A shot hit Vree straight through the chest and erupted out of his back spraying the struggling Tou and Tasya in yellow-green life-gunk.

Tasya had her knees dug firmly into the small of Tou's back and shifted her weight in her shoulders to rake the diamond garrotte through the skin of his neck. The knickers string ripped through his throat like a hacksaw through an orange. Tou spat out a wet cry of pain and protestation before the chain sliced clean through his throat and flopped his head over onto his back.

She pushed herself away, causing Tou's spurting, twitching mass to collide with Vree's spurting, twitching mass and sent them both onto the bundle of Luke, Phor and Phyve.

"You shtoopid bish!" Hwun bellowed through his broken jaw from the doorway and pulled his pistol from his overalls.

Tasya buried herself into the chaos of shadow, shelves and sex aids.

"You go too far, Tasha!" Hwun screamed and started taking pot-shots across the floor. He took a step forward after each shot in an attempt to drive her into an inescapable corner.

Phor and Phyve lifted themselves off the floor along with a semi-conscious Luke.

"Shall we get him in the car?" Phyve asked.

"Jus' kill him firsht," Hwun instructed.

Phor and Phyve looked at each other for support.

"Vey killed our bruffersh!" Hwun screamed. "Kill vem both. We can shay it was shelf defensh."

Tasya erupted from the debris again and lashed out at Hwun with a leather whip. It wrapped around his gun arm and she yanked it taught. He stumbled across the room and she swung out with her free left hand, around which she had wrapped a studded choker. As Hwun fell forward she caught him on the jaw again, this time ripping the lower mandible from its moorings and sending it twirling across the room and where it then landed on the amputee's display.

Hwun fell to the floor with his tongue flailing like a freshly caught fish, choking on his own juices.

The two remaining siblings stared at the jawbone in shock and revulsion, Phyve released Luke to go for his gun but Tasya was already on top of him and the pair tumbled into the shelving of body parts.

It must have been the 'kill him' instructions that made Luke come to his senses and then exceed them. He had already taken quite a pummelling and now that he had a free arm he decided it was time for a bit of payback. He swung his fist round at Phor and completely missed him. So Phor just wrapped his arms under Luke's armpits and around his back to hold him in an excruciating bear hug. Luke screamed as he felt his ribs bend to the point of snapping. He punched Phor on the side of the head and kicked him in his shins but nothing seemed to hinder the application of pressure.

Tasya was sitting on Phyve's back, repeatedly smacking his head on the floor. She might have done some serious damage if it had not been for the 'just like real skin' set of female genitalia that was in front of his face and softening each blow. He found some purchase under his hands and rolled her off his back. She crashed into the display case and paused to catch her breath. Phyve reared up and looked like he had some sort of parasite leached to his head - the final bounce that Tasya had inflicted upon him had caused the pubic portion to get suction stuck to his forehead. The pink, rubbery mass wobbled as if feeding greedily on its host and little fronds of 'real' pubic hair stuck out at the sides like multiple delicate tentacles.

Tasya laughed at him as he stomped over to her.

"Think that's funny, do you?" he threatened.

"I've heard of a dick-head before," she giggled.

"Laugh this off," he growled, curled his fingers into a fist and drew his arm back.

She leapt up inside of the punch so it just flew harmlessly past her ear. Phyve was surprised to see her launch at him again and even more shocked when she rammed a pair of love eggs into his mouth. He was absolutely, positively aghast when she followed them with a large bell-ended dildo which she used to ram the eggs down his throat like a pirate would load a cannon.

She kicked him away as he pulled the rubber penis from his mouth and scrabbled manically at his neck in a desperate attempt to dislodge the vaginal stimulators. Two bulbous lumps protruded from his neck like he had tried to swallow a dog's bone sideways. His face turned green, his eyes bulged and then rolled up in their sockets. He collapsed to the floor with an internal whimper.

"Please," Luke squealed as it became even harder to breathe. Phor stepped on a string of beads and fell forward.

Luke heard the cracks inside his body before the pain registered. He wanted to scream again but the remaining air had been blasted from his lungs so now he was suffocating too. He wanted to grab something that he might be able to batter Phor with and each hand discovered a tapered, silver-tipped vibrator. Without even thinking, he snatched them up and jabbed Phor on the top of his head. Phor yelped as the slick tips bruised his scalp but he could not relinquish his grip as his arms were pinned beneath the weight of both of them. He did, however, look up at Luke to warn him off from doing that again.

Luke buried the vibrators into Phor's eyes which popped like raw eggs and mucous ejaculated down the shafts and over Luke's hands. Phor roared in agony but he still could not let go. Luke's screams were a mixture of pain and sheer horror of his actions. He turned his head away and closed his eyes but could not block out Phor's gargled cries. Phor began convulsing and forcing more weight on Luke's battered ribcage. He tried pushing Phor away but simply forced the vibrators deeper until they hit something solid and would not penetrate further. As blackness threatened to engulf Luke's vision he managed to flick the small switches on the base of the vibrators and they tremored into life. The obstruction in Phor's sockets gave and he screamed for a second until his internal fluids flowed backwards through his cranial cavity, into his throat and spewed out of his mouth into Luke's face. Phor's grip slipped which allowed Luke to instinctively suck up a most desperately needed lungful of air but instead inhaled the free flowing life mulch.

Luke twisted the oscillations up to maximum and drilled the vibrators deeper in an attempt to get extra distance between them. Phor pushed himself up and away from the blinding agony but stepped on the beads again. His feet slipped out from under him and he fell, face first, onto the floor, thrusting the vibrators out through the back of his skull.

Luke could feel himself drowning on the acrid, viscous gel and had no air in his lungs to cough it all up. He desperately searched around for something that might help him expel the fluid from his chest but the flickering light was casting bizarre shadows amongst the bizarre objects at his feet. He looked up to find Tasya but could only see the last remaining mannequins seemingly animated to life in the strobe effect and then there was Phor. Luke was going to die and the last thing he was going to see was his skull punctured victim. He was not even *going to get the chance to ...*

Luke screamed as he jumped up from the bed. He hacked and coughed as if trying to clear something from his throat. He relaxed but remained doubled over in the corner of his cell and breathed deeply. He looked up and saw his guard with his gun aimed and ready.

Luke calmed his respiration and kept his eyes firmly sighted on his edgy protector.

"You've been fucked, mate," he whispered. The guard relaxed his stance slightly and cocked his head with incomprehension.

"That's all I wanted to say," Luke explained morosely and eased himself upright. "You've been fucked."

He gave a cursory inspection of his quarters and the guard's state of confused uncertainty. He weighed up a few of his options and, in the end, decided to just sit back down on the bed.

"Are you okay?" the guard asked as he took a step closer to the cell.

"Yeah," Luke replied. "Just having some bad dreams."

"About the invasion?"

"Something like that," Luke dismissed.

"Do you want me to get someone?"

Luke laughed silently and looked at his protector cum captor. "It was just a bad dream," Luke assured.

The guard lowered his gun fully. "I've seen people wake from nightmares before," he said. "And I knew what they had been through to be getting those bad dreams. You weren't having a nightmare, you were re-living something."

"Thanks, Doctor Freud," Luke replied, "but it doesn't matter what you call it, does it? It doesn't make them go away. If I call them dreams then at least I can pretend that they're not real."

The guard just stared at him.

"Do you know what's going on up there?" Luke asked

"They're settling the spectators down and the judges are having a word with the lawyers and the security alert. You should be going back up soon."

The pair of them fell silent until the guard had screwed his courage to the sticking point.

"If you don't mind me asking, who was fucked?"

"All of us, I think," Luke replied. "In the end."

The guard stuck his finger up to his earpiece and listened intently.

"They're getting ready for the off," he announced. "I'm to take you back up."

"I need to go to the loo first," Luke said and shut himself in the cubicle. They had not taken any chances with him in here. He may have had an element of privacy but the facilities were minimalist to say the least: no lock on the door, no toilet paper holder, no roll of toilet paper, just sheets, no toilet seat cover and a sealed down cistern lid. Someone had done their homework. However, Luke had made instinctive mental notes that the door could be easily removed from its hinges, the toilet seat had a bevelled rim and the flush handle would pry free with a bit of effort.

Luke urinated, flushed, exited the cubicle and rinsed his hands in the sink.

"I just wanted to take this opportunity to say thanks," the guard told him.

Luke nearly said, 'What for?' but decided he needed to mellow a bit. "It was the least I could do," he finally said and walked toward the cell door where the guard unlocked it and the pair of them made their way up to the courtroom.

"Where's my lawyer?" Luke asked.

"She's just leaving chambers now," the guard told him and escorted him to his seat. Luke sat down and the guard dithered on the spot.

"I don't think you have to stay," Luke told him.

The guard's eyes twitched around and clocked the position of each of his compatriots.

"To be honest," he whispered. "I don't know what the fuck I'm supposed to be doing."

"Go home then," Luke advised.

"It's tempting," the guard replied.

The side door opened and Kat walked through followed by Umri. The guard nodded to Luke and headed off backstage again. Kat's eyes were wide and she was biting back a grin that threatened to split her head in half. She quickly walked to her seat and slid in next to Luke.

"Am I going to have to ask?" he demanded.

She chewed on her top lip and watched as the court administrators entered and took their seats.

"I don't want to spoil anything," she giggled in return and then flashed him an excited grin.

"A clue, perhaps?" he urged.

She shook her head as she tried to order her thought processes. "It's," she started, "just too fucking funny. Look at him." She leaned back in her seat so Luke could get a clear view of Umri who looked thoroughly depressed and dejected.

"This could be *it*," she added.

"This mystery guy?" Luke asked incredulously. "What was his name again?"

"Robert Sescott," she said, over enunciating the 'Ses' to make her sound like a leaky pressure valve.

"And that's supposed to mean 'what' to me?" Luke asked.

"Nothing," she blurted and started to giggle to herself.

Luke scowled, folded his arms and slumped back into his seat. "Yeah, well I know something you don't know," he grumbled.

"Whatever," Kat replied with a snort.

The bailiff stepped through the side door and announced, "This court is now back in session. All rise."

Maybe it was because the audience had been getting to grips with this procedure or perhaps it was due to the volume of people had thinned even more since the last 'security threat' but everyone seemed more synchronised and stood as one.

The judges entered the room with another change around. Jameson took the farthest seat with Etienne in the middle and Farthing to her other side. After they sat, the rest of the room took their seats.

Etienne leant over to Jameson to discuss something, then addressed her microphone.

"Well," she sighed, "we have had quite an eventful imposed recess with some new and interesting details being brought to our attention. No doubt the word has spread that the young man who caused such a furore has to add to this hearing. Under normal circumstances his testimony would be inadmissible because of it being too late in the day for the defence or prosecution to accustom themselves to the details. However, firstly this is no normal hearing and secondly we have discussed the situation with notaries and they have both agreed that the man in question should be allowed to testify."

Umri and Kat looked across the divide at each other. She gave him a wide, toothy smile but he just stared back with a sullen gaze and then returned his attention to his paperwork.

"Please call Robert Sescott to the stand," Etienne instructed and the call went out.

The man entered through the usual door and was still wearing the same shabby clothes: a pair of dirty, torn dark blue jeans, a tattered white t-shirt and worn wax jacket. His dark brown hair and beard had, at least, been brushed to some sort of order. He was pale, emaciated and the thick, dark bruising around his eyes made him look very tired. He made his way up to the stand and was sworn in.

"Please state your name and relation to the defendant," Etienne said.

The man licked his lips before speaking. "My name," he paused. His voice was light but rasping as if he had been having a damn good shout just before coming out. "My name ith Robert Thethcott," he stated with an unashamed lisp.

The room was silent as the delivery of the information slowly sunk in.

"Rob The Scott?" Luke asked incredulously and a deluge of conversation spread through the auditorium.

Etienne allowed the conferring to continue for a couple of minutes and then slammed her gavel on the bench.

"That is enough," she ordered. "If everyone would kindly return to order." After quiet had regained its hold she turned back to Robert. "And what is your relation to the defendant?"

"I don't really have one," Robert replied. "Apart from I wath at the thame pub ath him on the twenty-eighth of February."

"Mr Sescott," Jameson addressed, "have you been listening to all the testimonies being given so far?"

"Yeth," Robert replied.

"And you are the person who has been repeatedly referred to as 'Rob The Scott'?" she asked.

"That ith correct," he replied.

"Do you have any form of identification?" she demanded.

"I don't, I'm afraid," he apologised. "I haven't carried any for nearly a month now."

"How were you able to prove your identity?"

"I was recognithed by Alec King, Jamie Argento, and Tony Hamilton back there," he stated and jabbed his thumb over his shoulder.

"How old are you Mr Sescott?" Farthing asked.

"I'll be thirty next month," he declared.

"You look like you're about fifty," the old judge stated. "Are you ill?"

"I have been travelling for four weekth," Robert told him. "I haven't been eating well."

"Where have you been?"

"I -" Robert stopped and corrected himself. "We were making our way through Europe. I got ath far ath Thpain before I came back."

"Who is 'we'?" Etienne asked.

"Mythelf and Barry Finkth."

"And where is Barry Finks now?"

"Dead," Robert replied bluntly. "He killed himself ath we were pathing through Franth."

Farthing tapped Etienne on the shoulder and the three judges leaned together to discuss something.

They returned to their positions and Etienne came to her microphone.

"Mr Sescott, will you just tell the court, in your own words, the events that transpired on the evening of the twenty-eighth, please," she said.

"I had met Barry Finkth and Dave Wilkinthon in the Wack 'n' Fank at about theven in the evening."

"Oh, fuck," Dave spat and tried to bury his head into his pint.

Barry widened his eyes and whipped his head around the half-full room trying to see what could have elicited such a reaction.

"Alright boyth," Robert called out from behind Barry and slapped his hand on his shoulder.

"Hallo Rob," Barry sighed and shot Dave a disdainful glance.

"Fuck off Rob," Dave ordered.

Robert swaggered round to stand between the two men. He was just over six-foot tall but looked considerably taller because of his slight frame, high back-combed fringe and, for some reason, the trousers he wore that were an inch too short in the leg. As an extra aid, tonight, he was standing next to these two men who were about six inches shorter than him. Dave had been mistaken for being albino in the past. He had very pale skin and near white hair that he had styled in a foppish quiff that threatened to engulf his right eye. Barry had ginger hair that he had shaved around the back and sides and cut back to the barest minimum on top. His face was freckled and he wore a pair of oval, gold rimmed glasses.

"There'th no need to be like that," Robert protested.

"I'm not subbing you tonight," Dave told him.

"That'th not a problem," Robert said. "I got a job."

"Fuck off," Dave said.

"Theriously, I've been doing a few odd-job'th here and there and I jutht got paid. Drinkth are on me tonight boyth."

"Nice one, Rob," Barry commended and Dave huffed his disappointment that he no longer had an excuse to send him packing so he just downed the remainder of his pint and proffered the empty glass to Robert. He took it with a smile, took the men's orders and made a quick trip to the bar and back again with three pints carefully grasped in his hands.

Robert passed them round. "Cheerth, boyth," he toasted and the all took a deep drink. "Who elth ith coming down tonight?"

Barry waited until a belch silently passed his lips before replying. "Tone, Jamie, Alec and maybe Juliet with some of her mates."

"Ah, the 'Team Thupreme' back together again, eh?"

Dave rolled his eyes. "You are such a twat."

Robert took the insult with a grin and another long sup of his pint.

"What's the job then, Rob?" Barry asked.

"You thouldn't athk quethtionth you might not want to know the antherth too," Robert advised.

"What? Are you in the S.A.S. or summink then?" Dave demanded.

"Calm down," Barry suggested.

"I've got a deal going on with Martin Dooley," Robert boasted and the two men just stared at him.

"Fuck off," Dave said.

"Dooley?" Barry asked.

"Thwear to God," Robert announced.

"Well you're possibly a bigger idiot then I ever thought possible," Dave told him.

"Whatever," Robert dismissed and finished his pint. "Want another?"

Dave and Barry nodded and watched as Robert returned to the bar. They turned to each other.

"Fuck!" Barry exclaimed and Dave just shrugged.

"Evenin' all," someone called from behind Dave.

"Alright Jimbo," Barry called. "Rob The Scot's at the bar if you want one."

Jamie rubbed at his flat, gelled scalp in mock concentration. "Hmm, 'If I want one'?" he pondered. "You muppet," he cajoled. "Rob? At the bar? I don't fucking believe it. The end of the World must be nigh."

"That wath latht week," Rob told him as he returned laden with glasses and suddenly the joviality slipped for a moment.

"You prick," Dave hissed.

Rob stopped in his tracks. "Thorry. I wath -"

"Fuck it," Jamie interrupted. "Rob's right, that *was* last week. Now get back up to that bar and get me a lager you Scotch git," he ordered and gave the skinny man a hearty slap on the shoulder that caused the drinks he was holding to slop over his hands and to the floor.

"Jimbo, you fucking mook!" Dave yelled as he jumped out of the way of the golden splash and Jamie laughed out loud.

The men drank. Sometimes they would pause to check out the other patrons but most of the time they interacted by seeing who could drink the quickest and visit the toilets the least. The pub slowly filled with more people and the piped music gradually increased in volume.

"There's Juliet," Jamie shouted and pointed through a gap in the milling crowds. They all looked at the group of half a dozen girls Jamie had pointed out and then searched the rest of the room.

"I don't see King or Tone," Barry noted.

"Maybe they didn't come together," Jamie bellowed back and gave his friends a knowing look.

"Oh fuck," Dave groaned. "Don't tell me they've had another row."

"She seems happy enough, now" Barry commented and watched the girls as they chatted and laughed their way towards a busy booth in the corner of the room.

"They've rowed," Dave concluded. "Now she's on the pull and Alec'll be on for a ruck."

"You might want to make a hasty exit, Rob," Jamie advised jokingly and Robert sneered back.

"You should go share that advice with the lads in the corner, there," Dave suggested. "Cos here comes trouble."

Alec and Tony shouldered their way through the crowd, making a beeline for their friends.

"Way-hay!" Robert called and raised his glass. "It's the ladies' men!"

Alec was looking decidedly unhappy and when he saw Robert he was able to look even more put out.

"What the fuck is he doing here?" he demanded and sniffed.

"Don't fucking start, Al," Jamie told him. "Rob's alright tonight."

"I don't want him taking the fucking piss," Alec warned and sniffed again. "That's all."

Robert held his hands up. "No worrieth," he apologised. "My bad."

"You tit," Dave said and laughed.

Alec looked to Tony who gave him an encouraging grin. "Who's getting them in then?" he bellowed and Rob swallowed what was left in his glass.

"My thout," Robert announced and wrestled his way through the throng to get to the bar.

Dave grabbed Tony's elbow and pulled him to the side. "What's up with him?"

"Jules dumped him, again" Tony said.

"They had a barney?"

"No, it's for real this time," Tony said. "Said she was seeing someone else."

"Fuck."

"Yup."

"You know she's in here," Dave said.

"Fuck."

"Yup."

"Th'cooth me," Robert hollered and stretched his bandy arms over a few shoulders to pass the drinks back to his band.

He rejoined them. "We thaw Juliet come in a minute ago," he announced and Alec's brows crawled down his forehead again.

"Where?" he demanded.

"Over there," Robert said, pointed to the corner of the room and was totally oblivious to the looks he was receiving from the rest of the men until after Alec had shoved his way through the crowd in the indicated direction.

"What?" Robert asked.

"Can you see anything?" Tony asked.

"No," Jamie replied and tried peering over shoulders and between arms.

"It'th alright, he'th coming back," Robert announced and sure enough, Alec staggered back to his friends looking pale and agitated.

"What happened?" Dave demanded.

"I dunno," I got over there and I saw Jules sitting next to this bloke having a right old laugh and I'm all ready to have a go and then I see who she's sitting next to."

The men leaned in closer.

"I think it was Luke Robinson," Alec said.

The men stepped back and looked at each other.

"You think? Or, it is?" Jamie asked.

"Yeah. No. It is. It's Luke Robinson sitting over there," Alec confessed.

"Fuck me," Barry said.

"I heard he used to live round here," Tony pondered.

"And he'th chatting up Juliet?" Robert asked.

"I'm gonna lamp you in a minute," Alec warned.

"What are you going t'do?" Barry asked.

"What can I do?" Alec retorted.

"I want to see," Dave declared and started to pass through the crowds with his cohorts close behind.

Their vision was blocked by a seemingly endless barrage of arms, backs and shoulders. Eventually they broke into an unnatural clearing where the patrons were either keeping their distance this side or crowding around the end corner booth. The six lads stood at the edge of the clearing and bobbed their heads from side to side in an effort to either see around the bodies of those flocking the booth or to mentally encourage them to shift away.

Then a group of girls stepped back and they got a clear shot of Luke, sitting next to blonde, pony-tailed Juliet, drinking and laughing with the people around him.

The lads collected around each other again.

"Fuck me," Dave gasped. "It's really him."

None of the young males looked at the other. They were all lost in their own musings. Alec peered over Dave's shoulder at the joviality beyond and quickly looked away again.

"Shit," he sniffed, "they're all looking over here."

Jamie was stood next to Alec so gave the corner of the room a cursory glance.

"No they're not," he reported.

"He was fucking eyeballing us," Alec insisted.

"I think I'm going to be sick," Barry announced.

"It doesn't matter if he's here or not," Tony told them. "It doesn't change anything."

"You're right," Robert replied idly. "It dothn't change anything. It thtill happened."

Barry slapped his hand over his mouth and barged his way through the toilets whilst his friends wrestled with their own consciences. Robert snapped out of it and looked at the others.

"I'll go thee if he'th alright," he said and wandered off in pursuit.

As he entered the men's toilets he found Barry splashing water over his face and staring at his reflection in the mirror above the sink.

"All right?" Robert asked.

"Nah, mate," Barry replied. "Anything but."

Robert stood there for a moment and watched Barry analyse his own face.

"I think I need to leave," Robert confessed and Barry turned to him.

"Where are you going? Home?"

"I dunno, I feel like I've just got to go thumwhere. Anywhere away from here. Away from me."

The men continued to stare at each other.

"Let's go," Barry said.

They quietly left the pub and started walking. They only stopped when a freight lorry picked them up off the side of *the road four hours later.*

"And from there you managed to get into France and then headed south?" Farthing asked.

"We weren't aiming to go anywhere," Robert said. "We jutht needed to keep moving."

"Why?" Farthing demanded.

"We didn't know if we were trying to run away or looking for thumthing. Looking for uth, I thuppothe. Theeing Luke in the fleth wath dithturbing for all of uth. I thaw that in all of them. I think it wath only Barry and I who thought it wath our problem to thort rather than thumone elthe'th fault."

"Mr Sescott," Jameson interjected. "You're talking in clichés and riddles. What was it that happened to cause such a dramatic reaction in you and your associates?"

Robert sighed. "Barry and I were looking for redemthon for the week that we thought we were going to die. The otherth jutht wanted to forget about it and hope that would mean it never happened."

Jameson sighed. "Are you talking about the week of the invasion?"

"Yeth."

"And do I have to coax the details of that week out of you as well?"

Robert shook himself and became slightly less aloof and enigmatic. "I am thorry," he said, "but after all of thith time wandering and hoping for an anther to come to me, it'th overwhelming to find my redemthun ith from a confethun to our thaviour."

Luke rolled his eyes.

"Mr Sescott," Etienne prompted. "Could you please tell us what happened to you during the week of the invasion."

"It was really jutht that Monday night. Everyone had given up on the idea that they we were going to die. The caretakerth had given tho many deadline'th and none of them had had any direct effect on uth. I had been th'taying at Tony'th flat and eventually everyone turned up there."

Robert was lying on Tony's sofa in a white vest and light blue boxer shorts. He was staring at the television at the opposite side of the room but not really paying attention to what the newsreader was saying. Tony stumbled into the living room swigging on a can of lager wearing jeans and a tight white t-shirt.

"Rob," Tony spat after swallowing a mouthful of beer, "get your fucking clothes on. The lads are coming over and I don't want them seeing you slumming all over the place."

Robert pushed himself to sit upright and lazily began to dress himself.

Tony took another long swig from his can the stared intently at his 'guest'.

"When are you going to piss off somewhere else?" he demanded.

"I gave my parent'th a call yethterday," Robert replied sullenly. "I can be out before thith weekend."

"Good," Tony said and finished his drink. He crunched the can in his hand and tossed it into a bin across the room. He checked the time on his wristwatch and rubbed at his cropped hair.

"What'th the plan for tonight?" Robert asked as he pulled his socks on.

"Just the usual," Tony muttered. "Although I think Alec and Julia have had a row so he might be a bit sensitive tonight."

"One of thothe night'th then," Robert commented.

Tony shrugged. "Probably." He turned and marched into the kitchen where he got himself another can of lager.

Robert turned the volume up on the television as an outside reporter caught his attention.

"… not entirely sure what to tell you," the young woman confessed. "The deadline is up, we have not heard any encouraging news about Luke Robinson's condition and we have received reports that a few heads of nations and religious leaders have advised that people should make their peace within the next twelve hours."

"Fuck me," Robert muttered.

"What's that?" Tony demanded.

"They've juth't thed we're all going to die."

Tony's face dropped and he stared at Robert with wide-eyed incomprehension.

"Seriously?" Tony asked and Robert shrugged, he waved his hands at the television screen.

"When?"

"Leth than a day."

Tony turned white and collapsed into an armchair. He breathed deeply and deliberately trying to control a surging wave of panic. His eyes searched the carpet for some kind of reality anchor.

Robert was taken aback by this reaction. "You okay?"

"No Rob, I'm not," Tony muttered. "I'm scared, mate." He blurted a laugh but there were no resonations of humour. "Christ, I'm really fucking scared."

"But you've known thith might happen, haven't you?"

"No, Rob, I haven't," Tony urged. "There are people -" he gesticulated wildly towards the front door, "- out there, doing stuff to stop this. Things like this don't happen."

Robert shook his head. "I'm thorry, I don't get it."

"Aren't you scared then?" Tony asked.

"I dunno," Robert replied morosely. "I gave up a long time ago."

The two men just stared at each other for a while until a loud knock at the door shook them from their contemplation.

Tony managed to build some resolve and answered the door. Barry and Dave were standing on the doorstep.

"Are you not ready yet?" Dave demanded and pushed his way past Tony into the living room.

Barry noticed something different about Tony's expression.

"What's up?" he asked.

"He's still got this Jock ligger hanging around, that's what's up," Dave shouted back.

Tony nodded to Barry to enter then closed the door behind him. Dave had taken Tony's vacated chair and was almost reclined in it. Barry sat next to Robert and Tony stayed by the door.

"You haven't heard then?" Tony asked.

"What?" Barry asked.

"They just announced on the telly that it's all over," Tony explained.

Dave just stared in stern silence.

"The caretakers are leaving?" Barry asked.

"No mate," Tony laughed. "Sorry. The other over."

Barry looked at Dave in confusion.

"Who said?" Dave asked.

"On the telly," Robert said.

"Fuck off, Rob," Dave spat, "I'm not talking to you. Who fucking said on the telly?"

"I didn't hear it," Tony explained. "Rob told me."

"You're fucking lying," Dave told Robert.

"They thed we have to make our peath," Robert said.

Dave sat upright and pointed his finger at Robert.

"You're a fucking liar," he accused. "You hair-lipped, freeloading, Jock bastard."

"What the fuck?" Robert asked rhetorically and Dave jumped to his feet.

"What did you say?"

"I athked, 'What the fuck?'"

"Stand up, you cunt."

"Steady Dave," Tony interjected. "What are you doing?"

"This lying piece of shit has had it coming for some time," Dave explained without taking his eyes off Robert.

"He's not done anything," Tony said.

"Hang on," Barry interrupted and directed their attention to the television where a depressed looking man sitting behind a news desk.

"We have received two separate reports: one from the Home Office and the other which has been distributed globally by The Pentagon. Both reports are stating that the efforts of the Earth's resistance have all been in vain and that the direct intervention of Luke Robinson has -" The newscaster's voice broke as he seemed about to burst into tears.

"Intelligence officers have stated that communication with Luke Robinson was disrupted at three o'clock this morning and they haven't heard from him since. Under the circumstances they can only presume that he has been -" Again he choked and then stared sincerely at the screen. "- defeated.

"The broadcasting network has decided to conduct five minutes of silence as a mark of respect at which point we shall be terminating our service until further notice."

"They're turning off the telly?" Barry remarked.

"It's really that serious," Tony said.

Dave flexed his fists a few times and breathed heavily.

"This ain't fucking right," he muttered. "This ain't the way we're supposed to die. Without a fight? Just like that? No."

"But there'th no one to fight, Dave," Robert explained. "That'th been the whole problem. That'th why we've never had a chanth from the beginning. It'th been up to Robinthon to and now -"

"Bollocks, you wanker," Dave bellowed. "Who the fuck do you think you're talking to?"

"Dave, calm it," Tony said.

"Fuck off, the lot of you, I done too fucking much to get here to be just swept under the carpet. I got too much still to do. I am not going to go out like this."

"What can we do?" Barry asked but never received a reply because there was another bang at the front door. Tony opened it and Alec barged in with tears rolling down his cheeks.

"Fucking bitch!" he screamed. "Fucking stupid bitch. She did it. She went too fucking far this time."

"Alec," Tony started.

"No, that's it now," he growled, "it's over for good."

"Alec."

"She just wouldn't fucking listen so I hit her. Course, then her old man steams upstairs, slaps me in the face and kicks me out."

"Alec!"

"What?!"

"Mate, it's all for shit," Tony explained. "They just announced on the telly that it's all over. The caretakers are going to do it -"

"Whatever 'it' might be," Barry added.

"- tonight. It's all for shit."

Alec looked from man to man hoping that one of them would burst out laughing or he might catch one giving another a wry, sideways glance but they all returned his stare.

"I gotta, I gotta call Juliet and explain and get it sorted," Alec babbled and rushed to the telephone.

"You fucking idiot," Dave sneered.

"Let him make his peace," Tony said.

"Don't talk to me like that, you tosser," Dave warned.

"Fuck off, Wilkinson," Tony spat. "I've had about enough of your bullshit."

"Don't fucking talk -" Dave started but Tony took one calm step forward and punched him in the stomach. Dave curled into a ball of pain and fell backwards into the armchair.

"Calm the fuck down," Tony ordered.

"Hello? Can I speak to Jules?" Alec begged down the phone. "Yeah, it's Alec. Can I - No, she - I really need to. Please?"

He pulled the receiver slowly from his ear and replaced it on the base.

"She's already gone into town with her mates," he said to no one in particular.

"That'th what we ought to do," Robert suggested. "Thith ith our lath't night."

"Yeah, come on, boys," Barry rejoined. "Rob's right. Fuck it, Dave's right. We shouldn't go out like this moping around and fighting each other."

Dave sucked back a revitalising breath of air. "Let's get wankered," he declared.

Tony marched into the kitchen, opened the fridge, pulled out two six-packs of lager and presented them to his compatriots.

"Let's get started then."

He split one of the packs and threw a can to each of the men. They all pulled the ring tops in silence and sipped the spewing froth that spilled to the floor. They all looked at each other.

"Fuck it," Alec toasted and they all raised their cans.

"Fuck it," they chorused and started necking their drinks.

One by one the first round of cans fell, crumpled to the floor.

"My shout again, boys," Tony declared and tossed the cans around the room again. "Help yourself to anything harder," he offered. "Fuck knows I ain't going to need it after tonight."

Alec caught his missile and popped the top. He drank again and quickly pulled the can away as the surging froth threatened to escape out of his nose. He swung his back to the room to disguise his faux pas and caught sight of movement through the living room window. He swallowed back his mouthful then belched loudly.

"There's something going on outside," he commented and Tony walked over to look out.

"Looks like a few other people are having the same idea as us," he said. "Better get our skates on boys or else the pubs'll get packed out."

Robert and Tony got themselves fully dressed as the others grabbed some bottles of spirits and filed out of the front door.

Soon they were all walking down the middle of the road towards the town centre, swigging liberally from their bottles and soaking up the intensifying atmosphere of wild revelry.

Dave knocked back the last mouthful from his bottle and indiscriminately threw it through the windscreen of the nearest parked car.

Barry jumped from the noise and unexpected violent outburst. The others laughed as the car alarm started blaring.

A front door opened and a man stood, silhouetted in the back-lit doorway.

"Oi! What the hell are you playing at?" he demanded.

"It's the end of the World, man," Tony screamed loudly.

"Yeah, fuck off," Dave ordered.

"You what?"

"I told you to fuck off," Dave reiterated and stood his ground. He pulled a half-full bottle of whiskey from a pocket and threw it through another car windscreen. "What are you going to do about it?" he asked.

"You stupid little shit," the man shouted.

"Don't fucking talk to me like that, you cunt."

"Fuck you. We're all in the same position but you're not making it any easier."

Dave started walking towards the man. "Come on then, you wanker," he challenged.

"Piss off," the man replied but edged his way back into his house and closed the door firmly behind him.

Alec jumped in excitement and threw his bottle at a car. The bottle shattered against the door and sprayed its contents over the roof. The alarm went off and Alec whooped with appreciation.

"I've always wanted to see if this worked," Tony muttered and flicked his cigarette lighter to life next to the alcohol pouring down the bonnet. The flame caught and quickly spread a weak blue flame over the surface of the liquid and the men roared with laughter.

Either by coincidence or from example, further up the road came another shattering of glass, blaring car alarm and a cheer of anarchic joy.

Robert ran across the road and jumped through the dwindling flames. He slipped on the slick surface and tumbled onto the path with his trouser leg caught alight. He quickly patted it out and jumped to his feet and his comrades applauded his act of daring do. He ran up to the next car and leapt onto its bonnet creating a huge dent in the bodywork. He climbed onto the roof and proceeded to jump up and down. A curtain flickered in the window of the house behind him and a woman's face peered out. Tony threw a can that slammed loudly against the window and the woman ducked away quickly.

"You fucking bastards," Tony screamed at the skies.

They heard shouting from along the street, picked up their pace to investigate and discovered another group of males attempting to roll a parked car onto its roof. They joined in and built up a rhythm to throw the car over. They all jumped around it like celebratory prehistoric huntsmen, whooping and hollering, and then someone ran forward and kicked the recumbent animal in its flank. Then a second joined in the senseless beating and then another. Stones were thrown, sticks bore down, it was thrashed with parts of its own rent body. Something ruptured, there came a shower of internal liquid and a hunter was doused with the felled creature's life source. A raw flame flashed out from the mob and landed in the puddle. Golden flames spread across the scene with such ferocity that it threw the nearest revellers off their feet. The fire arced across the gap between machine to man and ignited the baptised warrior who, at first, screamed in panic but soon cried with pain and frustration of not being able to escape the torture. His cohorts suddenly became his audience and turned him into their next focus of insurrection. Some regaled in his balletic plight whilst others pelted him with missiles. When his dance was done and he fell to the floor, the audience looked for other entertainment. They ran along the road attacking any object that dared to stand its ground against their torrent: cars, lampposts, letter boxes and even each other.

This was it. What else was there? These men - nee boys - had spent their lives trying to prove something to their friends, their family, the World in general and maybe even to themselves. At every turn, no matter how hard they tried, it never seemed good enough. Sometimes the quality did not even matter, sometimes it just was not enough.

And now? Who was there to prove to? What time was left in which to do it? What the fuck was it that they were trying to prove in the first place?

This was all that was left: a deep seeded anger at the society that had spawned them and deserted them, resentment at the world that had stopped them from getting the fulfilment that they deserved and jealousy for those around them who were satisfied with their lot.

Blue and red disco lights approached from the end of the road and soon the mutineers clashed with fully armoured defenders of peace but they had not anticipated their opponents' ferocity or single-minded intentions and were swiftly laid to waste.

Alec had earned himself a riot shield and baton; he bounded up and jumped on Dave's back.

"Fucking, yeah," he hollered and brandished his spoils of war.

"Did you see that bloke burn?" Dave shouted.

Alec nodded manically. "It was Tony that chucked the lighter in," he announced.

"Look there's Rob," Dave pointed to the side of the road where Robert was sat in the curb with his face in his hands. They ran over to him and Dave kicked him in the ribs. Robert rolled over, clutching his side and they saw blood all over his face where his nose had taken a pummelling.

"Serves you right, you fucking wanker," Dave declared.

Robert got to his feet as a window behind them shattered. They all ducked from the shower of glass then saw Tony and Barry clutching bricks and laughing.

Robert turned and kicked away the larger shards of glass that had survived the assault then climbed into the house. A television set came flying out and made the men jump clear. There was a moment's pause and then one of the top windows burst open and a bedside cabinet crashed to the street.

"Rock and roll!" Robert screamed from the bedroom.

They noticed people running back from the top of the road and could see a rolling mist, iridescent in the streetlights.

One boy stumbled to the floor near them; he had tears streaming down his dirty face and started throwing up.

Alec walked over and kicked the boy in the side of the head. He dropped to the floor, motionless.

Robert emerged from the house as the mass of ailing retreaters increased so they ran as well, all the time inflicting as much violence as possible on the things around them.

They passed the scorched, inverted car and then Dave made a beeline to a house. He threw his brick through the darkened window then climbed into the living room closely followed by the others.

There came a woman's scream from upstairs and a heavy scuffle of movement. Dave did not hesitate and ran up the flight of stairs. Before anyone could follow there was another scream, a brief exchange of male voices and then a heavy thundering as something came down the stairs. The man who confronted Dave earlier was lying, dazed on the floor. Tony and Robert grabbed him and dragged him out into the street then proceeded to kick and beat him.

The woman screamed again and came thumping down the stairs. She screamed hysterically until Barry kicked her in the face.

"Alec, get up here," Dave ordered and he unceremoniously stamped on the woman to get to the stairs.

Robert and Tony were still kicking the man and only stopped when his neck snapped and rolled limply to the side. They ran back into the house where Barry had crushed the woman's skull in on itself. They all piled upstairs, into a room where muffled noises were coming from. Inside, Dave was holding a teenage girl down on the floor. She had a gag in her mouth and was trying to scream. She had her nightdress pulled up to her neck and was being brutally raped by Alec.

"Fucking bitch! Fucking bitch!" Alec snarled with each thrust.

The girl stared imploringly at the three men in the doorway.

They stared back and *patiently waited for their turn.*

"We woke up early the next morning and were th'till in their house. The girl wath dead. We got out and went back to Tony'th. The telly wath on and they reported that the caretakerth had been beaten and left. Nobody thed anything. I don't know about the otherth but I don't think I wath happy about not being dead.

"Apparently there were riot'th all over the world. I think we could excuthe ourthelv'th by knowing that we weren't the only one'th, that maybe it wathn't our fault. But that didn't th'top it from having happened and when we thaw Luke in the pub we realithed how evil we were."

"Objection," Umri declared. "Mr Sescott is making a supposition as to how the others felt. He can only testify for his own emotions."

"Overruled, Mr Umri," Etienne stated. "I don't think there's any doubt in anyone's mind that the actions of these people was truly evil."

"But he -" Umri protested.

"Sit down, Mr Umri," Etienne ordered and he did.

"This is truly an astonishing confession, Mr Sescott," she told him. "but in all fairness I'm not sure how your testimony relates to these proceedings other than offering some insight into your friends' motives for attacking Mr Robinson. However speculative your account might be, I am sure the police will want to discuss it with you and the others implicated at further length."

Etienne look perplexed and turned to Jameson for advice then to Farthing.

"Ms Sabella?" Etienne addresses. "Do you think there is anything of any use you may derive from Mr Sescott?"

Kat pulled herself to her feet.

"Mr Sescott, I get the impression from your testimony that the kind of violent behaviour your friends exercised upon Luke Robinson is common practice. Is that so?"

"Yeth," Robert replied. "We didn't need much of an excuthe to th'tart a fight at the end of an evening."

"And, in general, did any of your victims defend themselves?"

"Rarely. We didn't give them the chanth."

"Thank you, Mr Sescott," Kat said and sat down.

"Mr Umri," Etienne prompted and Umri stood.

"Mr Sescott, were you the only group of men in your town who instigated fights?"

"No, there were quite a few," Robert replied.

"And were you a witness to the alleged attack on Luke Robinson?"

"No, I had th'tarted my journey."

"So whether Luke Robinson actually murdered David Wilkinson or was simply defending himself is an issue that only those present would know."

"Well, yeth. Of courth."

"Thank you," Umri said and sat down.

"You are excused, Mr Sescott," Etienne said. "The court bailiff will escort you from the room and take you into custody."

Robert accepted the information without reaction and allowed the guard to lead him out.

"Is there a 'the fucker deserved to die' route we can take?" Luke whispered.

"Morally? I think we'd get away with it but unfortunately we're in a court of law," Kat replied.

The judges were conferring again and rifling through their papers. Etienne leaned forward to the microphone.

"My apologies. What with Mr Sescott's impromptu appearance we lost track for a moment but we have found ourselves again. Will you call for Mary Hopkins please," she instructed.

Mary Hopkins was in her late forties, a short woman with dark brown, tight, curly hair. She was wearing a smart, purple dress suit that looked like the jacket was a size too small for her. She took to the stand and took her oath.

"Could you please give your name and relationship to the defendant please?" Etienne requested.

"My name is Mary Hopkins and I don't actually know Luke Robinson personally," she replied timidly.

"Mrs Hopkins," Jameson addressed, "you were driving the car that hit David Wilkinson on the evening of the twenty-eighth of February, is that correct?"

"Yes."

"Could you please tell us what happened?" Jameson asked.

Mary licked her lips and nervously looked around the room at everyone.

"I had been doing some food shopping and was driving home. It was about eleven o'clock at night and I was coming up Hurstpier Road. It's a long road and reasonably well lit so I could see the group of boys fighting at the top of the hill. As I got closer I saw that a couple of them were lying on the floor and two were standing by the edge of the road. One pushed the other and he sort of jumped out into the road in front of me.

"I tried to stop - really I did - but it was too late. I hit the boy and he rolled right over the top of the car. I was a few meters away before the car actually stopped. I couldn't move and it wasn't until the ambulance arrived that they managed to get me out of the car."

"How have you been since then?" Etienne asked.

"Not too good," Mary replied. "It's totally shaken me. I haven't been able to drive since, my nerves are shot to pieces, I can't sleep."

"Ms Sabella, do you have anything to ask?" Etienne offered.

"Just a couple of questions, Mrs Hopkins," Kat said as she pulled herself up. "If you are okay with that?"

"I'm all right," Mary replied.

"Thank you. Are you generally a careful driver?" Kat asked.

"I've never been at fault in an accident in the twenty-odd years I have been driving."

"Do you know what the speed limit along Hurstpier Road is?" Kat asked.

"I don't, I'm afraid," Mary replied.

"I presume that it is a route that you use regularly?"

"It is the way I have to go to get to the local supermarket."

"So what speed limit do you think is on that road?"

"Forty?"

"Thirty," Kat told her. "Do you usually drive within the speed limits?"

"Yes, of course," Mary replied defensively.

"I've got the police report from the accident here and it claims that from your testimony, the stopping distance of your car and the skid impressions on the road that you were driving at nearly fifty miles per hour."

"Oh, I doubt that," Mary stuttered.

"Can you be sure?"

"I -"

"Is eleven o'clock at night your usual shopping time?"

"Yes, the store is quieter at that time."

"Have you seen this sort of scenario on that road before?"

"A few times, yes."

"And it's your usual practice to just drive by?"

"Well, yes. What else am I supposed to do?"

"So the police report would probably be explained by you driving at forty miles an hour - thinking that was the legal limit - then accelerating to hurry past the scene. Is that a reasonable hypothesis?"

"I suppose. Yes."

"So in reflection, if you hadn't been driving ten miles over the limit in the first place and if you hadn't accelerated further then you wouldn't have been in the position to hit him, you would've had a shorter stopping distance and the collision itself might not have killed him."

"I don't -"

Umri jumped up. "Objection, Mrs Hopkins is not on trial here."

"I am simply trying to point out that David Wilkinson's death was more due to an unfortunate set of circumstances rather than any particular person's fault," Kat explained.

"Duly noted, Ms Sabella," Etienne said. "Do you have any more questions?"

"No, I'm finished," Kat told her and sat down.

"Mr Umri?"

"I have no questions, your honour," Umri replied and took his seat.

"Thank you, Mrs Hopkins, you may step down now," Etienne said and waited until Mary had left the room. "Please call Malcolm Ingrams."

Malcolm entered the room after a short while and stepped up to the witness stand. He was in his fifties, was bald from his forehead to the back of his scalp but what hair he did have was white. He wore a brown and tan, striped tank-top with a plain white shirt, green tie and charcoal trousers. He took the oath then sat down.

"Please give your name and relationship to the defendant," Etienne instructed.

"My name is Malcolm Ingrams and I saw the fight between Luke Robinson and David Wilkinson."

"Are you employed, Mr Ingrams?" Farthing asked.

"Yes, I own a newsagent's just on the edge of the town centre," Malcolm replied.

"How long have you been doing that?"

"Twenty eight years, so far."

When it was clear that the judges had nothing else to ask, Etienne said, "Please tell us what happened on the evening of the twenty-eighth of February."

"I had been out walking the dog in Hurstpier Park and was making my way home at about eleven-thirty when I noticed a group of lads coming up the hill over the opposite side of the road. There were five of them although one was a fair way ahead of the others.

"Anyway, although we had been up the park for three quarters of an hour, it was now that the dog needed to do its business so I stopped and just hoped they wouldn't notice me. It was then that the four boys at the back rushed up to the one on his own (who, it turned out, was Luke Robinson). There was an exchange of words then one of the four lads smacked Robinson in the face who then smacked him back. Then the rest of them charged in and was knocked to the ground. It was then that I thought I'd better call the police.

"The first lad got up again and squared up to Robinson who then gave him a shove. The lad kind of jumped back as if electrocuted or something and the car whacked into him. He rolled over the bonnet, across the roof and slapped on to the road. Robinson sat down on a bus-stop bench, the only lad still standing just collapsed on the curb and the other two didn't move until the ambulances showed up. The policeman took about five minutes to get there."

"Why did you say you hoped they wouldn't notice you?" Etienne asked.

"They were a gang of lads outside after closing time," Malcolm replied. "It's better to be safe than sorry."

"How long do you think the fight lasted?" Jameson asked.

"Not even a minute, I reckon," he said. "Slap, slap, throw, wallop, push, thump. How long was that? Robinson knocked them down like it was choreographed."

"Ms Sabella?" Etienne offered and Kat stood up.

"Mr Ingrams, I'll get straight to the point," Kat told him. "It was night time, there may have been a few street lights on but the incident was taking place over the other side of the road. Do you normally wear glasses?"

"I do, and I had them on that night," Malcolm told her.

"Okay, are you one hundred percent sure that the man who pushed David Wilkinson into the road was Luke Robinson?"

"Yes I am," Malcolm said. "I didn't take my eyes off him and when the policeman showed up I crossed the street and it was then that I recognised him."

"Okay," Kat conceded, "but can you reiterate for us that you saw Luke Robinson only push David Wilkinson away and that he leapt out of the way and into the path of the car?"

"I don't know if it was quite like that," Malcolm said.

"Isn't that what you already said?" Kat asked.

"No, I said he jumped away as if he had been electrocuted. It was more like his body was reacting to a sudden jolt but I couldn't see where it had come from."

"But Luke didn't push David Wilkinson into the road," Kat urged.

Malcolm sighed. "Look, I understand what you're trying to get me to say but ultimately I didn't see how and I don't know why the boy ended up in the road. He had his back to me but I did see Luke Robinson give him a shove to the chest. In my opinion I don't think that was enough force to create the reaction it did but something must have."

"Thank you, Mr Ingrams," Kat said.

"Maybe Robinson had a tazer in his pocket," Malcolm continued.

"Thank you, Mr Ingrams," she emphasised.

"Maybe the lad had springs in the souls of his shoes."

"Your honour?" Kat pleaded.

"Maybe Luke Robinson picked up telekinetic powers while he was away. Who knows what's happened to the boy?"

"Mr Ingrams," Etienne interrupted, "that's enough speculation, please."

"Well, she started it," Malcolm grumbled.

"Have you finished, Ms Sabella?" Etienne enquired.

"Yes, thank you," Kat replied and sat down.

Umri did not even wait for his cue before he was on his feet.

"Mr Ingrams, the actual fight itself: 'Slap, slap, throw, wallop, push, thump,' I believe?"

"Something like that, yes," Malcolm agreed.

"But not exactly like that?"

"Well, no, not really," Malcolm said. "I was just trying to explain the quickness of the event."

"And what about the control?" Umri asked.

"The what?"

"You said that Robinson fought as if it had all been choreographed; could you try to explain that?"

"Apart from the first punch none of them really laid a finger on him," Malcolm recalled. "Each assault was parried calmly and proficiently. The only time he seemed unsure of his actions was before he pushed the boy, Wilkinson."

"Unsure?"

"Yes. It was the only moment in which he looked like he didn't know what to do."

"He was hesitant?" Umri suggested.

"Objection," Kat shouted. "Mr Umri is leading the witness."

"Please allow Mr Ingrams the right to use his own words, Mr Umri," Etienne said.

"My apologies," Umri said, bowed his head to the judges then returned his attention to Malcolm.

"Mr Ingrams, would you say that there was a definite pause before Luke Robinson delivered his final blow?"

"Yes," Malcolm replied.

"Thank you," Umri said and sat down. Kat jumped up.

"Mr Ingrams, you stated that David Wilkinson had his back to you before he ended in the road, correct?"

"Yes, that's right."

"Was he holding anything? A weapon perhaps?" Kat asked.

"I don't know, I couldn't see," Malcolm said.

"Did he say anything?"

"I'm not sure."

"Well anyway, there are two reasons as to why Luke Robinson may have necessitated a pause during the course of him defending himself."

"I suppose," Malcolm said with disinterest.

"Thank you," Kat said and took her seat.

"Thank you, Mr Ingrams, you may step down now," Etienne said and Malcolm left the stand. The judges chatted between themselves before agreeing on their next course of action.

"We will take another brief recess," Etienne said. "Fifteen minutes."

The judges stood and the rest of the court followed suit. When the chambers' door closed behind them the court sat down and a gentle mumble of discourse spread around the auditorium.

"I think we're okay," Kat mumbled.

"That's not it, is it?" Luke asked.

"I think so, yes," she said. "They normally take a recess just before summation and if they were going to call you to testify they would've done that before the break."

"Unless, of course, that Farthing *really* needed to empty his bag," Luke hypothesised.

Kat was lost in thought then came round. "His 'what'?"

"Doesn't matter," Luke told her. "I think you're fooling yourself if you really think they won't call me."

"We never put you down to testify and the prosecution never put your name down either," Kat explained.

"That doesn't matter," Luke shrugged. "Rob The Scot wasn't on any list and on top of that there are a load of external parties that really want to find out what I know and what really went on."

"Why don't people know what really went on?" Kat demanded.

Luke sighed and rolled his eyes. "They do, Kat, but they don't want to believe the answers they've been given."

"I don't get it," Kat said dismissively.

"My point exactly," Luke huffed. "It's too simple an explanation, too raw an answer, you can't handle the truth."

Kat just stared at him. "How long have you been waiting to slip that in?"

"D'uh! All day. I was going to save it until I was up there. Do you think I could still get away with it?"

"You're impossible."

"No, just highly improbable."

"Look, we are so close to getting through this I just don't want you to fuck it all up," Kat explained.

"Do you really think I would?"

"Not on purpose," she said, "but you don't think like normal people."

"How's that?"

"You tell the truth, for starters," Kat blurted.

"I'm supposed to."

"Not the whole truth."

"But the oath states -" Luke started.

"I know what the oath states," Kat growled. "But most people, like those we've seen today, give answers how they perceive. You? You tell people stuff about themselves that they didn't even know."

"Everybody knows -"

"Don't do that forest for the trees shit," Kat ordered. "It's infuriating."

"This is my point though," Luke argued. "You people really can't handle it."

"And for god's sake don't do that," she warned.

"What?"

"That 'you people' nonsense, as if you *are* part of an alien species or something," she snorted derisively. "That will not go down well."

"Kat, I hate to tell you this, but I will answer those questions that are asked of me."

Kat looked disappointed. "You just don't seem to have any instincts of self-survival," she opined. "If you aren't at all careful up there they will crucify you. They will try you for murder and they will lock you away. Too many people are scared of you, what you have done, and what you might do. Personally, I think you are owed too much to be here and that's why I'm trying to help."

Luke just stared at her.

"I didn't save you, Kat," he eventually stated. "You don't owe me anything. I can't save you, only you can and you owe that to yourself."

Kat peered at him over the rim of her glasses and frowned slightly.

"I have no idea what you're talking about," she said.

"Yes you -"

"Stoppit!"

"Suit yourself."

"Be quiet."

"I am."

"Why do you always have to have the last word?" Kat demanded.

Luke was about to say something but a resurfaced memory stopped him and his manner changed instantly.

It did cause Kat some concern for a moment but she quickly contented herself with the fact that at least he had shut up. For now.

ACT 5: Who He Is

A bailiff stepped through the chambers' door and declared, "All rise, this court is now in session. Judge Etienne presiding."

The people in the room had it down perfect now and stood simultaneously. There was something disturbing about the way the amalgamated noise of people standing was sandwiched between two slices of intense silence.

The judges entered and took their seats. The audience sat and, again, the resounding thump of a couple of thousand pairs of buttocks padding against respective plastic seats unsettled everyone present. It was like every person there was embarrassed because they thought their bum had made that much noise.

Etienne gave the room an inquisitive look and mused that the uncomfortable silence felt like she had just walked into a room while someone had been talking about her. In this instance the feeling could be multiplied by the two thousand present.

"We seem to have uncovered an anomaly," she announced cautiously.

"Ah shit," Kat hissed.

"Would both parties please approach the bench?" Etienne requested. Umri and Kat walked to the front and Etienne pushed her microphone to one side.

"Why isn't Mr Robinson being called to testify?" Etienne demanded.

"Is he not?" Umri questioned.

"Mr Umri, are you serious?"

"We just presumed his name was on the list."

"Well it's not," Etienne informed him. "Ms Sabella? Any comments?"

"We didn't think it was necessary to put him through the public stocks, your honour," she said.

"I'm not sure I like your inference," Etienne warned.

"I'm just saying we believed that the all testimonies given would be enough without causing our client any further stress and disrespect at the hands of our opponents."

"Hey," Umri complained but Etienne held up her hand to quieten him.

"Nice try, Ms Sabella," Etienne said, "but we have agreed between us that we need to hear his side of the events of the evening in question so we may get as complete a picture as possible."

"Fair enough," Kat said, intoning as much nonchalance as she could muster.

"Let us proceed then," Etienne said and the opposing lawyers walked back to their places.

"I cannot believe you tried to get away with that," Umri muttered under his breath.

"Shove it," Kat spat back and sat down.

"Well?" Luke asked.

"Busted," she replied.

"We would like to call Luke Robinson to the stand now, please," Etienne requested.

"Show time," Luke whispered and Kat gave him an imploring look. The bailiff came over and led him to the stand. A slight murmur of excitement rippled around the audience that was quickly quashed by Etienne's gavel.

"I expect absolute silence and respect for this court from now on," she demanded. "And that goes for everyone." She allowed her gaze to wander from the crowd, pause on Umri, then Kat and to settle on Luke.

"Raise your right hand," the bailiff instructed. "Do you swear on the ruling deity of your life to tell the truth, whole truth and nothing but the truth?"

"I do not," Luke replied and Kat's head dropped the table.

"What?" Etienne demanded angrily.

"I don't have a ruling deity," Luke told her.

"It is purely a formality, Mr Robinson," Etienne said.

"I don't think it is," Luke replied. "The whole basis for me telling the truth being that if I don't I will receive punishment from the god that I happen to believe in. If it's 'just a formality' then there wouldn't be any downside to me lying to you."

"Apart from committing perjury and being held in contempt," Etienne warned.

"I think the prospect of eternal damnation is supposed to be a bigger threat than a material fine," he replied.

Etienne sighed. "Are you going to be this difficult throughout your testimony?" she asked.

"I'm just playing by your rules," he said. "My participation simply highlights the flaws in your system."

"Mr Robinson," Etienne addressed wearily, "do you promise to tell the truth and not tell any lies?"

"Okay," he said. "I can do that. I promise."

"Thank you. For the records could you tell us your full name?"

"My name is Luke Robinson."

"How old are you Mr Robinson?" Farthing asked.

"I'm twenty-six and could you call me Luke, please? My dad is 'Mr' Robinson."

"And what would you state your occupation as being?" Farthing continued.

"Unemployed," he replied.

"Really?" Farthing asked incredulously.

"Yep, I left my job just after the beginning of the invasion."

"And what was that job?"

"I was doing what is generally regarded as media sales but, in real life, is one of those professions that falls in the category of existential procrastination."

"Meaning?"

"It's not proper work, it's a self serving job. It's a job that's been created to keep someone employed and the people doing that job are only doing it because they either don't know what they really want to do or can't do what they really want to."

"I see," Farthing said uncertainly.

"Mr Robinson," Etienne interjected.

"Luke, please," Luke said.

"Mr Robinson," she repeated, "please answer the questions directly."

Luke just sat there in silence.

"Well?" Etienne prompted.

"I could be better," Luke said and had his attention drawn by a gentle rhythmic banging and saw Kat bouncing her head off the table.

"Mr Robinson, are you trying to make a mockery of this court?" Etienne demanded.

Luke leaned forward to his microphone and took a deep breath. "No," he said, exhaled and sat back.

Jameson patted Etienne on the arm.

"Luke, did you enjoy your job?" Jameson asked.

Luke pondered for a second.

"No," he said.

"Then why did you do it?" she continued.

"I didn't know what else I should be doing and I had bills to pay which meant I couldn't afford the luxury of taking time off to try to find myself," Luke said.

"So, you disliked your job?" Jameson suggested.

"No," Luke answered.

"Could you elaborate, please?" Jameson requested through gritted teeth.

"No," Luke said.

"Why?"

"Because she told me to answer the questions directly implying a distinct lack of elaboration," he told her.

"You shouldn't test the patience of this court with your facetiousness and attempts at wit," Jameson warned.

Luke turned to the judges.

"You are not in charge here," he told them. "I can make this very difficult for you. Don't test me."

Each judge had an extensive career of sitting before thousands of different types of case and heard testimonies from possibly millions of people and, during that time, of course they had been cajoled, abused and even threatened on numerous occasions. Sometimes the witness had even left the stand to try to get at the judge but was always intercepted by the bailiffs. Abuse was never taken seriously and always brushed off with the threat or administration of a fine and/or a spell in jail. This was the first time they truly believed what they were told.

"What were your feelings towards your employment, then?" Jameson asked.

"I just got on with it," Luke said. "It was something I had to do."

"How would you describe your personality prior to the invasion?" Farthing asked.

"Do you want me to describe myself from my point of view then or describe myself how I see it now?" Luke asked.

"Erm. Then," Farthing said.

"I was content - happy I suppose - and I was in love."

"And how would you describe yourself then, now?" Farthing asked and hoped the question made more sense to others than it did to him.

"I was, like nearly everybody else, ignorant, selfish and stupid."

"In what sense?"

"I was preoccupied with my own little bubble of existence," Luke explained, "not caring to give a thought about anyone or anything outside of it."

"And how are you now?"

Luke nodded sagely. "I am all too aware of the things that go on outside my bubble," he said with wide eyes. "My bubble has expanded."

"How was this enlightenment reached?" Etienne asked.

"Ultimately?" he asked rhetorically. "Through electro-shock therapy."

The judges waited for the punchline. Luke waited for the next question.

"Do you think you are a better person now?" Jameson enquired cautiously.

"Wow, that's a question and a half," Luke gasped. "'Am I a better person?' I suppose I must be. Enlightenment, for better or for worse, must make you better."

"How can enlightenment be 'for worse'?" Etienne demanded.

"The truth hurts," Luke said.

"Can you give us your version of the events that lead up to the death of David Wilkinson on the evening of the twenty-eighth of February?" Etienne asked.

"Gary and I had gone back to our respective parents' homes for the weekend and he dragged me out into town that night. We used to go to the Wack 'n' Fank when we were younger, although it used to be a 'normal' pub rather than the trendy wine bar cum nightclub it is now.

"Anyway, as was usual when we go out now, we managed to sneak into a corner booth so as to keep a low profile."

"Why did you do that?" Farthing interrupted.

"'Why'? Why do you think, 'why'?" Luke asked. "Because we go out for a drink, not to be mobbed by hundreds of people who think they're my best mate or worst enemy."

"But something like that is bound to happen if you go to a public place, isn't it?" Farthing continued. "You're just tempting fate."

"What? So I should just shut myself in my house and order take-aways for the rest of my life?" Luke asked. "I have a right to go out and try not to be recognised, you know?"

"But it's not going to happen," Farthing told him. "Ninety-nine percent of the population of the World knows what you look like. A study showed that eight of ten primary school children in the United Kingdom recognised your face first over that of Mickey Mouse."

"And yet you can't buy a novelty pair of my ears anywhere," Luke said. "Where's the justice?"

"The point I am trying to get to is that you know if you go out anywhere you won't get a moment's peace because you are an international celebrity. On top of that, it's as if you derive some pleasure from playing the victim when a 'fan' pays you some attention."

Luke unclenched his teeth and pondered on saying something about 'playing the victim' but caught that imploring look from Kat.

"Are you after Halfenshaw's job?" Luke asked. "I hate to say it but that's absolute bollocks. Film stars want to be film stars and they know the levels of adoration they might have to endure. That comes with the job. I never asked to be humanity's saviour and I like to think that maybe there is somewhere I can go where I can just be myself and that there are some people out there who might actually respect my privacy and desire to just get on with my life. Is that so unreasonable?"

Farthing did not reply.

"Shall I go on?" Luke asked and the judges nodded.

"Right. So, we're in the booth and Gary is getting the drinks in, as-and-when they're required, and we're actually having a pretty good time just chatting and then an ex-girlfriend of Gary's recognised him and came over to have a word. She brought a mate of hers over.

"They were catching up and we all started talking. Then a few more of their mates showed up and squeezed around the booth."

"None of them had recognised you at this point?" Jameson asked.

"I'm not sure, really," Luke said. "We were all just talking and having a laugh. Someone must have said something at some stage because when I looked up around the room there was this huge clearing around our booth as if everyone was trying to keep their distance. And then people kept staring over at us."

"But generally, people left you alone and certainly didn't bring issue to you and your exploits," Jameson said.

"Pretty much," Luke agreed. "Up until when that first twat came up."

Luke actually felt like he was normal again. He looked over at Gary who actually had his arms around two girls and was chatting them both up at the same time. Luke laughed at his mate's unadulterated brazenness and wondered why he had never been like that. He took a moment to look at all the girls around the booth, there were six of them altogether and they were all absolutely stunning. At first, he had felt a bit self-conscious. Although Gary's ex and her friend had been talking away to Gary and not minding him at all, he was just waiting for when they would turn to him and scream out or something but it never happened. Eventually he had been brought into a conversation, his natural defences kicked in and he said something morose and cynical but the girls laughed, thinking he was taking the piss. He relaxed and started enjoying himself. Then the other four showed up uninvited and made themselves comfortable. Again he withdrew and waited for the worse to come but it did not. The girls nattered amongst themselves mostly about boyfriends and on occasion allowed him to add a pithy comment here and there.

There was something else that made him feel slightly uneasy and that was that these were the first flirty girls he had been in contact with since ever going out with Carolyn and he did not know how to react. He remembered how awkward he had felt around Tasya at times. He had definitely felt some sort of attraction but could not quite put his finger on what it was. Now, he could most certainly put his finger on it and was secretly hoping he might get the chance to at the end of the evening.

They were all so spirited and full of joy. Their laughter was the most beautiful sound he had ever listened to. Sure, he had heard laughter but never really listened to it. It was so pure an emotion and such an all-embracing reaction and despite the smutty innuendo that triggered this particular burst of joy it was such an innocent pleasure.

Luke felt like he wanted to cry. It was almost all the justification he needed for everything that had happened.

Then he noticed the lad standing at the end of the table. Luke's jaws involuntarily ground together as he noticed the white shirt and thick gold chain that hung around his collar. He had gelled down black hair, bad acne and evidence of an attempted moustache. There was an obvious change in the jovial atmosphere around the table.

"S'up?" the lad asked Luke.

"Aw, piss off Jamie," one of the girls ordered.

"Shut yer mouth, Jules," Jamie retorted.

Luke flashed Gary a look that managed to prevent an outburst.

"'S'up' yourself?" Luke asked.

"You enjoying yourself?" Jamie asked.

"What do you want?" Gary demanded.

"You boys have been staring us out all night," Jamie told them.

"Don't flatter yourself," Luke blurted before he could think about it. The girls laughed.

"We've got far better things to keep our attention," Gary added and squeezed the females on either side of him.

Gary's ex slapped him playfully on the thigh. "'Things'?" she admonished.

"I come over to see if you've got a problem," Jamie said above the mockery.

"Thanks for your concern but there are no problems here," Luke said.

Gary leaned forward and Luke wanted to dive across the table and slap his hand over his friend's mouth.

"Do you know who he is?" Gary asked in a mock hushed tone.

All the girls turned and looked at Luke and he tried to disappear into the leather upholstery.

Jamie did not react. "I don't care who you are," he said, "but if you keep eyeballing us then there is going to be a definite problem."

Jamie turned away and wandered back into the crowd. Luke noticed the collection of Jamie's friends staring at them and his jaws flexed again.

"I want to go," Luke said.

"Shut up," Gary retorted.

"Oh my god," the girl called Jules gasped. "You're Luke Robinson, aren't you?"

"Oh, you're a bullet tonight, Jules," one of her friends ribbed.

"Oh right, and you all knew, did you?" Jules asked and the girls all nodded.

From that moment on Luke could not help himself but keep looking over at the boundary of people who stood watching and waiting. Two of Jamie's friends wandered off and did not return by the time last orders were called. The girls all excused themselves but invited Luke and Gary to their continued evening of merriment at the local nightclub. Luke declined before Gary had the chance to accept.

"Right, one more for the road?" Gary asked.

"Seriously, I want to go," Luke said. "There's going to be trouble."

"What? Those wankers? All mouth, mate."

"I want to go home now," Luke emphasised. "You have another drink if you want but I am leaving."

"All right, you grumpy bastard," Gary moaned. "I actually thought we were going to have a pleasant night out."

"We nearly did, pal," Luke told him.

They both pulled themselves out of the booth, slung their jackets on and left the pub without looking at anyone.

It was cold outside and Gary 'brrrr'ed his unhappiness with the air.

"Fuck it," he muttered. "That's why you never leave before time, 'cos there's never a cab around until then."

"The walk will do you good," Luke suggested.

"It'll freeze my fucking nuts off," Gary grumbled but started to tramp his way up the high street in the general direction of home.

Gary was rambling on about not very much: reliving the evening, the specific qualities of each of their female companions and what they might get up to for the rest of the weekend. Luke was quiet and more aware of the four lads who had followed them out of the pub and were still following even though they were a considerable distance away.

"Right," Gary announced, "you want me to walk you home?"

"Don't be soft," Luke replied.

"I'll see you tomorrow then," Gary said and took off down a side street. "If I haven't frozen to death beforehand."

"See ya," Luke called and continued his way up the hill.

Multiple footsteps from behind started to get closer and Luke ground his teeth together. He saw the bushes that grew to the left of the path; there were small sticks and loose earth underneath them. There was the road to his right and a man with his dog approaching from the opposite path. There was a bus stop bench just a bit further ahead.

"Oi," a voice called from behind him but Luke ignored it.

The footsteps picked up their pace. "Oi, I'm talking to you," the voice called again so Luke stopped and turned around.

Luke immediately recognised Jamie swaggering up the middle of the path and the others were his mates from the pub. There was a blond lad who must have had shares in hair-care products who walked on Jamie's right side, along the edge of the curb. The third had his hair shaved back and was on Jamie's left side. Leading the group was a short but stocky guy who seemed almost incandescent in the light of the street lamps. Luke waited for them to catch up to him.

"Go on, Dave," the cropped-haired lad urged.

"Who do you think you are trying to nick other blokes' birds?" Dave demanded.

"What?" Luke asked.

"You heard me," Dave said and lifted his hand up quickly to run his fingers through his limp quiff.

Luke did not flinch.

"Is this what it's really about?" Luke asked. "Those girls?"

"What gives you the right?" Dave asked and jabbed his index finger at Luke.

"You people," Luke groaned. "You exasperate me." He was trying to keep sedate about it all. "If nothing else, I have the right as much as you do." It was always the way though, and he had almost got used to the confrontations but tonight had been different. He had seen a good reason for all the pain and it had made it worth while. "If you *really* want a reason," he said through gritted teeth - this altercation seemed even more bitter because of the high of the evening - "then I have the right to do whatever the fuck I want because I'm the person responsible for saving your sad fucking life which, in retrospect, is probably the biggest mistake I have ever made."

Dave swung his fist up and over and caught Luke solidly on the jaw. Luke just stood there but his expression of rage changed as a smile spread across his mouth. As the corner crept up, a delicate trickle of blood escaped through his lips. He licked it away.

"That's all I needed," Luke whispered.

It did not seem like that much of a powerful move; Luke just swept his left arm around in an arc and slapped Dave across the face. Somewhere inside the movement was a hidden strength, it could have been in the momentum of his strike or the precise placement of the blow. Whatever it was, the action did not seem enough to have produced Dave's reaction. He was lifted from the ground and propelled across the path and into the bushes.

The others were taken aback for a brief second. Firstly because of their friend's overreaction to the assault, secondly because of Luke's lack of reaction to the initial blow, but mainly because Luke had actually hit back. Generally, that never happened but then, generally, they usually only approached lads who looked like they would not strike back.

The moment of shock lapsed and their testosterone, adrenaline and alcohol saturated instincts kicked in. Jamie grabbed Luke around the neck in an attempt to restrain him while Alec stepped forward.

"This is for -" Alec started but got to say no more as Luke deftly raised his hands over his head, grabbed Jamie by the shoulders then curled his body over into a ball.

Jamie's body was whip-flicked over Luke's back and he landed heavily on Alec's head which then thudded solidly on the path.

Tony was the last to move forward. It seemed to Luke that he was crying but there was no sorrow emanating from his gaze but steely hatred and anger.

"You fucking shit," Tony growled. "I'm going to make you wish you'd never come back."

"Pal, you made me feel like that before I'd even left the pub," Luke told him.

Tony tried a dummy punch with his left arm but Luke did not move until Tony's right arm had started its journey upwards.

Luke stepped forward so Tony swiped harmlessly beyond Luke's ear. Luke grabbed Tony by the chest of his jacket and threw him across the path on top of the recovering Dave.

Jamie staggered to his feet and shook the grogginess from his head. He looked down at his recumbent friend then remembered what was going on he turned to see Luke waiting for him. That look of raw hatred returned to his features and he stepped forward. Luke swung his leg forward and kicked Jamie squarely in the crotch.

Jamie was airborne again and shot three feet straight up with his legs running on the spot in mid-air. He dropped back down and landed on his feet. His facial expression had changed again; it was a blank look of shock which very slowly altered into unadulterated agony. Jamie opened his mouth as his body buckled over and his hands reached for his genitals but no real sound emerged. In fact, Jamie's scream was so intense that he managed to block his trachea and he was suffocating himself.

Luke watched with morbid fascination as Jamie's eyes bulged in their sockets, veins protruded violently across his forehead, his lips turned blue and his face reddened.

It was as soon as unconsciousness kicked in that he stopped straining to expel his agony, his body relaxed, throat opened and all involuntary organs continued to operate in the way they should.

Tony and Dave had scrambled to their feet and were making a redoubled charge. They put a bit of distance between them to approach from Luke's flanks but he did not wait for them. Two swift steps forward and Luke was within arm's reach of Tony and he punched him straight on the nose. Tony's olfactory organ exploded internally and crammed cartilage, fluid and pain up into his sinal cavity. He howled and clasped his hands over his face.

Luke turned to face Dave who was still circling like a preying lion.

"I hope you boys have learned your lesson," Luke said.

"Who the Hell do you think you are?" Dave growled as he reached into his jacket and flashed something silver in front of Luke.

Luke stepped back from the lash then moved back in when Dave's arm had overshot its mark. He pressed both his hands against Dave's chest and gave him a push. It did not seem like that much of a powerful move but Dave propelled backwards into the road and landed on his feet.

Dave seemed amazed that he had not endured any physical damage from the shove. "You fucking cu-"

Wheels and brakes squealed in harmony but Dave was already cartwheeling over the roof of the car. His body spun in mid-air then slapped to the floor at the same time that the car bumped *to a halt against the curb.*

"Not really any different to any other version that you've heard today," Luke added.

"Mr Umri?" Etienne offered.

"Your honour?" Kat called and stood just as Umri was getting up.

"Yes, Ms Sabella?" Etienne asked.

"I kind of thought that, because Mr Robinson is my client then I would be the first to -"

"Do I need to point out that despite him being your client I think you waived your right to address first when you failed to call him as one of your witnesses?" Etienne said.

Kat looked to Luke for some sort of support but he just winked at her. What was that? A signal for her to carry on fighting? A nod to give up? An ingrowing eyelash? What?

"Do you have something to say, Ms Sabella?"

"No, your honour," she conceded and Luke nodded.

"Very well," Etienne turned her attention back to Umri. "You may commence your cross-examination, Mr Umri."

"Thank you, your honour. Mr Robinson, is it all right that I may also call you Luke?"

"I'd certainly prefer it," Luke responded.

"Thank you. If you and you honours would indulge me, I would like to try to pinpoint a few of the differences between yourself, now, and the man you were before the invasion. I believe some of the more remarkable character differences that have occurred are imperative to decide whether you should and could be tried for murder."

The judges nodded their assent.

"I've got nowhere else to be," Luke sighed.

"Thank you," Umri said and checked through some of his paperwork. "Were you a happy child?"

"I think my parents were probably better at answering that," Luke said.

"As far as you can remember," Umri reiterated. "Generally, do you think you were happy?"

"I suppose," Luke pondered. "I get the impression there was quite a lot of disinterest during my teens but I don't recall any great bouts of unhappiness."

"So you don't have any issues with how your parents raised you?"

"They could only do what they thought was best and that involved not throwing me down the stairs, not stubbing cigarettes out on me and not sexually assaulting me in any way. They did okay, I guess."

"When your mother was testifying you made an outburst when she announced that your birth had not been planned, that you were 'an accident'. Does that information bother you?"

"I felt it was an unnecessary declaration for her to make," Luke explained.

"She embarrassed you?"

"My mum is a very open person and would rabbit on about anything. She could carry on a conversation along a thread of logical reasoning despite the conclusion ending with the global eradication of leeks. I didn't want my mum to go saying unnecessary stuff that you guys and the media might decide to use against her or any other member of my family. This is supposed to be about me."

"And she said that you did well at school," Umri stated.

"She did indeed," Luke agreed with a hint of confusion.

"And do you think you did?"

"I didn't get killed, I didn't end up addicted to any drugs, I didn't end up in prison and, instead, I ended up with a reasonable career and a woman who I shared affection with."

"Do you only grade how good something is by how few negative aspects are involved?"

"Don't we all?" Luke asked.

"No. Today, I am happy," Umri stated.

"Why are you happy?" Luke asked rhetorically. "Cos no shit is happening."

"Not at all," Umri argued. "I am happy because of the good things that are happening."

"You say that but, underneath it, you are really happy because the bad shit is happening to that guy across the way and not you."

"That's just not the case," Umri stated bluntly, "and I think you'll find that most people think like this. Most people are happy simply because they can appreciate the good things that are happening to them."

"But to be able to appreciate something you have to draw reference to an opposing pole," Luke urged.

Umri frowned. "Nonsense. If I like a painting I do not have to have seen a bad one to know that it is good."

"A subjective opinion has to have taken into consideration a spectrum of experience for a person to be able to place the subject matter in question in a relative position of ranking."

"Gentlemen!" Etienne hollered. "What is going on here?"

"I'm just answering the questions, your honour," Luke said.

"Mr Umri?" Where are you going with this?" Etienne demanded.

"I was, er, highlighting Mr - Luke's negative disposition on life."

"Done, now move on," Etienne urged.

"Back to your time at school, were you ever bullied?" Umri asked.

"Not that I remember," Luke replied.

"Do you suffer from memory loss?"

"I don't recall," Luke said.

"Mr Robinson," Etienne warned.

"No," Luke said.

"Then why is it that you don't remember if you were a happy child and now you don't remember if you were bullied or not?"

"Firstly, I didn't spend my entire childhood going around with a permanent grin fixed to my face. Neither was I permanently crying, hence why not one emotion particularly stands out more than another. Had I realised that there was going to be a test on my life I would've taken more notes. As for the bullying? I was probably teased as much as I might have teased other kids. What you want me to tell you is that I was constantly abused behind the backs of everyone who might have known and cared. That someone used to flush my head down the toilet, stole my dinner money or anally raped me behind the bike shed. Nothing happened to me as a child that I have stored as a repressed memory that might reveal some insight as to how I fought off those guys on the twenty-eighth."

Umri just stared for a beat.

"Do you need a moment to calm down?" he asked.

"Ha!" Luke blasted. "Do you think I'm angry at you?"

"Your outburst certainly seemed to display an intense amount of emotion."

"You don't rate on my list of people to waste emotion on," Luke told him. "I used a raised tone, elucidation and enunciation to try to get it through to you the answer that you wanted was not going to be given."

"If you say so," Umri said.

"And I do," Luke replied.

Umri physically had to stop himself from answering back. Luke was not like a normal witness: one who may be a bit nervous, unsure of themselves, maybe hiding something or, more usual, just plain stupid. Luke was smart and enjoyed a good argument.

Hell, Luke enjoyed a bad argument.

Umri flipped through his papers while he tried to compose himself.

"Your father said earlier that you have a marked respect for all levels of life," Umri read.

"He did," Luke said and Umri growled at the back of his throat.

"And that's true, is it?"

"I don't go around senselessly killing insects and stuff like that, no," Luke said.

"But you do kill them if it makes sense too?" Umri asked wryly.

"I have been known to," Luke replied.

"Can you give us an example of when it made sense to kill something?"

"Really?" Luke asked. "Are you sure you want me to answer that?"

"Your honour?" Umri implored.

"Mr Robinson, please answer the question."

A strange look passed over Luke's face: his eyes glazed over as his vision focused elsewhere and tears welled in their corners, every muscle around his face relaxed giving him a totally blank expression but then the right corner of his mouth curled up slightly and revealed a sadistic grin.

"They have these," he paused whilst his brain located the correct word, "animals that they use for special jobs."

"They?" Umri asked.

"Oh, I'm sorry. The caretakers. They have these special animals."

Luke was hog-tied and had been lowered into a rank smelling room. He did not know how long he had been unconscious for but knew he could not have been hanging there for very long because the rope had not fully completed its descent. The acrid air brought him to his senses quickly and immediately had him throwing up his stomach contents and then a few empty wretches of bright green bile.

"That's quite usual for your type of life-form," a voice called out above him. Luke recognised it as belonging to Evershine. "The interesting thing is that the papytick is actually a vegetarian. Of sorts. But becomes unusually sexually aroused by the scent of bodily fluids.

"Biologists believe it has something to do with the hormones that the females secrete during their mating practices. There's something very similar between those hormones and the scent given off by a humanoid organism's blood.

"Of course we've never seen how they react to a human's blood so don't think of this as a torturous death but more along the lines of advancing the course of scientific progress and, for that, we thank you."

Luke had a momentary panic and checked his body for lesions but relaxed slightly when he saw none. The calming caused him to exhale deeply which then made him inhale. He sucked back another lungful of soured milk, rotting meat and effluence and his stomach tried to turn itself inside out again.

Luke tried to stop the rivulets of bile escaping from his mouth but his throat was locked in a perpetual wretch and his mouth would not close.

A relief of sorts followed as his guts discovered something substantial to expel. Luke gasped with the relative satisfaction of regurgitating something until he opened his eyes and saw that it was not something that he had once devoured but actually a bit of him responsible for the act of digestion.

It was probably just blood and a fine scraping of his stomach lining but the way it had landed on a piece of detritus gave it a distinctive organ-like quality.

"Ah, there it is," Evershine commented.

For some reason the smell did not seem to bother him any more and his eyes desperately scanned the semi-solid surface below him. The oily skin undulated constantly and Luke found his paranoid gaze leaping from one lump of potential horror to another. Then he looked back down at his internal expulsion and froze in horror when he discovered it had gone and that a crustacean-like antenna was poking out from the depths. It twitched experimentally in the air around it then gently rose higher. Flotsam separated across *the pool in the wake of* -

"Mr Umri," Jameson interrupted and swallowed. "Is this line of questioning absolutely necessary?"

"I'd like to object as well, your honour," Kat added and Jameson sighed.

"On what grounds?" Etienne asked.

"Relevance, your honour," Kat said. "Luke Robinson is not here because he may have killed a few bugs in his life, no matter what their, er, size."

"I simply wanted to discover what Luke Robinson's boundaries were to killing something or someone," Umri remarked.

Jameson took a deep drink from her glass of water and looked at Luke.

"Sexually aroused?" she asked.

"In the mood for procreating is probably a better description," Luke said. "Apparently the male papytick does all the fertilising and spawning and the female is just used as a gestation box. The male grows its own pupa and then shoves it into a female where the larvae slowly ingests its host until it has developed enough to be able to survive on its own. The papytick is neither terribly intelligent nor at all discriminatory: he'll shove his kids into any hole that's being offered."

Jameson blanched.

"Sorry, did you want me to go on?" he asked and Jameson shook her head.

Etienne sighed. "Mr Umri, do continue but try to keep your line of questioning on some sort of clear-cut track."

"Luke, had you ever been in any kind of physical assault prior to the invasion?" Umri asked.

"You mean, like a fight?" Luke asked. "Why don't you ever just ask what you want to ask? Why has every question got to be so vague and open to interpretation? Yes, I had been involved in a physical assault prior to the invasion. I remember Jessica Melton giving me a Chinese Burn on my arm when we were eight because I wouldn't kiss her."

Umri rolled his eyes and pursed his lips. "I mean, had you ever been involved in a similar altercation like that on the twenty-eighth? A confrontation involving similarly aged males as yourself."

"I'd seen fights before but never been involved in them, no," Luke said.

"And had you ever taken any lessons in any type of contact sport or martial arts?"

Luke shook his head. "Nope. Although I was in a five-a-side team for about four months and that could get a bit physical at times."

"Five-a-side?" Etienne asked.

"Football," Farthing explained and Etienne nodded.

"Was there anything that used to make you angry?" Umri asked.

"Not really," Luke said. "The only time I got particularly upset was when Carolyn wasted an entire evening watching those stupid reality shows."

Umri's eyes widened. "And you got angry at you ex-fiancée over this, did you?"

"I'm sorry, no," Luke said. "I didn't get angry at Carolyn, I was angry with the people who were on the shows and the people who were behind them."

"Did you ever get angry at Carolyn?"

"We had our arguments - not that I can specifically remember any of them at the moment - but no, I was never 'angry' with her about anything."

"And you did love her, did you?"

"I was going to marry her," Luke said.

"That's not an answer to the question," Umri told him.

"And we judge others as we judge ourselves," Luke countered. "In my world, if I knew two people who were about to dedicate the rest of their lives to each other, I would say that they were in love until or unless they said otherwise. You are so totally going the wrong way with this," Luke told him.

"Am I?" Umri asked.

"Yes," Luke told him. "I was a nice, placid, normal bloke who didn't like confrontations. I couldn't react quick enough to defend myself verbally or physically so always attempted a resolution."

"So why didn't you attempt a resolution on the night of the twenty-eighth?" Umri demanded.

"I did," Luke said. "They attacked me, remember? Every single witness here today has stated that to be the case. I did what I had to do to try to minimise the violence."

"Were you looking forward to getting married?"

"Very much so," Luke said and thought back to those days. "I remember it was such a comforting feeling to know that, despite anything else, part of our future was planned out. We were going to be together. That was really nice."

"How did you think of the marriage plans after the invasion?"

Luke's expression hardened. "They felt a bit esoteric."

"Can you explain that for us?" Umri requested.

"My priorities had changed and the wedding wasn't up there any more."

"Had your feelings for Carolyn changed at all?"

"I don't know," Luke muttered. "I did still love her but I noticed she had changed as well. It was almost as if she wasn't entirely happy that I had made it back so I wasn't surprised when she split with me."

"Do you think that was fair?" Umri asked.

"I don't know if 'fair' is the right word," Luke pondered. "We had both been through a lot between us and we came out the other side as slightly different people. I'm pretty sure that if we gave the relationship a bit of time then something could've been salvaged."

"Carolyn stated earlier that she had a very good reason for being emotionally distant to you upon your reintegration in your relationship," Umri stated.

"Did she?" Luke said. "Was I here when that happened?" he asked the judges.

"Mr Umri," Jameson sighed, "Mr Robinson is already proving to be a belligerent and facetious witness. Please keep your questions more succinct and less verbose."

Umri nodded. "Carolyn stated during her testimony that she believed you had intimate relationships with the female known as Tasya, yes?"

"She did indeed," Luke agreed.

"And this was the woman who Agent Cummins declared was one of their department's special field agents."

"That's what he said, yes."

"Was Carolyn right to be jealous?"

"Objection, your honour," Kat spluttered. "What? What? What?"

"Mr Umri? Would you care to explain your reasoning behind this line?" Etienne asked.

"I am trying to uncover more of Mr Robinson's moral code to better define the man he is and was," Umri said.

"Carry on," Etienne instructed and waved at Kat to sit down.

"Do you need me to repeat my last question, Mr Robinson?" Umri asked.

"No but you might want to rephrase it," Luke said.

"Why?"

"Okay. It probably was right for Carolyn to feel jealous because she had constructed an illicit scenario in her head that she was convinced was true."

"And was it true?" Umri asked.

"I don't know," Luke said. "She never told me what it was."

"I'm asking, did you had an affair with the female called Tasya?"

"You can just call her 'Tasya'," Luke said. "There wasn't a male called Tasya that we might all get confused with."

"Mr Robinson!" Etienne spat.

"What happened to 'Luke'?" he asked. "All right. No, I didn't have an 'affair' with Tasya."

Umri was about to go on when he considered Luke's emphasis on 'affair'.

"Did you have any romantic associations with each other?"

Luke grinned devilishly. "Nope. No 'romantic associations'."

"Were you attracted to her at all?" Umri demanded, nearing his limits.

"There was something, Mr Umri," Luke said. "I can't deny it. And I seem to recall the ex-copper, Roberts, mentioned it too. There was something in her eyes," Luke explained and started to drift off, "when you looked in them, you could see a permanent expression of passion." He refocused. "But apart from that she wasn't particularly good looking, I don't think."

Umri checked his notes and was about to go on then realised something.

"Mr Robinson, did you and Tasya have sex?"

"How many times does he have to answer this question?" Kat screamed.

"He hasn't answered this one," Umri shouted back. "He is twisting the words and meanings to my questions."

"Well, if you just bloody asked a straight question in the first place he wouldn't be able to twist them," Kat argued.

"Ms Sabella," Etienne bellowed, "sit down. Mr Umri, get to the point."

"Did you and Tasya have sex?" Umri repeated quickly.

"We never had 'sex', no," Luke replied carefully.

"Graaargh!" Umri exclaimed and Luke looked around him in bewildered innocence.

"Will you excuse me for a moment, your honours?" Umri requested. "I need to compose my line of questioning."

"How long will you be?" Etienne asked.

"Just a couple of minutes, no more," Umri stated.

"Very well," Etienne said and Umri returned to his seat and started manically writing on his paper.

Luke gave Kat a raised eyebrow salute and she thinned her lips at him.

"Can I get a glass of water there?" he asked Jameson.

"Of course," she replied, poured him one and passed it across to him.

"Thanks," he said, drank it back then returned the glass.

"Out of curiosity, Mr Robinson," Jameson said, "why are you being such a hostile witness?"

"I'm in a tenuous position," he said. "I have to make sure the questions I am being asked mean the same as the ones I am answering."

"I'm not sure I understand," Jameson said.

"If I was to ask you if you loved Gershwin, what might you say?" Luke asked.

Jameson was taken aback for a moment then replied, "Well, yes. I suppose."

"Now I could derive from your answer that you've had a long-term, intimate relationship with someone called Gershwin."

"But I thought you were asking about the music," Jameson said.

"That doesn't matter what you thought though, does it? Not when I'm asking you the questions and trying to get a seedy answer," Luke said.

Jameson laughed. "But you don't have to worry about your answers being taken out of context here," she said. "This is just a hearing and you've been given the freedom to explain yourself to your heart's content."

"It's not you guys who are after the answers," Luke told her and sat back in his seat.

Jameson just frowned.

"Time is getting on, Mr Umri," Etienne stated.

"I am ready, your honours, and I thank you for your indulgence," he said as he got to his feet.

"Mr Robinson," he declared. "Did you fancy Tasya?"

"Oh my god!" Luke laughed. "No."

"Did you, by your definition of the word, love her?"

"Yes, I did. Still do. We went through hell with each other and I feel I am closer to her than I am to any other person I know."

"Did you kiss her?"

Something grabbed him by his hair and pulled him to the surface. He sucked back a precious lungful of air and saw Tasya's face as she dragged him to the bank.

"*I could kiss you,"* he gasped.

There were caretakers everywhere and there was nowhere to hide. Although there were hundreds of people roaming around the romantic nightspot they stood out like a sore thumb amongst them. Then Luke remembered the old 'hide in plain sight' ploy adopted on many films and he grabbed Tasya around the waist, pushed her to the wall and was *about to kiss her when -*

Evershine's black eyes stared mercilessly at him. It did not matter because he did not even have the strength to try to beg for mercy anyway. Tasya was lying unconscious next to him, she might even have been dead because she had been bleeding quite a bit and he could not tell if she was breathing any more.

Luke wobbled on his knees and took hold of Evershine's proffered hand. This was the end of everything. He pulled the hand towards his mouth and pursed his lips. As he rested them gently on the alien's knuckles his vision was filled by the garish blood-red gemstone set in the omega symbol of his signet ring. Luke raised the hand to stare at the man's palm, *then he pressed and prayed.*

"No, I never kissed her."

"Did you engage in *any* kind of sexually orientated activities?"

Luke chuckled. "No."

Umri was starting to get heated again and was running out of synonyms. He did not really want to use the slang and euphemisms but Luke was hiding something and he knew it.

"Did the pair of you ever exchange any kind of bodily fluids?"

"Mr Umri," Jameson chided before Kat could open her mouth.

"I am truly sorry, your honour," Umri apologised. "But Mr Robinson's caged responses are telling me that there is a matter of importance somewhere but I have to find the correct turn of phrase to get him to answer."

"Carry on," Etienne instructed and received a quizzical look from Jameson.

"Did you, Mr Robinson?"

"An exchange of bodily fluids?"

Tasya looked hesitant and panicky, then she overcame some internal struggle and *spat into Luke's open mouth.*

"Is that what you mean?" Luke asked.

"She did what?" Umri asked incredulously.

"She gobbed in my mouth," Luke repeated. "That was the first time I met her, too."

"No," Umri said feeling quite repulsed. "That's not what I meant and you know it."

"Okay," Luke said and took a moment to ponder.

The whip crack was so loud that it stung Luke's ears and overshadowed the uncomfortable sensation of the sweat pouring down his face.

The whip cracked again but Tasya had stopped crying out and he slowly built the courage to open his eyes to see how it was all coming apart this time. He could only prise one eye open and saw the whip slice at Tasya again. She flinched, which meant she was still alive. The leather flashed at her flesh causing a cascade of blood to arc across the room and shower over Luke's face.

Oh, so it *was not sweat after all.*

The motion detector was still activated, if they slipped now then the caretaker security would be in there in their hundreds.

Luke did not know how long he had kept himself propped up in that gap but his arms were starting to tremble. Tasya had managed to adjust herself slightly to bear a modicum of his weight but it was not enough to relieve him of the building pressure.

The heat was becoming unbearable but it was only supposed to need to rise another couple of degrees before they could then move freely out of the docking bay.

"Tasya," Luke whispered urgently.

"Hold on a bit longer," she urged.

"It's not that," he grunted. "I'm sweating."

"So?"

"I'm *really* sweating," he said. "You said any movement down there would set off the alarms."

She looked away from her purple 'phone' and tilted her head up to look at Luke's overhanging head. She could see the rivulets of sweat trickling across his forehead and gathering on his brow.

She quickly checked their progress on her phone again then leant *back and opened her mouth.*

"And then there was the time when she pissed in my ear," Luke added. "Only joking," he laughed.

"Did you ever stick any part of your anatomy in her?" Umri demanded and Etienne had to slam her gavel on the table to quell the rising level of mirth from the audience.

Luke considered the question carefully and decided not to go into the details of removing the shrapnel from her stomach with his fingers. Then he remembered something that he had not recalled since the moment it happened.

She closed the door behind them and checked the ammunition level in her pistol.

"I've only a few bolts left," she declared.

Luke tried to catch his breath and stop himself from throwing up at the same time.

"Mine's empty," he managed and threw the rifle to the floor.

She scanned the room and he took the time to take in his surroundings too. It must have been part of the engine systems, he presumed although he would openly confess to not being an expert of alien spacecraft. His experience thus far had lead him to believe that science fiction had completely lied to him: the caretakers' craft were very minimalist. They did not have rows of consoles with winking lights to indicate that something was doing something somewhere, nor dozens of little buttons and controls to carry out the simplest of manoeuvres. Things just seem to operate without anyone actually having to do anything.

"Okay, I think I know a place we can hide until the heat dies down," Tasya said.

"Excellent," Luke replied.

"It's in the ship's engine," she told him with a tone of apprehension that turned Luke's stomach even more.

"Do I want to know the pros and cons of this?" he asked her.

"Basically we are in a dead end at the moment," she said. "Emphasising the 'dead' if we get discovered. If we hide in the engine there's a good chance that they won't look there and a better chance that we'll survive as long as they don't decide to take the ship for a jaunt."

Luke held his head in his hands. "Okay. Whatever you say," he said.

"Take your clothes off," she told him.

He quickly pulled his head out of his hands to ask, 'What?' but saw that she was already disrobing so hid his eyes again.

"We can't get in there with clothes on," she said.

"Might they get caught in the gears, or something?" he asked and made no effort to strip off.

"No," she sighed. "In its idle form it's a geo-magnetic flux which automatically incinerates any synthetic material. If you're still wearing it then it'll fry you too."

Luke peeked through his fingers and saw a lot of flesh. Then he felt her hands upon him.

"I can do it myself," he whined.

"Get on with it then," she ordered. "Look." She walked over to a trapdoor in the floor, opened it and beckoned him over. He looked into the hole and saw what he could only describe as a torrential rainbow; a bottomless space filled with a spiralling spectrum.

"Whoa!" Tasya called and stopped him from falling forward. "I know, it's quite hypnotic, isn't it?"

Luke shook himself alert and started to take his clothes off. He kept an eye on Tasya to see if she tried to have a peek at him but made sure that he stared fixedly at her face and not any of her nudey bits. He watched as she dropped her clothes into the three-dimensional fractal. There was not even a puff of smoke, the items just instantly atomised. Then she dropped down their guns and started collecting his clothes.

"Come on," she told him and waited for his underpants.

He pulled them down and off and stood awkwardly hunched over as if trying to cover his penis with his stomach.

She dropped his underwear into the hatch then sat with her legs dangling down the hole.

"That too," she instructed and pointed to his finger.

Luke raised his hand and saw his engagement ring; he was not even aware that it had been there.

"It's silver," Luke argued.

"One hundred percent?" Tasya asked.

He tugged at the shiny band until it slipped over his knuckle and off the finger. He stared at it for a moment as if mentally delivering its last rites then flipped it into the trapdoor. He then returned his attention to the pale band that remained around his finger and felt more uncomfortable with that nakedness than with his genitals flailing around.

"Sit there," Tasya instructed and he positioned himself directly opposite her and tried not to look at her body but could not help it. "We need to lower ourselves in really slowly and holding together," she said. "It's a substance that acts just like a very viscose liquid in that it will hold us in place and we can move about but it is also quite prone to momentum and any sudden movement could carry you off for miles. If we stay together we will, in essence, be one object and so shouldn't get separated."

"I'll take your word for it," Luke said.

"Ready?" Tasya asked. She turned around and started to lower herself slightly into the mix. Luke also turned and dropped to his belly he dangled his legs in the air until they touched hers. They pushed themselves to drop a bit further until their bums touched each other, then their backs.

Luke discovered that although he was holding onto the edge of the trapdoor it was not a great effort as if he was hanging on to the edge of a swimming pool.

"Keep holding," Tasya told him. "I'm going to close the door."

She had to reach back out to pull the lid over and gently slid back into the pool. She wrapped one arm tightly around his chest as she dropped the lid closer to his fingertips.

"Let go now," she said and he did. The lid closed and the flux filled in all around them covering over their entrance.

"Can you still feel the ceiling?" Tasya asked and Luke stretched out with his fingers until he could feel the door still just above him.

"I can," he told her.

"Just give a gentle push so if they do look down here we'll still be below the depth of the flux."

He did just that and felt a momentary stab of uncertainty as to whether she was going to be able to get them out of this one.

He felt her hands move and she either rotated him on the spot or crawled around him until they were facing each other. She had her eyes shut.

"Why are you're eyes closed?" he asked.

"It helps keep an idea of our position and movement," she told him. "And besides, the patterns give me a terrible headache."

"This is amazing," he said. "The colours are fantastic, and it feels like I'm totally submerged in a huge, breathable bath. It's so relaxing."

"A womb," Tasya muttered. "Apparently this is the closest experience you will ever have to knowing what it was like in your mother's womb."

Luke closed his eyes as well and considered having a sleep. He was wrong to doubt Tasya's abilities, he was totally safe with her.

He started to drift off to sleep. He could feel her breathing against his chest and her breath against his neck. He thought he could even feel the rainbows wrapping themselves around his body and then sensed something else; a very gentle and calming vibration all around him.

He was so close to being asleep for the first time in fifty-odd hours. There was her breath, the all over body massage, her heaving chest and her loving eyes.

Her sudden gasp made him jump awake.

"What is it?" he asked and noticed that there was fear in her eyes.

"There's something in here," she stated.

"What?" Luke demanded and looked around him.

"Something is crawling up my leg," she said and then Luke experienced a different type of fear.

"Oh shit," he muttered.

"I've got it," she said through gritted teeth.

"No, wait," he told her but it was too late. She clamped her legs shut and his mouth and eyes burst open.

"What's the matter with you?" Tasya asked.

"That's me," he told her. "What you've got trapped there is me."

"What?" she asked and then realisation started to creep in. "Ew! Why are you doing that?" she demanded.

"I'm not doing it on purpose," he explained. "I can't control it. I was dozing off and getting comfortable."

There came a rhythmic tapping from above their heads.

"Shhh," Tasya warned. "They're in the room."

More footsteps proceeded the first and they wandered all around above their heads but all that Luke could concentrate on was the gentle vibrations of the flux that were throbbing through Tasya's thighs and enveloping his semi-erect penis from all angles.

The footsteps stopped by the hatch above their heads then they heard it open.

"How can I see if anyone's down there?" a voice asked.

"Don't worry about it," another replied. "It's just so we can say, 'Yes, we looked.'"

The hatch closed and the footsteps tapped off into the distance.

Tasya remembered where she was.

"Right, you can have this back then," she told him.

The undulating ministrations had turned Luke's semi into a fully.

"No," he blurted but it was too late and his erection stood up to full attention.

Tasya's eyes opened wider than they should have been able to. "What do you think you are fucking doing?"

"I told, you, I'm not doing anything. I can't help it."

"Luke, you are on the verge of entering me," she warned.

"I know," he sobbed. "It's not my fault."

"I suppose it's mine, is it?"

"No, it's nothing to do with you," he said.

"That's nice," she spat and carefully pushed herself up on his shoulders. "Let's get out of here."

It was too late for Luke to be chivalrous now as he mentally noted, *breasts, belly, bonnet,* as they *passed before his field of vision.*

"No," Luke told Umri. "I didn't stick any of my bits into Tasya, I didn't fondle her, I didn't jizz on her, she didn't fondle me nor stick anything in me. I did not have sexual relations with that woman and there is no blue dress to suggest otherwise. I was physically and mentally totally faithful to Carolyn. Without exception."

"Can we drop the subject now, Mr Umri?" Farthing enquired.

Umri looked defeated but tried to think of a way through this. Eventually his expression of concentration dropped and he nodded his admission.

"I take it you haven't finished yet, though, Mr Umri?" Etienne asked.

"No, your honour, thank you," he replied. "Mr Robinson I want to ask you to go over the details of your involvement in the invasion."

Luke flashed Kat an 'I told you so' look and she jumped up.

"What?" she screamed. "You want him to go over the entire scenario? Are you mad?"

"Your honour," Umri pleaded.

"Seriously, you waste a huge portion of our time rephrasing one question that has a tenuous (at best) relevance to the hearing and now you request Luke Robinson gives an account of events that took place over five days. Are you hoping that during that testimony *something* might just come up that will give you an insight into the events that happened over a week after the invasion?"

"Yes," Umri replied. "How can you presume that such a life altering incident could not have any relevance to this? Before, there is a man who is adverse to physical or verbal confrontation and then after, he has become a self-proclaimed killer and becomes involved in the death of a fellow human. And if my question is too open then I apologise. I can only request such a generalised testimony because I know so little about what went on that I cannot focus on isolated events."

"I'm going to allow it," Etienne said.

"What?" Kat exclaimed.

"Really?" asked Farthing. "I thought the main aspect of this hearing was the altercation itself rather than anything that happened during the invasion."

"I believe that there may be something in his account that may reveal more of a motive behind his actions on the twenty-eighth," Etienne explained.

"I disagree," Jameson added. "I think such a wholly unconstructive testimony will distract from the intent of this hearing."

"Well, I am in the chair," Etienne boasted.

"Would you like to be removed?" Farthing asked her. "You are outnumbered in this judgement and can be replaced if pressed."

"This is disgusting," Etienne sneered. "How dare you question my decisions."

"But that's why so many of us were appointed," Jameson explained. "So we could all keep each other in check."

Etienne just scowled into the distance. "Very well," she grumbled. "Mr Umri, you must be more specific in your line of questioning."

"Yes, your honour," he said and watched Kat take her seat again. "Mr Robinson, can you tell us how many times you consciously had to kill someone during the invasion?"

Luke frowned. "By 'consciously' do you mean that I went out of my way to kill them rather than me inadvertently killing them?"

"Something like that," Umri agreed, "but as well as an 'inadvertent' death you could include a killing that was conducted as an act of self-defence."

"Okay, in which case, never," Luke said.

"Are you saying that at no time did you enter a situation in which part of your intent was going to be the death of a caretaker?" Umri asked.

"That's right."

"Even when you destroyed one of their spaceships? You didn't intend any of the crew to die?"

"Ah well, you see, that was an unfortunate occurrence that stemmed from a series of misunderstandings," Luke said.

"You mean you didn't mean to blow up the entire spaceship?" Umri asked.

Their escape pod accelerated away from the gleaming starcruiser. Luke had his head hung low in shame while Tasya was still frowning with her lips pursed tightly together.

Luke peered up at the shrinking ship and could just make out the glints of dozens of other pods jettisoning from their bays.

"They'll never get the distance," Tasya said before he could make a silver lining out of it. And as if to clarify her point the entire craft reverberated, crumpled all around its hull, imploded at its centre and then detonated. A solid shockwave of matter and flames rippled out from the craft like an inflating fiery balloon and evaporated each of the escaping lifeboats as the deluge washed over them.

Tasya turned to him. "You were only supposed to blow the *bloody doors off,*" she scolded.

Luke had a sheepish grin on his face and shrugged his shoulders at the judges. "I'd class that as inadvertent deaths," he said.

"And every other killing was only conducted during the course of self-defence?" Umri asked.

"I'm afraid so, Mr Umri," Luke said. "Tasya was proactive, I was reactive."

"And back to Tasya," Umri said, "did she ever say why she got you involved?"

"Why don't you ask her?" Luke asked.

Umri frowned. "Because she's not a witness."

"But why not? You've brought in every other bugger who had the slightest thing to do with it."

"Please answer the question, Mr Robinson," Etienne said.

"Blimey, you two are proving to be quite a team," Luke commented.

"And what is that supposed to imply?" Etienne demanded.

"There was no implication," Luke said.

"Good."

"I was simply applauding that you two are working well together."

"Mr Robinson," Etienne barked. "How would you like to be held in contempt?"

"Wouldn't be the first time," Luke muttered.

"Continue, Mr Umri," Etienne ordered.

"Did she tell you why she got you involved?" Umri repeated.

"I have to say that I am absolutely stunned that she has not been subpoenaed or whatever it is," Luke exclaimed. "She has to be a key witness and nobody seems to give a shit about where she is or anything."

"It's already been explained why she can't be here," Umri said.

"That special agent bollocks?" Luke laughed. "Listen, if she was that bothered about losing her undercover anonymity then she shouldn't have broadcast her fucking face over the World's television networks."

"Ours is not to reason why, Mr Robinson," Etienne said.

"Of course it is," Luke bit back. "If we can't ask why then who can?"

"Can you disprove Agent Cummings claims that she was one of their agents?" Umri asked.

"Of course I can't," Luke sighed. "I can tell you how I know she's not but that doesn't mean you'd believe me or those spin doctors couldn't explain it away."

"Try us," Umri suggested.

"It was the first time that I came face-to-face with Evershine," Luke told them and his gaze drifted off into the distance. He turned his attention to the camera that had its red light on and looked directly into the lens. "Is there any way I can get a flashback wobble thing going on here?"

Luke could not remember the last time he had ever needed to kneel. It was such a bizarre and unnatural feeling but could remember that it was something that he used to do when he was a child but did not know why he had ever given it up. If that was the correct term to use, of course. Was it something that you gave up doing? Or was it just something that you stopped doing? Like blowing milkshake bubbles through a straw, eating bogeys or chasing pigeons.

He adjusted his weight slightly and felt a kneecap slip in protestation. Would it have been less uncomfortable had he set aside ten minutes a day to have a good kneel? Maybe he could have hardened himself up in preparation for when something like this might happen.

If he got out of this one he would have to consider getting his skipping up to scratch.

The four large caretakers who had picked them up and brought them here just stood in each corner of the white room and watched them.

Tasya was not doing very much either. She was curled up in a ball and he wondered whether she was conserving her strength, in dire agony or asleep.

The other kneecap clicked out of place and brought him slightly to his senses. He was very tired and physically drained. Technically the pain in his knees and the ache in his shoulders and wrists from having his hands tied behind his back was not much more than a distraction. He wondered what future torture he could be saved from if he took up 'running around in circles until he fell over' for five minutes every day.

The door swung open and a middle-aged man walked in wearing a fur trimmed black suit. He was incredibly skinny and each stride seemed to be a precarious step on eggshells but at a hurried pace. His face reminded Luke of a fish, in that it was so angular that it looked like his eyes were on the sides of his head rather than at the front. This was probably more down to his large, pointed nose that split through his fine, but solid black, wind wafted hair like the bow of a frigate ploughing through the stormy seas.

"I am sorry to keep you waiting but I do so enjoy giving my prisoners the time to consider their predicament," he announced.

Tasya still did not raise her head so the man turned immediately to Luke. It was only when he had approached within a couple of feet that Luke realised his irises were black too.

"So, she gave the code to you, did she?" the man demanded.

"I don't have anything," Luke protested.

"I don't have time to play games," the man yelled. "I am on a schedule here and it's all falling behind because of you two." He allowed his gaze to fall on the back of Tasya's head.

"Have you given it to anyone else?" the man asked in a soft tone.

"What?" Luke asked.

"The code," he growled. "Have you passed the code on to anyone else?"

"Of course he has, Evershine," Tasya shouted and made Luke fall over with surprise. "You know what they're like."

"Yes, I know what they're like, Tasya," Evershine said. "That is why I am trying to carry out my job."

"No, this isn't your job," Tasya argued as Luke struggled to get himself upright. "There are procedures."

"You annoying little bureaucrat," Evershine spat. "You are nothing but a paper shuffler, Tasya. All you are and all you ever will be. A little brown-nosing do-gooder. It would take years to get back and go through the procedures just to get us back here in time to see these people escaping the boundaries of their own ignorance and colonising other planets. Do you really want that?"

"That's not the point," Tasya said.

"Of course it's not, dear," Evershine purred. "It never is. But how much trouble do you think I'll get into when we get back? They'll not even give me a slap on the wrist. I'll show them the files and they might even promote me. You could've been a part of that, too. Not now."

Evershine nodded to one of the goons in the corner of the room. He stepped forward carrying a small satchel and handed it to Evershine.

"Thank you," he said, flipped the bag open and pulled out a palm sized tubular device. It was made of dark chrome with a red and green button on the side.

"I'm sorry Tasya," Evershine said with no conviction at all.

"You can't let that off here," she said. "There's no way you could cover that up."

"I'll cross that bridge when I come to it," he sighed. "But I do have to let it off as I have to make sure I get rid of the code and its carriers before it's too late."

"I already said -" Tasya tried.

"I know what you said but I don't believe you and that's all that counts at the moment," Evershine told her and pressed the red button.

Nothing happen.

"Gentlemen," Evershine called and the goons gathered around him. "We are so sorry to see you go," he said to Tasya.

Luke managed to haul himself back up onto his knees to see Evershine hold his palm up to his face then press a blood-red opal on his signet ring. There was an electrostatic buzz in the air and the ring expelled a gelatinous, silver goo that wrapped itself around Evershine and his men. When they were completely covered it billowed out to become a perfect sphere.

"Quick, help me get these ropes off," Tasya called and edged herself backwards to him. He turned his back to her and they fumbled with each others' knots. Luke's hands became untangled first and he grabbed the device.

"What is it? A bomb?" he asked.

"Of sorts."

"Do I just press the green button to turn it off?"

"NO!" she screamed and he nearly dropped it. "That just makes it blow up now," she told him. "We've got a few seconds so untie me quickly."

Luke carefully put the bomb on the floor and helped Tasya with her binds and freed her hands.

"There's only one way out of this," she commented, delved into her rucksack and pulled out a roll of, what looked like, sticky tape.

"Why do you have that with you?" Luke asked.

"For times like this," she told him and started to wrap the tape around the bomb then applied more tape to stick it on the side of the sphere.

"Give me a hand," she ordered and pressed her back against the sphere and gave it a shove.

Luke tried to push it as well and it just moved slightly.

"What is this thing?" Luke grunted.

"It's like a solid liquid," she explained and pushed again. "Totally impenetrable."

They gave another heave together and the sphere moved again but this time kept its gentle momentum. The pair pushed harder and the sphere picked up speed.

"Come on!" Tasya screamed and the sphere upped its pace.

"Where the fuck are we pushing it?" Luke demanded.

"Just out."

They had managed a brisk walking pace just as it reached the end of the room and then it continued through the wall as if it had been made of children's blocks. From there, the sphere continued its journey across the field and over the edge of the cliff. Tasya grabbed Luke and pulled them both to the floor.

Luke tried to ask, 'What the hell is happening?' or at least swear as the impact on the floor bruised his ribs but for some reason the sound could not get past his lips. A focussed gale picked up out of nowhere and tried to blow them closer to the cliff edge but they clutched on to the tough grasses and buried their heads into the ground. But still there was no sound: no sound of the wind rushing past his ears, no shouts from Tasya, not even a noise from inside, his breathing, his heartbeat in his ears or grinding joints. If it had not been for the ferocity of the wind it could have been an incredibly calm and serene moment which then would have been spoiled by his internal dialogue screaming, *I can't hear anything! I'm deaf! Am I dead! What the fuck is happening?*

The wind dropped and every ambient noise returned like slap around the ears.

"Run," Tasya instructed as she picked herself up and started sprinting back to the mobile cabin. Luke may have still been a novice in the world of espying potential and imminent threats to his life but he had learned to react instinctively whenever an order from Tasya suggested that he ran away. So he was up and pounding his legs before his brain could try to work out what they might be running from.

The deafening silence had been nothing compared to the noise of the explosion that followed. It started a deep bass growl emanating from the depths of the chalk cliffs and he could feel it vibrating up through his feet as the hurried to get away.

A roar of flame and debris geysered over the cliff edge and pierced the clouds above. As it continued to flare into the sky, the ground trembled harder and started to crumble away at the edges to join the flight to the skies.

The floor shook and tried to bring the escaping couple down at the same time as meteors of flaming rock showered thunderously around them detonating the unstable and brittle earth into sprays of shrapnel that ripped into their clothes and skin.

They were about to jump into the cabin when a red-hot boulder plummeted through the roof and ripped it to shreds. Chunks of prefabricated wall sliced through the air around them like oversized shuriken.

As he picked himself up, Luke glanced over his shoulder to see the elemental fountain swathing a path through the cliff-side. It ripped chunks of the ground into its devourous heart and then spewed them out into the sky.

He tried to push himself up from his heels but he tripped over Tasya's scrabbling body and the pair tumbled into a heap of flailing limbs, impotent to the advance of utter destruction.

Then it stopped.

Luke breathed and turned to stare directly at Tasya.

"Is that it all over?" he asked. "He's dead?"

She shook her head. "The sphere can survive a blast like that easily," she told him. "It'll just delay them for a while. We'd better get moving."

She jumped to her feet and tried to pull him with her but he refused to move.

"What is it?" she asked.

"Two things," he said. "First, you two talked as if you know each other."

Tasya looked confused. "Well, we do," she said.

"How?"

"I'm a caretaker," she told *him. "Didn't you know that?"*

"Are you trying to tell us that Tasya was actually one of them?" Umri asked. "An alien?"

"That's right," Luke confirmed.

"That doesn't make any sense. Why would she put her life on the line to try to save us?"

"You'd have to ask her that," Luke said. "If you bothered to try to find her."

"You must have asked."

"Why must I?" Luke demanded. "Why should I give a shit why she was doing it? I was too busy trying not to die."

"But you said you became close," Urmi said. "You said that you loved her."

"But that doesn't mean I supported her cause or gave a shit about it," Luke said.

"So she did have a cause?" Umri asked.

"Well of course she did," Luke spat.

"But you still don't know what it was?" Umri asked.

"I never said I didn't know what it was," Luke said. "I just asked why should I have known or asked what it was."

"So what was her cause?" Umri asked.

"Not on your life, mister," Kat called.

"Overruled," Etienne blasted. "You will answer the question."

"What?" Kat demanded.

"It's all right, Kat," Luke calmed. "I don't mind."

Kat lowered herself slowly but scowled angrily at Etienne.

"Tasya's 'cause'," Luke said and laughed. "The reason Tasya was trying to stop her fellow caretakers from wiping out this entire planet was because of her job."

Luke left a dramatic pause.

"Which was?" Umri prompted.

"She was an accountant in the fleet," he announced. "You see, they're called caretakers for a reason. It's not the name of their species, for they are comprised of a variety of different lifeforms. Those that interacted with us were better suited to our environment. They go around the universe and clean up messes. All kinds of things: ruptured cruisers, extinguished suns, black holes, anything that might be considered a general threat to the wellbeing of the universe on a whole.

"It was Tasya's job to balance the sheets for every job undertaken. There was an obvious budget for each project of which the accounts had to match every level of expenditure. Just like any other business.

"The problem was, you see, that the caretakers had just happened to come across the Earth and its populace on the way through to another job. Evershine assessed our existence and decided that we were the equivalent of a slowly filling bucket of oil. Eventually, if left unchecked, the bucket would spill over into the surrounding galaxies and make a mess of everywhere else."

"But mass genocide was illegal and Tasya took it upon herself to defend a lesser species?" Umri hypothesised.

"Ha! You wish," Luke laughed. "No, Tasya's involvement was purely from the perspective of company policy and procedure. The correct ethos was that they didn't do a clean up without it going through the correct channels: project management, budgeting, damage control, et cetera. However, we are such an isolated community with zero impact on the universe outside of our own solar system that it would have been a relatively cheap and inconsequential job to wipe us out on their way through and then just write the cost off as, say, a business lunch or suchlike."

"Wait a minute," Umri interrupted, "if we are so isolated and inconsequential then why not just leave us alone?"

"Evershine was a jobsworth man and knew that we wouldn't be isolated forever," Luke explained. "Like I said before, humanity is a slowly filling bucket of oil and eventually we are going to burst our banks. When that happens it would take ages before word of our spread of pollution reached galactic civilisation and then when the clean-up had gone through the correct departments the job would've escalated considerably."

"What's to say that humanity wouldn't have changed its ways so as not to be such a destructive force?"

"Humanity's history," Luke said pointedly.

"So Tasya wasn't trying to save the Earth?" Jameson asked.

"Well, sort of," Luke shrugged. "I guess she felt she should give us a heads up as to what was going to happen eventually."

"What could've happened," Jameson corrected.

"No," Luke said with a smile. "What's going to happen."

"I don't understand, you beat them and now they've gone, yes?"

"Well, yes," Luke agreed. "Basically. But haven't you asked yourself where they've gone? They've gone back to the office to fill in the proper forms. They'll come back. Maybe not in our lifetime but they'll still be back to clean up our mess."

"Isn't there anything we can do?" Farthing asked.

"As a race you could try to change your attitude," Luke suggested. "Stop manufacturing, stop wasting, stop bickering. That would show that you were willing to make an effort. I'm not sure you could do it or that you'd be willing to really try. Or, of course, that the caretakers would actually believe you."

"What about you?" Umri asked.

"What about me? You'll have me locked away in some comfy cushioned room doped up so much on Prozac I wouldn't even know what day of the week it was."

"No, you keep saying that 'you' will have to change," Umri said. "Implying that you are setting yourself aside from the rest of humanity."

Luke looked mildly amused and confused.

"You seem to me to be quite a clever man, Mr Umri, and you've certainly showed that some seemingly inconsequential matters haven't skipped your attention. Don't tell me that you've forgotten?"

"What?"

"Well, I've still got the code," Luke said.

"The code that stopped the invasion?" Umri asked.

"Er, no," Luke said. "There wasn't any such code."

"Then what was the code for?" Umri demanded. "Disarming a bomb? Evershine's safe? What?"

"It's a genetic code," Luke said with marginal surprise. "Didn't you know that? Tasya bumped into me, passed me the code -"

"By injection?" Umri suggested.

"Spit, Mr Umri," Farthing shouted. "Keep up, man."

"Thank you, your honour," Luke said. "And that altered my genetic structure as explained by Doctor Gregg, yes? The whole DNA thing."

"Why would that have caused Evershine so much problem?" Umri asked. "Why didn't he just kill you as well?"

"He tried," Luke said. "Really tried. You have to admire his persistence but at the start he didn't know where I was and my alteration would have protected me against the global viral assault he wanted to do the job. Evershine couldn't run the risk of anyone surviving this clean up."

"Why?"

"He could've lost his job," Luke said.

"That's it?" Umri squealed.

"Then later, he couldn't be totally sure that I hadn't passed the code onto anyone else."

"And had you?" Umri asked.

"You are joking, right? Why would I do something like that?"

"To ensure our safety as a race," Umri said.

"Which would ensure the pollution of the rest of the galaxy in time," Luke said.

"We could learn to be better," Umri suggested.

"Look, no offence right, but it took a week of intense pain and suffering for me to learn to be better and even then I don't think I've got it a hundred per cent right. What makes you think that if I was to spread the secret of good health and longevity around the World that people would decide to start living more cleanly and stop fighting rather than carry on smoking, drinking and have to create more diabolical ways in which to try to kill each other?"

"I don't think that's up to you to decide," Umri said.

"I'm the one with the fucking code, pal. Who else is there to make that decision?"

"I am so confused, Mr Robinson," Umri stated. "You sound so cold as to the fate of the human race and yet you went to all that trouble of saving us. Why do that if you don't care if we live or die?"

"I didn't save your lives, I saved mine. It's called self preservation. At no point during that week did I ever think, 'Oh, I must save the Earth and all its inhabitants,' or go out of my way to ensure your safety. My thoughts and everything I did were solely focussed on my survival. You people staying alive was simply an after effect.

"You want a real hero to idolise? Tasya, she was the one who really tried to save you. An intergalactic accountant was not only doing her job but also took the time to look out for your safety and where is she now? I bet she wasn't even allowed to leave the planet. You've got her locked up in some lab somewhere, prodding and poking her. You see what you people do to your real saviours? And you think you have the right to live in this universe."

"Is that why you killed David Wilkinson?" Umri asked. "Because he didn't have the right to live?"

"Nice try, but I'm sorry no, I did not kill David Wilkinson," Luke stated.

Umri almost shook his fist with frustration. He had managed to get Luke to talk about something that he was passionate about and thought he might catch him out by slipping that obvious question in.

"So you did not kill David Wilkinson?" Umri asked.

"Yes," Luke said.

Umri's eyes lit up. "'Yes'?" he asked.

"'Yes,' I did not kill David Wilkinson," Luke emphasised.

"So, how do you explain his death?"

"Well, d'hur, the car," Luke said.

"But how did he get in front of the car?"

"Look, I know what you are trying to do," Luke told him.

"Which is?" Umri asked.

"You're trying to get me to say something that didn't happen."

"I am just trying to get you to give a straight answer," Umri told him.

"Well, maybe you should try asking some straight questions," Luke suggested.

Umri flapped his hands on his sides and dropped his papers on the table. "Your honours, may I have it recorded that Mr Robinson is a hostile witness?"

"Hostile?" Luke squealed. "You don't know what hostile is. I swear to God I've tried to be humble about all this. I've so desperately tried to get back into a normal lifestyle even though the people I love most dearly seem to have deserted me.

"Nobody can ever know exactly what happened, no matter how many times I explain it. Even though you all know the final outcome and a general summary of the events that went on, you'll never appreciate the physical and mental torture I had to endure unless you have to experience it first-hand yourselves. So, let it be known now, that despite any motivations or intentions, I did save this World and I did save the lives of every person on this planet. That means, ultimately, you all owe me. It doesn't matter if I get locked away somewhere because that place will be far more comfortable than the hell I had to go through to get here. However, know that I have finally recognised that there is a debt to be paid and maybe, one day, I might come knocking on your door to claim it."

"Mr Robinson," Etienne said, "are you threatening the human race?"

"That's not a threat," Luke said. "It would have been more like a threat if I'd said that I'd saved your lives which meant your lives belonged to me and that I could take them back whenever I wanted."

"But that is not what you said?" Etienne asked.

"Nah, I just said that there's a debt."

"Are you that aggrieved to have gone through it all?" Umri asked.

"God damn it," Luke groaned. "Are you not going to be happy until I've poured my soul out to you and drowned in a flood of my own tears? 'Aggrieved'? Do you know that I physically and mentally cannot relax any more? Halfenshaw noted it, I am permanently on edge. Anywhere that I go, I catch myself checking every person in the room as a potential threat. On top of that I immediately assess every room I go through for escape routes and ascertain the lethal properties of the various inanimate objects around the place."

"What does that mean?" Umri asked.

"It means that I look at everything in the room and then give it a mental ranking as to how each object would fare if I had to try to use it to kill someone."

"Everywhere?" Umri asked.

"Everywhere," Luke stated.

"Even here?"

"What part of 'everywhere' don't you get, Mr Umri?" Luke asked.

"Can you give us an example?" Umri asked.

Luke rubbed his forehead and chuckled. "You are killing me," he said.

"How so?"

"That's like asking a dyslexic to spell dyslexia," Luke said and then closed his eyes. "For starters I've got wrought steel barricades here." He patted the witness box. "I've got three untrained easily dispensable people to my right and in front of them are glassware, pens and paper."

"Paper?" Umri asked. "How lethal is that?"

Luke opened his eyes. "You ever had a paper cut?" he asked and Umri nodded. "That's caused by the paper edge being of the right tension, the right angle and moving at the right speed. If you get all those elements *really* right, you can open someone's throat.

"Shall I go on?" he asked. "The pens are obvious stabbing tools but would only be of any use in close-hand combat. However, Judge Farthing on the end there is using a particularly weighty Paperweight which I could probably use effectively up to a distance of about a hundred yards.

"Also back here, I've got chairs that can be used entirely or broken and use the shards. Again, a decently torn chair leg could be propelled a fair distance. Farthing has a collection of loose change, Etienne has got at least half-a-dozen hair grips and Jameson has dentures."

"You can't expect us to believe that you could use a set of dentures as a lethal weapon," Umri scorned and Luke's eyes lit up.

Luke found himself sitting on the back of Cholmes with his knees pressed tightly into the big caretaker's arms. The blood, mulch and sweat poured down Luke's face and stung his eyes. Everywhere on his body seemed to be screaming with some sort of pain but there was only one thing on his mind; *Bloody revenge.*

Luke grabbed the flailing assassin by his hair, lifted his head and slammed it back down onto the tiled floor. Cholmes' skull made an almighty thud on the ground and the man yelped with the pain but that was not enough. Luke lifted his head and slammed it down again. This time Cholmes bucked his body, almost finding the purchase and strength to throw Luke off.

Luke's own strength was starting to desert him and his resolve was waning. He knew that if he passed out now then he would never wake up. This needed to be finished.

Without even thinking about it, he reached up to the table beside him and found the set of false teeth. He pulled at the back of Cholmes' head and slipped the dentures on the floor. He then slammed the alien's head down on them.

Instead of the thud there came a crack and this time Cholmes screamed in agony and furiously struggled to get Luke off him. Luke repeated the action and received the same bone-grinding crack then a pool of snot coloured liquid started spreading across the floor.

Luke slammed Cholmes' face down a third time, the big man stopped wriggling but Luke did not cease ramming his face into the ground until he felt the caretaker's body release all its tension and feel as if he was sitting on a water mattress.

Only then did he let go of Cholmes' hair and fall to the floor with exhaustion. He looked over to the caretaker and saw that Cholmes' head had rolled over to return his gaze. Luke stared dispassionately at the repeated teeth lacerations up his face, across the bridge of his nose, his empty sockets where the teeth had burst through his eyes and finally the embedded dentures sat squarely in his forehead.

"Bite me," Luke told him.

Jameson distractedly pressed her false teeth firmly against her palette with her tongue.

"What is the point of this?" Kat demanded.

"Your client is displaying distinct symptoms of severe paranoia and persecution," Umri said.

"That's what Halfenshaw said," Luke added.

"I want to know how extreme it is," Umri finished.

"Mr Umri," Luke said calmly, "as I walked in here this morning I had already clocked the shooter from earlier as well as about two hundred other potential threats."

"Why didn't you do anything about him then?" Umri demanded.

"Because as I walked past he didn't try to kill me then, so assumed he wasn't going to be a threat to me at all."

"But you didn't care that he may have been a threat to anyone else?"

"You're catching on."

"So you didn't really care that David Wilkinson died?"

"The guy was an obvious hazard to the well-being of life on this planet, never mind the rest of the universe."

"Can you explain that?"

"Him and his mates were responsible for destroying lives," Luke said. "Aside from their last night of madness that we only have the word of Rob The Scot for, they physically and mentally destroyed the humanity of every bloke they ever had a pop at."

"How do you know that they had done it before?" Umri demanded.

"Oh piss off. You can't throw circumstantial, hearsay, third person bollocks at me. These guys have issues and have had for thousands of years. They're inherent. They're fucking idiots. It's these type of people who will hold back the rest of humanity if you ever do try to improve. Their demise is a boon to the gene pool and would improve your chances for future survival."

"Are you preoccupied with death?" Umri asked.

"I think I'm one of the only people who really accepts its inevitability," Luke said.

"But you are a young man," Umri stated, "you've still got maybe sixty years ahead of you. Why have such a fatalistic outlook on life now?"

"Do you think sixty years is such a long time?" Luke asked. "The majority of people die before they are eighty, either naturally or before their time. Say you do manage to live that long: the first twenty years are spent under the care of the education system, the next twenty is trying to establish a niche in society, the next twenty is slogging it out to ensure you can survive the last twenty during which time your body and mind slowly evaporates. What's the point of all that? You die. Maybe you've managed to find the time and finances to propagate your family name (which you're very proud of achieving, of course) and within two generations you've been forgotten and all your effort has been for nothing.

"The human race is a short-term species which is currently having long-term detrimental effects on its environment and nobody gives a shit. Why should I?"

"I find your explanations to be quite dichotomous," Umri said. "On the one hand you display a total nihilistic outlook on human life but then you still seem intent on trying to educate and, ultimately, save us all."

"I'm here, ain't I? I have to live with you shmoes and while I am stuck here I'd like the chance to maybe breathe some fresh air," Luke said.

"'While you're here'? What does that mean? Where are you planning on going?" Umri asked.

"There's a whole Universe opened up out there now and I'm thinking I want to get away from this place before the caretakers get back and do some official cleaning up."

"And how are you going to leave?" Umri scoffed. "Hitchhike?"

"You forget, I know someone who knows how the Universe works. I was hoping that this little charade was going to lead me to where she might be but I realise now I'm going to have to take matters into my own hands."

"That's it?" Umri demanded. "You think that's the end of this hearing? Just because you didn't get some answers that might not actually exist then you're going to be allowed to get up a just walk out of here?"

"Not quite as simplistic as that but generally, yes."

"This is an affront to this court, to the judicial and legal system of this planet and to every single human on the planet," Umri stated. "Who the hell do you think you are?"

Luke smiled at Umri.

"What?" Umri demanded.

"That's the last thing Wilkinson said before the car mashed him," Luke said.

Umri took a step back and nearly fell over his seat in his attempt to escape Luke's steely gaze.

"Was that a threat?" he stuttered.

Luke frowned. "It wasn't a particularly good one if it was," he said.

Umri opened his mouth to say something but suddenly all the events of the day caught up with him: humanity's saviour, the assassinations, the violence, the heart attack, the blood, the conspiracies and now the threat. He was alone with nothing between him and potentially the most dangerous man on the planet and his easy access to a heavy biro.

"I have no further questions your honour," he babbled and took his seat.

"I must say," Etienne sighed, "that has to be the most intense testimony I have ever heard. Mr Robinson, are you truly without any remorse concerning the death of David Wilkinson?"

"Totally without remorse," Luke said.

Etienne raised her eyebrows with surprise and resignation.

"Ms Sabella," she addressed, "do you have any questions that may enable you to salvage this testimony?"

"I have one question that I truly believe is the only one that needs to be asked in this hearing, your honour," Kat declared as she rose. "I think the main reason for this hearing seems to have escaped the attention of the prosecution and yourselves."

"Be careful, Ms Sabella," Etienne warned.

"No, your honour," Kat argued. "Luke Robinson has been brought here to see if he should be taken to court to answer the charges of murder. The incidents of the invasion which seems to have preoccupied the attention of everyone here is largely circumstantial. Regardless of whether Luke Robinson saved the World, or what his motivations for doing so were, the question is whether Luke Robinson intended for David Wilkinson to die on the night of the twenty-eighth."

Luke just stared at her.

"Mr Robinson?" Jameson prompted.

"Was that a question?" Luke asked.

"Did you intend for David Wilkinson to die on the night of the twenty-eighth?" Kat asked.

Luke blinked a few times. "Wow," he said and Kat's eyes widened.

"Oh no," she muttered.

"Do you know," Luke chuckled. "That's the first time I've been asked that?"

"Oh no," she muttered.

"What a brilliantly pertinent question, Kat," Luke applauded. "Well done."

"Oh no," she muttered.

Luke smiled. "Yes," he nodded. "Yes, I fully intended for David Wilkinson to die on the evening of the twenty-eighth.

"I hadn't intended it to be the car, mind you. That was accidental. The move I had made on him directed a huge surge of focussed kinetic energy directly into his chest which would've caused him to have a massive heart attack about the time he was flipping over the bonnet.

"Him, his mates and other idiots out there need to be taught a lesson that they can't just indiscriminately go around looking for fights because, one day, they might be picking on me and I'm not going to put up with that kind of shit any more."

Kat closed her eyes and slumped into her seat.

The court was silent.

"Is that it?" Luke asked.

"You can return to your seat, Mr Robinson," Etienne instructed cautiously.

Luke got up and was escorted back to his table by one of the bailiffs. Kat did not look up.

"Ms Sabella?" Etienne asked. "Would you like to make a summation?"

"I've nothing else," Kat mumbled.

"Mr Umri?"

Umri's confidence had returned somewhat and he lifted himself up.

"There are a few points I would like to address," he stated. "Aside from the obvious and long-overdue confession from Mr Robinson concerning his intentions, which I believe is all that is needed to obligate a judicial trial, there is still an argument as to whether Luke Robinson should be tried based on his actions during the invasion. I believe that Mr Robinson has waived any rights to be considered Earth's hero based on the testimony of his motivations of self-preservation. Here lies the simple implication that if Luke Robinson should be so uncaring for the safety of his own species then how could he be held in a position of high-regard amongst them?

"With that comes the question as to his actual species. We have heard from Doctor Gregg and his own testimony that, technically, he is not human any more but does, in fact, hold a key into the future safety of our race. Not human implies that perhaps he cannot be governed by the laws of humanity and if he is so unwilling to share the key then maybe it should be taken without his consent.

"Thirdly, and perhaps most important, is Mr Robinson's precarious state of mental health. Doctor Halfenshaw testified that it was his professional opinion that Mr Robinson's acute paranoia and persecution complex makes him an incredibly dangerous person. I believe that Mr Robinson's own testimony has also proved this beyond a doubt and so request that your honours take into the consideration that Mr Robinson should be institutionalised for the safety of everyone around him."

"I don't think there is anything else, your honour," Umri stated.

"I think you're right, Mr Umri," Etienne agreed.

The judges conferred for a second then Etienne came forward.

"We are going to take another brief recess to finalise our judgement," she announced and they stood and hurriedly left the room.

The room started to come alive with excited chatter.

Luke just stared ahead and Kat had her head bowed at the table.

"What a waste of time," she mumbled.

"Yep," Luke agreed.

"How dare you," she snarled and turned viciously to him. Luke did not flinch. "How dare you make me care about you. How dare you let me admire you and make me think that I owed you and make me think that you really cared when all along you are the most callous of all people. Dispassionate, unloving and hateful." She had tears welling in her eyes.

"No," she bit and wiped them away. "I will not cry for you. I will not give you the pleasure of thinking that I still care when these aren't tears of sorrow or hurt but tears of pure rage.

"I feel I could kill you right now for everything you have put me through. For everything you have put everyone through. The false idolisation, the false sense of security, the false hope of a better tomorrow and the false belief that you might actually be the only really decent human on this planet."

Luke exhaled a silent laugh.

"Fuck me, Kat," he said. "You haven't taken notice of one fucking word I've said, have you? All the way through this I've consistently enforced the idea that there is no better tomorrow, that things won't turn out all right and that I'm not the man you all believed me to be.

"You have just displayed the exact reason why humanity is doomed, you listen but because it doesn't fit into some delusional ideal you've built in your head, you don't believe. And if you don't believe you can pretend you never heard.

"I cannot win with you people. I am despised, hounded and attacked because of one thing and when you finally hear the truth I still get despised, hounded and attacked. The only time I'm ever going to get any peace is when you're all dead."

Kat's fury waned for a moment. "Bullshit," she hissed.

"Don't do it, Kat," Luke warned.

"This is bollocks," she said. "There's more to this."

"No there's not," Luke urged. "Can't you see? You're doing it again. Not listening."

The judges' chambers door opened and they marched through to their seats. Umri, Kat and Luke all stood as Etienne made herself comfortable in front of her microphone.

"It has unanimously been decided that due to the intense physical and mental ordeals Mr Robinson had to suffer during the invasion that he is currently not in a fit mental state to go to trial for the charges of the murder of David Wilkinson."

The audience muttered unintelligibly.

"And that Mr Robinson will return to the care of Dr Halfenshaw until such time as it is deemed he has recovered and is safe to reintegrate with the rest of society. At that time the charges will be reviewed again."

Etienne raised and slammed her gavel on the desk at the same time that general cries of protest broke out from the audience.

The sounds filtered through Luke's hearing and his jaw stiffened.

The judges were already preparing to make a swift exit and a number of extra guards had emerged from the rear rooms in case any major trouble broke out. Two guards were approaching him with handcuffs and Kat was silently gathering her papers together.

Luke peered over his shoulder at the unsettled masses and caught site of a bearded man wearing a large duffel coat, staring fixedly and calmly at him.

The man seemed to take this eye contact as a cue and raised himself up onto his seat. Luke's guards noticed first, paused in their approach and edgily reached for their weapons. The people around the man began to panic and tried to scramble away, then hysteria grew and spread throughout the courtroom.

Kat turned and watched as the man pulled his coat open. Underneath was what looked like a black floatation jacket but this was made out of very heavy-looking bricks.

Something tugged on her jacket sleeve and she involuntarily stepped backwards with the pull. The pressure remained and she slowly moved whilst remaining hypnotised by the sight before her. As she continued backwards, the guards pressed forwards.

The man started to shout something but he could not be heard over the screams of the crowd and the bellowed threats of the guards who all aimed their guns at him. Whatever he was saying, he was either extremely fervent about or very scared of because he had tears pouring down his face and was manically waving a hand held device all around the room.

Kat stumbled up a step and was vaguely aware of being led around to the back of the witness stand. She could see everything now: the judges were as paralysed as she thought she was, the guards had surrounded the man, people were trampling each other underfoot in an attempt to escape. Then she was pushed down into the hollow of the witness stand and she saw Luke standing over her just calmly watching the scene. He then gripped the top of the stand and pulled. The expression on his face was a display of an immense exertion of force and she felt the stand begin to fall over her. She heard the bolts being wrenched from the floor, then Luke tucked himself inside and the entire metal booth fell over them like a cask.

Just before all external light and sound was extinguished Kat swore she heard the man yell above all the other noise and then there was a solitary female scream.

Then there was black inside the box.

Then there was a noise that was more like a physical force. It beat down on their cover from every angle with such ferocity that Kat thought her head might cave in. She tried to scream but any noise that came out of her mouth was drowned by the assault around them. The box jolted a meter or so and made them tumble over each other. Then the top and sides crumbled slightly as the World fell down on them.

Then there was black *and* silence.

Prologue: March 31st. 3:45 pm

It was a small room. Too small for any person to stay in comfortably for too long. There was only a mattress against one of the walls and there were no sheets. There was no window and the illumination for the room came from a sealed panel that was flush against the high ceiling. The room was all white and the walls seemed to be made from padded material.

Luke was in this room. He was kneeling in its centre. He had his arms wrapped around his chest and he was gently rocking backwards and forwards. In this position of peace it did look as if he was wrapping his body in a caring self embrace but every now and then his head would jerk up violently and he would mutter something through his teeth. The sound was distorted because of the tight clench of his jaw and the copious amounts of saliva pouring from his lips, but it sounded like this, "T'sha!"

Eventually his eyes rolled up into their sockets, his lids closed and he rolled to the floor. From this position it could be seen that his arms were not wrapped around his body of his volition.

www.ingramcontent.com/pod-product-compliance
Ingram Content Group UK Ltd.
Pitfield, Milton Keynes, MK11 3LW, UK
UKHW041439180426
11947UKWH00007B/518